Darkness

Laurann Dohner

ELLORA'S CAVE
ROMANTICA®
ELLORASCAVE.COM

An Ellora's Cave Publication

www.ellorascave.com

Darkness

ISBN 9781419971525
ALL RIGHTS RESERVED.
Darkness Copyright © 2014 Laurann Dohner
Cover design by Allyse Leodra.
Cover photography by Anetta.

Electronic book publication September 2014
Trade paperback publication 2015

Prologue

Katrina Perkins barely contained the anger that simmered inside. Robert Mason, her boss, always made her wish she could just draw her sidearm and shoot the bastard. It wasn't a matter of if she wanted to put a bullet in him, it all boiled down to what body part she'd aim for first. It was a tough decision at times between his nuts or his big mouth. She fisted her hands behind her back to resist the urge to target both.

"I'm going to prove these New Species bastards are criminal. They use their sovereign status to get away with shit. No more!"

Katrina watched her boss pace. She wanted to stick her foot out and trip him every time he passed. He often ranted about his paranoid and idiotic theories that New Species were really public enemy number one. She was tired of hearing it. He'd been on a real tear for days after she'd overheard him ordering other agents to track the movements of a man named Jeremiah Boris, otherwise known as Jerry Boris. The person seemed to have disappeared and her boss believed the NSO was involved. It felt personal to Kat, though, as if her boss knew the guy or had a special interest.

"I'll keep digging until I can prove they played a part in the disappearance of Jerry if it's the last thing I do." He shot her an angry look. "He works for them."

She took a deep breath. "At Homeland or Reservation?"

"Fuller Prison."

That surprised her. "I've never heard of the place. How is the NSO connected to a prison?"

"It's classified." He lowered his voice. "Unofficially, it's where they incarcerate anyone who used to work for Mercile Industries."

Her respect for her boss lowered even more. She'd be fired and he'd bring her up on charges if she shared restricted information the way he just had. She didn't pry, not willing to be a party to his breach of conduct. Curiosity tugged at her though, making her wonder where it was located and if the NSO actually ran it.

"Jerry is a good man but he is afraid of them."

She kept her lips sealed, refusing to be baited. Anyone who was a friend of Mason's couldn't be upstanding. She'd wondered how he'd gained the position ever since he'd been transferred to lead her department. He was rash, too emotional, bordering on nuts in her opinion. The only explanation she could think of was that he'd either kissed some major ass, blackmailed his way to the top or was related to someone important enough to call in some favors.

"They also do vile things to women. I think they drug them and get them addicted to something similar to heroin. It's the only reason women would allow those bastards to stick their peckers in them."

She decided to try reason again. "Sir, I don't believe that's true. I've watched a few of those women interviewed on television and didn't spot any indication that they were drugged."

He glared.

"Their pupils appear normal, their speech clear and their movements are fluid," she explained, resenting that she had to. Signs of drug use were taught to every agent.

"Maybe it's a hormone thing," her superior muttered, pacing again. "You know, like making them nuts. Someone would have to be insane to allow one of those animals to screw them. It's sick. Women might as well start going on all fours in front of their dogs and just avoid the NSO completely."

She flexed her fingers, which were almost itching for her gun again, and hated her boss with a passion. She took that insult personally. "It's not their fault what they are, sir. They were created by Mercile Industries and didn't have a say when someone messed with their genes. It was against their will. They are victims."

He glared at her. "Right. You have a dog. You're an animal lover. You probably want to protest the standard procedure of putting down dogs that kill people when they attack."

It depends on who they kill. I'd reward a dog with a juicy steak if he tore into your ass. I'm not forgetting your remark about women who own dogs either.

She silently watched him. Nothing good would come out of her mouth at that point and she didn't want to be placed on suspension for insulting her superior. She did manage to shake her head, the appropriate response, which she figured he expected.

"I am assigning you to a mission, Special Agent Perkins." A gleam lit Robert Mason's eyes. "I'm sending you into Homeland, undercover. You're going to find out their secrets and expose those animal bastards for what they are. I also want you to locate any information about Jerry Boris. He's probably a prisoner there. You will assist in his escape if you locate him."

Surprise tore through her. "What?"

He nodded. "You're perfect for this assignment. You're very attractive. They'll be drawn to you like bees to honey. You look very feminine so they won't realize what a hard-ass you are." He chuckled. "You're going to be very helpful."

She swallowed back a protest.

"You're the right man for the job." He reached out and clasped her shoulder. "They'll think you're a harmless set of tits but we both know what you really are."

She was too stunned to even punch the son of a bitch for what he'd just said. *Is he losing his damn mind?* It wouldn't surprise her in the least.

He winked and squeezed tighter. "I did a full background check on you. There's no reason for alarm. You look a bit pale but it's perfect. You're perfect. I'm the only one who knows your secret. We have a hell of a lot in common, Perkins."

Mason calling her a man with a set of tits suddenly seemed tame in comparison to the new insult. They had no similarities. They both worked for the FBI, in the same building, but that was where the connection ended. She also had no idea what kind of secret he spoke of.

"Those animal bastards are going to want to fuck you but you'll be immune to them. I'm sure your girlfriend will understand you going on assignment. We're both the men of our families and I just tell my girlfriend how it is. I need you to pretend to be a real woman while you're there. I hope that won't be too hard for you. Hell, in a pinch I could pretend I find men attractive so I'm confident that you'll be able to play it straight."

She stared at Robert Mason and just nodded numbly. The moron thought her roommate and long-time best friend was her lover. She had to battle the urge to laugh in his stupid face. *Oh, this is just priceless. Wait until I tell Missy.*

"Yeah," she finally got out. "I can do the straight thing."

He winked. "We're going to take these bastards down."

She suddenly imagined what it would be like when his plan blew up in his face. He'd have to explain to his boss why he'd wasted money, time and resources. She had to follow orders but it didn't mean she couldn't file a complaint detailing how erratic and unreasonable Mason had become. Her suspicions were confirmed. He somehow knew Jerry Boris and was sending her to Homeland for personal reasons. He'd lose his job over it in the end. She'd make sure of it.

She smiled. "I love helping pin assholes to the wall." She closed her mouth. *Like you.*

Chapter One

ൟ

Darkness stared at the mirror. Steam filled the small bathroom from the running shower but he remained still instead of stepping under the spray of water. A few blood spatters marred one cheek and his forehead.

He glanced down at his hands, where he gripped the edge of the sink. One knuckle was swollen from the force of a punch. Jerry Boris was alive but he needed medical attention. Part of him regretted not killing the bastard. Another part of him was surprised he'd been able to stop. The door opened behind him and he turned his head to stare at the female.

"I wanted to check on you," she whispered.

He saw no horror in her look, only sadness and worry. "I'm okay, Bluebird."

She hesitated before stepping into the bathroom and closing the door behind her. "They sent him to Medical. He'll live. You did what you had to do. The task force will assemble a team and put the location under surveillance. They want more facts before they rescue the Gift. The person who has her might own more homes and they want to locate them and enter all at once in case she has been moved, if she's still alive."

He pushed away from the sink, reaching for his bloodied shirt to remove it. "Thanks. I'm going to shower and then I'll return to duty."

She didn't leave. "Do you want help?"

The offer stunned him and he swung his gaze back in her direction. "I can shower myself."

"Do you want company? I know that had to be tough on you but he refused to break. Sometimes violence is the only resort."

"How would you know?" He regretted the words as soon as they left his lips. It wasn't her fault the interrogation had gone that way. The human had refused to give up the location of the Gift until he'd been beaten within an inch of his life. "I'm sorry. That was uncalled for."

"You're kind, Darkness. You try to hide it but I know you didn't enjoy hurting that human. You couldn't get out of that room fast enough once he told you what we needed to know. It took inner strength I don't possess to force him to speak. You probably saved a life. That Gift might be recovered because of your actions."

"I hope so."

She glanced down his body. "I could make you forget what just happened."

"You could distract me for a short time but I won't ever forget."

She peered into his eyes. "You're too hard on yourself."

He kept quiet, not willing to tell her it was deserved.

"You are," she insisted. "I don't know much about your background because you don't speak of it but I realize it was harsher than most of us endured. Do you want to talk? I won't repeat anything you say. You should have someone to open up to. It's an important part of the healing process."

"Some wounds are just too deep," he rasped.

"It doesn't help when you won't even try." She stepped closer. "Let me soothe you. I'm offering friendship and comfort."

"I appreciate that but sex isn't the way."

Her chin lifted. "Fine. We don't need to share sex but you should talk to me."

"What do you want to know?" Anger stirred but he buried it. Her intentions were good. He accepted and trusted that. "I was trained to kill and the violence you witnessed was just the beginning of what I was taught. It made me cold inside. I refuse to allow anyone to get too close."

"You know the problem then. Change. We're free now to make anything possible if we want it."

"I don't want to depend on others or care overly much about anything. I enjoy being numb."

"You care about Species."

"I do but there's a line I won't cross." He pointed to the tile on the floor between them. "There it is. I need to shower and get back on duty. I appreciate your offer but I decline. Don't take it personally. It isn't."

"Am I not to your liking? Everyone has a preference. Do the Gifts appeal to you? Perhaps one of the primates? You were around humans a lot. They are smaller and softer than most Species females. I could speak to some of them to find out if any are interested in sharing sex."

"It's not a matter of size or strength, Bluebird. It's any woman."

Her eyes widened. "You prefer males?" She swallowed hard. "I don't know any who are sexually attracted to other ones. We could see if any of the human employees are though."

"Goddamn." He ran his fingers through his hair, forgetting that they were bloody. He needed to get it cut. It almost touched his shoulders, longer than he liked, and was just another reminder of a past he wanted distance from. "That's not it either. You're the second person to ask me that. I am attracted to females. It's just that…"

"What? Finish what you were going to say. I won't judge."

He dropped his hand to his side and sighed. "I don't ever want to feel that much again and females are a weakness. I trusted the wrong one once and people I cared about paid the price. Something inside me died and I'm not grieving its loss. I like being solitary and in control. I am free and that's my choice."

She accepted it with a nod. "Don't you ever feel lonely though? Long to hold someone or be touched?"

"No. That's just a reminder of the past. The only time I'm completely at ease is when I'm alone."

She stared at him. "I'm so sorry for whatever was done to you, Darkness. Just know we care about you and if you ever change your mind, all you have to do is reach out. We'll be there."

"Thank you. It means a lot."

She turned away but paused at the door to glance over her shoulder at him. "No one would blame you if you ended your shift early and went home. That was intense for everyone."

"I'm different," he reminded her. "Give me fifteen minutes and I'll be back in uniform."

"You're stubborn." She smiled though. "You hold my respect."

He watched her leave and then stripped off the rest of his clothes. The last thing he wanted was to go home and listen to the silence. He'd relive every moment inside that interrogation room. Boris was a real son of a bitch who deserved everything he'd done but the fact that he'd enjoyed inflicting pain on that piece of shit didn't sit well with him.

He scrubbed his skin and washed his hair. It only took him ten minutes to dress and return to Security. He glanced around but no one seemed surprised or uncomfortable upon his arrival. Bluebird was the only one who smiled from her seat in front of a bank of monitors that provided live feeds around Homeland.

"What's going on?"

"Not much," Flame answered. "We just allowed two trucks inside to deliver food supplies. Justice finished one meeting with a reporter doing a story on us and he's got another one coming in about fifteen minutes."

"Poor bastard," Darkness muttered.

Flame nodded in sympathy. "I'm glad I'm not the one who has to answer all their questions. The task force left to assemble at their headquarters. Do you want to know what we have so far?" He pointed to two males at the far end of the room with their attention fixed on their computers. "They are tracing all information they can gather about the name Boris gave up."

He didn't want to be involved. He'd obtained the Gift's location. It wasn't his job to go after her. He liked to remain within NSO lands. "What else is going on?"

"Not much." Flame held a portable electronic device, scrolling as he read. "Oh. The new instructor is due to arrive soon."

"What instructor?" He frowned.

"A forensic one." Excitement laced Flame's voice. "Tiger hired someone to come in to teach us all about police procedures for gathering evidence. It will be fun."

Darkness arched an eyebrow. "Fun?"

"Don't you watch those shows on television? We'll be solving crimes before you know it. I'm looking forward to learning how to take fingerprints."

"What crimes? This is Homeland. It's the outside world we need to worry about and the task force handles them."

Some of the joy faded from Flame's features. "Tiger asked what we'd like to learn and we voted on a forensic science instructor."

Regret stabbed at Darkness. He hadn't meant to deflate the other male's good mood. "I don't watch much television but I'm certain it's very interesting if it earned the majority vote. I'll be sure to stop in to check it out. I might learn something new and I'm sure we'll find the skills useful."

Flame smiled. "It's fascinating."

"I'll take your word for it. Where is this instructor going to stay? Are the human accommodations already prepared? A background check run?"

"It was last minute but I'm sure we're on top of it."

"Double-check."

"Okay." Flame hurried away.

The door opened and Breeze entered. She grinned as she approached him. "Good job, badass. I heard you broke that son of a bitch and made him squeal like the pig he is." She stopped, lifting one palm above her head.

He eyed it, frowning.

"High five. Put it right here."

He refused to slap her palm with his.

"Kill-sport," she muttered, dropping her arm. "Reporting for duty. I know I'm an hour early but I was bored. Anything happening?"

"Typical stuff. Deliveries, reporters and some new instructor."

"Awesome." She grinned. "The forensics one? I can't wait. I made a list of questions I want to ask, starting with why it takes so long to get toxicology results after an autopsy. Did you know it can take weeks?"

"I didn't."

"Is he here yet? I might as well pick his brain."

"He's due at any time."

"Great. I'll suit up and work the gate." She walked a few feet away before turning, a smile on her face. "I hate wearing the helmet but I don't want the humans falling in love with me. They couldn't handle all this." She winked before disappearing into one of the rooms.

The corners of his mouth lifted but he resisted laughing outright. Breeze always amused, saying outrageous things. She put everyone at ease—a rare gift. His was instilling fear in others. Those grim observations darkened his disposition as he crossed the room, watching the monitors.

"It's a calm day for the protestors," Bluebird announced.

"Good."

The door opened again and Trey Roberts entered. The human task force team leader glanced around, finally met his stare and approached. Darkness tensed.

"I was looking for you."

"Did the human die from his injuries?"

Trey shook his head. "Pricks like that don't die easily. I'm here to work with the guys looking for more intel on our target. Tim wanted someone to relay the info while he's putting together a plan of attack with the rest of the teams."

"They are working on that over there. Make yourself at home. You know where the fridge and coffee machine are located."

"You New Species have me addicted to caffeine."

"Is that a complaint?"

"Hell no. Just an observation. I'll go be useful and get out of your hair. Great job in there. Tim might not have said it but I will."

Darkness watched the human join the two males at the computers before he spun around and went to the room where they kept their gear. He put on a bulletproof vest, grabbed a helmet and headed outside.

He climbed the ladder to the walkway near the top of the wall and peered over the edge as he lifted a weapon, his intention to look intimidating. One glance showed him two cars and a van in line, waiting to be searched before entering the first gate. He sighed. It was boring walking the wall but it was better than staring at the ceiling from his bed.

* * * * *

Katrina was excited as she drove through the first set of gates at New Species Homeland and hit the down button on her window. She already had her identification out, having shown it to the first guard. It had passed inspection, being an official license. She also had a full background cover. A second guard approached her driver's side window.

It fascinated her that all the NSO officers were completely covered, from their combat boots to their gloved hands and tinted face shields. She studied the person intently but couldn't see a hint of skin. The broad shoulders, tall frame and bulky arms implied it was a male but she had no way to tell if he was human or New Species. It was a brilliant tactic to prevent protestors or potential threats from distinguishing the exact identity of each guard.

"Hi. I'm Kathryn Decker but call me Kat. I'm from the crime lab in Bakersfield. I'm the consultant."

He accepted her license and touched the communication device attached to his ear. He spoke softly enough that she couldn't hear the words. It would be procedure to verify her identity once again and that she was expected at Homeland. She glanced at the gates that closed behind her and looked toward the second one about fifty yards in front of her. There was plenty of space separating the sides of her rental car from a guard shack and more walls.

"So you wave people through the first gates one vehicle at a time and recheck them in this area?"

He slid his glove up the side of his protective headgear but said nothing.

"Sorry. I'm just curious. I'm with the crime lab, remember?"

The guard released his earpiece and handed back her license. "You need to pull up there and leave the engine running. Our team has to go over your car and then we need to search you. A female will do that. Just step out of your vehicle and she'll meet with you." He pointed to marks that had been painted on the pavement.

She accepted her license and drove forward. It put her dead center in the open space. It made sense. They'd have room to go over the vehicle and it was a good blast zone if anyone drove explosives inside. She put the car in park and exited the vehicle.

A second guard stepped outside the shack and approached. Kat surveyed the person from head to foot — exact outfit, no unique marks, generic identity. The figure was tall and fit but there was noticeably less shoulder and arm mass. The woman's breasts were hidden under the thick Kevlar vest. She wouldn't have guessed her sex if she hadn't been told to expect a female.

Kat's heart rate increased with excitement at the prospect of having interaction with one of the New Species women. They were elusive and not much was known about them. No photographs had ever surfaced and no one knew what they looked like. She grinned. "Hi."

The figure paused a few feet from her. "Why are you so happy?" The voice was a little gruff but definitely that of a woman.

"I'm just happy to be here. I'm really looking forward to getting to know New Species. I'm Kat Decker from the crime lab in Bakersfield."

"I'm aware of who you are. We're looking forward to your classes." Her tone softened. "I love crime shows."

"It's not exactly the same as you see on television. Those shows have a lot of high-tech equipment that we don't really use."

"Oh."

"The classes will be fun though. I spent two days reviewing things to teach." Kat didn't want to disappoint the NSO. She might be there under false pretenses but she'd decided to make the most of it. Robert Mason could kiss her ass if he thought she was going to follow his exact orders. She'd view it as a vacation of sorts, one where she got to interact with New Species and share some of her knowledge on how to combat the latest criminal trends.

"We don't frighten you?"

"Only if you plan on kicking my ass because you all appear to be in really good shape."

The tall woman laughed. "I'm Rusty."

"Is it bad manners to offer to shake hands?"

Rusty offered a gloved hand. "Nope."

Kat shook it. "NSO stands for New Species Organization, right?"

Rusty nodded. "When in uniform it also stands for New Species Officer. Take your pick. We're good at adapting."

"Very cool."

"I need to search you. Would you mind turning around and assuming the position?"

Kat spun and spread her legs. She reached into her front pocket and removed her cigarettes and lighter. She set them on the roof of her car in clear view. It was a reminder of why she had come to Homeland and how torn she felt about it. Smoking was a bad habit she fell back on every time there was a lot of stress in her life. She spread her arms wide and gripped the top of the car. The pat-down was thorough and Rusty even checked her cigarette pack and lighter, handing them back when she was done.

"I need to check your purse now."

Kat reached inside her car to retrieve it. Rusty placed the handbag on the hood of the car and carefully searched inside as Kat watched.

"Here you go," Rusty said as she tried to return it.

Kat refused to take it, instead asking, "May I make a suggestion?"

Rusty nodded. "All right."

Kat accepted the purse and placed it back on the hood. She motioned Rusty closer. "You don't want to just examine the contents. You need to search the purse as well. I'm here to teach your officers the latest tricks criminals use and this is one of them. I put a few things inside my purse to see if you would find them. You missed them. Watch."

Kat dumped out the contents and then handed the purse back to Rusty. "Squeeze the purse. Feel every inch."

Rusty did so and tensed. Kat stepped back. "Both sides of the lining have two fake knives that are plastic. They aren't sharp but they could have been. Running a metal detector over the purse wouldn't have worked to find them. I also put a tube of water along the bottom of the purse that you probably mistook for cushioning. It could have contained poison, a biological weapon or a gel explosive that could be ignited with the lighter you handed back to me. You have to feel every inch of something you search and investigate every bump or inconsistency. Never allow any substance through security, even if you believe it's just simple water. Your best option is to secure purses and bags in a separate location when you have day visitors. Take their possessions away from them when they enter and return them when they leave."

Rusty discovered the hidden linings and removed the objects. She sighed. "I see."

Kat nodded. "I could have killed someone if I'd been a bad guy."

Screams suddenly erupted from the direction of the front gate. Kat turned in time to spot a van with tinted windows tearing through the shrubs next to the line of cars waiting to enter Homeland. It nearly plowed into a few protestors before it scraped against those vehicles. The grill had been modified into a battering ram. She caught a glimpse of what appeared to be two packages taped to it. Those packages exploded on impact with the gates. The hinges of the gate gave way and it came crashing forward onto the pavement.

Shock held her immobile for precious seconds while the van tried to drive over the downed metal barrier. The guards along the top of the walls opened fire. Their bullets ricocheted off the sides of the vehicle. Rusty grabbed Kat and both of them hit the ground next to her rental.

Kat lifted her head and took in the unfolding hell. Two of the van's tires were stuck in the damaged gate but it wouldn't take long to get free. It backed up and then the driver shifted gears and advanced again. A bent part of the gate hung him up but he was almost clear of it.

The too-close-for-comfort view she had of the grill revealed no sign of more explosives taped to the front. The driver was probably intent on using engine power and force to breach the second gate but her rental car stood in his way. He'd have to skirt around it and that would slow him down.

She struggled to get out from under the New Species woman who'd taken her to the ground. One look revealed that Rusty was okay and not in the way of the tires that were about to be pushed forward when the van slammed into her rental. The engine was still running. She got to her knees and lunged through the open car door, grabbed the emergency brake and yanked it on. It wouldn't stop the van but it would make pushing the car a bit more difficult.

She backed out of the car, landing on her ass, an instant before it was rammed. Her attention fixed on the van. Bullets were still bouncing off it, not doing any damage except for what appeared to be some faint scratch marks.

"MOVE!" Rusty yelled. "Follow me."

Kat turned her head as the New Species got to her feet. She pulled her weapon but didn't fire at the van. Kat reacted, her years of training taking over before she could think. She yanked the handgun from Rusty's hand, rose and flipped off the safety.

"Shoot the tires," Kat yelled.

She took a shot at the windshield where she saw two assailants sitting. Both wore tactical assault gear with full-face shields. The vehicle windows held, which meant she couldn't do any damage but that went both ways. Movement in the back of the van assured her there were more of the bastards. She advanced, ignoring the gunfire, hoping the guards on the wall didn't target her.

The driver turned his head as she stopped next to his door. She grabbed the handle but it was locked. She gripped the gun with both hands. He pressed on the gas, tires squealing, and the smell of burning rubber assailed her as he pushed her rental a few feet. She moved with it and scanned the door for a flaw. The lock was exposed so she fired into it. The hole that appeared seemed to surprise the driver and she might have hit him but the bullet wouldn't do much damage with the chest rig he wore. She yanked open the door and aimed for the two inches of skin revealed at his throat when he looked her way and made the mistake of glancing up at the wall, lifting his head. She fired.

The passenger attempted to raise a military-grade assault rifle to shoot her but he snagged the end of it on the center divider, between the seats. She fired at him but the bullet didn't pierce his face shield. He did lunge back. The driver choked, blood flowing over his vest. He wasn't wearing a belt. She fisted one of the straps of his vest and yanked hard. She turned as he fell out, putting her side against the van, out of the passenger's sight line. The driver fell to the ground and she released him.

Bullets tore into the open door next to her and she knew if she swung forward to fire at the passenger again, he'd hit her. She focused on the dying man at her feet. She bent, careful to keep out of the open door of the still-running van but it wasn't moving forward anymore. Her car prevented it. She yanked his handgun free of its holster and spotted two objects that looked like grenades.

Holy fuck. They aren't screwing around. She dropped the guns on the ground and grabbed the two explosive devices. They were handmade, by her guess, but looked deadly. She didn't have time to ponder exactly how they worked or what they would do. She feared the other assailants would burst out at any second and attack. She saw the switches and used her thumbs to activate them, praying they wouldn't instantly blow. She risked exposure when she threw them inside and leaned over to grab the door. She slammed it closed, spun and sprinted away.

"Run! Bomb!" she shouted at two advancing NSO officers.

One of them followed orders by diving behind some kind of barrier they'd set up near the guard house but the second one kept coming.

"It's going to blow," she got out. At least she hoped it would. It would be really bad if she'd just set off two chemical weapons, thinking they were explosive devices. She'd had mere seconds to examine them.

The guard still coming at her had to be at least six-foot-five. He didn't point his gun at her, which was a blessing. She tucked her head when his arms opened as if to grab her but she tackled his waist. It knocked the air from her lungs when she slammed into his solid frame, reminding her of hitting a wall at full speed. They both went down though.

BOOM!

The sound nearly deafened her and something slammed into her back. She wasn't sure if she'd been hit by a flying object or if it was just the shock wave from the explosion. Her ears rang, she felt numb and was unaware whether she was hurt. The big body under her moved. She was sprawled on top of him. He rolled over and she suddenly felt the unforgiving pavement under her back. His weight pinned her as she managed to open her eyes, not even aware they had been closed until then.

Her hearing improved somewhat as the trauma lessened. The guard was heavy, crushing her between him and the ground. He'd turned his head to look behind him. She stared up at a tan throat, revealed beneath his tinted face shield, and even noticed his square chin. Popping noises and a hissing sound filled the air.

"Son of a bitch." His voice gave her chills. There was a gruffness to it that wasn't quite human—too deep, almost a snarl.

He pushed off her and she sucked in air, her lungs starved for oxygen. She got her first glimpse of the van, or what was left of it, when he rolled to his knees then got to his feet.

She sat up enough to stare mutely at the destruction. The windows had blown out at the front of the van and the back doors were open. Flames shot from both sides of it and black smoke rolled upward. A body lay near the driver's door—the man she'd shot in the throat. He wasn't moving and she didn't expect him to. The bullet she'd fired had been a kill shot.

Her attention returned to the van and the dark object hanging out the back, to the ground. She was able to focus enough to make out what it was. Bile rose as she identified the shape of a head and arms. He wasn't moving. She managed to choke back the urge to throw up. It sank in that she'd just killed at least three people, unless the passenger had exited the other side before the explosion. The NSO guard moved but she couldn't take her horrified gaze off the burning van.

Orders were shouted in the background but she ignored them. *I did that. I killed them.* It sank in and she couldn't force her limbs to move. Kat didn't flinch when the guard leaned down and grabbed her arms. He easily jerked her to her unsteady feet. She swayed a little but locked her knees. Her training demanded she snap out of it and get with the program but all she could do was watch the burning van. She could smell burning flesh under the thick stench of rubber and whatever else was on fire.

"You're under arrest," that deep voice growled next to her ear.

The feel of handcuffs being snapped on her wrists finally pulled her out of her shock. She turned her head and peered up at the guard. He was over a foot taller than she was and massive. He'd snapped the cuffs on her wrists in front instead of behind her back and now gripped the chain between them.

She swallowed, trying to find her voice. "I can explain."

"You blew up that van." He growled. "You stole a gun from one of my officers. Who are you?"

She turned her head. Black-clad officers had rushed forward with fire extinguishers, trying to put out the blaze. She wanted to order them back in case the gas tank hadn't already blown but they were keeping a safe distance. The New Species at her side expected an answer. She remembered that and looked at him. "I'm Kat Decker. I'm the crime lab consultant."

"Bullshit."

She inwardly winced at his harsh tone. Her mind began to fully function again and she realized she'd fucked up. She'd have laughed outright at someone if they'd just done what she had then claimed to be some lab jockey from forensics. She didn't regret her actions though.

He spun her and a hand firmly clamped around her upper arm before he shoved her gently. "Move."

It came as a shock when she saw the destruction done to the guard shack. Part of the roof had caved in, the entire side facing the van having taken heavy damage. "Is everyone okay?"

"I don't know." He definitely snarled. "We're checking."

Rusty rushed forward. Kat identified her by her shape and empty gun holster. "I'm so sorry, Darkness."

"Save it," he snapped. "Take her to a holding cell. I have to check our people. Strip her down to her underwear and make damn sure she's not hiding anything."

"Of course." Rusty sounded stressed as her voice broke.

He pushed her toward Rusty. "Calm. Take a deep breath."

Kat admitted she followed his advice too, though she knew it wasn't meant for her.

"Do you think any of ours died?" Rusty sounded close to tears.

"I don't think so. I need to check. Move. Take her now and watch her closely. No one is to go near her until I get there. I'll interview her."

Rusty gripped her handcuffs and tugged. Kat followed her around the damaged building, taking in every detail. Officers had rushed to the scene and she spotted movement through an intact window when they rounded the side. One man was lifting a section of roof off the floor.

Kat had no words as she was escorted to the back of the long building. Its much smaller appearance from the front had been deceiving. More officers rushed out in full gear. They didn't take time to stop or question who she was as Rusty just pushed her against the wall to get out of their way.

"Come on," Rusty whispered.

Kat didn't argue. She needed to think up a good lie to explain what she'd just done. "I'm sorry about taking your gun."

Rusty growled. "Silence. You heard Darkness. No talking until he comes. He'll be the one to interrogate you."

That didn't sound good at all. She was led down a hallway at the very back corner of the building and the door was shoved open. Kat glanced around the room—maybe fifteen feet by twenty-five feet. There were no two-way mirrors. A chair was bolted to the floor near a drain. There was a hook at the top of the wall behind it on one side and a long table with two chairs on the other. The walls and ceiling had been painted to match the dull-gray concrete floor.

The first twinges of fear shot up Kat's spine. It wasn't like any interrogation room she'd ever visited in a police station. It reminded her more of one she'd recently seen in a movie. The guards had nearly beaten the prisoner to death. Blood had soaked the walls and floor of that room, the drain on the floor there for easy cleanup. She really hoped the NSO hadn't seen a similar film and taken notes.

Rusty fished out a key and removed the cuffs. "Remove everything but your undergarments."

Kat winced at the thought of a cavity search but she didn't resist. The room was chilly as she stripped and placed her clothing in a folded stack on the table, her shoes next to it. She faced Rusty, wondering if it was policy to keep the face shield and helmet on.

"Hands in front again."

Kat meekly offered her wrists, accepting the click of metal without a word.

"You don't appear injured. Do you need a medic?"

She was far from okay but nothing hurt physically except a little throbbing in her back. It didn't seem important, though, or serious. Her emotions were a mess but a medic couldn't help with that. "I'm okay."

"Have a seat."

She sat. Rusty picked up her clothing and shoes. "Don't get up. Stay put. Darkness will be here soon."

"May I have some water, please?"

"I'll forward your request to Darkness."

Rusty was gone in the next instant, the click of metal a certainty that she'd locked the door. Kat glanced around the room grimly. *At least there was no cavity search.* That was the only good news for Kat.

Chapter Two

✠

Darkness stripped out of his uniform and put on a tank top and sweat pants with NSO imprinted in white on the black material. It wasn't the ideal outfit for an interrogation but the lockers had been damaged in the blast. His discarded uniform lay in a heap on the floor, covered in dust and drywall powder. The makeshift changing room was filled with other Species.

Bluebird rushed in with another armload of clothing. "Here you go. This is all Supply had on hand. It is too hot for sweatshirts."

"Everyone is okay." Flame entered the room. "The last one of our officers is accounted for. There are only minor injuries."

Darkness bit back a snarl. "What of the humans?"

Flame held his gaze. "Four died but one is barely alive. He's been airlifted to a trauma unit in the out world. He suffered severe burns and internal injuries. Our medical staff doesn't believe he'll survive."

No sympathy for their deaths bothered Darkness. "Too bad. I wanted to question them."

Snow stomped in, removing his uniform. "We barricaded the front gates. Homeland is officially closed. Justice is handling the media while Fury is waiting for the task force to assemble to begin the investigation. Trey was already here so he's spoken to Tim." He sneezed. "I don't think I'll ever get the smell out of my nose. I inhaled a lot of that shit."

"The dust isn't harmful." Bluebird began gathering the dirty uniforms. "At least that's what Trey said. It's mostly

28

debris from part of the building collapsing. He said new buildings don't have poisonous materials."

"Good to know." Snow sneezed again. "But I was talking about the smoke from the fire."

"Oh." She paused, her arms still full. "I'll get more clothing from Supply." She spun and rushed away.

Rusty entered next. "Is everyone well?"

"Only some cuts and bruises," Flame answered. "We didn't lose anyone."

Darkness stepped forward, drawing her attention. "I told you to stay with the prisoner."

"She's locked in interrogation room three. It's the farthest corner from the damage. She wasn't carrying anything in her clothing. I checked and tagged it as evidence. She wants water. Is it okay to give her some?"

"Yes. Go stand guard. I'll be there in a moment." He sat, debating whether he should put his boots back on. They were coated with white powder. He stood. "Fuck it."

"Excuse me?" Snow was dressing, too, but paused and looked up.

"I'm going to talk to our prisoner like this."

"You're going to interview a suspect barefoot and out of uniform?" Flame's eyebrows rose.

Darkness pointed to where the dressing rooms for the males had been. "If you want to go in there where the ceiling lights crashed into the metal lockers and risk being electrocuted to retrieve my spares, go right ahead. I don't have time to rush home first either. We need answers. We were attacked."

Flame closed his mouth and nodded sharply.

"Do you want help?" Flirt moved forward, already changed from his uniform to running clothes. "Two of us may intimidate the male more."

"It's a female." Darkness strode forward. "I'll handle this alone."

"I didn't think you interrogated females. I'd like to volunteer to do it." Snow was putting on his shirt.

"I'll make an exception this time. I saw what she did. She's well trained and a soldier isn't just any female. They are far more dangerous."

"I'd really like to interview her," Snow persisted.

"No."

Darkness didn't wait around any longer for more conversation. He needed answers and he would get them, regardless of what he had to do. Rage simmered as he maneuvered through the building. Every Species had heard the news and rushed to duty. He passed them, feeling a little pride at the unity and calm they showed under the circumstances.

He paused outside the door of the interrogation room and it sank in that he'd have to go in there and do whatever it took to make the female talk. Homeland had been attacked and it could have cost a lot of Species lives. He'd been on his way to take out the driver of that van but admitted it probably would have cost his own life attempting it. He'd leapt from the top of the wall to the roof of the security building once it became clear their bullets were useless. The female had done his job instead.

Why? Her tactics had been clean, too precise. She had skills that she should not possess. He'd have been hard-pressed to do what she had. He spun and stormed over to the phone. Security picked up on the second ring.

"Tell me everything you've learned about the female in holding."

He listened, his rage building. He needed to stop thinking of her as a female. She was a threat. He needed to remember that. Normal tactics wouldn't work. He'd have to outsmart her and keep her off guard. A plan formed and he took a few calming breaths. Anger was the last thing he needed to use against someone with her probable background.

* * * * *

Kat kept her eyes closed and tried to ignore the chilly air. Adrenaline had left her emotionally drained. It was a normal reaction under the tense circumstances. She'd just faced death, had taken the life of the driver she'd shot and probably his accomplices. *That's at least two dead for sure. The one hanging out of the back of that van was burnt toast.*

She flinched at the food comparison her mind came up with and shifted her weight on the metal chair. It wasn't helping her get any warmer. She debated pacing the room but decided against it. The risk of incurring more suspicion from the NSO would be higher if she failed to act the role of the frightened, timid mouse. That's what they would expect and that's what she needed to give them if she had any chance of recovering her undercover persona.

The click of a lock preceded the door being thrown open. A dark-haired man entered. He was seriously tan with piercing dark eyes, which looked black. He stared at her, his features shadowed. She put him at about six-and-a-half feet tall. *Darkness. That's got to be him. Holy shit, he's huge and intimidating.*

She took note of his densely muscled arms and very broad shoulders. The tank top stretched tightly over his upper body and tapered down to where he'd tucked it in the waistband of black drawstring pants. They weren't tied, the white laces just hung free. He had shapely, muscular thighs, evident even through the thick material, and at least size-sixteen bare feet. His very casual attire wasn't what she'd expected.

"Who are you?"

It confirmed his identity. She'd never forget that deep voice. "Kathryn Decker but everyone just calls me Kat for short."

The door slammed, sealing them inside together. She glanced at it, waiting for it to open a second time.

"No one else is coming in here. There will be no rescue."

She focused on his face. He stood still, a few feet inside the door. "Isn't a woman supposed to be present?"

A soft, frightening sound came from him. It wasn't exactly a growl but it wasn't friendly either. "Do you realize you're not inside the United States anymore? You were in NSO territory once you passed those gates. Tell me the truth because believe me, you don't want me to make you talk. Your laws of interrogation don't apply here."

Fear edged up Kat's spine but she pushed it back. "You can't kill me."

He stepped closer and lifted his head enough for her to get a better look at his face. Her breath caught in her lungs. He had one of the most masculine faces she'd ever seen. His cheekbones were pronounced, possibly American Indian. A square jaw sat under a pair of full lips with a harsh angle, due to his frown. It was the shape of his eyes, though, that really startled her. Justice North had the catlike shape but his weren't nearly as fierce. She still couldn't tell the exact color of those eyes but she'd guess dark brown. Unusually long, thick eyelashes framed them.

Breathe, damn it. She sucked in air, forcing her lungs to work again. The way he dressed had to be a tactic to throw her off her game. She needed to keep her shit together. It was difficult to do with that grim expression and the predatory stare aimed her way.

"I actually could. Are you ready to tell me the truth now? Who are you really? What are you doing here?"

He's bluffing. She hoped. "My name is Kat Decker," she lied. "Check my driver's license. Call my boss. I was asked to come to Homeland for two weeks to teach forensic science classes and brush up your security on some of the newest trends in criminal behavior."

He took another step closer. "Are you Army? Marines? Special forces?"

She shook her head. "Crime lab."

He snarled.

Kat tried not to react but failed. Her body tensed at the frightening, dangerous sound. The layout of the room didn't make her feel any safer. There were no cameras. She'd looked for signs of how they could monitor her but hadn't found any. They really were alone in the room.

"Where did you learn how to take out that armored van?"

"I watch too many action movies and I learned all that through them."

His mouth pressed into a tighter angry line, assuring her he wasn't buying that bullshit. She tried again.

"I love watching movies. Blow-them-up-shoot-it-out-save-the-world kind of stuff. Would you believe I wanted to grow up to be an action-film star when I was a little girl?" She couldn't resist. "Bruce Willis is my idol."

His hands fisted at his sides, his only reaction. She might have gone too far with that answer but hoped he'd have a sense of humor. He didn't.

"I'm not in a mood to play games. Take my words as a warning. My patience is nearly gone."

Kat took a deep breath then blew it out slowly. She knew she was on thin ice and she'd have to give him something valid. "The bullets were bouncing off the van. It doesn't take a genius to figure out it was armored. I yelled at them to shoot the tires but I don't think anyone heard me over all that racket. Maybe they didn't see it from their angle but I was kind of up close and personal since it was trying to break free of the gate. I realized they'd shove my car out of the way to attack your second gate."

"How did you know their plans?"

"I didn't. I made an educated guess. It was just common sense. I only wanted to stop them. Your bullets weren't working so I grabbed Rusty's gun to look for a weak spot. They didn't plate the lock on the driver's door." She hesitated. "I saw that the driver and passenger were wearing full assault gear. Something had to be done fast. I reacted before I really thought it out. I remember the last time vehicles got past your gates. How many died? Sixteen people?"

"Seventeen," he growled.

She studied him and it was clear he didn't enjoy being reminded of the breach that had taken place after Homeland first opened. "I saw a way to get the driver's door open and took it. I shot out the lock on the door and took out the driver. Disabling the driver wasn't going to stop them. The passenger could have just scooted over to drive and I saw movement in the back. That meant there was at least one more assailant. It would have been a bloodbath. Have you ever seen what bad guys with guns and full assault gear can do? I have. I told you I watch a lot of movies. I looked down and saw grenades strapped to the driver. I tossed them inside and closed the door."

"How did you know what they were?"

Kat was starting to get irritated. "Because I'm not a moron. That is what they looked like, to me. I wasn't exactly sure what they'd do but they were obviously meant to be used against the NSO. I used them instead."

One of his eyebrows arched. "You weren't sure what they'd do?"

"They looked like homemade explosives with switches, is what I meant. I didn't see any cylinders, which would indicate a chemical bomb, so I assumed they just went *boom*! I was right. I didn't exactly have much time to mull it over since I was dodging bullets from the passenger, who was intent on killing me."

Darkness unfurled his fists and crossed his arms over his chest. "Four humans inside that van are dead and the fifth one won't live long."

They were bad guys but it still hit her hard. She'd never killed anyone before. The training she'd had didn't cover the reality of learning that news.

"You killed humans. Do you understand that?"

She nodded sharply, not trusting her voice. The assholes might have deserved it but the reality was rough. They probably had families and friends who would suffer their loss. *Even evil shitheads have mothers.*

"Answer me," he demanded in a harsh tone.

"Yes." She grew defensive because it helped her deal with the stress. "Do you understand that they didn't batter down your gates in an armored vehicle, wearing full military assault gear, to bring you cupcakes and a we-love-you message? I was trying to protect New Species."

Darkness moved fast enough to make her flinch when he closed the distance between them, bent and gripped the sides of her chair. He pushed his face almost nose to nose with her. His eyes were shadowed with his head tipped forward but they appeared very menacing. She tried to lean back but there was nowhere to go in the metal chair pressed tightly against her spine.

He growled deep in his throat, proving he was not completely human. "Do you expect me to believe you are a crime lab technician when you just single-handedly took out five humans?"

She forced a smile and ignored her rapidly beating heart. "I'm really good at my job. I see a lot of bad stuff and don't forget my love of action films."

He hissed, fanning her with the scent of chocolate and mint. She hoped her breath smelled as good since their lips were mere inches apart. The urge to glance at his mouth was too strong to pass up but she regretted it as soon as she did.

Her eyes widened in surprise and fear at the sight of two long, terrifying fangs.

"Holy shit." She hadn't meant to say it aloud.

His upper lip lifted a little to give her a better view of them. It had to be on purpose. His next words killed any doubt.

"I'm nothing like you." His tone deepened. "I'll show you mercy if you start giving me honest answers. Were those men sent here to die to fool us into trusting you?"

That jerked her out of the stupor caused by his scary fangs. She stared into his eyes. "What?"

"You heard me. Was that some type of show played out to gain our trust?"

"Are you on drugs?" She'd been excited to visit Homeland but it had turned into a nightmare. Her cover was pretty much blown unless she could talk her way out of the situation. To be accused of being in cahoots with the assholes intent on killing New Species flipped her bitch switch.

"I don't know if you rushed out of that guard house or if you were already outside but that prick on the passenger side tried really hard to turn me into Swiss cheese. Those explosive devices could have gone off in my hands before I threw them into that van. I could have been blown to bits right along with those pricks. How dare you?" She glared at him. "You think you're the only one having a bad day? I just wanted to come to Homeland to have some fun, meet New Species and teach some classes. That was my only agenda. Now I'm locked in a room with a paranoid idiot."

The silence was absolute. She replayed what she'd just said to him and closed her eyes. *Shit. Get hold of yourself, damn it. I'm falling apart faster than a recruit on day one of training.*

He released the chair, gripped her rib cage and yanked her right out of her seat. Her feet didn't touch as he walked across the room and dropped her ass-first on the table. He grabbed the chain linking her handcuffed wrists in front of her body and forcibly raised her arms by jerking them up. He sidestepped the table and she fell back as he hauled her along the surface, only stopping when she was stretched out flat atop it.

"Fight your way up," he snarled, bending enough to get in her face again. "I dare you. Show me how skilled a crime lab technician is at hand-to-hand combat."

She lay still. He hadn't hurt her. She might have a bruise or two on her ass from the hard surface when he'd dropped her but that was the extent of it. The tabletop was cold. He kept a fisted hold on the chain to keep her arms restrained above her head. It was imperative that she defuse the edgy situation. She could use her legs by bending them up and kicking out at him, try to knock him back, but it would only prove that she wasn't who she claimed.

"I'm sorry I called you an idiot. I was just really upset that you accused me of such a horrible thing. I risked my life out there. It wasn't staged."

He reached down and grabbed the front of his pants. Kat had forgotten that she only wore a pair of panties and a bra until that moment. Real fear shot through her that he'd sexually assault her. He was a big bastard, really strong, and probably weighed double what she did. She was tough but doubted she could fight him off for long. Every muscle went rigid in preparation to at least try. He didn't expose his dick but instead tore the drawstring tie from the sweatpants.

She slightly relaxed until he began to secure her to something above her head. She twisted enough to look up and saw the bolted-in ring then peered at his face.

"What are you doing?"

"Making sure you stay exactly where I want you."

She felt exposed, stretched out practically naked on her back. "I want to sit in the chair."

"I want the truth." He straightened and took a step back.

Kat tugged on the handcuffs but the thick cord held. She glanced at the sides of the table but couldn't roll over without falling against the chairs on the left or into him on the right.

"Who are you really? Let's stop playing this game. Your ID was good but my officers are better. Someone fucked up when they created your history. Our security check only tracked you back three years then you end. There's nothing on you."

She stared up into his eyes, hoping he might be bluffing, but she saw the truth reflected there. *Shit.* That rat bastard Mason had screwed up the paper trail and, in fact, had blown her cover.

"I got divorced," she lied. "I took back my maiden name." It was worth a try.

He smiled but it didn't reach his eyes. "Here's an interesting twist. Checking the current database showed you exist but when we searched outdated internet sites that social security number belonged to an Eleanor Brinkler. She was a seventy-year-old housewife who died ten years ago." He slowly raked his gaze down her body then back up. "I'm no expert on what an eighty-year-old looks like but I'm certain you're nowhere near that age."

Kat panicked but tried to mask her features, struggling to think of something to say.

He stepped closer. "You don't look dead." He stared at her chest. "You're breathing." His gaze met and held hers. "What is your real name? Who sent you and why?"

"This has to be some horrible mistake." It was all she could say. She was nailed and Robert Mason had sent her into one hell of a mess. Her cover identity had been a muddled rush job.

Darkness leaned forward, putting his face close to hers again. "I don't want to hurt you." His voice lowered to a rasp. "Don't make me do that, sweetheart. I have enough memories to assure I suffer nightmares almost every time I sleep. Just tell me who you really are and why you came to Homeland. You're busted."

She licked her lips, tempted to tell him the truth. Mason never should have sent her to Homeland undercover. It would probably get them both fired, but it would be even worse if she talked. No one wanted an agent working for them who cracked under pressure. Darkness was just doing his job and he was good at it. She respected that.

"You look so soft and fragile." He paused, watching her. "Let me tell you a few things about me. Have you ever heard of a human named Darwin Havings?"

Kat blanked her features but her heart rate jumped. Havings was currently number thirty-two on the list of the Department of Homeland Security's most wanted. He'd been a rich bastard with businesses mainly in the Middle East and ties to third-world countries. He was also suspected to have invested heavily in Mercile Industries. That last association had earned him a hard look from authorities and what they'd uncovered was some pretty nasty suspicions but no actual evidence. Havings was rumored to be wrapped up in drug and sex-slave trafficking. They'd also found indications that he might be guilty of stealing from the US military in Afghanistan and selling the stolen weapons to rebels. That had put his name on the wanted list.

"Nope. Is he an action star?" A crime lab technician wouldn't be familiar with that name because it hadn't been in the news.

"He's a bad human I've met."

She had to remember to regulate her breathing, something that was tough to do since she was frantically trying to figure out how that meeting was possible. *Why? How? When?* A horrible suspicion gripped her that her dickhead boss might have been right. *Are they in business with Havings? The NSO would be the perfect place for him to hide. We don't have jurisdiction at Homeland or Reservation. He could flip us off from inside the gates and there wouldn't be a damn thing we could do about it.*

"I was one of a group of Species he took from Mercile."

"Why?" She relaxed slightly. That meant it had happened in the past when Darkness had been a prisoner of the company. Havings would have had access to New Species then. *Is the connection still active?*

"It was a test." He growled, cocked his head and continued to watch her eyes. "They put explosive collars around our necks. We were biological brothers and they knew we were aware of the connection because they showed us proof. We were birthed from the same batch of embryos they'd created from two particular humans they had matched up. They always created multiple embryos, often from the same pair of humans, sometimes by pairing one or both with other donors for different physical characteristics. Our animal genetics varied but our human DNA showed a familial match. That was why he wanted us. He knew we'd protect each other and do anything for our brothers."

Jesus. Some of her control slipped and she knew her expression revealed the sympathy she felt. "Why explosive collars?"

"We knew they'd set them off and kill our brothers if we didn't follow orders."

"That's fucked up." *Also a terrorist tactic — an extreme one.* She didn't mention that last part.

He cocked his head and leaned in. His nose tickled as it brushed against her throat. He inhaled deeply, seeming to smell her. Kat didn't protest but it made her aware of him in a new way. It was kind of sexual.

"We're protective of our own by nature and they used that," Darkness whispered. "Do you want to know what they made us do?"

"Sure." Her gut twisted from a bad feeling that she wouldn't like the answer.

"They taught us how to fight and kill. We were four breathing weapons with faster reflexes, stronger bodies and keener senses than humans." He lifted his head and came at her neck from the other side, inhaling again. It brought his chest into light contact with her breasts. "Our teachers were mercenaries with strange accents. They were brutal."

Fuck. The strange accents he spoke of were a tipoff. Darwin Havings only hired his bodyguards from his Middle Eastern contacts. They were the sorts usually linked to presumed assassinations. It was really bad news that they had trained Darkness. She could just imagine the things he'd been subjected to.

"I learned everything about how to torture someone into telling me whatever I want to know."

Suspicion confirmed. She took another deep breath, shaking inside, terrified. She'd been trained to withstand torture but not the hardcore stuff he'd probably learned. Would he use it to break her? If so, he'd do whatever worked to get answers. It meant it could get ugly and dangerous, with the possible loss of body parts or death.

He moved again until he could stare directly into her eyes. "You're frightened. I can smell it on you. Just tell me the truth."

She wasn't sure what to do. "Is that why you're sniffing at me?"

"I'm not human."

She really didn't need the reminder. "May I have some time to think about it?"

His eyebrows rose. "You want me to wait while you try to come up with more convincing lies?"

"I want to tell you the truth but can't."

He braced both hands on the table, one on each side of her chest, and leaned in closer until he was almost half on top of her. "Do you know how animalistic some of us can be?"

"Not really. I read the papers and have watched interviews."

"You see what we want you to. I'm not Justice North."

She could believe that. Mr. North seemed downright friendly, even cuddly on television. He displayed a quick sense of humor and an easygoing personality. Darkness was none of those things.

He parted his lips and showed off those fangs again. Kat stared at them and hoped he wasn't implying he'd use them to bite her. That would probably hurt like hell.

"Imagine honing predatory instincts, combined with being encouraged to become the worst of humanity. That's what I was made to be when I was pulled from Mercile and sent to those humans, if they could be called that. Tell me the truth or you'll see what I'm capable of. It will be brutal."

Real tears filled her eyes and there was nothing she could do but blink them back. He was a master at instilling fear since she believed every word he'd said.

"Honestly. I had no hidden agenda. I just wanted to stop those men from hurting your people." She stared into his striking eyes, hoping he'd see the truth. "I don't want any New Species hurt. I was looking forward to teaching some classes and getting to spend time here at Homeland. I thought it would be cool, almost a vacation."

His eyes narrowed. "Don't do that, sweetheart."

"I swear on my life that every word I just said was absolutely true."

"I meant don't cry." He closed his eyes and tucked his chin to look away. "Fuck."

His reaction astounded her. He was either an amazing actor or a master at deception. Otherwise she'd think he was feeling a twinge of empathy. He looked at her again and the tortured expression on his face stabbed at her heart.

"I can't do this." He shook his head. "It's not worth my soul or what's left of it."

"Can't do what?"

"Pretend you're a female from my past so I can effectively do my job. I actually admired your skill out there. I don't think I could have done as well as you did or dealt with those humans as quickly. You either think fast on your feet or it was a brilliant strategic move. You're one of the best assassins I've ever met if that's the case. If I'm wrong…" He looked at her chest. "It makes you exceptionally sexy."

Kat didn't know if she should be flattered or offended. She said nothing.

He blinked a few times. "You pose a problem for me, Kat. If that is your name."

"It is. Everyone calls me that."

"I doubt it."

"Why? What's so unbelievable about my name?"

"You're at the NSO and have the name of a feline?"

It sank in. "It's spelled with a K."

"I don't care. Why not use a more human name like Mary?"

"That's not what my parents stuck me with. I'm actually named after my grandmother. She died while my mom was pregnant with me." That was also true. "It's just a weird coincidence."

He didn't look convinced.

"It's too obvious if you think about it. I'd have to be dumb to pick that name and I didn't even make the connection to cats until you brought it up. I'm not an idiot. I would have done a fantastic job at building a false identity for myself."

"That, I believe."

"Good."

"Who do you work for?"

"Bakersfield Police Department, crime lab."

"What color is your bra?"

"Black." He was testing her, trying to gauge facial expressions or her tone of voice to determine if he could spot a sign that she lied. She'd done the same thing to suspects.

"My hair is brown. So are my eyes. I'm five-foot-five. Don't bother asking my weight. I'm not telling. Everyone lies on their license about that."

"You're about a hundred forty pounds. No need. I lifted you out of that chair."

He was good. She was actually a hundred thirty-eight pounds.

"You appear to be lighter, about one twenty-five, but you have good muscle tone. That tells me you work out or train often." He studied her breasts. "No plastic surgery." He lifted away and stood, his gaze raking over her stomach and thighs. "No children."

"How do you know that?"

"You have scars on you. Your upper arm, one near your calf. They are noticeable. It is telling. Pregnancy would have marred you as well and left signs. Your lower belly and upper thighs are flawless. No signs of stretch marks."

"Not all women get them." She admired his skills of observation. It was kind of hot.

"Not all but most have at least a few."

"I don't have kids," she confirmed.

His focus returned to her face. "You don't wear makeup. It also explains your plain undergarments. No lace on them and your bra isn't a padded one to give your breasts a larger appearance. You don't want to draw attention to yourself from men. Why is that?"

"Maybe I just didn't have time to do my face this morning. As for my bra, pushups are uncomfortable as hell."

He regarded her, expressionless, and she would have loved to know what he was thinking.

Darkness hoped fear provided the last push he needed to get the female to break. Everything he'd told her was true. He did admire her. An image flashed of what would happen if he struck her or broke bones. She'd scream. He'd feel like the monster the humans had tried to create. He couldn't hit her.

She had beautiful, expressive eyes. He hoped he could read her correctly and that the males who'd attacked the gates weren't with her. It would anger him if she were evil. He'd already fallen for one female who had betrayed him. He could use that anger on Kat but one glance at her frail build stopped him cold. There was no honor in harming Kat. She was helpless and, damn it, he really liked her.

Frustration came next. It was his job to get answers and find out who she really was. He just couldn't do it effectively. He considered his options. Someone else would have to take his place. He didn't even want to be in the building, knowing what would go down in that interrogation room. A wave of compassion and protectiveness washed over him. Queasiness pitted in his stomach, thinking about another male inflicting pain on her to make her talk.

He stared into her eyes again, torn between duty and the unexpected desire to just escort her to the gate. That would put an end to it all but that wasn't possible. He decided to try one more shot at intimidation and fear.

Chapter Three

∞

"Look at me." He removed his tank top.

"I am." Kat studied Darkness.

"All of me." He backed away from the table a few feet. "Tell me what you see."

"You're tall." She took in his naked chest. "Very fit." The tight, well-defined muscles displayed across his abs were perfection all the way down to the waistband of his sweats. She jerked her attention to his face.

"Never entice a predator into playing a game you can't win," he rasped. "The NSO isn't to be fooled with. I don't want to hurt you because I have an issue with hitting females but others won't have that same problem. Tell me everything, the whole truth, or this is going to get extreme."

"I don't know what you mean." She really didn't.

He stepped closer and her heart pounded when he braced his hands on the table on each side of her breasts and leaned over. He pressed his nose against her throat, inhaling. She turned her head to give him access and to keep her face away from his scary teeth.

"I can smell your fear, yet you won't break. Fine. I'm going to get someone else in here." He reached up and untied the cord then straightened and gripped her arm, hauling her into a sitting position. "I strongly suggest you talk to whoever replaces me. I would hate for you to see the inside of Medical." He let her go and glanced down her body. "Something so beautiful should never be bloodied and battered."

He spun around and stalked toward the door. It sank in what was happening and Kat panicked. "Wait!"

He halted and slowly turned to face her. "You're willing to tell me the truth?"

"I've already told you what I can. That's about as honest as I can be."

"That's not good enough. Just sit there. Someone will be in shortly."

"There's got to be another option."

"It's beat it out of you or…" His dark gaze lowered to her breasts.

"Or what?"

"I could seduce it out of you."

Kat was stunned for a few seconds, letting his words sink in. "Oh."

"That's against the rules." He actually smiled.

It transformed his features and Kat just gawked at how handsome an amused Darkness was. She did her own once-over of his body. He had the best one she'd ever seen and the idea of getting up close and personal with him was oddly appealing. "You don't look like someone who plays by the rules." *That came out of my mouth.* She cleared her throat, slightly embarrassed at her slip. "I mean, that sounds better than taking a beating."

His grin faded. "I'll go get someone else."

Kat bit her lower lip as he gripped the door handle, turned it and swung it open a few inches.

"You could try."

He froze.

"I mean, it might work. The seduction thing."

The door slammed and he spun, anger on his features. "Are you trying to bait me?"

"Maybe." Her gaze traveled down his length again. "You know you're seriously hot."

He advanced a step, paused. His hands fisted at his sides. "This is a dangerous game, Kat. *If* that is your name."

"I told you it is. Everyone really calls me that." She licked her lips. Darkness was the type of man she'd always fantasized about. Big, sexy, and he probably didn't follow the rules. She slid off the edge of the table, ignoring his command for her to stay in place. She might never get another chance to be with someone like him. "I'd rather have a battle of wills than be on the receiving end of a beat-down."

He drew closer and growled softly. She advanced, meeting him halfway. Only inches separated them. It made her aware of how much taller he was, how much bigger. She wasn't afraid though. He'd been willing to walk out of the room rather than hit her. It made him even more appealing. A lot of muscular men she'd met were bullies. Darkness had a sense of chivalry. That was a rare trait.

"This is a mistake." He reached out, though, and gently encircled her hips with his warm hands. His head lowered and she tilted hers to give him access to her neck.

"Maybe." She hoped he'd go for her throat again. She'd liked it before when he'd sniffed at her.

She smothered a moan when he brushed a teasing kiss under her ear. His lips were soft and his tongue hot as it swiped at her skin. A shiver ran down her spine when his fangs pressed against her throat. He didn't bite but instead lightly used them to trail a path lower to the curve of her neck.

He used his tongue and teeth to explore her throat and shoulder. It was amazing and her body responded when his chest touched hers. He was feverishly hot but it felt incredibly good. She'd been cold but he warmed her. She resisted the urge to lift her cuffed hands up and loop them around his neck.

He nipped her with his fangs. Her entire body jerked at the sudden jolt of sensation. It didn't hurt but it had been hard enough to shock her system. He growled. Her nipples ached where they touched him, the thin material of her bra doing nothing to lessen the vibrations that originated from his chest. His lips trailed upward to her earlobe and he stopped kissing her.

"Tell me who you really work for."

She tried to clear her mind. He was good. She had almost forgotten she was still being interrogated via seduction. She was turned-on and he had the sexiest voice ever when he spoke in that gruff whisper.

"Bakersfield Police Department, crime lab." She tensed, hoping it wouldn't piss him off.

He chuckled, to her surprise. "I'm going to break you, sweetheart. It's going to be a pleasure for both of us."

She tried to turn to look at him but he dipped his head and started kissing her neck again. He caressed the curve of her hip and his thumb hooked beneath the band of her underwear. He pulled it down on one side and she was very aware of the material lowering, dangerously close to exposing her mound.

"No real foreplay first?" She longed to have him actually touch her there.

"I'm motivating you to tell the truth."

His hand moved and the back of his fingers played with the skin he'd exposed. He nipped her again on the curve of her shoulder. She jerked against him and gasped. It seemed to encourage him to trail hot kisses up her neck while rubbing slow circles with his fingertips precariously close to her sex.

She clenched her teeth as a slow throbbing began in her clit and heat spread to her belly, causing it to ache too. *Ignore it. You're making this too easy.* Her mind knew it but her body didn't listen. In desperation, she decided to spread her palms on his chest. The handcuffs restricted her movement. He reached between them and gripped the chain, jerking them to the side so she couldn't touch him.

"I should be able to touch you back."

That made him lift his head and arch an eyebrow in question. "You're the one who said I shouldn't play by the rules. There is no 'fair' in this room, sweetheart."

"That's your plan? Only you can do the touching?"

His nostrils flared and his sexy smile curved into a smug grin. "Yes. I can smell how you respond to me."

He's full of shit. It made her angry and she latched on to that feeling, hoping it would help her resist him. "Bullshit."

"You're getting wet."

"It takes more than a few kisses to get me that hot."

He chuckled. "That's a bold lie." His fingers stilled their stroking. "Should I prove it?"

He turned his hand and inched lower, keeping it between her underwear and skin until it was the only thing that covered her pussy. The feel of his palm was shocking but he wasn't done. He traced the line of her slit and slid one fingertip between her pussy lips.

She tried to buck her hips away from him but he released the chain and hooked his arm around her waist, jerking her body against his. He slowly moved his fingertip enough to press against her clit. She moaned at the pleasure.

"Wet," he confirmed. "Very wet." His fingertip applied a little pressure to her clit and stroked.

Kat rested her forehead against his chest and closed her eyes. She battled her body, trying to block the pleasure that radiated through her system. She had never been trained to resist an attack on the most sensitive spot on her body.

"That's so not fair."

He leaned in and started to kiss her throat again. Her knees threatened to buckle but he kept her upright. She wanted to do a little tormenting too.

The finger rubbing her clit stilled and he ceased kissing her throat. "Who do you work for? Don't lie, sweetheart."

"Do you stop if I tell you?"

"Yes."

"The crime lab."

His hot breath fanned her skin. "At this pace, you're going to beg me to make you come in about five minutes or less." His voice deepened. "I'll stop long enough for your passion to cool and we'll start again. I can do this for hours until you're drenched in sweat and hurting so bad to come that you'll tell me anything I want to know just to make the agony stop. It will turn into that."

"That's mean."

He lifted his face and their gazes held. His eyes were beautiful in a fierce way. His voice came out raspy. "Just tell me what I want to know. I'll reward you."

"By getting me off?"

"Yes."

Kat was tempted to blurt out the truth. She couldn't remember a time when she'd wanted a man more. Her day had been insane and it seemed fitting to be in that room with him, doing things they both would get in serious trouble for if their bosses found out. It was completely unprofessional to want to have sex with Darkness. It didn't feel wrong though. It was one thing to break some moral codes but another altogether to completely screw over her agency.

"I wish I could. I guess you're going to have to try harder."

"This will be worse for me than you."

"What does that mean?"

His gaze lowered to where their chests were smashed together. She glanced down and saw the way it created a lot of cleavage. She looked back into his dark eyes.

"It's going to be a battle of wills that I don't look forward to, sweetheart."

She didn't understand. He must have read the confusion in her eyes or expression.

"You're going to beg me to fuck you and I'm going to want to, regardless of whether you keep your silence. I've avoided females for some time but you tempt me like no other. I'm depending on my resolve to never be led by my sexual desires ever again to keep my will strong. Otherwise…"

His voice trailed off and she wanted to know what he would have said. "Otherwise what?"

"You don't want to see me snap. You'd end up with more than you could handle. You'd have two hundred forty-five pounds of raw male unleashed on your ass." The color of his eyes seemed to darken before they narrowed. "I mean that. I'd carry you to that table, bend you over it and fuck you like you've never been fucked before. I'm not sure you could survive it. I've got years of pent-up sexual frustration and all of it would be pounding into you."

He twisted his pelvis and pressed his erection against her hip. Even through the material he felt really hard and big. His words, the meaning behind them and the feel of his dick amped up the sexual tension. It also turned her on even more. No man had ever spoken to her that way. She bet he was one guy who wasn't all talk and he could back it up.

"Little pretend-cats shouldn't ever play with actual feral, bigger ones. Do you understand? I'm not as domesticated as you might think."

Her heart rate raced and she sealed her lips, otherwise she might have asked him to do just that.

"So do us both a favor and just start telling me the truth because once this plays out further, it might end really bad. See how honesty works? It's giving someone the absolute truth. I will get you off but I won't fuck you. I might hurt you."

He was a big guy but she wasn't afraid. She hated to see the conflict in his eyes though. To put him in that situation was the last thing she'd meant to do. Inexplicably, she really liked Darkness. Maybe asking him to seduce her hadn't been her best idea. He had a job to do and had someone to answer to as well.

"My name is really Kat and I came here to teach. I'd never hurt your people. That is the absolute truth."

"Who do you work for?"

She hesitated, knowing he wouldn't accept the lie because he was smart. It was tempting to just say FBI but she couldn't give that up. Her boss might have sent her to do his personal bidding but she had no plans to really snoop on the NSO or try to find dirt on them. "I'm not an assassin or someone who'd ever want anyone at Homeland hurt."

"Who. Do. You. Work. For?" He rasped out each word.

"A jerk." She was skating around lying to him by giving honest answers, just not the ones he wanted.

"Does he want to harm us?"

She didn't mean to look away from his direct stare but she was off her game and the reflexive movement couldn't be taken back. She held his gaze again. "I'm not a big fan of my boss. He really is a jerk. I don't follow his orders to the letter. I came here to meet New Species and teach them forensics. I would never hurt your people. I don't wish them harm. I swear."

"What is your boss's name?"

"Dickhead. I also call him prick." She closed her eyes. She wouldn't lie to Darkness anymore but she couldn't give up her boss even if she didn't agree with why she had been sent. It put her in a hell of a moral dilemma.

She'd admired New Species since they'd been freed, reading and watching everything in the news about their struggles. She was a fan, even. Robert Mason's connection to them or the reasons for his hatred wasn't clear but she knew it must be personal for him. She was just a pawn but that didn't mean she had to make any moves against anyone at Homeland.

"Look at me, sweetheart."

She did as Darkness ordered and held his gaze. His were really beautiful eyes. She believed everything he'd told her about his past. To have survived that hellish experience made her admire the hell out of him. Lesser men would have broken, died during the ordeal or taken their lives just to make it end. He deserved her respect, especially since she was pretty certain she could guess what he'd been taught. He wasn't beating the hell out of her, snapping bones just to hear her screams or flaying her alive. He had to have seen it done plenty of times.

"What is your boss's legal name?"

"I can't tell you. I want to but I can't. It's a matter of obligation. Do you understand?"

"It's my duty to make you answer my questions."

"We're in a hell of a mess then, aren't we?" She blinked back tears because the situation felt heartrending. "I never wanted to be considered a bad guy by you. I guess that's where we stand right now, isn't it?"

"You're not a bad guy. You're all female. I'll make you aware of it as much as I am. Do we continue this or do I stop?"

"I don't want you to stop."

He slid his fingertip off her clit to stroke the seam of her pussy. She didn't look away from him or protest. He'd warned her of what he'd do in great detail and she only hoped she wouldn't give in and tell him everything. Darkness might be able to get her to that point. He was just too sexy with that brooding expression and tragic past. He was the type of guy who could be her downfall.

He brought his face closer until his warm breath feathered across her lips. She wanted him to kiss her but he tilted away at the last second and dipped his face into the crook of her neck. She closed her eyes and fisted her hands together when his tongue traced her earlobe. He sucked on it, growled so the vibrations teased her nipples and his finger returned to her clit to slowly stroke it.

Kat wanted to dig her hands into his hair and hold him closer. It looked silky and thick but she couldn't reach him since his arms kept her from lifting up. She even parted her thighs to give him better access to play with her sex.

She was lost in the sensations. His mouth was heaven on her neck, only second to the building ecstasy flooding through her brain. She tried to remain as still as possible in hopes it would lessen the sexual tension. It didn't. She tensed and moaned when she couldn't hold back anymore. He growled in response and pressed his groin tighter against her. The feel of his rigid cock made her aware of how empty she felt. She wanted him inside her. Just imagining what it would feel like had her grinding her pussy against his finger. She was going to come.

He stilled and stopped kissing her. "No."

He eased off her clit and yanked his hand out of her underwear. Darkness gripped her inner thigh. Calloused fingertips stroked the sensitive skin of her hip, almost touching her pussy. He paused there and began kissing her throat again. He ran his fingers along the center of her underwear from the outside, teasing her. His fangs nipped her. She jerked from the shot of pleasure.

She stood there as he explored her with his free hand. He left her underwear alone to tease the skin on her lower belly then cupped her mound. He rubbed but when she moaned he retreated to her inner thigh, caressing it then starting the process over.

Darkness was in hell. The scent of his prisoner's arousal was strong enough to threaten his control. He fought his desire to lay her over the end of the table, shove her thighs far apart and just bend over until he could actually discover if she tasted as good as she smelled. He'd have feared drooling if he'd been canine.

The promise of the carnal high from hearing her cries of pleasure and the way she'd move against his tongue nearly broke his will. It had been too long since he'd gotten lost in the taste, feel and softness of a female. He resisted because he would get lost. He'd make her come and she'd scream his name. Nothing would stop him, at that point, from fucking her. Just imagining how hot and wet she'd be, how she'd feel as he thrust into her made him snarl. That wasn't the objective in their battle of wills. He couldn't allow her to come until she told him everything he needed to know.

His dick hurt. It was steel-hard, a heavy weight of pure torture trapped inside his sweats. He spread his legs a little to alleviate the pressure in his nuts. They wouldn't actually rupture from how tight they had become but it felt that way. He tried to ignore everything below his waist and focus on his little pretend-cat.

Sweat had broken out on her the way he knew it would. He licked some of it. *So sweet.* He used his fangs to bite down on a tendon in her shoulder. He didn't use enough force to break skin but she moaned in response. Her breasts pressed tighter against his chest as she writhed against him. The thin material of her bra did nothing to diminish the impact of those pebbled nipples.

Don't go there, he reminded himself. He wouldn't risk removing her undergarments. He didn't trust his resolve if she was completely bare. He'd suck on her breasts and move lower down her body. That would put his mouth between her thighs and he wouldn't be able to stop until he flipped her over and fucked her.

You're here to get answers. Remember that. He had to chant it inside his head when he caught himself rubbing his dick against her body. Even that slight break in his control alarmed him. He wanted her bad and couldn't ever remember desiring a female more. She was strong and beautiful. *Delicate and human. Don't forget that.* She was an unknown threat who had lied about her identity and purpose.

Memories of the past helped. He latched on to the ones of the female he'd once trusted, who'd betrayed him. She'd been beautiful too. *Treacherous. With pleasure comes pain.*

The door to the interrogation room opened and Darkness tore his mouth away from his pretend-cat's neck and snarled at the person who dared enter after he'd given orders that no one was to interfere. He used his body to block hers.

Snow jerked to a halt, his eyes widened in shock and his nose flared. He paled, staring back at Darkness.

"Get out."

Snow didn't move. He did, however, school his features to hide his emotions. "You need to step out now."

"Get out," Darkness repeated.

Snow tried to crane his neck to view the female but Darkness knew he couldn't see much. The Species would be able to hear her, though, and smell her desire. She was breathing rapidly, almost panting. Darkness growled to draw his focus. The male responded by growling back when their gazes clashed.

"You are to step outside."

"You don't give me orders."

"Justice does. Some new information has come in. Outside now."

He gave a sharp nod. "I'll be there in a moment."

"Now," Snow demanded.

Darkness turned and rose to his full height. He had to release Kat to do it but he stepped to the right to keep most of her blocked from the Snow's view. He snarled, "Leave. I'll be there in a moment."

Snow hesitated but then backed out. He left the door open. Darkness tried to leash his temper but failed. He turned and looked at Kat. She stared at him and had to notice his attention on her breasts. They rose and fell rapidly with her breathing. A sheen of sweat coated her skin. He would have liked to take time soothing some of her tension but Snow would return.

"I'll be back." He reached out, lifted her and carried her to the table where he gently set her on top of it.

He strode across the room without a backward glance. He felt guilty leaving her in that condition though he couldn't afford that useless emotion. He closed the door to the interrogation room. It was soundproof so she wouldn't hear anything they said. He stepped closer and used his chest to push Snow back. It was a display of dominance but he was furious. He did make sure the front of his pants didn't come in contact with the male. It would be awhile before his dick softened.

Snow stumbled back but righted, his fists clenching at his sides. "What the hell were you doing in there?"

"My job. Never argue with me in front of a prisoner."

"You were about to mount her."

"What is going on?" Justice turned the corner and stopped, apparently reading their body language.

"Darkness was touching the female," Snow accused.

"Would you have preferred I beat on her? I would never treat one of them the way I do a male." He straightened his shoulders and glared at Justice. "I wouldn't have actually mounted her. She refused to tell me who she really works for. Unfulfilled sexual frustration can be more effective than inflicting pain, if done right. Do you have a problem with my tactics?"

Justice opened his mouth, closed it, and then sighed. He shook his head. "I trust you. You didn't hurt her at all?"

"No. I don't molest females." He shot a dirty look at Snow. "Or beat on them or inflict any kind of pain on them."

"Enough," Justice stated. "I had Snow pull you out because we know who sent her. We got a call from Jessie's father."

"The Senator?" Darkness frowned. "What does the human government have to do with this? Is she military?"

Justice hesitated. "He has a friend with the FBI. It seems they sent an agent to Homeland today. We're unclear of why she is here but we're certain she is their agent."

"The Senator couldn't give you more details?" Darkness wanted to return to Kat and find out.

"We're lucky we even learned they were sending someone in. Jacob's friend knows Jessie lives here and was worried about her safety. He asked if she was in danger and if they could be of more assistance since only one agent had been assigned." Justice paused. "He thought we'd requested one of their agents. We didn't."

Darkness crossed his arms over his chest, trying to think of why they'd secretly send an agent to Homeland. He couldn't think of a reason.

Justice seemed equally at a loss. "Jacob and I discussed the matter. Do you remember when they sent agents here to question Jeanie Shiver? They weren't happy with our refusal to hand her over to them. I'm having True and his mate transported to Reservation right now. Their helicopter should leave in twenty minutes."

"You believe she came here to kidnap True's mate to be handed over to the FBI?" Darkness was furious.

"Possibly." Justice's eyes gleamed with the same emotion. "It won't happen."

"I'll escort her to the front gates and walk her out." Darkness turned but Justice gripped his arm.

"Wait."

Darkness hated the way his stomach churned. He faced Justice. "She caused no harm to us. You said she works for the FBI. It means she was given orders. They aren't ones we agree with but I don't believe she should be taken to a holding cell or transported to Fuller Prison. Allow me to escort her off Homeland. She'll go back to the FBI empty-handed and that will be punishment enough. She's not from Mercile or a hired mercenary. She's law enforcement, as misguided as her mission was. We also owe her something for effectively handling the threat at the gates."

Justice released him. "I was thinking more along the lines of allowing her to stay and pretend we believe her cover story."

The stunning words cured Darkness of his painful erection. "Why?"

"We assume she came here for Jeanie but what if she's here for another reason? I'm curious."

None of it sat well with Darkness. "Why else would they send someone here?"

"I'd like to find out. Jeanie will be safe. We'll allow the FBI agent to teach classes while we keep an eye on her every move. She'll let her guard down and reveal the truth." Justice smiled coldly. "Then we'll decide what to do about it. I'm having Security clone her cell phone and install tracking devices on her belongings in case she slips by our officers at any point. We'll constantly have her under electronic surveillance. I'm sure, with her training, she'd spot anyone in physical proximity. I'll assign someone to stick within sight, though, or she'll become suspicious."

"I could go back in there and continue working on her. I'll find out why she's here and what she was ordered to do."

Snow snorted. "You mean you just want to mount her after you got her all hot and bothered?"

Darkness took a threatening step toward him and snarled.

The male held his ground and flashed fang, prepared to fight.

"Enough!" Justice's voice deepened. "Snow, leave Darkness alone. He's good at what he does for a reason."

"Step into that room and breathe deep. You'll know what he's been doing." Snow frowned. "He's good at attracting a female. I couldn't get away with those tactics if I were allowed to interview her."

"You don't have his background or his control over his physical responses, Snow."

"I saw how much control he had and you would have too if you'd looked at his crotch when he stepped into the hallway." Snow glanced at the front of Darkness' pants. "He's got it under control now."

"I wouldn't have mounted her," Darkness growled. "What is your problem?"

"Stop," Justice snapped. "Darkness is an excellent judge of what it requires to get a prisoner to talk and each prisoner is different. Darkness, I know you could learn her secrets but she is FBI. I'd rather take a less aggressive approach since she comes from a government agency. Let's call it a professional courtesy and do it to appease my curiosity."

"Fine." Darkness inclined his head. "What would you like me to do?"

"Go in there and blame someone on our end for the mistake. Pretend to buy everything she tells you and take her to human housing. A team is there now to make sure every room is covered. She won't do anything without us knowing about it."

"All right."

Justice glanced between them. "I'm leaving now. I have some calls to make. The press is going crazy over what happened at the gates and every law enforcement agency is calling us to ask if we need assistance. No fighting. We have enough to deal with. We're all stressed."

Darkness waited until the sound of Justice's footsteps faded. He glared at Snow. "What is your issue?"

"I can see why you didn't want me to go in there with you."

"Do you know the female? Is there a personal connection?"

"No."

"Then what is your problem?"

Snow clenched his teeth. "I want experience with interrogation. You didn't want the job so I thought I could work here full-time doing it."

"You mostly live at Reservation."

"I want to stay here."

"Then tell Fury and Slade not to assign you anywhere else."

"I don't want to walk perimeter or work the gate. I want to do something useful."

Darkness sighed, relaxing. He hadn't liked the idea that the male had a personal interest in Kat but it wasn't about the female, it was his job. "I don't do interrogations often and only with special cases."

"Only important ones."

He studied the Species. "What is really going on?"

Snow hesitated. "I feel useless."

"You aren't."

"There are Species who stand out and get special treatment. I want that."

"I don't stand out. I get no special treatment either. I live in the men's dorms, as you do."

"Our people fear you and you have special skills. You heard Justice. You can seduce a female prisoner and he doesn't even question it. I'd be sent to Medical for evaluation if I did that. They'd worry about me having a meltdown."

Frustration rose but he pushed it back. "I didn't force any of that. She was the one to initiate my actions. We'll discuss this later. Right now Justice is correct. We're all stressed because of the attack. It's normal to feel ineffective after such an ordeal. You wish to do something to help our people."

He wasn't good about dealing with males who were experiencing emotional upheaval but he liked Snow. The male was easygoing most of the time and had a quick wit. He also didn't avoid direct eye contact, something Darkness appreciated.

"We'll work out a solution. I need to go in there and act stupid. It will be difficult." He smirked.

Snow nodded. "Sorry. I didn't mean to take it out on you."

"It hasn't been a good day. Why don't you work off some of your energy by helping with cleanup? The front of the security building is a mess. They'll need to rebuild as fast as possible and that means removing the debris."

"I'm on it." Snow stalked away.

Darkness watched him go and took a few deep breaths. Kat, or whatever her real name was, worked for the FBI. It alleviated his fear that she was a hired killer sent by someone associated with their enemies but that didn't make her a friend either. She'd come to Homeland for an undisclosed reason. He was going to figure out what it was. He just wouldn't be doing it by keeping her on that table. Part of him regretted that, while part of him felt relieved. She was too tempting.

He opened the door and entered. She slid off the table and watched him. He closed the door behind him and approached her slowly.

"We need to talk."

Wariness filled her eyes. "About what?"

"Someone in Security messed up. They are new. Some Species are learning their jobs and this one was in charge of running your background check." She'd accept the excuse easily if he gauged her right. She desperately wanted them to believe her cover identity. "Another ran your information and everything came back just as you said. Your name is Kathryn Decker and you work for the Bakersfield Police Department as a crime technician." He grimaced, hoping it passed for a show of regret. "I apologize."

She blinked rapidly and he could almost see that information spinning in her mind. "Good." She licked her lips and straightened, her shoulders going back. "Great. I told you that."

"You did." He reached in his pocket, located the key to her cuffs, leaned over and unlocked them. She withdrew her wrists and rubbed the skin. "I am sorry for what you suffered at my hands."

Her cheeks colored and she broke eye contact. "You have nothing to apologize for, except for being a tease. I'll survive."

He could still smell her. His dick stirred but he quickly imagined the worst moments of his life. That killed his sexual desire. "I'm certain you'll want to leave us now, rather than being escorted to guest quarters. Your car was damaged but we can provide your passage home. We'll return the rental to the company you leased it from after repairs are done to it. It's the least we could do." He knew she wouldn't go. She was formidable and didn't disappoint.

"No. I came to teach classes. Shit happens. I'm good. I wouldn't mind some clothes though."

He admired her spirit. Some females wouldn't recover quickly from facing a difficult situation to dealing with a new one. The only flaw in her armor was the slight trembling of her legs. He noticed everything about her.

"Of course. Stay here and I'll retrieve your clothes. Would you prefer someone else bring them to you? I'm sure I'm not your favorite person." He couldn't resist baiting her.

Color rose in her cheeks again. "I don't care who brings them." Her chin lifted and she held his gaze with determination.

She was so appealing. He wanted to smile but kept the grimace in place. "Is there anything I can do to make it up to you?" He purposely lowered his gaze down her body. "I owe you."

He caught the quick intake of her breath and the way her eyes widened. He'd shocked her with his subtle sexual offer. She didn't answer immediately.

"It's probably best for both of us if we leave it as is. Just get me some clothes. It's cold in here. It would be nice to know if my suitcase survived so I have something to wear tomorrow. It was in the trunk of my car."

"I'll look into that. Relax, Kat. Welcome to Homeland." He spun and stalked to the door, picking up his discarded tank top on the way. "Someone will be in shortly with your things. Stay here. There are a lot of males outside who would enjoy the view of you in so little."

He walked out and closed the door behind him. He'd be keeping a close eye on that female and she'd be dealing with him often. First he'd have to change his current living arrangements. He looked forward to seeing her surprise when he became her neighbor.

Chapter Four

✂

Kat walked around the small home after her shower and appreciated how well the NSO accommodated guests though she wasn't allowed to leave without picking up the phone and calling for an escort. Visitors weren't permitted to roam Homeland without one.

The two-bedroom cottage had charming furnishings and a comfortable feel. Her suitcase had been searched and delivered. Some new damage showed on the plastic case but she was grateful it had survived the explosion. All her clothes had been put away in one of the bedrooms that faced the cute little patio area.

The doorbell rang and she tensed, not expecting anyone until morning. She opened it, though, feeling safe. NSO had security up the ass. A female stood there, one she hadn't met before, and held out a covered tray.

"Darkness asked me to deliver your dinner. I know you're stocked with food supplies but he told me this is his way of apologizing for being mean to you."

Kat was surprised. "Thanks."

"Move and I'll bring it in."

"I'm Kat, by the way." She stepped aside and waved her arm. "Come on in."

"I'm Sunshine."

The tall feline New Species was pretty. "I love your hair."

The woman turned and flashed a smile. "Thanks. It's natural."

That surprised Kat. The woman's tresses had to be at least six different colors. She didn't mention that it reminded her of her neighbor's pet or that she could guess what breed of cat they'd gotten her DNA from. She'd never look at Calicos the same way again.

"I know the layout. Most of these cottages have the same floor plan." Sunshine walked into the kitchen and placed the tray on the counter. "Are you okay? I figured Darkness must have done something really bad to ask me to deliver food. He's frightening."

"I'm great. There was just a little mix-up at the gate."

The woman arched her eyebrows. "We were attacked and you made the bad guys go *kaboom*!" She grinned. "Everyone is talking about it."

Kat had to admit she hadn't thought about much else since she'd been shown to the cottage. Men had died. They had planned to do harm but that didn't mean she wasn't going to have some issues to deal with. The report she'd have to write when she returned to her office would be a nightmare. She would also want to look up their backgrounds. It would probably help ease some of her distress about the incident when she checked their priors.

"Great." She hoped her sarcasm didn't come across.

"We got lucky. None of ours died, although my friend Breeze was trapped under part of the ceiling. It collapsed on top of her."

"Is she okay?"

"Yes. Breeze is tough. The roof actually fell on top of the desks but she'd hit the floor first so it didn't crush her. She just needed a shower once she got home. The males took over the only working showers so all the females on duty came to the dorm to get cleaned up. She was just angry that it happened."

"It shouldn't have."

"The main gates are closed. They are going to have crews come in tonight to work on them but it's going to take at least two days."

"That's fast."

"Money talks, bullshit walks." Sunshine beamed. "Is that the right saying? We pay out a lot of money by having contractors working around the clock when we need something done fast."

"You nailed it." Kat wanted to change the subject. "Do you know anything about the classes I'm supposed to start teaching tomorrow?"

"Of course. I'm signed up."

"Where are they going to be held? No one said."

"The bar. It's big enough to house everyone who wants to come."

That surprised her. "I'm holding class in a bar?"

Sunshine opened cupboards and removed a plate. "It's not like the ones in your movies. We dance there and they mostly serve caffeine. That's an amazing thing."

"Dancing?"

"Caffeine."

Kat grinned. "I'm partial to it myself."

"Most of us don't drink alcohol. It tastes horrible and with our metabolisms it's tough to get and stay drunk." She curled her lip and revealed her fangs. "I don't see the draw in it. Alcohol makes you lightheaded and stupid. Where is the fun in that?"

"I'm not sure. I'm not much of a drinker myself."

"Good. A lot of us signed up for your class. We rarely have human guests who hold classes. Everyone is excited but I should warn you that some of the males will be there because you're female."

Kat opened the fridge. "Do you want a soda?"

"No thank you. Do you want me to leave?"

"Stay. I enjoy the company. Why are guys coming just because I'm a woman?"

"Some of them are looking for mates. Justice strongly discourages them from talking to the protestors or the mate hunters at the gates."

"Mate hunters? What are those?"

Sunshine took a seat at the counter. "Females who show up looking for one of our males to mate them. Most of them are a bit...what is that saying? One nut shy of a full bag of peanuts?"

Kat laughed. She opened the lid on the tray and stared at the biggest steak she'd ever seen. It had to be over twenty ounces. "Wow."

"You don't like meat?"

"It's enough for two. I can't possibly eat all that."

"Good! I'm hungry." Sunshine slid out of her seat and took out another plate. "That is if you don't mind."

"Nope."

Sunshine found silverware, cut the steak in half and passed one of the plates to her. "Here you go."

Kat sat at the counter and opened her soda. "Thanks. So tell me more about these mate hunters. I'm curious."

"They flash their breasts at us. I walk the wall by the gates and they can't tell which of us are male or female. I'm tired of seeing boobs."

It was funny. "I bet."

"As if a little breast flashing would be enough to drive our males into a sexual frenzy. Maybe if they tried that at the Wild Zone. Some of our males there would go for it. Those humans would be so sorry if they lured one of those males into taking them home."

"Why?"

Sunshine paused. "I don't know if I'm allowed to say."

The implied secret piqued Kat's suspicious nature. Where they hiding something?

"Well, I guess it would be okay to say it's called the Wild Zone for a reason. Some of us aren't as civilized as others. They were badly mistreated at Mercile so humans aren't their friends. They live there to avoid running into any except for mates. Ta..." She stopped. "A mate lives there year-round. Of course her mate is very protective so she's safe from anyone being mean to her."

"She's human?" It was a calculated guess.

"Yes. There's no harm in telling you that."

"So why would a woman be sorry to end up with a Wild Zone mate? I am curious."

Sunshine cut into her meat and glanced at her. "Wild. Get it? They aren't so polite. Your females see Justice on television and assume all have his manners. They would be wrong. The Wild Zone males wouldn't use polite words and conversation with a female. They'd just want to seduce a female. They aren't into extended discussions first, if you know what I mean. They like sex and can get a little carried away. A male would get a woman to say yes and then go right for the good spots. I know human females are used to human males taking things much slower. Species love burying their faces between a female's thighs. Often."

"Oh." Kat took a bite of her steak. It was delicious. She thought about what she'd learned. "They just go for it, huh?"

Sunshine grinned. "It makes for hot sex but they are a little rough. I don't know if a human could handle it. They wouldn't hurt them or force the issue but it would be a wild ride."

Darkness flashed in her mind. He'd implied he liked rough sex. "How rough?"

"Our males are strong. I haven't shared sex with one of yours but I've seen porn videos on the internet." She hissed. "I don't want to share sex with one of your males. I'd break his jaw if he called me some of the things I've heard them say to their partners and they seem very selfish." She snorted. "Ever see the massage videos? They play with the female but don't get her off, then shove their dicks at them. How is that mutual pleasure? They find it but the female gets the shaft. Did you notice my innuendo there?"

Kat laughed.

"Most of them don't know what to do when they go down on a female either. How is it satisfying to have them lick around your clit? It looks annoying."

"Those videos are pretty sad."

Sunshine peered at her curiously. "How are human males in reality?"

"Not like those videos or they wouldn't have sex often. I'd never have sex if even half of that shit is what really goes on in a bedroom. Those things turn my stomach."

"Do you have a mate? I don't smell a male on you but you've recently showered."

"No. I'm single."

"You're an attractive female. I thought all of you wanted mates. I assume you chose not to have one."

Kat shifted in her seat, reminded of her last conversation with her mother. It had been more of a lecture. She wasn't giving the woman grandkids and that apparently was a disappointment. "I work a lot. Some men are intimidated by my job and don't appreciate knowing they come second on my list of priorities."

"You solve crimes. That's important. They should be proud."

"I think they mostly feel irritated or neglected because I love what I do. I admit my last relationship ended because of a case I worked. I missed his birthday party and then stood him up a week later at his best friend's wedding because of work. He gave me an ultimatum and didn't like my answer."

"What was the ultimatum?"

"Him or my job."

"Oh. That's sad." Sunshine took a bite.

That summed up Kat's life. The job came first and everything else second.

"I have recently considered taking a mate."

Sunshine's announcement brought her out of her thoughts. "Really? What is he like?"

"I haven't chosen one yet. It would be difficult. The males I share sex with all have their good qualities and flaws."

"How many are you sleeping with?"

"I don't allow them to sleep in my bed. That would imply a commitment I'm not willing to make yet. Our males tend to get possessive fast if you don't set boundaries. They respect those. Your world is different from mine. Sharing sex with many males is considered bad where you come from. Here?" Sunshine smiled. "Have you seen our males? I am a female with a healthy sex drive. We don't have to worry about sexual diseases or pregnancies. It would be strange not to share sex often with different males unless we wanted a mate."

Kat wasn't one to judge. "I was just curious. I don't know much about New Species."

"To allow a male to spend the night in your bed would give him the idea that he could just sleep there every night. There's a saying you'd know. Give them an inch and they will take a mile. They are aggressive so you have to be just as aggressive. Remember that while you're here because some of the males will come after you. They view humans as more submissive and easier to dominate."

"Okay. I'll remember that."

"Kick the male out of your bed if you allow one to share sex with you. Tell him to leave afterward. Don't cuddle with him. Well, unless he's a primate. They tend to need that or their feelings get hurt but cut it off after about five minutes. Otherwise they'll try to press you to stay. They can be persuasive."

Persuasive was an understatement. She would have begged Darkness to fuck her if he hadn't been called away from that interrogation room. She'd come dangerously close to breaking a few times. He had been that good at tormenting her body until she'd been physically hurting to come.

"They see the mated pairs and wish to have someone depend on them that way."

Mason's accusation popped up. He thought the women were addicted to the men. "How are they dependent?"

Sunshine finished her half of the steak and frowned. "Your females enjoy the constant cuddling and the way the males are protective of them. We call it annoying but your females seem to think it's endearing when they snarl at other males who get too close to them. The males really seem to crave a female to love them." She paused. "We never had that. They also enjoy feeling needed by a female. Does that make sense? To be the most important person to another after we were just numbers is a remarkable thing."

It broke Kat's heart a little. "I see."

Sunshine's mood brightened. "Your females also seem to appreciate the sex and I don't blame them. Our males are not anything like your males in those porn videos. No Species would ever call a female bad names or strike them. Our males have a high sex drive but aren't selfish. They will do whatever it takes to give pleasure over and over."

Not Darkness. He'd tormented the hell out of her. She'd never gotten turned-on so fast or experienced sexual frustration at that level before. Sunshine's words did blow Mason's theory out of the water. Great sex and a guy who paid them a lot of attention would be reasons enough for women to want to live with a New Species. As for the men, it probably would be desirable to have someone to share their lives with after all the hell they'd survived.

"I should go. I'm assigned to a shift tonight. We've doubled our patrols and increased security to handle the human workers coming in. I'll see you at the bar tomorrow. I'm really looking forward to learning." Sunshine offered her hand. "It was good to meet you and thank you for sharing your meal."

Kat shook her hand. "Thanks for bringing it to me and for the talk."

"Thank Darkness. You never answered my question. What did he do to you?"

She wasn't going to answer that. "We just got off on the wrong foot when I entered Homeland. It's nothing worth talking about." *Fat liar.* She forced a smile. "Have a good night. I hope nothing else happens."

"I do as well. We've had enough trouble to last us a month."

Kat led her to the door and waved goodbye. She spotted the Jeep parked down the street with a guard inside. He was probably there to keep an eye on her. She closed and locked the door.

She wasn't used to down time. Her job kept her busy and when she was home she and Missy were working on the house. They were about to start their remodel on the outdated kitchen. She longed to call her friend but couldn't risk it. The NSO had access to her new cell phone when she'd been in that interrogation room and might keep tabs on any calls she made. It would lead them to her true identity.

She walked around the house, admiring it. She hand-washed the few dishes, bypassing the dishwasher. Adding one to her house was a dream but she wasn't going to waste it on a few plates and silverware. She walked to the slider, unlocked it and stepped out onto the small patio.

It was a cool evening and she stared up at the sky. It was beautiful seeing so many stars, something she missed in the city. She was about to turn when the flare of a small light caught her eye and drew her attention to the house next door.

A big figure stepped out of the shadows and Darkness met her stare.

He held a cigarette in his hand and seemed to be watching her as he lifted it to his lips, took a drag and blew it out. She was surprised he smoked since she hadn't seen any Species do it. It was also a reminder that her cigarettes and lighter hadn't been returned. She had a few packs stashed in her suitcase though.

He moved closer and stepped over the three-foot wall divider between their patios, entering hers. He looked really tall and was dressed in silky black pajama pants with no shirt. She tried to keep her eyes up and not admire his chest. She said nothing as he approached until he was close enough to touch. She tilted her head up to keep eye contact.

He turned his wrist and offered her his cigarette. She didn't hesitate. Smoking was her one bad habit. She accepted it and took a long drag. Her eyes closed and she held it in her lungs before slowly blowing it out. She looked at him and offered it back.

"Keep it. It's yours." He reached inside his pants pocket.

She followed the movement and admitted to staring a little too long at his abs. He had great ones, every muscle displayed beneath his firm skin. He withdrew her pack and lighter. He held them in his palm.

"I wondered where those got to."

He removed a second cigarette from the pack and lit it then leaned over and placed the pack and lighter on the patio table. "It's not healthy."

She'd heard that a million times. "Everyone has a vice. This is mine. I don't smoke all the time but I do when I'm stressed. It's been a tough week for me. I didn't know you smoked."

He took a drag and blew it out. "I don't."

She cocked an eyebrow and took another drag on hers. "It sure looks like you are."

"I wanted to try it."

"So?"

"It tastes like shit and smells bad."

Her hand paused on the way to her lips. "Then why are you doing it?"

"I'm trying to figure you out."

"So you're smoking my cigarettes? How is that going for you?"

He took another drag, turned and walked over to a potted plant. He bent, showing off a muscular ass in those silky, drawstring pajama pants. He ground the cigarette out in the soil, turned and approached her again.

She didn't try to stop him when he jerked the cigarette from her fingers and smiled. "Find another vice." He leaned sideways and picked up her pack and lighter. "We don't sell cigarettes here at Homeland."

"Good thing I brought more then."

He grinned. "Did you?"

She'd seen them when she'd unpacked. She had thought she might need at least a few packs to get her through the ordeal of being at Homeland. "I did."

The soft chuckle was nice. "Are you sure?"

"What does that mean?"

"Good night, Kat. Sleep well. I'm next door if you need anything." He flashed her cigarette pack in his palm before returning to his patio. She watched him put out her cigarette on the way before he entered his house through the back slider.

She stood there for a few seconds before going back inside and directly to the master bedroom. She had left her suitcase on the floor next to the bed and lifted it, setting it on the mattress. She opened it and cursed. The four packs she'd brought were no longer inside the zippered section of the lid. It was unzipped and empty.

He must have sneaked in and taken them. She examined the window and discovered it was wide open. It hadn't been. She ground her teeth together and wondered what kind of game the tall New Species played.

"Shit."

Did he expect her to bang on his door and demand the return of her cigarettes? Maybe break into his house to steal them back? She suddenly grinned. It was tempting to do just that. Her humor faded though. He might be tempting her to do something that would get her thrown out of Homeland. She couldn't risk it.

She sat down and sighed. It wouldn't be the first time she couldn't smoke. She usually stocked up on gum first though. She didn't have any and wondered if Homeland had a convenience store open at night. She doubted it.

"Damn."

Darkness watched the screen and smiled at Kat's frustrated look. He sat back and leaned against the soft pillows, adjusting the laptop higher on his thighs. He wondered if she'd confront him about the theft. She hadn't found the hidden cameras in the house or looked for any. He'd been viewing her since she'd arrived, with the exception of her shower. He'd used that time to sneak inside her home to gain access to her suitcase. He wanted her to know he'd been there.

She stood and walked to the window, shutting and locking it, before drawing the curtains. He followed her through the house by clicking on other camera feeds. She checked the locks on every window and closed all the curtains. Part of him felt a little guilty. She should feel safe at Homeland but it had been a strategic move to show her he could get to her at any time.

Kat entered the bedroom and closed the door. She twisted the lock and went into the bathroom. He had a camera in there but didn't activate it. She deserved some privacy. He could see her cell phone charging on the dresser. He would have turned on the camera if she'd taken it with her, in order to see what she was up to. Within minutes she exited the bathroom and shoved the suitcase off the bed.

He grinned over her display of temper. The loss of her cigarettes would irritate her and keep her off balance. That's what he needed. She'd make a mistake. The cell phone next to him buzzed and he reached for it, seeing it was Security.

"Darkness here."

"I thought you'd like to know we're set up for surveillance of the Gift location."

"Thanks for informing me, Fury."

The male grunted. "You got her location from Boris. I figured you'd want an update."

"I appreciate that."

"Do you wish to be the one to make first contact if we recover her alive?"

"No. I have no desire to ever leave NSO lands to venture into the out world."

"I thought I'd offer it to you instead of Jaded. He's flying in tonight."

"Why? He enjoys being at Reservation."

"There is a charity event for an animal rescue group that he planned to attend."

"Ah." That explained it. Jaded had made fundraising for animal rescue charities his undertaking. "Tell him he can make first contact."

"You blocked the security feeds to our guest."

He had hoped Security wouldn't share that information but wasn't surprised. "I'm allowing them access to the feeds when I'm unable to watch the female."

"Why block them at all?"

He didn't enjoy the idea of anyone watching Kat or knowing that he'd sneaked inside her home to snag her precious cigarettes. He also didn't want them witnessing his interactions with her. "I'm in charge of this investigation."

"Justice told me what Snow said. Is this going to be a problem? Are you attracted to this female?"

That angered him. "I'm not thinking purely with my dick. Are you asking me to pass this investigation to someone else?"

"No. Are you are attracted to her?"

He clenched his teeth. He didn't want to lie but admitting the truth might make them question his judgment.

"I see."

"I didn't answer."

"Your silence spoke for you. I know you must feel lonely since you keep everyone at arm's distance. Is this going to be a problem or can you be unbiased if the need arises?"

"My job is to find out what she's doing here at Homeland and learn her mission. That's exactly what I plan to do."

Fury sighed. "That's a given." He paused. "I guess I'm asking you if you're all right."

"I'm fine."

Fury hesitated again. "Let me know if there's anything I can do if this turns sideways."

"What does that mean?"

"She could be here to do harm. That might become a conflict for you if you are highly attracted to her. I'm stating that I'm here for you and I'm offering help if you find yourself in trouble. That's what family does."

"I have no family."

"Damn it," Fury growled. "You once helped save my life. Why must you deny our connection? Do I have to be dying again to get you to admit what we are to each other?"

"I need to go. Is there anything else you want?"

"I'd tell you to watch your back but you always do. Just let me know if you need anything and I do mean anything. You will have my support."

"Thank you." He hung up and laid the phone on the edge of the bed.

Guilt surfaced but he pushed it back. Fury was a good male but he didn't want a close relationship to him, despite the blood tie from their human DNA. He'd learned his lesson and wasn't willing to ever risk losing someone he cared about that way again.

Darkness leaned back and relaxed by viewing Kat as she took her pajamas into the bathroom. He found it amusing that she would go in there to change. That enjoyment faded when he pondered the idea that perhaps she was aware of the hidden cameras. She exited the bathroom a few minutes later, pulled back the covers and climbed into the bed.

She appeared small and lost on the big mattress when she rolled onto her side into a fetal position. It was odd that she left the lights on. He glanced at the clock. It was earlier than he'd thought she would turn in.

He waited until he was certain she slept then transferred the camera feeds back over to Security and stood. It was too tempting to break in again and share that bed. An abundance of energy prodded him into changing his clothing and stepping out the patio door. He couldn't resist staring at his neighbor's home.

"Damn."

There was no denying why he felt wired. He forced his gaze away from her bedroom window, leaped over the wall and broke into a run. He needed to burn off all that sexual tension or he'd end up finishing what he'd started in that interrogation room.

Chapter Five

ဢ

Kat was thrilled that over five dozen New Species filled the bar. It was a bigger turnout than she'd hoped for. They filled the tables along the dance floor and in the higher section near the bar. Some even stood around the edges. She smiled and spoke in a loud voice to make sure everyone would be able to hear her in the back of the room.

They had been receptive to her "murder scene" with the "body" that she'd made with pillows, a blanket and a few belts. She'd wanted to bring one of the life-size rescue training manikins but hadn't been able to acquire it in time. She'd staged a mugging gone wrong. It had been fun to show them how to treat a crime scene and collect evidence.

"Any questions?"

A woman at a nearby table spoke. "Why do humans steal from each other?"

The question confused Kat. "Why?"

"They don't understand greed."

Kat spun, startled by Darkness' voice. He stepped out of the shadows behind the stage and stared at her. He wore a blue muscle shirt, jeans and a pair of black boots. His tan arms were on display. He looked good. Their eyes met and he frowned.

He strode out onto the dance floor where she stood and addressed her class. "We appreciate the things we have since we never had anything before. Some humans are deeply flawed and crave what others have. They will rob and sometimes kill others to take it. For some it is a lack of morals or pride, to others it is a sport and some become addicted to drugs. It's a money-based system in the out world so some acquire that money by taking it from others."

"Oh." The female nodded. "I see. That's sad."

"Yes, it is." Darkness turned and stared down at Kat.

She was mute until another woman spoke. "Is it true that some males harm their females and even sometimes kill them?"

Kat turned and located the speaker. "Yes. Domestic violence is unfortunately a common crime."

"Why?" A male stood. "Males are superior in strength and there is no honor in harming a female. They should be protected."

"They should kill the male if he attacks," one of the women hissed from the corner. "Why don't your females fight back and take the male down? I would if one struck me."

The questions weren't what Kat expected.

"They aren't like us," Darkness stated. "Humans believe males and females are completely equal." He chuckled. "So they don't value the differences or acknowledge physical limitations."

A guy at the bar snorted. "Equal? Males are physically stronger, while females are more prone to be superior in tactical strategies. We each have our own strengths but they are not the same."

One of the women laughed. "You mean you males are impulsive while we take our time to plot everything out."

He laughed. "Exactly. That is an advantage you have."

"Don't forget sex," one woman added and chuckled. "We have the advantage there too." She stood and waved her hand down her body. "We have what you want."

A howl broke out in the back and Kat was startled by the animalistic sound.

Darkness grinned at her response. "That was an agreement." He faced the class. "Focus on the techniques she taught to process evidence but don't expect her to explain human nature. We'd need her to move to Homeland indefinitely to cover those topics. Humans are flawed and their crime rate is high. Just accept that they don't make sense to us."

Kat resented his words. "Not all humans commit crimes."

"Not all but a lot of them do." He shrugged. "Let's have lunch. Class is over."

It stunned her that he'd cut her time short. It also pissed her off. Her students started to talk amongst themselves and she reached out, gripped Darkness' arm. He looked down at her fingers on his forearm and then met her gaze.

"Can we talk?" She wanted an explanation for him interrupting her class.

"Sure." He motioned toward the stage. "Back there unless you want to be overheard."

She released him and marched behind the stage. He followed and she turned on him when they had privacy. "What was that about?"

"Saving your ass. Did you really think they wouldn't question why a human would rob another one for something as petty as a wallet when you used that scenario?"

She stared up at him, unsure how to answer.

"You're not in your world anymore. Species don't rob other Species. Teach them something they can actually use. They won't be solving a homicide like that here."

Kat tried to cool her temper. "Fine. What kind of crimes do you face?"

"Most of it happens at the gates. We pass those investigations to our human task force."

"Then why am I here?"

"Blame your crime shows. It made my people curious about humans and those are the reactions you'll mostly get from them. They'll want you to explain why humans are so fucked-up. Good luck with that."

"You're human too—mostly."

He took a step closer and she backed up, finding a wall there. He lifted his arms and rested his open palms on each side of her, pinning her in place. "We're nothing like you. Never forget that. Do you know how we were created?"

"Mercile Industries."

"They vetted human donors for targeted physical and mental attributes, used them to create embryos and then let a geneticist splice away with specific animal DNA, manipulating it to create traits they desired. They culled all the bad shit or killed any infants born with defects or flaws they hadn't aimed for. We were birthed by surrogate mothers. They just carried the fetuses to term and didn't give a damn about anything except the money they were paid. Our childhoods were spent chained to walls while they shoved drugs into our veins or down our throats to benefit your world. We didn't have parents or people who gave a shit about us unless it was one of the doctors who depended on us to gain whatever results they wanted. In those situations they protected us against death or severe abuse but only until the study was over. Hell, having an actual bed and the ability to see daylight is treasured by us. We're nothing like you."

Her heart ached for him and the others. "I didn't mean it that way. I meant you are physically like us, for the most part."

He leaned down, getting in her face, and opened his mouth. "Really?"

The show of fangs didn't scare her that time. She could tell he was angry and wanted to defuse the situation. "I realize you're different too."

"I can bench-press five hundred pounds without really straining," he rasped. "I can endure pain that would leave one of your kind screaming and probably fainting. Look to your left. See that ten-foot ledge? I can reach it without the use of a ladder. You have no idea what we can do because we don't publicize it. Your kind is already afraid of us." He sniffed at her. "My senses aren't as good as a canine's but they are far better than your average human. I can tell what shampoo, conditioner and body wash you used this morning. I can even identify what kind of laundry soap you buy. Your toothpaste."

He tilted his head and nudged hers aside. "Stop wearing perfume. It's not pleasant to us. You dabbed some of it at the back of your neck." He lifted his head. "I can smell some of your emotions if they are strong. Fear. Desire. Hell, even anger. Can you do any of that?"

Kat stared into his eyes. "No."

"Then stop saying we're anything alike."

"You are part human though. A genetically enhanced version but—"

He moved so fast that she gasped when he gripped her hips and yanked her off her feet. She found herself dangling a foot above the floor until they were face level. Her hands automatically gripped the tops of his shoulders.

"We're not the same. Here's a lesson, teacher."

He growled and his chest vibrated against hers. The low, dangerous sound sent chills down her spine and the color of his eyes seemed to darken. It might have been a play of the dim light since they were far from the windows but he looked terrifying. Her heart rate quickened and she wondered if he planned to hurt her.

"Try to fight me," he snarled.

"I won't." She knew he was attempting to provoke her but she wasn't dense. His body felt as hard and solid as the wall at her back. It wouldn't be a fight she could win.

"Exactly." The growling stopped and the vibrations ceased. His tone lowered to a harsh whisper. "Never believe we're amenable creatures who could conform to your way of life. We have an entire section at Reservation that is full of failed examples of what happens when idiots attempt to make pets out of animals not meant to be tame. They live with us for a reason. Take the blinders off. We have more in common with rescued ex-circus animals than with you."

He shifted his hips closer and the press of his groin rubbed against her inner thigh. The rigid length of his erection couldn't be mistaken for anything else. Most women would have begged to be put down or pleaded with him to cool his temper. She thought he was kind of sexy when he was hostile.

"We're not too different though." She eased her hold on his shoulders and trailed her fingertips down his chest. "You want me. An ex-circus animal wouldn't be sporting a boner from having me this close."

His eyes widened and he hissed. "Fuck."

The sound he made reminded her of a pissed-off large cat. "Sorry that your plan to intimidate and terrify me isn't working." She felt no regret though. "Did you expect me to burst into tears?"

The low growl that came from his slightly parted lips was sexy. She liked the way he glanced at her breasts before meeting her eyes again. She traced her palms upward to curl her fingers over the tops of his shoulders.

"You feel like a man to me. That makes us compatible as people."

"Don't," he rasped.

"Don't what?"

"Provoke me."

She was tempted to. "I'm just stating the obvious. You can keep denying we're comparable but your body doesn't believe what your mouth is saying."

His hold on her eased and she slid down his body. He backed up the second her feet touched the floor to release her completely. "Teach them the tricks your people use to lie and deceive our officers. That's how you can be useful. Rusty told me what you did with your purse. Show all that you know. Tomorrow tell them about the weapons they aren't aware of."

She appreciated the suggestion. "Okay."

"Don't sugarcoat humans either. We don't deal with nice ones, for the most part. Tell them about the worst of your kind."

"I resent that. Not every human being is a criminal."

"You drove through our gates. Did you see the protestors?"

"I saw the supporters too."

"Do you believe all of them are there with good intentions?" He tilted his head, staring deeply into her eyes. "What does your training tell you about those who try to seem harmless, when in fact they are a danger to the NSO?"

She swallowed, feeling that question was directed at her. He was smart, though, and she wouldn't treat him otherwise. "It's possible that some are pretending to be supportive to spy on the ones who really are or to gain the trust of your officers in hopes that they'll be able to launch an effective attack."

"Exactly. Teach them that."

"I just don't want to leave them with the impression that all people are bad. You seem to already think that."

"Supposedly your job here is to help us learn how to protect ourselves more effectively."

"Supposedly?" Was he still suspicious of her? She studied his dark eyes but he gave no emotion away.

"I don't trust anyone. I made that mistake once and learned. It's how I've survived."

She wondered who had betrayed him. Something he'd said when they'd been in that interrogation room tugged at her memory. "A woman?"

He scowled. "Did I say that?"

She should just let it drop but couldn't. There was just something about Darkness that made her want to know more about him. "You said something about pretending I was someone else to effectively do your job. I got the impression you meant a woman. You said 'a female from your past'."

"You read too much into it."

"Did I?" She wasn't convinced. He was good, though, keeping his tone unchanged.

He leaned in a little and ducked his head to stare down at her. "Let me give you a little advice, sweetheart. You're very inquisitive but your skills of observation are a little too refined for your background. I'd watch that."

He spun away and strode out into the main area of the bar. She hugged her waist and leaned against the wall, taking a few deep breaths. It was a warning, plain and simple. He suspected she wasn't who she claimed. He had a point though. She was trained in ways a crime lab technician wouldn't be. They were skilled at determining data at a scene, not delving into behavioral or verbal observation and clues.

"Well hell," she muttered.

She pushed away from the wall and dropped her arms to her sides. She stepped out from behind the stage, forced a smile and glanced around the room. Darkness was nowhere to be found but plenty of New Species seemed to want her attention as they indicated they'd like to speak. It was time to be sociable.

"Hi." She kept her voice cheerful.

"I have a question."

"Ask away."

* * * * *

Darkness plowed his fist into the punching bag without restraint. The chain that held it suspended groaned. The bag swung out and came back. He threw his left fist into it. The top of the bag ripped at the hook and the weighted container slammed to the floor four feet away.

"That was impressive but you aren't supposed to break our equipment."

He clenched his jaw and slowly turned to stare at Bluebird. She was the last person he wanted to talk to, besides Kat. "Hello."

She glanced at the bag then up at him. "That's a whole lot of frustration. Is there anything I can do to help?"

"I'm fine."

"I was at the class earlier. I saw you take our teacher behind the stage. I was curious so I crept forward enough to see what happened. You want her."

He didn't enjoy being spied on. "How did you come to that conclusion? She needed to be instructed on what to teach Species and was irritated that I intervened during the class."

"You've never pinned me to a wall when we talk."

"You're smart enough not to insult me."

"So that's what it takes to get your hands on me?" She arched her eyebrows.

"I don't want to share sex. I told you not to take it personally."

"I'm a caregiver. It's my nature, it seems. I'm drawn to damaged males with anger issues."

"It's not an issue."

She glanced at the downed bag again and smiled. "The equipment would say otherwise if it could speak. I imagine it would be crying right now or at least muttering *ouch*."

Her sense of wit amused him. He smiled back, relaxing a bit. "I suppose it would."

"I'm attracted to you. Call it a flaw of my nature but any time I see a very aggressive male it turns me on."

"All of us are aggressive."

"True, but you more so than others. Perhaps I miss the sense of danger when undressing for a male who doesn't have his emotions under control."

"I'm in control."

"For now." Her smile faded. "You are on the edge. I watch you closer than any other male because I want you. It's only a matter of time before you break."

"I'd never allow it to happen."

"I just insulted you but you don't have me pinned against a wall."

"You're testing me?"

"I'm just proving what I said. You feel something for the teacher."

Bluebird irritated him. "Fine. I am attracted to her but I'd never act on it."

"Why not? I didn't see her struggling or yelling for help when she could have. That implies she didn't mind your hands on her."

"Mind your own business."

"Fine." She took a step back. "You know you don't have to talk to her during shared sex. She'll only be here for a short time unless you were to ask her to stay. I don't see that happening since I was working the day she arrived. We both know she's not who she pretends to be. You've never shown interest in a female before. You should take advantage of it."

"Use her?" He didn't like the concept.

Bluebird shrugged. "Humans used us. You're walking a fine line, Darkness. I don't care how tough you are. Everyone has a breaking point. I don't need to tell you that though." She paused. "Perhaps I do. You're damaged, by your own words. You avoid our females but she isn't one of us. She won't have any expectations if that's what you worry about."

He scowled.

"I don't mean sexual worries. I'm certain you're skilled. We expect to be treated a certain way but she wouldn't know that." She seemed to appreciate the sight of his body. "You're full of sexual frustration. I can spot it a mile away." She looked into his eyes. "Unleash some of it on her and release the pressure. You're about to boil over. She's perfect for that. You know not to trust her and she's playing games. I think you're a master at that too."

She turned without another word and strolled away. Darkness clenched his teeth and spun, wishing to hit the bag again. It remained on the floor, damaged. "Fuck."

Bluebird had a point. A few of them, actually. He was sexually frustrated. Kat wasn't anything like a Species female and she also wasn't some innocent human. She'd come to Homeland with a hidden agenda. A highly trained individual never took sex personally when they were on a job. He couldn't hurt her feelings and she wouldn't expect any commitment.

I could have her. His dick stirred and it pissed him off. It was a matter of pride. He'd never fall into that trap again. It had cost him too much.

He left the training facility and returned to the guest cottage. After a quick shower, he sat on the bed with his laptop open. He watched Kat in the home next door. She fixed a sandwich for dinner and ate it at the bar.

His fascination with her wasn't healthy. She was the exact type of female he needed to avoid the most. It frustrated him that she was also the one who piqued his interest. Why couldn't he have formed an obsession with a harmless human?

The answer came easily. He'd destroy some soft-hearted female with his cold ways. They'd want to be with a male who could feel and show emotion. He kept everything inside where it was safe. Memories surfaced but he pushed them back. It only brought pain to remember the one female he'd ever allowed to get close to him. She'd fooled him and the price had been far too high. *Lesson learned.*

His cell phone beeped and he blindly picked it up. "Darkness here."

"How are you?"

He growled low. "Fine."

Fury paused. "I heard you destroyed a poor weight bag today. What did it do to you?"

"Don't you have anything better to do with your time? I bet Ellie and your offspring would enjoy you talking to them."

"I'm worried about you."

"Stop."

Fury growled back. "I can't help it. I wish it wasn't so but those are the facts."

"I'm fine. I hit the damn thing too hard. End of story."

"This female is getting to you. Do you want to assign her to someone else?"

It was tempting.

"You think you're the only one who has ever experienced this? There are things you don't know about me."

He watched Kat rise from the chair and begin washing her dishes. Darkness kept his gaze on the screen but he was curious about Fury's remark. "Like what?"

"I hated Ellie once. I believed she'd betrayed me."

That actually amused Darkness. "That female is so in love with you that I don't buy it. She's also very easy to read. She's about as dangerous as a kitten."

"She worked at Mercile."

"I'm aware. She was the one who provided the evidence that blew the lid off them and got us freed."

"A technician had it out for me and came into my cell. He…" Fury cleared his throat. "He did bad things and was about to do worse."

"They were assholes."

"He sexually assaulted me," Fury snarled.

Darkness closed his eyes and leaned back. Pain stabbed at his chest. That was one indignity he'd never been subjected to. A strong sense of compassion rose in him over what Fury had suffered. "I'm sorry."

"Ellie came in and bludgeoned him to death with her testing kit."

That astounded Darkness and he opened his eyes. "Ellie?"

"Ellie," Fury confirmed. "She killed him and then set it up so it appeared that I'd done it before the paralytic drugs he'd given me took effect. She'd been kind to me up to that point but as I lay there helpless, realizing what she was doing, I felt betrayed."

"I can't believe she'd do that. I mean, you were mistaken, right? No female is more loving than she is toward you."

"She'd acquired evidence that day that she needed to smuggle out to save all of us. She felt sure that I wouldn't be killed for the crime and had to blame me. They would have killed her if they'd known she'd taken the male's life. I didn't understand that until much later. I attacked her on sight after Homeland opened. It was the first time I'd seen her since the incident. I couldn't let it go even after I learned the truth. She'd seen what that male had done to me. It was a matter of pride and rage. I never got the chance to make that male pay. She became a target to me."

"I understand." He did.

"I became obsessed to the point that I stalked and kidnapped her. I took her to my home for payback."

Darkness flinched. "You hurt her? I can't see you doing that. You love that female."

"I was fucked up," Fury admitted. "I had her tied to my bed but I couldn't follow through with all the horrible things I wanted to do. Luckily. I still wake up some nights in a sweat, imagining the horrible consequences if I'd allowed that rage to take control. She's my life. I would have lost her forever."

"I'm glad you regained control of your emotions."

"Me too." Fury took a few breaths. "Kathryn Decker must remind you of the female who betrayed you."

"They look nothing alike." He lifted the laptop off his thighs and quickly stood. "You are out of line with that comment."

"She's here under false pretenses for an unknown reason. You're attracted to her but you know she'll betray us in some way. We all expect it. It has to make you relive the past. Tell me I'm wrong without lying."

"Fine. I have been having issues with the past but I know she's not Galina. I did have the ability to get my revenge on her."

"You never told me that part."

Darkness wanted to toss the phone into the wall and smash it into a hundred pieces. "She's dead." He left it at that.

"You killed her?"

He clenched his teeth and spun, pacing the confines of the room. "I don't want to discuss this."

"I'm not judging you. We're brothers," Fury rasped. "You did what you had to do."

"We share the same human DNA. That doesn't make us brothers."

"Does that make it easier for you if you say that?" Fury growled. "We are brothers. Not all of yours are dead. I'm still here."

"I'm fine. Good night. I have a job to do." He hung up and resisted smashing the phone.

It rang just seconds later. He looked down and saw the name. He used his thumb to turn off the ringer. He didn't want to speak to Fury again. Not while he was in a bad mood. It had been a trying few days. He needed to be calm. Fury had gotten under his skin. He glanced down at the phone a minute later and saw a message had been left. He turned it on and dialed Security.

"I'm sending you the feeds to the human's cottage. I'm going for a jog. I'll be back in about forty minutes."

"Good deal," the male announced. "We're ready on this end."

He bent and typed in the commands. Kat sat on the couch, watching the news. She was oblivious of the hell he felt. He switched the feeds over and slammed the laptop closed. He needed to run and expend his energy.

Chapter Six

❧

Darkness approached his current residence and stopped running. His nose flared and he growled as he faced the male who stepped out from behind a tree near the patio doors. He shouldn't have been surprised to find Fury waiting for him.

"I told you that I don't want to talk."

Fury shrugged. "I told you that I'm worried about you."

"Stop."

Fury took a step forward. "Family can be a pain in the ass."

"We aren't family."

Anger flashed on the male's features. "I'm tired of waiting around for you to heal enough to deal with what the tests revealed. We are family. Maybe it doesn't bother you to refuse to acknowledge me but I'd like you to be part of my life. We're the only blood ties we each have. No one else matched my DNA test."

"Only the human part."

"I'm canine and you're feline. Big deal." Fury came a little closer. "I see a resemblance. We both ended up with dark hair and brown eyes. We have the same chin too. We got those traits from our humans. Do you ever wonder who they were? I do."

"No. I never consider it. The records were destroyed so we'll never know."

"Have you ever thought about putting your DNA out there to see if we can find a human match and possibly find other relatives? They have adoption registries that might help us find close relations."

The concept horrified Darkness. "No!"

"I have. These are things family should talk about. We could have fully human siblings."

"Don't do it." Darkness advanced until they were a foot apart. "They are nothing like us. The connection died the moment the humans were paid by Mercile."

Fury frowned. "I'm talking about the children those humans could have created. Not the parents who made that choice."

"I want no part of it."

"That's the problem. You want no part of anything."

Darkness leashed his temper. "Stop taking it personally."

"How can I not? I know I can't replace the full-blooded siblings you lost. I'm not trying to. I just want to be closer to you."

"No." He unfurled his fists.

"Did they look like us? They were my brothers too. Tell me something personal about them."

Pain stabbed at Darkness' chest. "Stop."

"Did they have our hair color? Our eye color?"

"STOP!" He hadn't meant to shove the male but Fury stumbled back, assuring him that's exactly what he'd done.

Fury rubbed his chest and snarled.

Darkness lifted his hands, not willing to fight. "Sorry. I don't want to discuss this."

"Too damn bad." Fury took a menacing step forward. "Do I have to beat it out of you?"

"You don't want to do this."

"Are you going to kill me?" Fury kicked off his shoes. "You hold everything inside. Stop blaming yourself for something out of your control. I know you somehow blame yourself for their deaths but it's just survivor's guilt."

"You don't understand."

"Then make me. Tell me everything that happened when they took you away from Mercile. Why do you blame yourself for the deaths of our brothers? Why are you such an asshole by refusing to accept our bond? Talk to me because I'm tired of waiting. I deserve answers."

"It's better if you don't know all the details," he admitted.

"I never took you for a coward."

That infuriated him. "I'm not."

"Then tell me more about them," Fury snarled. "Talk to me, damn it."

"I'm going inside." He tried to walk around the male but Fury grabbed his arm.

"This isn't over. I'm not leaving until I have answers."

He glanced down at the fisted hand gripping his forearm. He held the male's furious gaze. "I won't fight you."

Fury released him. Darkness relaxed. He understood the male's frustration and wasn't even surprised by it. Fury had tried repeatedly to get him to talk. He just didn't want to share the details. It would hurt the male, the last thing he wanted.

"Some things are better left unknown." It was the best advice he could give.

"That's bullshit. You're going to tell me everything that happened when you were taken from Mercile and exactly how our brothers died. All I know are the barest basics. They died there and you were the only one to survive. There was a human female there who helped train you but she betrayed you. I want the information you won't share."

He faced Fury. "It's not a good story."

"I don't care."

"It's best you never met them. You didn't get to know them the way I did so you can't ever know the loss I feel. That's a good thing. Be grateful for it."

"That's it," Fury snarled. "You think I don't care? They were family. Share the burden and get it off your chest so you can accept me as your brother. This thing is like a wall between us and I want it torn down."

"Good night." Darkness turned away.

Fury howled with rage, the only warning he got before the male attacked. He spun in time to catch a fist to his jaw. It sent him reeling back. The force of the blow almost made him fall. He regained his balance and braced his legs.

"Stop it!" he yelled.

Fury shook his head and raised his fists. "I'm tearing down that wall even if it means we both end up bloody, in Medical." He threw another punch.

Darkness jerked his head to the left, barely missing a direct hit to his mouth. He threw out an arm and nailed Fury in the ribs. The male stumbled back and snarled. He advanced. Darkness retreated.

"Stop it. This is immature."

"Brothers sometimes fight." Fury waved his hand toward his chest, urging him to come at him. "Let's figure out who is the toughest, bro."

"Goddamn it," Darkness hissed.

The fight was on. Fury grabbed his shirt and nailed him in the ribs with a knee. He groaned but regained the upper hand when he managed to land a blow to the male's chin. Fury stumbled back but Darkness didn't retreat that time. The male wanted to fight and he was up for it. He tackled Fury around the waist, taking them both to the ground.

They rolled, exchanging punches. He heard someone approaching but ignored the audience they seemed to have drawn until males pulled them apart. Security had surrounded them quickly. He glared at Fury, who was being held by two other males.

Fury actually grinned. He had blood around his mouth. "Tell me that didn't feel good."

"What is going on here?" Jinx glanced between the two of them.

"A little harmless competition," Fury announced. "Release us."

"Harmless?" Jinx shook his head. "You're both bleeding."

"We're bleeding the same blood type though, aren't we?" Fury arched an eyebrow at Darkness.

"Release us," Darkness repeated. "The fight is over."

"But the discussion has just begun. I'll be back tomorrow night and every night after until we work this out," Fury warned.

"You're crazy," Darkness accused.

The males restraining Fury released him. "No. You could have done a hell of a lot more damage to me if you wanted but I'm your brother. You were playing with me or I would have broken bones. I've seen you fight."

"You caught me by surprise."

Fury snorted. "See you tomorrow night. Talk or it's on again."

Darkness watched Fury walk away and ordered the males to go with him. The male had lost his mind if he thought they'd fight again. It amazed him when he found himself smiling though. He admired Fury. He even liked him. He turned to go into his home to shower.

Kat stood on the grass next to her patio. He could see her shocked expression and tell she was upset by the way she hugged her middle. His good humor died, knowing she'd witnessed the fight. She approached him cautiously.

"Are you okay?"

He didn't want to deal with her or more questions. He spun and stalked toward the pond. He lifted his shirt and wiped at the blood on his mouth and forehead with the material. It was mostly from split knuckles. Fury had a point.

Their blood was shared, even if it was just from their human side.

His keen hearing picked up soft footsteps and a female curse. He slowed his pace. Kat followed him. It was tempting to leave her behind. She wouldn't have a chance of finding him if he sprinted off but curiosity rose. He reached a shadowed area under a tree and sat on the ground, staring out at the pond. Lights reflected off it, the water slightly rippling from the wind.

She approached but he didn't turn his head. When she reached him, he glanced at her once, really taking in her appearance. The oversized T-shirt she wore was three times too big and thin cotton pants hugged her legs. Her bare feet caused him to frown. They were probably too tender to go barefoot outside since humans were rarely without shoes. It wasn't his concern though. She'd made the choice to follow him into the night.

A sudden weariness settled in. He was tired but it wasn't the kind that sleep could cure. Fury had been right. He'd carried a burden alone and the male deserved to know the truth. He might not like the answers he received. It might even make them enemies.

Was he willing to risk it? He almost wished he could go back in time and just tell Fury the truth. Then he'd know for sure. It wasn't as if things could get worse. He was a loner at the NSO. There were mental walls he had put in place. Perhaps it was time to tear them down, as Fury had suggested.

Kat sat down under the tree next to the brooding man she'd followed. Darkness turned his head. Enough moonlight peeked through the trees for her to make out most of his features.

"Hi."

"I allowed you to trail me and you did. Why are you here?"

"I was worried about you." She shrugged, getting more comfortable. "Are you all right? That looked pretty intense. Do you fight with other New Species often?"

He sighed, looking away. "I'm different."

Sympathy welled. "Because of what was done to you by that guy who took you and your brothers?" She really hated Darwin Havings at that moment and hoped he'd screw up soon and make it possible for the authorities to capture him. He'd never know freedom again once the government got their hands on him.

"Yes."

Darkness wasn't the most talkative person. She glanced around. The park was abandoned at night and the water in front of them looked pretty and the muted sounds were soothing. She looked at him.

"Do you come here often?"

"Yes." He watched her as well. "It gives me a sense of peace."

She let that information sink in. "Demons are a horrible thing to live with."

He was silent for a full minute and she wondered if he was done talking. It might have been a mistake to follow him but she just hadn't been able to resist after the scene she'd witnessed.

"He was angry because I don't talk when I should." His words were spoken so softly that she strained to hear them.

"That was what the fight was about?"

"Yes."

The silence stretched again. She wanted to help him somehow. "Do you want to talk about it? That can help at times."

"That depends."

She waited for him to say more but a good minute passed. She finally broke the silence. "On what?"

He took a deep breath, blew it out. "Who are you going to repeat it to?"

"I don't understand."

"Yes you do."

She really didn't. He cleared it up though.

"Are you on duty or off right now, Kat?"

She wondered again if he still suspected she wasn't who she said she was. "I'm off duty. What is said will stay between us. I know you don't trust me but you can." She meant it.

He hesitated, turned his head and stared out at the vast darkness of the water. "Fury wants to know more about what happened to my brothers."

"Aren't they here somewhere?"

He shook his head. "No."

"Reservation?"

He was quiet for a full minute. "They are dead."

Bad scenarios filled her head. Had Havings had them killed? Had they been returned to Mercile Industries and died there? Some had died when it had been seized by government agencies. Others had died during rescue attempts at other locations. There'd been that explosion linked to a facility associated with Mercile Industries. Everyone had died according to the news reports. The NSO didn't share too much information with the general public but she got her intel from reliable sources. The NSO had tried to breach the lower floors of the company but it had been rigged to explode. Everyone below ground had died before they could be rescued.

"I'm sorry." She wanted to ask for details but resisted.

He stared out across the water. "I am as well. Fury wants me to speak of them but I refuse."

"Why?"

"It's not a happy story to tell. I don't want him to suffer. He's a good male."

She let that sink in. "Why would he be hurt?"

"They were his brothers too."

Shock rolled through her. "You're related to Fury North?"

He jerked his head in her direction and growled low.

"Sorry. I didn't mean anything by it. I just didn't expect that."

"We're half brothers. Are you going to share that information?"

"No."

She was tempted to ask him who he thought she'd tell but refrained. She had been stunned when she'd heard noises and stepped out onto the patio to see Darkness fighting another guy. Security had rushed to the scene and broken it up pretty fast but she'd identified his opponent. Fury North was an NSO celebrity, almost as popular and well-known as Justice North.

"He wants us to be closer but I don't allow anyone to get too close."

Darkness might suffer from post-traumatic stress disorder. She guessed he'd seen a lot of shit go down when Havings had him. None of it would have been good. "Are you getting counseling?"

His scowl was answer enough. She sealed her lips, not one to preach that seeking treatment might help.

"I don't need it."

She disagreed. He was an Alpha-male type and most of them refused to admit they might have severe and lasting issues until it was too late. Of course he wasn't like anyone she'd ever met before. His childhood had been a nightmare so he'd never had an easy time of it. "So you're dealing with it by getting into fights with people who care about you? How is that working out?"

He turned away. "I don't want a lecture."

Fair enough. "What do you want?"

"Do you really want to know?"

Kat scooted a little closer but not enough to touch him. "Yes. I wouldn't ask if I didn't."

He stared straight ahead. "I want to forget."

She could understand that.

"But Fury won't let this go. He's going to keep pushing until I tell him how they died. I don't want him to hate me."

"Why would he?"

"I was there." He paused, taking a few deep breaths. "He knows that but not all of it. I was asked to write a summary report but didn't include many details."

"Is it too tough to talk about? That's understandable."

Darkness was silent for so long that she thought he'd totally shut her out. She peered out at the night, just sitting by him. He took a deep breath.

"We were kept in tents next to each other during the training." He paused, his hands rubbing his pants over his thighs. "It was the first time we were made aware of each other's existence and our blood connection. They made us do things." His voice changed, deepened and turned raspy. "We did them. They said the humans we were ordered to kill were enemies, rebels who murdered innocents. They were well armed but were no match against us."

Her stomach roiled a bit as her imagination filled in more blanks. She just hoped they hadn't been US soldiers.

He seemed to guess where her thoughts had turned. "They didn't speak our language. There were camps of them in the mountains. We hit at night. I didn't feel so bad after the third time. We found the remains of a male child. They'd mutilated and murdered him. He couldn't have been more than twelve."

Kat blinked back tears, staring at the pond too. The sight of that poor kid's body must have been horrific. The urge to reach over and curl her fingers over Darkness' hand, still rubbing his thigh, struck her but she resisted.

"We had no choice." He cleared his throat. "If one of us disobeyed, they'd have killed the others. They were my brothers and we wanted to survive. It's against our nature to give up. We're stubborn."

"That's a good thing. Sometimes that will keep you going no matter what."

Silence stretched. "One night they ordered us to sneak into a camp and kill everyone. We got there but there were no armed males. It was only females and children." His voice deepened into a snarl. "They were terrified when they saw us."

Her gut twisted. She didn't really want to hear any more. She liked him too much. "You don't have to tell me this."

"We refused to kill them."

She turned her head to stare at him, their eyes meeting. Relief washed through her. "What happened?"

"The humans in charge of the project ordered us to go back and kill all of them." His chin lifted and his handsome face was clearly visible in the moonlight. He was suffering. "We refused again."

She had a sinking sensation that she wasn't going to like what happened next.

"Number Four didn't feel pain. It was too fast." He paused. "*Boom!*"

His sudden loud outburst startled her.

"That was how quickly he died when they detonated his collar."

Tears filled her eyes, understanding they'd murdered his brother.

"It didn't take much of a charge to separate his head from his shoulders."

Jesus. She reached over. Her fingertips traced the back of his hand, so warm and larger than hers. She wanted to comfort him.

"They ordered us again to go kill everyone in that camp. I looked at my brothers and saw the same emotion in their eyes that must have been in mine. We refused."

She guessed what was coming.

"Number Three closed his eyes and it was over. I saw fear in his expression though. He felt that before he died."

"I'm...so sorry," she whispered.

His hand twisted under hers and he laced long fingers through her smaller ones, holding her hand. He looked away to stare into the night again.

"They demanded again that we kill. Number Two stepped forward and said he'd do it. His survival instincts were strong and he was so enraged that he no longer cared who died. He just wanted to kill something out of revenge. It didn't matter to him anymore if they were innocent. They were human. That was enough. I could see he'd snapped."

She couldn't blame his brother but it was horrific, knowing that Darkness had been a party to killing innocent people, despite being forced. It was the worst scenario to ever expect someone to be in.

He grew silent and she watched him until he looked back at her and suddenly leaned in closer. "Do you want to know why you should walk in the opposite direction when you see me?"

"You had no choice, Darkness. It was a kill-or-be-killed situation."

"I snapped his neck with my bare hands." His voice came out a snarl. "I couldn't allow my brother to kill babies and helpless females. I will never forget the look in his eyes when I lunged forward and he realized what I was about to do. I saw betrayal and shock in them." He released her hand. "I didn't hesitate. I knew they'd kill me before I could take him out if my reflexes weren't faster than the human with the remote for my collar."

Kat blinked back tears, her chest tight with emotion that threatened to choke her. She wanted to tell him he did the right thing but she was afraid she'd start to cry if she did. It took everything she had not to fall apart. It broke her heart and made her respect him even more.

He lifted both hands with his palms facing her. "I clean them but the blood and deaths of others are stained here. I never forget." He rolled away, gracefully getting to his feet. He kept his back to her. "Do you think Fury will still want to be a part of my life when he finds out I killed one of our brothers?"

She got to her knees, then to her feet. She trembled all over, emotionally overwrought. "You did the right thing and I think he'd understand," she finally got out. "Why did they allow you to live?"

"You caught that. I knew you were smart. It was a test." His tone came out raspy. "They needed to find out if we'd follow orders or die first. They didn't count on the fact that I was willing to kill my own brother to save others. The test was deemed a failure and I was sent back to Mercile to the same fate as the other Species but I had to suffer the guilt of what I'd done."

It was worse than cruel. "A failure of what kind of test?"

"To see if they could make us mindless killers by keeping us under their control. It didn't work. They believed we didn't have souls but they were wrong."

"I'm so damn sorry, Darkness."

He shrugged. "The past can't be changed." He turned his head but didn't look at her, just stared into the night, his features in profile. "I'll return you to your cottage to make sure you don't get into trouble. You know you're not allowed to roam Homeland without an escort. Let's go."

"I don't want to leave you alone right now."

He turned to stare at her. "Return to your cottage, Kat. Don't follow me ever again or you might catch me in a moment when I'm not feeling so talkative. I don't want you to be hurt if I'm in a defensive mood. That's what caused that fight you saw."

"I don't believe you're dangerous to me."

He ran his fingers through his hair before he fisted his hands at his sides. "You'd be wrong."

"You wouldn't hurt a woman. You said so yourself."

She could sense the danger. It hung in the air thickly as if it were a scent or a sensation, almost tangible. She refused to back down though. It was probably stupid but she did trust him with her life. He was tortured by his past but he was a good man.

"I've killed a female before."

The news should have surprised her more but she remembered the vibe she'd gotten when he'd interrogated her and what she'd called him on after her class. "What did she do to you?"

He took a deep breath and let it out slowly. "I want you so bad sometimes I have to fight myself not to take you."

Her heart raced. She was attracted to him too but noticed he'd changed the subject. Part of her wanted to push for an answer about that woman but she was afraid he'd shut her out again. "We're talking sex, right?" She wanted to be sure they were on the same page.

His gaze lowered down her body before jerking up to hold her curious stare. "I'm not mate material."

"What does that mean?"

"Some of my kind have taken humans as mates. They aren't as tormented inside as I am. They adjusted to freedom better and can provide those females with positive emotions and tenderness. I have neither. I am restless and wouldn't take to a stable relationship well. I don't have a heart to give. I don't do commitment."

The air froze inside her lungs until the jealousy passed. "You mean you sleep around with other women?"

His jaw clenched, the muscle taut. He hesitated. "I don't seek female companionship. I scare most of them. They see me as too cold. I'm saying I would never offer anything more than physical pleasure."

He was hot. She totally disagreed with the female New Species assessment if that's what they really thought of him. "Understood. You're not looking for anything long-term."

"I don't stay in one place for long. I transfer between Homeland and Reservation often. I will visit the Wild Zone for days or weeks at a time without bothering to stay inside the cabins provided there. I enjoy sleeping outdoors. Mates need a full-time male who is always there to protect them. That won't ever be me."

Message received. He was offering a one-night stand. She took a deep breath and stepped closer to him. "I'm kind of good at taking care of myself and I'm not looking for anything long-term either. I'm married to my job. I travel a lot too."

"Are you married to it right now?"

"I'm not working at this moment. This is my own time."

His clenched fingers opened and he crossed his arms over his chest, regarding her with a frown. "You're human."

"I am."

"They wish for more than to just share sex with a male."

Amused, she smiled. "Are you an expert on them? If so, here's a lesson. We're not all the same."

He wet his lips with his tongue. "You want to fuck me?"

She took another step closer, had to lift her chin to keep staring into his eyes, and knew she was playing with fire. He was blunt. She did want him, though, and had since they'd first met. There wasn't a time she could recall of ever having been more attracted to a man.

"You like direct, don't you?"

"Yes." His voice deepened.

"Okay. I want you, Darkness. I'm not looking for an engagement ring or a lifetime commitment. I'm bad with the whole relationship thing. Tried it and failed miserably. Men tend to resent my job and my independence after a while. They are also irritated when they know I could take them in a fight."

"I'd win if we tussled."

She glanced at his powerful arms and well-built body, agreeing. She lifted her hand and placed it on his forearm. His skin was hot to the touch, just like him. "You don't scare me."

He slowly unfolded his arms and firm, large hands encased her hips. One jerk and she was flattened against his chest roughly enough to make her gasp. Their bodies pressed together. The bulge against her belly assured her he was interested in her too.

"This is one game you don't want to play."

"I'm not playing."

He lowered his head while staring at her face. She wished she could see his beautiful eyes better in the dim night. The scent of his masculine cologne, or whatever it was that smelled so good, teased her nose. The urge to get closer became strong.

"You should tell me no while you can."

"I don't want to."

He drew in a ragged breath, his chest invading her space and pressing against her breasts. "I'll take you. Do you understand?"

"Your place or mine? Let's go."

He glanced around and his hold on her loosened. "Yours. The patrols will be by here soon." He held her gaze. "Or I'd take you where you stand."

Sexy. She'd totally do him on the grass but wasn't about to admit that. "Let's go."

He stepped back and his hands dropped away. "I come with conditions, Kat."

"What are they?"

He hesitated. "You do what I say when it comes to sex."

"You're one of those." She felt a little disappointed. "I'm not the Master-and-slave type. Sorry but I won't drop to my knees on command to blow you or enjoy being smacked."

"That's not what I meant. I'm going to tie your hands to the headboard so you can't touch me. Will you agree to that?"

"Why?"

He hesitated. "Remember when I had you in interrogation? I would have lost control of the situation if you'd had your hands free. That's part of the terms. There will be no hitting involved but I'm not one of your humans. I just want to fuck you while I'm in control of it. It's safer for both of us that way. Don't ever forget what I said to you about an out-of-control male."

Everything they'd shared inside that interrogation room flashed through her mind. "You want to repeat what happened between us before but this time you plan to finish what you start?"

"Yes. That's half of my terms."

"What's the other half?"

He lowered his head and stared into her eyes. "Don't lie to me this time. Everything that comes out of your mouth will be the truth when I have you naked or don't say anything at all."

His intense stare reminded her of why she was really there. That really dampened her mood. "Why would you want to take me to bed if you think I'm going to lie to you? That's what you're implying."

"This is just about sex. Trust is earned but we're strangers. I'm making that a term, Kat. No lies between us when we're naked. Lie to me any other time and I won't take it personally. You never want me to feel betrayed by you. Do you understand? It would be dangerous."

She did and that scared her. He had made it clear that he suspected she was at Homeland for other reasons than to teach her classes. It was there between them, larger than life.

"I understand and accept the terms."

"Also, this stays between you and me only. No one is to know what happens between us sexually. Do you agree?"

She wanted him. "Yes."

It was a bargain she hoped she wouldn't regret. He'd given her the option of not talking at all if something he asked her crossed a line where she'd have to lie. She appreciated that but silence would be as telling as just blurting out the truth. It was stupid to follow him back to her cottage but she wanted him enough to risk it. Even if it meant putting her career on the line.

Chapter Seven

∞

"Go inside and wash off that perfume," Darkness ordered the moment they entered her back yard.

"I forgot what you said about it bothering your nose. Do you want to join me in the shower?" She glanced at his hands and face. "You've got blood on you still."

"I'll wash up next door and return in about fifteen minutes. Don't bother putting anything on. Just a towel. Leave the slider unlocked."

He expected her to protest. She was a strong-willed female but she just nodded curtly. "Okay. See you in fifteen."

He hurried next door, snatched up his cell phone and dialed. It rang while he opened the laptop on his bed. Security answered.

"Hi, Darkness. You ready to take the feed over again?"

"Yes." He punched commands into the keyboard. "Thanks." He disconnected the feed to Security.

The screen showed that Kat paced in the bedroom. She didn't seem too eager to take a shower and he wondered if she'd changed her mind. Darkness locked down the feed so no one else could view the cameras that watched her every move. He'd rather be safe than sorry. He rose and entered the bathroom, tearing off his clothing.

When the blood washed off he saw that the fight with Fury had left him bruised. There were some minor cuts on his hands. He put on a pair of silky sleeping pants, entered the bedroom and he sat on the bed. Kat wasn't on screen. He changed the location of the feed until he found her in the bathroom.

She had washed her hair and body and had a towel around her middle. Her hand lifted and she wiped steam off the mirror to peer at her reflection. Her lips moved and he activated the sound. Did she have some type of listening device they hadn't found to talk to whoever she worked for? It infuriated him since he'd purposely not invaded her privacy in that one room until then.

"Fine," she whispered. "You want him. He wants you. What's the worst that could happen?" She straightened and closed her eyes, taking a few deep breaths. "I'll regret this if I chicken out." Her eyes opened and she leaned forward again, taking in her reflection. "I'm not a chicken. It's going to be fine. He won't hurt me."

He studied her ears, looking for listening devices but saw none. *Who is she talking to?* He couldn't hear anyone else.

"Okay, enough of the pep talk before he shows up and hears me talking to myself."

He relaxed. She turned away from the mirror and exited the bathroom, flipping off the light as she went. He switched the feed. She entered the bedroom and stared at the bed. The vulnerable look on her face made him regretful. He had asked her to trust him when he wasn't willing to do the same. No female would ever be allowed to tie him to a bed. He shuddered at the thought.

He closed the laptop and rose. A quick trip to the bathroom gained him what he wanted and then he left through the backdoor, quickly scanning the area to make sure no one saw him cross to her yard. It was clear of patrols so he entered her home through the slider, closing and locking it behind him. He even closed the curtain over the glass.

Kat turned when he entered her bedroom. The expression on her face smoothed out and she attempted to hide her fear. The slight tremble of her hands as they reached up to grip her towel gave away her true emotions. She noticed his hand holding the box of condoms. Her eyebrows arched.

"What are those for?"

"Us."

She licked her lips. "I don't have any diseases and everything I've ever read stated you're immune to sexually transmitted diseases." She held his gaze. "Was that bullshit?"

"Do you want every Species in your class tomorrow to know I fucked you? They would unless I pull out. That's not my preference. Our sense of smell is as good as I said it was. You'd have to soak in a bath for a long time to make certain every drop of me was washed away. Are you willing to risk that or would you rather take precautions?" He glanced at the box then her. "As I said, I want this kept just between us."

She took a deep breath. "I understand."

He moved to the wall shelves, removing a roll of condoms as he went and placed the box in front of the hidden camera. It would just show the color of the box and not allow anyone to see what happened in the bedroom. He couldn't be sure that Fury wouldn't override his secure access and watch Kat if he believed Darkness might be a danger to her. He also used his thumb to crush the tiny audio transmitter located on the same shelf. Security feeds to this room would now be blind and deaf to everything they did.

He faced her and shoved the roll of condoms in his front pocket. "I'm going to borrow your pantyhose."

"How do you know I own any?"

"I searched your suitcase before it was delivered. How are you doing without your cigarettes?"

"That so wasn't cool."

He didn't feel regret. "They stink. Where are the pantyhose?"

"Top drawer, to your left."

He turned, found them. He tested their strength and was happy with the results. He approached the headboard. "Drop the towel and get on the bed."

She swallowed hard but allowed the towel to fall to the floor. He could see her wariness and kept his gaze locked with hers so she didn't feel uncomfortable being completely naked before him. He only glanced down her body when she lay flat on her back in the center of the bed, raising her arms upward until her fingertips curled around the wooden slats of the headboard. She gripped them a bit tightly, again showing her bravado was strained.

"Easy." He sat on the edge of the bed, giving her his back to help put her at ease. "I won't hurt you. You'll have a little movement with the way I attach your hands to the headboard."

"I'd feel a little better if I wasn't actually tied down. You could just trust me to keep hold of the headboard."

It was tempting but he shook his head. "Trust is earned, Kat. We've been over this. I need to be in control."

"Right." She closed her eyes. "I'm supposed to trust you but you don't trust me."

He wasn't being fair. "I see your point but these are my terms."

"Fine. Do it."

She had delicate wrists. He tied the pantyhose around them and knotted the silky material so it wouldn't tighten if she struggled. He kept her arms close together and secured them to the same bar. The headboard was solidly made and she wouldn't be strong enough to break free. He rose and reached for the waistband of his pajama bottoms. Kat opened her eyes and stared at him. He saw a little fear in her gaze. It made him pause.

"You'll enjoy this." He decided to wait until later to strip out of the pants. She was already leery and he'd heard males complain that some human females were intimidated by the sizes of their dicks. The last thing he wanted was for Kat to change her mind. "Relax."

"Easier said than done," she muttered. She cleared her throat and swallowed. "Okay. What next, Mr. Control?"

He liked her spirit. She was a bit frightened but refused to give in to it. He rounded the bed, studying her. She was beautiful. Her body was fit but not overly muscled. Her frame was much smaller than a Species female with more fragile bones. Her pale skin would probably bruise easily if he didn't touch her with care. He used his knee to brace his weight on the bed and leaned forward.

"Spread your thighs."

"Just like that, huh?" The soft growl was a warning. "Okay. That's kind of sexy."

He smiled. "You think so?"

"Yeah. I like it when your voice deepens too."

"Give me a few minutes and you might hear me snarl. You don't scare easily, do you?"

"It depends on whether you're angry or not."

He allowed her to see some emotion on his face. It was hunger. He wanted her bad. "I'm going to make sounds because I'm Species. Are you prepared for that?"

He wanted to groan when she wet her lips with her pink tongue. She ran her upper teeth over her bottom lip next. "Bring it on but just remember I'm not into pain."

"It's going to be all pleasure. Spread your thighs wider and bend them up. Give me access to you."

She only hesitated for a second before following his orders. She looked appealing as hell with her pussy exposed and in that position. He stretched out on his stomach as he came down on the bed and slid his arms next to her hips, bent them at the elbow and wrapped his hands around the tops of her legs. It pinned her open, leaving his face inches away from the sweet sight of bare, pink skin. She had no hair there.

"No landing strip?" His voice came out a bit husky but he didn't try to tone it down. She'd said she found that appealing.

Breathing her in made his dick hard. She wasn't turned-on yet but that would change soon.

"I occasionally decide to torture myself by getting waxed."

He lifted his chin and stared up at her. One eyebrow arched in question.

"It hurts like a son of a bitch. I usually have it done right before I go on vacation during the summer."

"You're not on vacation."

"It depends on who you ask. I am according to me."

That sparked curiosity but he pushed it back. His throbbing dick didn't want to interrogate her at that moment. He dipped his head, more interested in her sex than conversation. He'd missed studying a female...and the taste of one. She was beautiful all over. He wet his lips and opened his mouth, aware of his fangs. He wondered if Kat remembered them. He'd remind her soon.

The tightening of his chest and a tingling in his throat warned him to mute his reaction to her. He wasn't about to purr. It might alarm her before she was too distracted to notice. He fought the urge and won.

"Relax," he ordered, feeling her legs tense in his hold.

"I'm trying. It's been awhile since I had someone up close and personal down there who wasn't wearing a doctor's coat. That would have been my last checkup a few months ago."

That spiked his interest. "How long has it been since you had sex?"

She didn't answer.

"You can't tell me the truth about that?"

"Almost a year. I keep busy."

He ran the tip of his tongue over the pink, fleshy bundle of nerves. She sucked in a sharp breath and he repeated the process, going at her slowly and tenderly. He needed to keep in control or they both would be in trouble. It had been years since he'd allowed himself the pleasure of sex. He pushed those thoughts back, not wanting the past to ruin the present.

Her legs tensed in his hold and he gripped her more firmly. Her scent began to change as he used the tip of his tongue to play with her sex. The sweet smell of desire and arousal was a stimulating drug to him. Kat tried to wiggle in his hold and her soft moans increased. The headboard creaked but he didn't look up, certain she couldn't break free even if she struggled.

"Oh god," she whispered. "I'm not going to last."

He applied more pressure. He wanted to get inside her too bad to wait long. He had to adjust his hips to shift weight off his swollen dick. He couldn't get any harder than he already was. He growled, using vibration to increase her pleasure as he pressed his open mouth tighter against her clit.

She jerked in his hold and cried out his name. He sucked on the small bud again then gently released her and lifted his head enough to view her pussy. She was soaked now, wet and ready to take him. He lifted his chin and stared up her body. Kat's head was thrown back, her mouth open. Her muscles started to relax, including her legs, still pinned by him. He let her go and sat up.

Kat opened her eyes, her breath coming in rapid pants. "Sorry."

He dug a hand in his pocket and removed the roll of condoms. "For what?"

"I came pretty fast. Should I be embarrassed?" She smiled though, a teasing look in her eyes. "Or are you proud that you're that good at it?"

"This time doesn't count."

That subdued her humor. "No? I disagree."

"This is just a warm-up. I need you really wet." He straightened to his knees, used his thumbs to hook his pajama bottoms and shoved them down. He watched her face as he revealed his dick. Her expression blanked. It took her a few seconds to react. Her lips parted and he could see surprise.

"I'll fit." He tore off one of the condoms from the roll and tossed the rest of them up near the top of the bed. She didn't seem so certain or fearless anymore. It amused him. "I'll go slow. You're tough. I promised not to hurt you."

"I don't think that's an option. You're size-proportioned, that's for sure. I guess those big feet of yours should have been a clue. Do you carry a permit for that?"

He laughed, understanding the joke. "I thought about flipping you over first and not allowing you to see me." He looked down and carefully rolled on the condom. He had a flashback of the past but immediately looked at Kat's face. She was there, not the other female who'd always made him use condoms. He focused on Kat's still-spread legs. She'd put her feet down on the bed but kept open for him. "I'll be gentle."

"You'd better be." She bit her lower lip, studying his cock.

He had to make a decision and chose to take her facing away from him. It would put less weight on her small frame and he could control his entry better. He reached down and gripped her calves, lifted them and flipped her over before she could protest. He released her legs.

"Get on your knees." He helped by getting between her legs and shoving them apart to make room. His hands carefully slid under her hips and lifted.

Kat gasped. "You could have just told me to get on my stomach first."

He chuckled again, amused. "I thought I did. I said I wanted to let you see me first though. You did."

She crawled a little closer to the headboard and gripped it with her hands. The pantyhose allowed her that much movement but kept her wrists inches apart. She looked over her shoulder. Uncertainty flashed across her face for a second. He caught the emotion.

"Easy, sweetheart. I'm going to be careful."

121

He inched closer and had to put his legs on the outside of hers. She was shorter and he needed to spread his legs wider to put their hips at the same level. She faced forward and stiffened, her shoulders tightening as she appeared to get a death grip on the headboard. It was clear she expected rough treatment but he was about to disappoint her.

He bent over her until his chest rested lightly against her spine. He fisted the top of the headboard beside one of her hands. It was a reminder of their size difference. He wanted to get inside her but he used his other hand to reach between her parted thighs and play with her clit with his fingertip.

She was soaked and jerked under him, probably still a little sensitive. He gentled his touch, rubbing slow circles. Her posture relaxed and she lowered her head to rest against her outstretched arms. Her ass tilted upward and drew his attention. She had a nice one and it made his dick twitch. The throbbing sensation of having all that blood pooled there wasn't painless but he'd given Kat his word. It had been a long time and he could wait a little longer to make sure she was as into wanting him inside her as he wanted to be.

Soft moans came from her and she moved under him, rocking slightly. He released the headboard and straightened. He kept playing with her clit though, not easing off. He gripped his shaft and hated the way he trembled slightly as he backed up a little and pressed the head of his engorged shaft against the opening of her pussy. He leaned back a little, staring down. She appeared small and he clenched his teeth. He applied a little pressure and pushed forward slowly.

"Relax," he demanded.

"You're big," she stated softly.

It wasn't a request for him to stop so he pushed farther. The desire to drive into the heat of her snug body was strong. It would feel good but he resisted the urge. He watched her take him. The sight of the condom-covered head of his dick disappearing inside her pussy made him want to purr, combined with the warmth and tight fit. She felt amazing. He'd forgotten how good sex was.

He entered deeper and released his shaft. He couldn't watch anymore. The feeling of being inside Kat was too good and with visual stimulation it was almost too much to withstand. He leaned forward again and blindly gripped the headboard, coming down over her, settling her under him.

He rocked his hips, easing into her a little deeper with each thrust. Kat moaned louder and said his name. His control started to slip. He moved a little faster but made sure to be gentle. His chest rumbled and his throat tingled. He made another choice. He allowed his lips to part and let the sounds out, preferring to focus on his other physical reactions. *Gentle.* He chanted that word over and over in his mind.

Kat turned her head a little and bit into her upper arm. It did muffle some of the sounds she was making. Darkness was inside her and he kept rubbing her clit. The pleasure was too much and her vaginal muscles clamped tighter with each glide of his hips. He moved faster and it notched up the level of ecstasy. The deep purring near her ear was background noise and she knew it came from him. It was sexy, adding to the experience.

She tried to move against him, to shove back when he surged forward, but the arm around her hip tightened as he stroked her clit with more pressure. He fucked her faster. The climax struck. She lost the ability to think and didn't even care. Pleasure slammed into her brain so hard she wondered if she'd even survive. She couldn't breathe at first.

The stimulus to her clit stopped and Darkness hooked her waist with one muscular arm. He almost lifted her off her knees and more of his weight pressed down against her back. Hot breath fanned her shoulder and he snarled her name.

The bed creaked loudly as he shook from the force of coming. She could feel him inside her, as if his cock had a pulse. His thrusts slowed until he came to rest, buried deep so they were completely connected. Some of his weight eased off her back.

They were both panting while they recovered and the purring noises had stopped. Kat opened her eyes and lifted her head enough to stare at her arm. She could see her own teeth marks marring her biceps. Her fingers ached slightly when she released the headboard.

Darkness slowly withdrew from her and she hated the loss. She feared he'd just back away from her and climb off the bed. He didn't though. He kept close, his legs trapping hers between his. The arm around her waist remained too.

"Are you okay?"

She shivered at the husky, deep tone of his voice. Kat licked her lips and twisted her head to peer at him. "I'm great."

His eyes amazed her. The color appeared to have lightened slightly. It made her wonder again if his eye color could change with emotion. At that moment they were a soft brown with flecks of yellow. He blinked and arched an eyebrow.

"What?"

"You have beautiful eyes."

He looked away and cleared his throat. The compliment almost seemed to embarrass him. "So do you."

"Do…never mind." She didn't want to ruin the moment.

He stared back at her. "Do I what?"

"Never mind."

"I purred." His mouth creased into an unfriendly line. "I warned you that I made noises a human wouldn't."

"That was hot. I like the sounds you make."

His expression cleared. "Good. What was your question?"

She studied his eyes again. The color was darker, the yellow hints gone. "They do change!"

"What?"

"Your eye color. I kept thinking I imagined it or it was just the lighting."

"I need to throw away the condom. I'll be right back."

"Can you untie me first?"

"No. I'm not done with you yet. I told you. That was a warm-up."

He slowly eased away and crawled off the bed. Kat turned and sat up, a bit awkwardly since she was still secured to the headboard. She watched with a grin as Darkness strode naked into her bathroom. He had a great ass. It was muscular and perfectly rounded. He also was tan all over, no lines.

"No pancake ass for you."

He returned in seconds. "Pancake ass?"

She laughed. "I like firm asses and you have one of the best I've ever seen."

He halted, cocked his head and lowered his chin. He looked down his body then back up at her. "What about the front?"

"You need to get a concealed weapon permit." She winked. "I have no complaints except I'd love to touch you." She openly appreciated his abs. "You have no idea how much I want to trace those muscles with my fingertips. You're almost begging for it."

Darkness scowled.

She found that amusing. "Let me loose."

He approached the bed and put his knee on the end. He leaned over and grabbed her ankle. She gasped when he jerked hard, pulling her down the bed until she lay flat, the pantyhose pulling on her wrists. He was on top of her a second later, his hot flesh pressed against hers, though he leaned to one side so he didn't crush her under his weight.

"No." His lips hovered above hers. "I do all the touching."

She wanted to kiss him and pointedly stared at his mouth.

"None of that either," he rasped.

She saw no give in his determined stare. "Why not? Do I have bad breath or something? I brushed my teeth."

Her joke fell flat when he didn't even crack a smile. "It's too personal."

"And this isn't? We're naked and as close as two people can get."

He adjusted a little more to rest on his side against her. One hand opened on her stomach and slid lower until he cupped her pussy. He teased her clit with the side of his finger. "You agreed to my terms."

It was tough to form arguments when he dropped his head and his mouth opened on her nipple. He ran his tongue around the tip and then closed it over the areola. He sucked and she gasped, not expecting the jolt of pleasure.

"That's not fair." She arched her back to help him get better access to her breast.

He released her nipple and leaned over her a little more. "I never said I would be." He captured her other nipple and sucked on it. His finger brushed her clit, rubbing.

Kat closed her eyes and spread her legs to give him free access. "That feels so good."

He sucked harder on her breast. She thought it would hurt but instead it seemed to connect the sensitive area to her clit. It was as if the nerve endings were the same. She moaned and tried to turn her body into him. Darkness wouldn't allow it though, tossing one of his thighs across hers to keep her in place.

She writhed on the bed as he continued to use his mouth and fingers to tease her. Sweat broke out along her body because he'd ease off her clit every time she tensed, ready to come. She fought the restraints but they held. She wanted to dig her nails into his skin.

"Please," she urged.

Darkness lifted his head, releasing her breast. The yellow flecks were there in his eyes again and so was the hungry look she loved. He was a beautiful man when he was turned-on. She looked down his body. He'd tucked his cock between his thighs but there was no missing that he was hard again.

"Let me go," she pleaded.

He reached behind him, snagged the condoms and used his teeth to tear one of the packets from the roll. He dropped them behind his back and gripped the edge of the foil, his fangs flashing. The thing opened with a jerk of his head and he shifted his hips back away from her. He parted his thighs and his dick sprang free. He rolled on the condom and came down on top of her. She spread her legs to accommodate him.

He entered her slowly and she moaned. He felt amazing. She wrapped her legs around his hips, hugging him close since it was the only way he'd allow her to hold on to him.

He braced his arms next to hers and nuzzled her face. She turned to give him access to her neck and he nipped her. The sharp bite didn't break the skin — it felt good. She tightened her thighs around him and wiggled, urging him to move.

"You're dangerous, little pretend-cat."

She wanted to ask him why he thought that, what it meant, but then he drove into her. She cried out. He paused, buried deep inside her.

"Too rough?"

"No. I can take you. I like it."

He growled low and kissed her neck. He almost withdrew from her body and then surged forward. It drove her ass against the bed but there was no pain. Just pleasure. No one had ever taken Kat that way. She moaned and went for his shoulder with her teeth, lightly biting him.

The snarl didn't scare her and she licked his skin. He tasted good, slightly salty and all man. He moved faster, a bit rougher, and nipped her shoulder again. Kat moaned, lifting her thighs a little higher on his waist to give him freer movement with his hips. He rolled them, thrusting into her at a new angle.

She cried out and he rode her harder, hitting *that* spot over and over. She fisted the nylon restraints and squeezed her eyes closed. The pleasure kept slamming her as hard as the headboard hit the wall. She knew what two hundred forty-five pounds of unleashed, raw male felt like and it was amazing.

Chapter Eight

Kat tugged at her long-sleeved shirt to cover the marks on her wrists from the night before. They were faint but still showed. The skin hadn't actually bruised but it was a bit irritated from the nylon. She didn't want anyone to ask about the slight redness.

The second day of class had gone better after she'd shown everyone the purse trick. They'd also gone over other ways criminals hid items to get past security checks. There was no sign of Darkness.

A tall man with catlike eyes approached. He had light-brown hair and soft brown eyes. "Hello."

She smiled, giving him her attention. "Do you have a question?"

"Would you like to go home with me to share sex?"

She tried to hide her surprise. It took her a few seconds to recover. Sunshine had warned her that men might approach her and she knew New Species just said it like it was. She'd have considered slapping a normal guy for being crude but rejected that reaction. She'd encouraged them to ask questions, after all. Her sense of humor sparked.

He grinned, flashing fangs. "I promise you a very good time."

"I'm certain you would but no thank you." He was a handsome guy but there was only one man who interested her.

"Find me at any time if you change your mind." He spun away and crossed the room to the area where pool tables were.

"You handled that well."

Startled, she twisted her head to find Darkness standing a few feet behind her. "Can you not sneak up on me and how did you get in? I didn't see you."

"I came through the backdoor and stayed in the shadows to observe your teachings. You did a good job."

It was slightly irritating how that stirred warm feelings. She didn't need his approval but liked it. "Thank you. I remembered what you said."

He gave her body a once-over. "How are you feeling this morning?"

Sore. She wasn't about to admit to a little tenderness in a few areas of her body. "Great."

"I hope the bath helped."

Images flashed through her mind. They'd had sex twice and then he'd untied her. He'd entered her bathroom to remove the condom but she'd heard water running. He'd stayed in there a few minutes. Curiosity had drawn her to follow him. He was bent over her bathtub with his hand under the running water. He'd looked at her then.

"This is for you. The temperature should be perfect." He straightened. "Good night, Kat."

He'd left, taking her bathroom trash with him. She'd relaxed in the tub for a while and when she'd gotten out all traces of Darkness had been removed. He'd taken his condoms with him, the empty wrappers and had even returned her pantyhose to the drawer.

He drew her back to the present. "You didn't answer. Did the bath help?"

"Yes. Thanks for that."

"Did I leave bruises on your arms or throat? It's warm out today."

She hesitated. "My wrists got slightly chafed from the nylon. It's nothing major. I just didn't want to risk anyone making assumptions or having questions about the marks."

"I'll come up with something else that won't mar your skin. You could just say they were from when you first arrived at Homeland. Everyone knows you were taken to interrogation."

He planned to see her again. She was relieved about that. "Does that mean you're coming over tonight?"

"I'm on duty."

"Oh."

"I might stop by late but I'm not certain if I'll be able to. Would you mind?"

"No."

"I get off at eleven." He lowered his gaze to the front of her shirt, his focus on her breasts obvious. "I need to go."

She watched him cross the room and stop to chat with a few men. One woman approached him and Kat hated the prickly sensation that rose. Jealousy was an emotion she didn't enjoy but it was there. The woman was pretty and beamed up at Darkness, even reaching out to run her fingers along the center of his shirt. He didn't flinch away or seem to mind.

Kat looked away. He wouldn't let her do that to him. He'd have blocked her hand if she'd pulled that stunt. She couldn't help but look back at him. The urge was too strong. He still stood there and now the woman talking to him had stepped closer, only inches away. She reached up again and laid her palm over his upper arm, stroking it. He didn't react in any way, just stood there allowing her to touch him.

"Jerk," she muttered, shoving the plastic inserts and gel bag she'd used for the demonstration back inside the purse.

"Are you well?" Sunshine walked over.

Kat blanked her features and forced a smile. She refused to glance over at Darkness. It was just going to infuriate her if that woman was still touching him. "I'm great. How did I do today?"

"Very well. I learned a lot. We don't receive many gift baskets at Homeland but I'll be more careful now that you warned us to double-check for false compartments hidden in delivery containers. I won't assume a truck with a business name painted on the side is safe either."

"Delivery trucks can be stolen and employee uniforms are easy to come by. It's better to be a bit paranoid than not. Call and confirm with the company before accepting anything."

"Humans can be very devious."

"They can be. It's unfortunate that you have to deal with so many of the worst of humanity."

"They are frightened of us because we're different."

"Yes." It was a good way to sum it up. She didn't want to get into the other dozens of reasons the NSO would be targeted. "I wanted to ask you something."

"Go ahead."

"You're aware of what happened when I came to Homeland. When I was taken into custody they handcuffed me to the front instead of behind my back. A cavity search wasn't performed either. Is that normal?"

"I see where you're going with this." Sunshine smiled. "I paid close attention to everything you said. We usually do a more thorough search but we were off our game that day. Is that the right way to put it? Rusty was shaken up. We don't usually have females in custody. The males wouldn't have made those mistakes."

"Okay."

"I could see if they will allow you to tour Security and go over procedures if you wish. You might find ways to better them."

"I'd like that."

"I'll make inquiries. I don't see why they wouldn't allow it. It would be beneficial to us. We have the task force team but they usually search all humans before they are brought to us.

132

The head of the team would have yelled a lot at Rusty if he'd known she left you alone and hadn't followed procedures to the letter." Her voice lowered. "Tim shouts often. He's not a pleasant human but it's because he's protective of us. We get treated as if we're children at times. We try to keep our sense of humor about it, especially with him. His intentions are good."

"I'm sure they are." Kat hoped that was the case.

Sunshine seemed to read her uncertainty. "Tim is devoted to the NSO. He's loud and vocal to everyone he cares about. I'd worry if he were silent. He's what you would consider a father figure and he's adopted us. We've been told loving parents can be stern. That's Tim. We appreciate his loyalty. I'd trust him with my life, as would other Species."

"That's good." It also made Kat sad that New Species had never had parents. She hoped whoever Tim was, he never let the NSO down. They'd had enough disappointments.

"Are you hungry? Some of the females would like to talk to you but it won't be about your class." Sunshine laughed. "It's about human males and sex. Some of them are very curious. We were ordered not to ask any of the task force team members questions while on duty and we rarely spend time with any of them when they are off. Tim has forbidden them to interact with us in any way sexual, including discussions on the subject. We also were asked not to pester the mated human females."

"Why?"

"We were assured it was rude and not the best idea to ask them about having sex with other males before they met their mates. Species are extremely possessive. Breeze said one of their males could overhear and decide to 'track down and put the hurt on some poor bastard'. Those are her exact words."

She remembered the name. "How is your friend? She's the one who had a roof fall on her, right?"

"She's well. She meant to come to your classes but something came up." A spark of humor glinted in her eyes. "I hope you aren't shy, Kat. They will ask you everything that comes to mind."

"Okay." It beat returning to her cottage and sulking about Darkness' interaction with that other woman. "Lead the way." She shoved the rest of her things inside the purse. Darkness had left and she didn't see the woman who'd been with him.

Images of them together flashed through her mind and she hated every one. That no-commitment talk only served to remind her that he could screw anyone he chose. It didn't mean it wouldn't rub her wrong. She followed Sunshine to the bar area and spotted the woman who'd been mauling Darkness. She was one of the four seated at the table. *He isn't somewhere having sex with her at least.* That improved her mood.

Sunshine introduced her to the women but the name Bluebird stuck in her mind. She paid more attention to her than the rest. Her warm, friendly smile had Kat feeling a little guilty over her instant dislike. It was Darkness' fault. He was the one who stayed aloof and had his conditions. *I agreed to them though. I'm an idiot.* She sat.

* * * * *

Darkness stood at the end of the bed watching Kat sleep. His shift had ended later than expected. One of the protestors had decided it would be a good idea to throw sealed cans of soda at the officers on the wall. His aim had been poor but they'd called the local police to haul the male away. He'd been stuck answering their questions, then volunteered to clean up the sticky mess since it would attract bugs.

The clock on her nightstand showed it was just after one in the morning. He'd read Security's notes and knew she had a class scheduled for eleven. It would be best if he returned home and just went to bed. Yet he stood there.

Kat made a soft sound in her sleep and rolled onto her back. She kicked at the blanket, one foot slipping out. He smiled and his fingers gripped his vest. He applied light pressure and slowly removed it to keep the noise at a minimum. She still slept. He dropped it onto the floor and bent, removing his boots next. Within minutes he was naked and dropped to his knees. The sight of her aroused him enough to put on a condom. He reached out and wrapped his fingers around her ankle. Humor sparked. He wanted to find out if Kat would react with any defensive measures.

He jerked her hard, yanking her body down the bed. She gasped and blindly kicked out. Her foot was tangled with the bedding. He caught it and growled. She shoved the blanket off her head and sat up enough to stare down in his direction. It was pitch dark in the room, leaving her blind.

"That better be you, Darkness. Otherwise, I'm about to kick your ass."

He chuckled. "Who else would be in your bedroom?"

She slumped back on the bed and peered at the clock. "I thought you weren't coming."

"I was held up." He released her ankles. "Why do you sleep with the lights on?"

"Why did you turn them off?"

"Answer me first."

"It's an unfamiliar place. There's nothing worse than waking and forgetting where you are. I travel a lot so it's just a habit I've picked up. Now it's your turn."

"I wanted to see how you'd react."

"You're kind of a dick. You scared me."

"Your reactions are slower than they should be. I would have pounced on you if you'd pulled that stunt."

"I bet you have better night vision." She lifted a hand above her face, waving it. "I can't see a thing. Will you turn on the bathroom light at least?"

"No." He threw off her covers and gently ran his fingers along her calves, trailing them upward. "Why do you sleep in clothing?"

"It's a nightshirt."

"And panties. Stop wearing them."

"You're demanding for a guy who has no give in him. What do you sleep in?"

"It depends on where I am."

"Right. You said you live at Reservation sometimes in the Wild Zone. I'm disappointed, thinking you're not running around the woods naked."

He found her statement amusing. "The other males wouldn't appreciate it, although they do wear very little during the summer months."

"How little?"

He didn't like the idea of her imagining other males. He spread her thighs until her knees were bent over the edge of the mattress. He released her, gripped the narrow band of her underwear and tore the material easily, destroying it. He tossed it aside, leaving her bare.

"Those were the bottoms of a matching set I have."

"Buy new ones."

He dipped his head over her lower stomach, which was exposed with her shirt trapped around her ribs. He wanted her breasts but he'd settle for any exposed skin. "Keep your hands off me."

Her slight protest ended the second he opened his mouth to trail his tongue just under her bellybutton. His hands opened on her inner thighs, shoving them wider apart and caressed upward.

"I love your hands," she softly admitted. "Your mouth isn't too bad either."

He almost laughed. She was a good sport about the way he'd woken her. He stopped exploring her with his tongue and gripped her knees, lifting them. He rested her legs over his shoulders. It was easy to slide his hands under her ass and raise her hips to his mouth.

She sucked in a sharp breath when he fastened his lips around her clit and licked at the bundle of nerves. He growled, purposely creating vibrations as he mercilessly attacked her senses. Her scent changed fast. The sweetness of her need became intoxicating and her low moans ratcheted up his aggression. He liked it when her inner thighs pressed the sides of his face, holding him there as if he were about to stop. Nothing could have pulled him away from her until she cried out his name.

He loved the way she bucked her hips when the climax struck and she rubbed her pussy against his mouth. Her heels dug into his back too. He eased her ass to the bed and reached up, got a firm hold under her knees and jerked her almost off the bed. He looked down between them and adjusted his hips until his rigid dick was in the right position then pressed forward, entering her.

Kat clawed the bed and moaned. The tingling in the back of his throat and his chest began. He didn't mute his instincts. She had said she found the noises he made sexy. He closed his eyes when he was buried deeply within the inviting confines of her pussy. He wanted to just stay there, to enjoy the feel of her, but desire drove him to move.

He tried to be gentle but the more he fucked her, the less control he was able to maintain. He increased the pace, her moans growing louder over the sounds he made. Kat came hard, her vaginal muscles clenching and unclenching around his dick. He rode out his own release and was oblivious to everything for the next few seconds until the magnitude of it passed and only their heavy breathing remained.

He wanted to climb on the bed with Kat and hold her in his arms, remove her shirt and press his skin to hers. Just keep her close. She relaxed under him and he eased her legs down. It came as a shock when she suddenly reached for him, her fingers splaying on his chest and lower stomach. He jerked but didn't withdraw from her body.

Her hands were soft and gentle, almost petting him. He looked down, watching them caress his flesh. His softening dick stirred and it reminded him of the spent condom. He captured her wrists and removed her touch.

"Don't."

Her hands fisted. "Fine. Sorry."

He let her go and eased away. The separation of their bodies left him feeling cold. He stood and entered the bathroom, disposed of the condom. He lingered for a full minute, debating. The smart thing would be to leave. He didn't want to go just yet. He returned to the bedroom. Kat had the bedside lamp on and was sitting against the headboard with the blanket covering her from her breasts down. She smiled.

"I like seeing you."

He wasn't sure how to respond. Her gaze lingered over parts of him, especially his chest and groin area. He held still, not minding her examination. She could look all she wanted but he didn't want her to touch him. It was too personal.

"I'll draw you another bath." It gave him something to do.

"No." She shook her head and lifted a hand, curving one finger. "You could come over here, though, and join me."

He tensed. "No."

Disappointment and a flash of pain showed in her eyes. "Okay."

"I should go home. You have a class in the morning and I have a meeting."

"You could sleep with me," she offered. "I don't snore."

It steeled his determination to keep away from the bed. It was tempting to agree. "I can't."

"It's a big bed." She inched over a little to make more room. "I'll even let you pick which side you want."

"Kat," he warned, his tone deepening. "Stop."

"Fine."

He dressed and retrieved the condom box then grabbed the bag from her trash. She stopped him before he could escape. It felt as if he were about to do just that.

"Why do you always do that?"

He paused, turning to face her. "Do what?"

"Take the trash with you."

"Security does sweeps of your home while you're gone."

"They come in here?" She frowned. "Why?"

"It's procedure." He didn't tell her they did checks on the cameras and audio devices to make certain they worked properly. "It also lets them know if you're low on any supplies you may need. It's not as if you can shop for new shampoo or food."

"I guess that's nice."

"We like to take care of our visitors."

"Just not sleep with them."

"I'm sure many males would be happy to share your bed." It pissed him off even saying it. He'd wanted to punch the feline male who'd asked to share sex with her. He might have if she'd accepted the offer. Anger boiled under his skin just thinking about someone else stripping Kat bare.

"Just not you."

"I told you I'm different."

"Are you sleeping with Bluebird?"

He was so surprised he didn't think he hid the reaction but masked his features fast. "No."

"I met her today. I also noticed she's allowed to touch you."

Darkness noted the way her fingers were clawed on the covers and the slight anger in her tone. "We're friends. Are you jealous?"

Her lips pressed together. "No."

He growled. "You're not dressed and I think that's a lie." Had she forgotten their agreement to be truthful when she was naked? "Do you want to try again? You're agitated."

"That's a polite way to put it. I just assumed you didn't like anyone touching you but I guess it's just me. I'll admit that's not the best feeling in the world."

Regret surfaced. He wasn't being fair to Kat and knew it. "Bluebird doesn't interest me." He should have left it at that but hated the way she looked at him, as if he were hurting her. "I'm not immune to you. Good night, Kat. Sleep well."

He left before he could change his mind. He did a sweep of the outside perimeter before going home. He showered to remove Kat's scent but the memory wouldn't fade. He took a seat on the bed and peered at the laptop he'd left on after taking over the security feeds.

Kat lay curled on her side facing away from the lamp. Her eyes were closed but the restless way she kept moving assured him she didn't sleep. It was as if she couldn't get comfortable. He lifted the laptop and set it on his lap. His finger, just an inch from the screen, traced the outline of her body. He wanted to touch her again.

"Damn," he muttered.

Kat sat up and threw off the covers. He tensed, part of him hopeful that she'd come after him. He'd given her reason to be angry. Kat was a confrontational female. He tracked her out of the bedroom but she didn't go near the slider. She fixed a sandwich instead and plopped down on the couch.

The morose expression on her face while she turned on the TV and ate tugged at him. She'd been sleeping peacefully before he'd woken her. She curled up on the couch eventually and drifted to sleep. He found himself rising before giving it thought.

It was easy to sneak into her home and take the comforter off her bed. He crouched down next to the couch, watching her sleep. He took care not to wake her when he tucked the material around her body.

I could just pick her up and carry her to bed.

He rejected the idea and left her cottage before he changed his mind. The protective urges he felt toward Kat were only growing stronger. It was a bad sign. He couldn't afford to form an attachment to her. She wasn't a female he could ever fully trust. None were though. He refused to make that mistake again. Caring meant pain. He'd had enough of that to last him a lifetime.

He sat on his bed and moved the open laptop to the night table, turning it so he could keep watch over Kat's still form. He lay down, leaving the lights on for once as he prepared to sleep. He wanted to understand the female. A well-lit room didn't give him a sense of security. He preferred the dark. It was just a reminder of how different they were.

Darkness reached out and turned up the volume to the listening device in her living room. The TV had been left on, the movie she'd been watching was still playing. He could detect her light breathing though. He closed his eyes, focusing on it instead of the human voices. He should switch the feed back to Security but didn't.

Chapter Nine

❧

"That was a great class." Jinx grinned. "Thanks for having lunch with the males today."

Kat smiled at the ten males who were jammed around three tables that had been placed in a row. "Thank you for asking me."

"We behaved," Flirt muttered, shooting Jinx a dirty look.

The male grinned. "I threatened them with punishment if they brought up sex." He stood. "I'm in charge of chores in the men's dorm this week. None wanted to scrub toilets in the downstairs bathrooms. Are you ready to go on the tour I promised?"

Kat set her napkin next to the plate. "I am." She really wanted out of there. New Species were nice but the way they'd watched her every move had been a little unsettling. They were curious, she understood that, but it made her self-conscious. She followed Jinx outside to a waiting Jeep. He motioned for her to climb inside.

"We'll go to the training facilities first. Do you have to train to be a crime lab technician? Physically, I mean. Of course you went to school to learn all the techniques you know."

She put on her seat belt, noticing that he didn't. He just started the engine and threw it in gear, only glancing behind him once to make sure he didn't pull out in front of traffic. There wasn't any.

"Some." She kept it vague.

"Good. There won't be any sessions right now but sometimes we drift in to work out our frustrations or extra energy."

She studied the feline male. He had gorgeous blue eyes and a carefree personality. The muscular body displayed in a T-shirt and snug jeans proved he was fit. Long black hair whipped freely around his shoulders as he drove fast, barely slowing for a turn. She gripped the edges of her seat.

"Are we in a hurry?"

"Sorry." He slowed. "Darkness put me in charge of giving you the tour and I don't want to mess it up."

Her interest peaked. "You're afraid of him?"

"No." He chuckled. "He's definitely intimidating but he's fair. It's just that he never asks anything of anyone so I want to make sure I do exactly what he said. You're to tour the training rooms and then I'm to take you to Security."

"Is he on duty?"

"Not yet. He assigned me to you because he felt you'd be more at ease because he's just not friendly. He asked Sunshine first but she couldn't trade her shift today. I was his second choice."

He parked in front of a building and turned off the engine. "This is it. It doesn't look like much from the outside but it houses sparring rooms, weight rooms, some offices, showers, and we even have a climbing wall. That was added after we took over."

She paused by his side as he used a card scanner to unlock the door. "I noticed all the common areas have those, except the bar."

"It's for security reasons. This place was built as a military base but we were given it when it was complete. Upgrades were made. It assures us that if the gates are breached we're able to be secure inside the buildings." He tapped the glass as he held open the door. "Weapons grade is what I think you would call it. Bullets don't pierce the glass and metal shutters slam down in case of an emergency." He pointed up, showing her where they were hidden above the interior doors.

"Impressive."

"Unfortunately, we've had to use them."

"The breach when Homeland first opened?"

He growled softly. "Yes. We're always upgrading our security. That was a lesson."

Kat let the subject drop. He showed her the reception area. It was a lounge setup with a hallway leading past closed office doors. None of them were marked. He opened a door to a room that held weight benches and free weights.

"May I ask you a personal question?"

"Sure. What do you want to know?"

"It's about your name."

He laughed. "Say no more. I tease that anyone who causes me harm will have bad luck but the truth is…"

Seconds ticked by. "The truth is what?"

His expression grew serious. "I was heavily abused as an adolescent. I have damage to one ear after suffering a blow to the head. It can't be fixed. It messes with my equilibrium. I didn't want to call myself clumsy so Jinx sounded better."

"I'm sorry." She regretted bringing it up.

"It's all right. I was one of the lucky ones. Damaged Species were usually killed but they spared me because of my intelligence and because I have a pleasant disposition. It wasn't a happy place at Mercile but you lived longer if you played their games. I was good at pretending I didn't hate everyone who worked there."

He touched his left ear. "This was done by orderlies. I was being taken to one of the scientists for some sort of testing and came across other orderlies escorting a female. One of them had her cornered and was kicking her for some unknown reason. She might have resisted going with them or one of them could have touched her wrong. The others were laughing and helping him keep her trapped. I attacked to defend her. They all turned on me with their batons. We're good fighters but ten on one wasn't good odds. I wasn't fully grown."

Kat reached out and touched his arm. "I'm so sorry."

"You didn't do it. I don't blame all humans for the actions of Mercile or the other facilities. I was taken to a second location then later freed. The humans planned their assault badly. They should have struck all the Mercile facilities at once but instead they did it over a matter of days. It gave some of the staff time to transfer small groups of us out before all the locations were searched."

"Your task force found you?"

"Yes. See? Some humans are our heroes." He nodded, patted her hand and turned away, breaking their physical connection.

"May I ask you another question?"

"Sure." He closed the door and led her down the hall to a room full of mats. It was obviously used for wrestling and sparring.

"How come most New Species are feline or canine? I hardly see any of the primates."

"There used to be more ape primates but few made it out alive. They are pretty aggressive, with short tempers." Jinx threw open a door. "Welcome to my favorite place."

Kat peered in and grinned. "Wow!"

"Do you want to have some fun?"

She stepped into the room and stared up at the sixty-foot wall. The entire surface had been sectioned into three parts. The first was covered in rocks, the middle smooth with handholds and the third appeared to be a flat cliff face with small cracks running through it, as if nature had put it there.

"Our climbing room. We added this. The original ceiling wasn't high enough. Would you like to try one? I'd suggest the handholds. That is the easiest."

She stared at the ceiling. "I don't see safety lines anywhere."

"The mat is thickly padded. It won't kill you if you fall."

She turned to him. "You don't use safety equipment?"

"What would be the fun in that?" He laughed. "Watch but don't stand directly below me. I wouldn't want to fall and land on you. That would hurt."

He crossed the room and kicked off his shoes. In seconds he was climbing the rock section. He used his fingers and toes to hold his weight while he changed each handhold. He made it to the top in record time and turned his head to grin at her from above.

"It's fun."

"It looks dangerous," she called.

"Not for us. Watch."

He kicked off and Kat gasped when he flipped in the air, falling. He landed in a crouch and stood. "Easy."

She was too stunned to speak. He approached with a grin.

"Felines are good at leaping and landing. The floor is very padded. I wouldn't want to do that on solid ground. Our bone density is stronger than yours but they can be broken. Anything over thirty feet is iffy."

"You look pretty agile to me."

He laughed. "That's easy. Don't watch me run on a six-inch-wide balance beam. I can't make it twenty feet without missing a step. I actually wanted to land a little closer to you."

"I couldn't do that."

"Try the handholds. I'll catch you if you fall. You'd have to slip to do that. They are for..." He sobered. "Um, beginners. I have faith in you."

It was her turn to laugh. "I'm glad someone does."

"Have a little fun, Kat."

She bent to remove her shoes. "Okay. I know you guys have an onsite medical center, right? I might need to use it. I'd hate to go home with crutches or an arm in a sling." *Or dead.* That fall could kill a human, no matter how thick the mat was.

Jinx cleared his throat. "You might want to leave those on. Your toes are human."

She straightened. "And?"

He bent a leg up to show off the bottom of his foot. "See the padding on my toes? You could compare them with calluses. I'd hate for you to hurt yours or get a blister. You'll also have better traction with your shoes on so you don't slip." He dropped his leg.

"Okay." She blew out a breath and approached the middle section. She'd done indoor climbing before but not without being in a harness, rigged to a rope in case of a fall. "I wish I had gloves."

He took her hand and turned it, studying it closely. One of his fingertips brushed over the tip of her index finger. He frowned. "Perhaps you shouldn't climb. We don't have gloves. I didn't think about that."

"I'm good."

She grabbed one of the handholds. It was curved in a way her that fit her fingers comfortably and the rim seemed solid. The inside and top even had rubber to help a climber keep a firm grip. She caught one a little higher. There were no footholds until about five feet off the ground so she had to use her upper-body strength to hold her weight until she could climb high enough to brace her feet.

"You've done this before."

"It's been awhile." She was a little out of breath but it was fun. "I forgot how much I like it."

"Take your time."

She twisted her head to stare down at him. She'd made it about ten feet off the ground. He stood under her. "Maybe you should back away in case I slip. I'd hate to land on you."

"Just twist in the air so you fall sideways and I'll catch you. Tense your body if it happens."

"I think I'll climb up and then down. I don't have your grace. I'd just go splat!" She faced the wall and reached up for another handhold.

"What the hell?" The snarled words startled her.

Kat's hand slipped but she managed to recover since she had solid footholds. She turned her head again and watched Darkness across the room. He looked furious as he glared up at her.

"What are you doing?"

"Climbing."

"She's doing well," Jinx assessed.

"I told you to give her a tour, not allow her to use our equipment."

"She has experience."

"Kat?" Darkness bent and tore off his boots. "Don't move."

"I'm fine."

He ignored her and pushed Jinx back. He bent at the knee and she gasped when he jumped. He landed on the wall beside her, grabbing onto handholds and finding footing. He maneuvered next to her and used his longer arms to stretch around her until he pressed against her back.

"Turn and wrap around me."

She refused to let go. "I've got this."

"Do it," he snarled.

The look on his face wasn't something she could ignore. He was enraged and his eyes were almost black. He bent a little and braced. "I can take your weight. Just release with one hand and twist your body. Wrap one arm around my neck and then the other. You won't fall."

"I wouldn't have fallen anyway."

"Kat," he hissed, "do it or I'll tear you off and just fall back so you land on top of me. You could get hurt that way."

He braced his arms wider and gave her room to move. She followed directions and ended up clinging to him. He pressed her body against the wall and let go with one hand to hook an arm under her ass. He hefted her higher.

"Wrap your legs around my waist."

She did, with his help. Her upper arms were braced against his shoulders. He climbed slowly down until his feet reached the floor. She eased her hold and slid down him until she stood in front of him.

"I was fine."

He growled low but fixed his angry stare on Jinx. "We'll discuss this later. Take her to Security to finish the tour. Don't let her play with our weapons while you're there, either, or put her in a uniform and take her to the wall to discover how rude the protestors are...for the fun of it."

"Can we have a minute alone, Jinx? I have a few words to say to Darkness that aren't for polite company."

"Um, sure."

She waited until the door closed behind him. That was her cue. "What is wrong with you?"

"Me? You could have fallen."

"I was doing fine until you almost scared the hell out of me."

"You're not Species. You could have broken your neck if you'd fallen from higher up."

"I would have been fine. You were also really rude to Jinx. He was just trying to make the tour fun. It *was* until you arrived. Is he in trouble? That's messed up, Darkness. It's my fault. I insisted on climbing." It was a little white lie. *I'm dressed.*

His lips pressed into a tight line.

She tried to notch down her temper. "I don't know why you're acting this way. Just don't tear Jinx a new one, okay? He didn't do anything wrong."

149

"You're protective of the male?"

"I guess. He shouldn't—"

Darkness moved fast and grabbed Kat around her waist, yanking her off her feet. She slammed into his chest hard enough to knock the air from her lungs. He held her so tightly that it took her a second to suck in a breath.

"Do you want to share sex with him?"

She stared into Darkness' eyes and felt a shiver of fear. The cold look in them would have frozen lava. "No."

His nose flared.

She opened her hands cautiously and placed them on his biceps. "Are you jealous?"

He didn't say a word to admit or deny it, just held her gaze. Some of her fear eased. She had faith that he wouldn't hurt her since the worst thing he'd done was to put them at face level in a bear hug that wasn't painful.

"Don't start mind games," he warned softly. "Do you understand? I'm not a male who plays well."

"I'm not."

"Are you interested in Jinx?"

"No."

He blinked and his hold eased. "Yet you are defending him."

"He didn't do anything wrong. For someone who doesn't do commitment, you're acting irrational. You realize that, don't you?"

He lowered her to her feet and backed away, letting her go. "He's waiting to take you to Security."

"You don't want to talk about this?"

"No. Forget it."

As if. She stepped forward but didn't touch him. "You're jealous," she accused.

"I was worried."

"About me wanting to nail Jinx?"

His upper lip curled and his fangs showed. "Stop, Kat."

"Fine. Are you coming by later?"

"Yes."

"Okay. I'll see you then." She spun away and crossed the room, refusing to glance back. He was jealous, whether he wanted to admit it or not. She opened the door. Jinx paced the hallway but stopped when he saw her. "Ready to show me your security setup?"

"Sure." He flashed a dubious look toward the door.

"He's not friendly. You were right." She walked away, hoping to lure Jinx from the doorway before Darkness appeared. He needed some time to cool off and she wanted to analyze what had happened. She did cover for him though. "Darkness is bent out of shape, thinking how bad it would look to send me back to work at the crime lab if I sprained an ankle or something."

"That makes sense." Jinx hurried to her side. "We're always worried about bad press. Some humans might accuse us of purposely harming you."

"Journalism has really taken a dive in the past ten years. It's a valid worry. They seem to print any damn thing nowadays."

Darkness climbed the sheer wall face, wanting to punch it instead. It had infuriated him when he'd walked into the room and found Kat in danger. Jinx had been staring up at her shapely ass. Any male would.

He muted a roar of rage and shoved away from the wall at the top, free-falling. He tensed before impact with the floor but loosened his knees just enough to prevent injury. He landed, straightened to his full height then sat hard and put his boots on.

"Jealous." It had him seeing red. It didn't anger him that she'd called him on it but that she'd accurately read his emotions. "Get control of yourself."

The door opened and he jerked his head in that direction, expecting Jinx to come apologize. Slade entered. He paused.

"Sorry. I thought I'd be alone."

"I'm leaving."

"Did Jinx come through here already with our guest?"

"Yes. He's escorting her to Security now."

"That's what the officer said but I wanted to make sure." He removed his cell and dialed. "All clear."

Darkness stood. "What is going on?"

Slade grinned. "Forest was bored and Trisha needed a break."

The door opened and Fury entered with Forest and Salvation. The young males were grinning, their excitement clear. Darkness tried not to stare at Fury's son. He was a replica of his father in miniature size. Both young ones spotted him and froze.

Darkness twisted his lips up in a smile to put them at ease. "Hello."

Salvation glanced at his father. Fury nodded. "You remember Darkness."

The young male glared. "You fought with my daddy. Mommy was pissed."

"Sal," Fury rasped.

"Sorry. She was angry. She doesn't like it when you fight."

"No, she doesn't." Fury chuckled. "It's rude to mention those things. Species fight. It's in our nature but we don't hold grudges. It's just how males work out their differences sometimes. No real harm was done. Darkness and I are friends."

Forest reached over and slapped Salvation's arm. "Like us. We fight sometimes but you're my best friend."

"I thought you two wanted to climb," Slade reminded them. "Less talking. Go!"

The young males rushed to the center area of the wall and jumped. Salvation caught a handhold but Forest missed, inches short of reaching it. He landed on the floor and growled.

"I'm taller," Salvation chuckled. "Climb me." He gripped two handholds, dangling there.

Forest jumped again, this time grabbing hold of the slightly bigger boy around his waist. He hugged him around the middle with one arm then gripped Salvation's shoulder. He scrambled upward until he could reach the handholds. They stayed close together.

"Not bad for a pair of canine young," Slade whispered.

Fury nodded.

Darkness knew he should leave. It was a family moment, shared between fathers and sons. He didn't though. He watched the children and tensed as they reached the thirty-foot mark.

"Do they ever fall?" He worried about their bones breaking from that height.

"Sometimes. They are tough," Fury answered. "We are good at catching them."

"Forest is more likely to tire out. He's still working on his upper-body strength," Slade whispered. "But he's improving."

Darkness moved closer to the wall. He climbed faster than a canine. He could also leap to reach them. He kept his focus on each movement the children made, ready to go after them if one needed assistance.

"We should install safety lines and harness them." Darkness decided he'd ask for the improvements, regardless of Fury or Slade's opinion.

Fury moved to stand next to him. "They do this often. We come every few days. They haven't been hurt yet."

"Yet." Darkness scowled. "I'll make certain that rope lines are added by this weekend."

Slade moved to the other side of him. "It might encourage the task force to come in here. Trey is the only one who's attempted it. He didn't fall but he was sweating it." He chuckled. "He didn't try again. Once was enough."

Fury bumped Darkness' arm. He turned his head to find the male grinning at him. "You care."

"Of course I do. No one wants to see young ones harmed." Darkness stared up, intent on taking action if either child needed help.

"They need to learn," Fury added. "They are our future."

"They won't be if they get hurt." Darkness softened his tone, not wanting to startle the children. "They are too high."

Fury bumped him again. "Relax. Watch. Move a little to the left and back three feet."

Darkness moved and Fury took his spot. "Sal? Emergency drop!"

The boy pushed away from the wall and turned in the air as he fell. Darkness wanted to jump up and catch him but Fury opened his arms. The child landed safely in them. Giggles erupted from the boy when Fury tossed him in the air once and then set him on his feet.

"Emergency drop," Slade called out.

Darkness tensed again but expected it when Forest shoved off the wall and fell. He curled into a ball. Slade caught him and put him on the floor, tickling him in the process. They both laughed.

Fury winked. "See? We have this down. They not only are learning how to climb but gaining upper-body strength in the process."

Slade gave him a meaningful look. "In case of emergency they know to follow orders without pausing to give it thought. He'd have dropped for you too if you'd asked, trusting you to catch him."

Darkness nodded. "Species only, I hope."

Fury shook his head. "We don't discuss that. They are still too young. Their mothers..."

Darkness understood. He could finish what Fury hadn't said aloud. Their mothers were human and therefore they'd only been exposed to love. "That will be a tough conversation."

Slade captured his son and hoisted him high, putting him within reach of the handholds on the wall. "Go for it."

His son laughed and started climbing again. Salvation didn't have to be told. He ran at the wall and jumped, that time managing to catch two handholds at once. He quickly reached Forest but stayed next to the other young one.

It confused Darkness. "Salvation is taller and stronger. Why doesn't he climb above Forest?"

Fury answered his question. "They are a team. If Forest slips, Sal will help him." He shot Darkness a pointed look. "They are like brothers. They will always be there for each other."

The words were meant to sting and they hit their mark. Darkness felt guilt. "I need to go. I'm late for my shift." He quickly left.

Chapter Ten

ဆ

Kat smiled and glanced around the main room in Security. The banks of monitors were impressive. It was a top-of-the-line system. She felt honored to get a tour.

"What do you think?"

"It's great." She pointed to one wall. "Those are all exterior monitors there?"

Jinx nodded. "Yes. They cover the wall sections. To your left is the interior of Homeland in general areas. The right is the exterior shots of Homeland, beyond the gates."

She peered right. Protestors paced the sidewalks and cars drove by on the street. On another screen was the view of a nearly deserted street. The monitor under it showed a park. She glanced at each screen, realizing they had views of everything within about a block of their walls.

"Do you get a lot of people who try to breach the walls at various points?"

"Not often. We have officers on the wall and the humans see them. It dissuades most from attempting it."

"What about by air?" She knew the answer already but a crime lab technician wouldn't.

"We have a mile radius no-fly zone around all NSO lands. We closely monitor air traffic. Anything incoming needs prior approval."

"What if someone does breach the air space?"

"We have the means to take them down."

She pondered that, questions forming.

"I can't discuss it further," Jinx murmured. "Sorry. Some precautions are classified."

Kat let it go. "No problem." She knew the military had worked with the NSO and their task force to protect their land. Her attention drifted left and she watched the monitors covering the front gates. At least thirty people were working to repair the damage, repaving the scarred ground and putting up new gates. A redhead caught her attention. There was something about him that seemed familiar.

"Can you zoom with these cameras? Do they move?"

"Sure."

She walked forward, hoping it didn't seem suspicious. "Can you show me? Like, zoom in on this guy here?" She pointed to the construction worker smoothing freshly poured concrete over the scarred area where the van had exploded.

"Do it," Jinx ordered.

The image was sent to a larger monitor at the front of the room and the operator of the security system brought the man into sharp focus for close inspection. The face of the construction worker filled the screen and he glanced around, lifting his chin just enough for her to get a really good look at him. Her anger simmered.

"Show her the mobility of the cameras," Jinx ordered the woman at the controls.

The camera angle moved, panning across the other construction workers. The man behind the wheel of the concrete truck came into view and Kat clenched her teeth. She studied each face on the monitor.

"Very cool." She tried to make her voice sound ordinary.

"Would you like a tour of our interrogation rooms?"

"I've seen one of them already. I'll pass."

Jinx winced. "Sorry. I forgot about that."

"Speaking of, is there any way I can talk to Darkness? I had a question for him and want to make sure he's still not irritated with us."

"Ask me." Jinx inched closer.

"It can wait." She forced a smile. "I'm ready to leave now. Thank you so much for the tour."

"Do you have any suggestions?"

"I do better when I think about things for a bit. We'll discuss it tomorrow. Is that okay?" She wanted to get out of there before she lost her temper. It was burning hotter by the second and she had to hide it.

"I'll take you out to your escort, who will drive you back to your guest cottage."

"Thank you."

He led her out of Security and she was happy to see Sunshine waiting behind the wheel of a Jeep. She waved to Jinx, thanked him again, and climbed into the passenger seat. The woman grinned at her.

"Did we meet your expectations?"

"What?"

"Our security measures?"

"They are great."

"I'll take you home unless there's somewhere else you'd like to see. I'm on duty for a few more hours but they told me to take you wherever you want to go."

Kat hesitated. "Do you have Darkness' number? I really need to ask him a question."

"Sure." The woman reached inside her shirt pocket and withdrew her cell phone. She tapped the screen a few times and handed it over.

Kat took it and slid out of the seat. "Give me a minute." Her heart began to pound as she listened to the phone ring twice. It was stupid and she knew she should just keep her mouth shut. She was putting her ass on the line if she actually spoke to him. His deep voice answered.

"Darkness here. What do you need, Sunshine?"

"It's Kat."

"Why do you have the female's phone?" He didn't seem happy.

"I borrowed it with her permission. She's about ten feet away, staring at me."

"What do you need?"

She hesitated.

"Kat? Is something wrong?"

Just say no and hang up. You can't do this. Just keep your damn mouth shut.

"Kat?" His voice deepened. "What is it?"

Fuck it. "Is there any way you can get near the front gate?"

"I'm actually very near there. I just came on duty."

She closed her eyes. The sick feeling in her stomach increased. She had to make a decision and it was a tough one.

"Kat?" He softened his tone in a way that reminded her of the night before. "What is it? Are you well?"

Shit! She opened her eyes and focused. "You know how you expect me to trust you but you don't trust me?"

"You want to discuss this now? I said I'd see you later." Irritation sounded in his tone.

"I'm trusting you because this could get me in some serious shit. Do you understand?"

He was silent for long seconds. "What is it?"

"See the redheaded guy getting a sunburn and smoothing out concrete? Look at the driver of the truck who's working nearby? Also, the woman with black hair who is helping install that new gate, on the right side facing the main street? Watch them closely, okay?"

Darkness growled. "Why?"

She bit her lip and then decided she'd already crossed a line. "We work for the same dickhead. I'm putting my ass on the line. That's all I can say."

"Are they a danger to the NSO?"

"I don't know why they are here. That's the truth. There could be more of them but those are the ones I recognized. They might have come to get a look inside your gates to see how much damage was done. I just don't know."

"How did you know they were here in the first place if you don't know why they came?" He sounded angry.

"I just toured Security. I spotted them on the monitors. Just…watch them, okay?"

"We're going to talk more about this later."

"I imagine so."

"Would you be in trouble if they were to suspect you pointed them out?"

"Big time." Her stomach roiled, just considering Mason's reaction.

"I'll handle it. Are you still at Security?"

"Outside. Sunshine is about to return me to the cottage."

"Go and stay there. I'll see you soon." He disconnected.

It sounded like a threat. She uttered a silent curse and returned to the Jeep. She passed the phone over and climbed back into the passenger seat. "Thanks."

"Is everything okay? You look a little pale."

"It's fine. I'm just tired."

"I'll take you home."

"Thanks."

Kat wasn't sure if she should regret what she'd just done or not. Why would Robert Mason send other agents into NSO, undercover? Their access would be limited to the area where they were pretending to be construction workers. Did they plan to sneak away to search for Jerry Boris? She really needed to discover what his connection to her boss was. Why was the guy so important that Mason would risk sending in a group of agents? It bothered her.

Sunshine pulled up in front of her cottage. "Are you well? You really don't look so good."

"I think I have a headache coming on." It wasn't far from the truth. Her boss was a pain. "Thanks for the ride home."

"Any time. I'll see you tomorrow for your class."

Kat forced another smile. "I look forward to it."

Kat escaped inside the house and leaned against the closed door. She didn't bother locking it. Darkness would come and she had a feeling it would be soon. He'd want answers she really couldn't give. She'd already said too much.

"Damn! I should have just kept my mouth shut."

Did they really have Jerry Boris? If so, she believed it had to be for a good reason. *Why?* It would be so much simpler to just ask Darkness but that would mean laying all her cards on the table.

"What do I do?" The silent house didn't hold an answer for her. She pushed away from the door and walked to the master bedroom. She changed out of her clothes into a comfortable oversized T-shirt that doubled as a nightgown. Her mind was abuzz with unanswered questions. What a dilemma. Mason's orders went against the grain in every way. "It's still my duty," she muttered. "But does it count when the boss is out of line?"

She entered the kitchen and yanked open the fridge. It had been stocked with sodas, milk, juice and even wine. She didn't drink alcohol much but it was tempting to grab the bottle. She bypassed it for a soda. The last thing she needed was to get rip-roaring drunk. It was unprofessional to drink on the job but she had gone off the rails already when she'd had sex with Darkness.

The front door banged open when he walked in. It slammed closed behind him with enough force to shake the house. She regarded him over the kitchen/living room divider as he approached. He was in uniform but had left the helmet somewhere. The only skin that showed was from the neck up. His expression would have frozen ice.

"What the hell is going on?"

She cringed at his snarled words. "I don't know."

He rounded the corner and halted a few feet away. He looked at her bare legs then jerked his dark gaze upward. He growled again. "You thought to distract me by showing skin?"

"No. I wanted out of my bra and to be comfortable."

"Who do you work for? I want a name."

She turned to face him and leaned back against the counter, taking a sip of the soda. She placed it down a few feet away. "We're dressed."

"What does that mean?"

"Remember your rules? I do. I work for the Bakersfield crime lab."

He lunged forward and she tensed, closing her eyes. He didn't touch her. She braved peeking at him and he stood inches away, glaring down at her. She relaxed. They stared at each other for a good minute.

"Why warn me about those humans if you won't tell me more?"

"I don't know." She looked at the white lettering on his vest. "I didn't think about it. I risked a lot though. Doesn't that earn me any points?" She lifted her gaze, studying his beautiful eyes. He was still furious. "I take it you're having them watched since you're here?"

"Yes."

"Did you tell anyone why?"

He shook his head. "I just said they were acting suspiciously and I had a bad feeling. We doubled our teams out there to keep an eye on the workers. They won't be able to do anything without it being noticed. The larger presence of officers should dissuade them from attempting any activities they might have had planned."

That made her feel a little better. "Thank you for keeping my name out of it."

He cupped her cheek. The feel of leather against her skin was odd but kind of sexy. "What can you tell me, Kat?"

"Not much."

"Do you know why they would come here?"

"I haven't been in contact with anyone since I arrived at Homeland. It was a surprise, seeing them."

"Do they plan on doing us harm?"

"I really don't know why they are here." Frustration rose. "I hate this dance, don't you?"

"So stop. Just talk to me."

"I already risked too much when I called you. I shouldn't have done it."

"Then why did you?"

She chose her words wisely. "I don't think they should be here."

"Do you think you should be here?"

"No."

He backed up and dropped his hand to his side, no longer touching her. "So why do you stay?"

"I'm supposed to."

"Do you always follow orders?"

"Not quite to the letter, in this case. I came to teach classes. That's it."

"Were you supposed to do something else?"

She bit her lip, staring at him.

"Yes or no?"

She said nothing.

"Damn it." He gripped her waist, his hold gentle, and pulled her away from the counter. "I'm done."

She gasped when he bent and his shoulder hit her hips. He lifted her and carried her over his shoulder into the master bedroom. She didn't struggle or protest until he dumped her on the bed.

"What are you doing?"

He walked over to the shelves and tore off his vest, shoving it onto one of them. He bent, tearing at his boots. "Strip."

She sat up, astonished. "You want to have sex now?"

"Rules," he hissed. "No clothes, no lies. Take off that shirt before I shred it."

"I still can't tell you what you want to know."

"Strip," he snarled.

She got to her knees and pulled the shirt over her head. Then shoved down her panties and tossed them on the floor. Darkness shed his pants, briefs and shirt. He breathed heavily when he stood naked before her, still looking furious. He took off the gloves last.

"Lie flat and grip the headboard."

"No." She sat on her legs, peering at him. "I can't tell you what you want to know. Did you hear me? I have no idea why they were sent. All I can think of is that they might have wanted to see the damage firsthand."

"Did they cause it? Was that van sent in by them?"

"NO!" Her own temper flared again. "I already told you I had no association with those assholes. It wasn't some plot to gain your trust. I'm not an assassin either. Isn't that what you called me? Totally not true."

He stepped closer. "Look at me."

She studied him from head to toe. He was semi-aroused and a sight to see when he was naked and breathing heavily, even if it was because he fought his temper. She could read his emotions by the tense lines of his body and the way his lip curled up just enough to flash a little fang.

"Do I look as if I want to play games?"

"I'm not playing. I made the call, didn't I? I risked my ass by doing that. It could get me in deep shit but I still did it."

"Why?"

"Because I'm stupid. Obviously. Look where it's gotten me. You're ready to lunge at me again."

"Tell me something then."

She swallowed and took a deep breath. "It's possible they might be looking for someone."

"She's not here."

That caused Kat to frown. "She?"

"The female they seek."

Why does he think they're after a woman? "It would be a man."

He looked surprised. "A male? Species?"

Kat hesitated. "Can you keep this just between us?"

"No."

"You won't tell anyone we're getting it on but you have a problem keeping this secret?"

"Don't play head games, damn it. Are they after a Species?"

"No."

He regarded her with suspicion.

"Naked, remember?" She waved her hands at her body. "I promised never to lie to you when we were this way. It's not a New Species they might be looking for."

"A task force member?"

She shook her head. "I don't think so."

"You don't think?"

"I don't know much about this guy, okay?"

"Give me a name."

The line was there—she could mentally see it between her job and Darkness. "I can't. That's asking too much."

He put his knee on the bed and glared down at her. "Tell me a name."

"I can't." She felt frustration more than fear. "I'm guessing and I've already said way too much, Darkness. Give me a break, okay?"

His hand snaked out and gripped her shoulder. He pushed and knocked her over onto her back. She gasped but then he grabbed her legs, yanked her flat. He came down on top of her, pinning her under his weight. They were nose to nose.

"Give me a name."

"I can't."

"Do you know it?"

She nodded.

"Then tell me."

"I can't."

He snarled, flashing those sharp teeth.

"Go ahead and bite me." She didn't fight him. He was too strong and she knew it would be pointless. "I still can't do that without losing my job and getting into a shitload of trouble. Hell, I'm already in it if that phone call ever comes to light."

Some of his anger dissipated. "Why would you take that risk? Just tell me that, Kat."

"I don't agree with some things, okay? I feel protective of the NSO."

"Were you supposed to look for this male?"

She should have seen that question coming. "I just plan to teach some classes. That's all."

"But you were asked to do more?"

She barely nodded. "Not that I'd do it."

"A human? Just look into my eyes."

She stared into his dark gaze and shrugged. "I don't know why he'd be here but I got the impression he wouldn't hang around if he had a choice. That's all I can say."

"A prisoner?" He studied her eyes. "A prisoner. Your eyes widened and you sucked in a sharp breath."

She closed her eyes. "That's my assumption. It's not as if the NSO lets anyone else know what is going on or why they'd keep someone here. I'm done now. I can't say anything else."

Darkness leaned forward and ran his nose along her throat, growling softly. "Don't shut down on me."

"Don't push me so far there's no way back. I did you a solid today, Darkness. Can't that be enough?"

His lips brushed her ear. "No."

She wiggled beneath him and opened her hands on his chest. His firm, warm skin felt wonderful. She loved his body and all the memories that came with the last time he'd had her naked under him.

"Damn you, Darkness."

"The same to you, my little pretend-cat."

She smiled. "You're such a dick."

He adjusted his legs and shoved hers open, pressing the solid, thick length of his cock against her thigh. "What about it?"

"I took a risk today. Can't you just say thank you for the heads-up? That was even after you made me angry in the climbing room. As if I'd go to bed with Jinx. I could punch you for that. I just happen to like you for some reason that escapes me at this moment."

"Look at me."

She refused to open her eyes. "Why? So you can hit me up with more questions and guess the answers because my guard is down when you're this close? It's not fair."

167

"I never said I would be."

"I never said I'd be easy."

He chuckled. "Look at me, Kat."

She opened her eyes when he lifted his head away from her face, betting she would regret it. All the anger was gone from his features and he actually smiled.

"Thank you."

That surprised her. "You're welcome."

"How much trouble would you really be in if anyone found out about that phone call?"

That killed the moment. "Shitloads."

"Why take the risk then?"

"You wanted trust. I gave it to you. I hope it works both ways."

He peered deeply into her eyes. "What can you tell me? It stays here."

"You won't have to repeat it to anyone?"

"No."

She hesitated. She wanted to trust Darkness so much that her chest ached from the longing but her career was at stake. "Theoretically, there might be someone here that my boss wants pretty bad. It's personal to him."

"Why?"

"I don't know. It's driving me nuts. How does he know this person and why would he go to all this trouble to um, ask someone to help him leave?"

Darkness' expression hardened. "You were asked to help someone escape?"

"I just plan to teach classes. How many times do I have to say it?"

"Blink twice if you were asked though."

She hesitated and then blinked twice.

He cursed and rolled off her to lie on his back next to her. She turned onto her side to watch him. He glared up at the ceiling and his hands were fisted above his head. That had killed the mood. He didn't look interested in sex anymore.

"You have to give me the name."

"I can't outright cross the line. My future is pure shit if I do that. Don't you understand? There's no way for you to link this guy to my boss otherwise."

He turned his head. "This is important."

"They can't get to whoever it is here, if he's here. I don't know that for sure. Nor does my boss. He suspects."

Darkness sat up and left the bed. Kat watched him with a heavy heart. He was angry again and she knew whatever relationship they had would probably end the moment he walked out the door. He might even have her tossed out of Homeland. She'd risked her career by telling him about those agents. He'd hang her out to dry with the NSO. They'd open a full investigation and eventually it would lead back to Mason. Her boss would know where to pin the blame.

He bent to get his pants. "I'm sorry."

It was just as she suspected. He was calling it quits between them. "Me too."

He straightened, plastic zip-tie cuffs in his hands. He glanced at them then her. "Just tell me the male's name, Kat. Don't make me do this."

He wasn't getting dressed. "Do what? Are you going to arrest me?"

"Worse." He bent and grabbed her ankle, jerking her down the bed.

"What are you doing?"

He flipped her and she struggled, too late though. He was faster and stronger, pinning her with his knee on her ass. She gasped as he pressed her against the bed, securing her wrists behind her back. He let go the second she was cuffed. She rolled onto her side, staring up at him.

"Darkness? You're arresting me?"

He put on his pants.

"At least let me get dressed." She struggled to sit upright.

He shook his head.

"You're going to take me in naked? This better just be a threat."

He fastened his pants and then reached out, knocking her back onto her side. He grabbed the corner of the bedding and wrapped it around her.

"Let me get dressed first. This is beyond fucked-up, Darkness."

He lifted her and she ended over his shoulder again. The blanket fell over her face, blinding her.

"Goddamn you!" She was furious. "Do you think I'll run? Give me a break. I've seen your security measures. I'd never make it off Homeland unless someone allows me out the gates. Put me down and let me get dressed."

"Shut up, Kat. I'm not taking you to a holding cell."

"Then where are we going?"

"My house."

That didn't bode well but it beat being arrested. "Why?"

"I have my tools there."

A chill ran down her spine. "What does that mean?"

"You're going to talk to me, one way or another."

He paused and the glass door slid open. Her bare feet felt the breeze though she couldn't see anything.

"Don't do this."

"You're leaving me no choice."

"Take me back."

"No." His strong arm across the back of her thighs kept her in place when he stepped over the short divider wall between their houses. Seconds later he entered his house and closed the slider.

Chapter Eleven

ഇ

"Darkness, what are you going to do?" Kat hated the way her voice quivered.

"Make you talk."

"You're going to hurt me?" It was shocking. They didn't exactly have a solid relationship but there were feelings. Could he torture her? Maim her? Her mind instantly went to Darwin Havings and what he and his thugs had done to Darkness. He'd learned from the worst of humanity but he wasn't a monster. She'd seen that. Darkness was tormented by his past. A man without remorse wouldn't have regrets. Darkness was a good man with plenty of them.

He dropped her on something soft but rolled her before she could try to evaluate where she was. She tossed her head, freeing it of the blanket, to find herself on a bed. She twisted enough to stare up at Darkness. He grimly regarded her.

"Tell me the human's name. Let's not do this, Kat."

"Damn it, Darkness, I already said too much. How many prisoners do you have here? Look into all of them. At least that way it will look random and won't pin a target on my back if you come up with something."

"I appreciate it. Now understand this. I'm going to make you tell me everything. No more games or half-truths. No more dropping hints. You're going to start at the beginning and tell me everything. Otherwise..." His voice trailed off.

It pissed her off. "I'm sorry I tried to help you. I thought we were friends."

He shook his head. "Never."

The stabbing pain that one word created really hurt. She raised her chin. "Fine. My name is Kathryn Decker and I work for the Bakersfield crime lab. You can take your rules and shove them up your ass."

"Understood."

He crossed the room to his closet, yanked open the door and disappeared inside. She fought tears. She'd slept with him and started to care about him. He'd obviously felt nothing for her in return. She glanced at the window. Patrols went by often but it would be dangerous to throw herself through the glass, even tempered glass, and hope an officer heard the noise and came to her rescue. She would likely end up in their medical facility. Darkness would still get his hands on her. They'd just turn her over to their number-one interrogator.

He exited the closet with a bag and dropped it on the floor. She stared at it and then watched him stomp out of the room. Her attention returned to the bag. Those were his tools. What did he plan to do to her? The possibilities were horrible and limitless. He could break bones, yank out teeth or carve her up with a knife. She shivered, feeling exposed.

He might be bluffing. She hoped so. He returned, carrying an office chair. She frowned when he slammed it down on the floor and straightened. He stormed over to her and bent, grabbing her around her waist. She gasped as he lifted her and dropped her into the chair.

"What are you going to do?"

He dropped to his knees next to her, reached out, hooked the bag and dragged it closer. "Stay still."

She shot up, trying to flee. Her hands might be behind her back but that didn't mean she was helpless. He moved faster than she would have thought possible. One arm hooked around her waist and she gasped as she was thrown back into the chair. He snarled at her, fury flashing in his look.

"I said sit."

"Fuck you. I'm not playing this game. I told you what I could."

He withdrew elastic ties and, though she struggled, secured her at the elbows to the arms of the chair, at the back. He easily subdued her. He rose and went to the bed, grabbed a pillow and returned. He got behind her and she gasped when he shoved the pillow between her lower back and the chair. He straightened, came around and dropped to his knees in front of her. He got more elastic ties from the bag.

"Don't make me bruise you."

That was a good indication that he didn't want to inflict pain.

"Spread your legs a little. Heels against the chair."

He was going to make certain she didn't get out of the chair. She hesitated but did it. Her fear level had dropped considerably. "You're frustrated. I get that. Why don't we both just calm down a bit and rethink this?"

He secured her ankles to the chair legs so she couldn't lift them. He reached around her and hooked her waist, yanking her ass to the edge. He adjusted the pillow then let go and shoved her thighs wide apart, exposing her pussy. She tried to wiggle back but the pillow wouldn't allow it.

"Is this going to be sexual torture? As opposed to just seducing it out of me, like last time? Okay, new approach. This is starting to look a bit kinky." She tried to use humor.

He arched one eyebrow.

"I'd prefer that over real torture. The whole bleeding-and-in-pain thing would suck." She allowed her feelings to show. "I'd never forgive you."

"Nor would I," he muttered.

"I'm glad we agree."

His mouth twisted and he frowned. "Do you think I'd really hurt you? That I could?"

"I hope not."

174

His features hardened and all emotion was wiped away. "I could but I wouldn't. Don't ever forget that."

It reaffirmed her faith in him and the feelings she'd started to have for him. He bent a little and reached into the bag once more. He straightened and held out a ball gag. She'd seen them in sex films. "No way."

"Open your mouth."

"I thought you wanted me to talk."

"I don't want anyone to hear you scream. Species have excellent hearing."

"Then it's a 'hell no'." She clenched her teeth and showed him that she had by parting her lips.

He grinned. "Really?"

She nodded.

He dropped the gag and reached into his bag again, pulled out duct tape. "This hurts coming off. Your lips are sensitive, Kat. One way or another, I'm going to have to muffle you."

"You wouldn't."

One eyebrow arched.

"Why are you doing this? We both know there are limits on what we can say to each other. That's been an understanding between us."

"Give me the name. It will end here."

"Cut me a break."

His chin lowered and he closed his eyes. She relaxed. Her instincts had been right. Darkness hadn't hurt her when she'd been a stranger. They'd shared intimate moments since then. He'd opened up to her and they'd become a lot closer. She understood his frustration, feeling it too.

He jerked his head up and snarled, snapping close to her face with his fangs. She gasped and pulled back, not expecting it. He shoved the rubber between her teeth. She tried to use her tongue to shove it out and twist her head at the same time.

Darkness fisted her hair at the nape of her neck until it actually hurt, holding her still while his other hand kept the rubber in place. He pushed it in more and then grabbed her jaw, holding it closed around the ball. He snagged the rounded loop over her head and secured it.

He let go and she tried to curse. It came out muffled. She leaned back, trying to rub her hair against the chair back to wiggle the strap up. Darkness yanked her forward and shook his head. He kept her there while he pulled out a clip from his bag and stood, leaning over her. It dug into her hair, securing the thing in place. She seethed, glaring at him.

He bent and shook his head. "Surprise always works. It's a natural reaction for someone to scream or gasp when frightened. That opens the mouth right up. Did you really think I'd remove your nose? It's too cute."

She stared at him until he broke eye contact. A deep sigh came from him. He looked up, regret twisting his lips a little, then leaned in and gently removed the clip and strap, allowing her to spit out the ball gag.

"Fine. Keep it down. I can't stand you looking at me that way."

"Thank you."

"Just keep it down, Kat. I mean it. Otherwise we're going to have company and I'd rather no one else see you tied to that chair."

"I wouldn't like that either." She glanced down her body and muttered how wrong it would be.

He chuckled. "What? I didn't understand you. Were you calling me a name?"

She glared at him rather than speak. He was being a controlling bastard but not as much of one as he had been. He sat back on his legs and looked down, unfastening his pants. He left them on but the front gaped open, revealing a line of tan skin and evidence that he hadn't taken the time to put on briefs.

Kat tested the ties holding her in place but couldn't get free. She wasn't exactly uncomfortable in the plush chair and the restraints weren't too tight. He gripped her inner thighs and shoved them apart then rose to his knees to put his hips between them so she couldn't close them again.

She stared into his eyes and wondered what he'd do to her. Some of his evident amusement fled.

"Don't look at me that way."

Is he kidding? "How am I supposed to look? You have me tied to a chair."

"I'm not going to enter you. I just didn't want my pants digging into my dick because I know I'm going to react to you. You have a way of making a male pretty uncomfortable."

He reached into the bag she had begun to hate. She turned her head, worried about what he'd pull out next. He hesitated until she looked back at him.

"I thought it might come to this at some point. I did a little shopping with you in mind. Overnight delivery is a great option you humans have. I like to be prepared." He paused. "Things have changed between us now. I *know* you better and I put a lot of time into considering how to go about doing this."

He lifted his arm and her eyes widened. He held a tube of lubricant. He even turned it so she could read the label. It was warming gel. She looked back at him. He placed the cold tube on the top of her thigh and reached into the bag again.

Part of Kat was flattered. She had a suspicion that the bag held sex toys. No man had ever done that for her before and it was exciting.

The second item he withdrew made her swallow. She stared at the large vibrator. It had a rounded rubber head and a long handle. Darkness allowed her to stare at it for a few seconds before he picked up the lube, uncapped it and doused the tip of the vibrator with the clear gel.

"I'm going to make you orgasm again and again." His voice deepened. "You ready, my little pretend-cat?"

"That's why you wanted me gagged?"

"Yes."

She'd had fantasies about a man doing that to her but he was about to make it a reality. She nodded. "Do your worst." She licked her lips. "Or your best."

He dropped the gel to the floor and brushed his fingertips across her nipple. It hardened at his touch. He used his thumb to circle the tip and she responded instantly.

"Let's see if you purr."

He turned the vibrator on. The sound was loud in the room and she guessed he had new batteries for that sucker since it seemed at full power. She tensed when he lowered it and held it inches from her pussy. She looked down and then at him. Her heart rate increased and excitement had her almost panting before he'd even started.

One arm wrapped around her waist and he pulled her to the very edge of the seat. "I've got you. Just feel. Are you going to tell me the name?"

She shook her head. "You know I can't."

"Are you ready? How tough are you, sweetheart?"

She lifted her chin. He hadn't gotten the name from her before and he wouldn't do it now. It was a kind of extremely sexy game between them actually, in a twisted way. She accepted that surprising insight and didn't struggle. She wanted him to continue.

He adjusted the speed of the vibrator to something slower and touched it against her clit. She jerked, the sensation instant and intense. Pleasure radiated upward and she closed her eyes.

He rubbed it against her clit and she moaned. His arm tightened, holding her in place. She tried to grab hold of him, only to be reminded that her arms were restrained. She wanted to touch him. He upped the speed and she moaned louder. The orgasm hit fast and hard. She threw her head back and opened her eyes, staring into his as her body rode through the force of it.

He pulled the vibrator away and she relaxed, breathing hard. The look on his face told her he was affected. He had that hungry, sexy look she'd seen before. She looked down, noticing that his cock was hard.

"Are you going to fuck me now?" She hoped he would.

"Not yet."

She lifted her gaze to his.

He flipped on the vibrator. "We're only beginning."

He pressed it against her already-sensitive clit. She cried out and tried to twist away but he held her still, forcing her to feel. It was too much but she couldn't tell him since nothing intelligible came out of her mouth. He increased the speed and she knew hell. It hurt so good, though, and she came a second time. Darkness turned off the vibrator. He leaned in, pressed his chest against hers and his lips brushed her ear as she tried to catch her breath.

"Imagine an hour of this," he growled. "Fuck, you smell good. I could eat you. You're dripping wet, sweetheart. That's why I chose the vibrator though. This is about breaking you, not me. One taste and I'd be lost." A light thud sounded. She guessed it was the vibrator. His fingers played with her clit then rubbed down the seam of her sex. "I want in."

"I want you in."

"Tell me the name."

"I can't." She wished she could but her pride wouldn't allow her to cave that easily. It had become a battle of wills.

One of his fingers slowly breached her pussy and she moaned. He slid it in then almost withdrew it. He hesitated before pressing back in deep.

"My dick is so much bigger. Remember how we fit together?"

Her vaginal muscles clenched around his digit. He made that purring sound she found sexy. He moved his finger again, fucking her with it. She spread her legs wider to give him better access.

"Do you want me?"

She nodded.

"Damn." He withdrew his finger. "It's hell torturing you. I don't know which one of us is hurting more."

She stared into his eyes.

He hesitated and pulled his arm away. "Just give me the damn name, Kat."

"You know I've given you as much as I can."

"So we keep going?"

"I'm having fun. I like this a lot."

He grinned. "I'll remember."

"Want to torture me some more?" She grinned. Kat suspected he'd initiated the confrontation because he enjoyed the verbal sparring as much as being in complete control of their encounters. His need for answers was his job but his need for this was his pleasure. Still, she was glad when he removed the chair restraints.

Darkness freed her ankles first, then her upper arms. He stood and gripped her arm, helping her stand. Her knees trembled a little and the wetness down her thighs was proof that he was really good at making her come hard, twice in a row. "Now my wrists." She turned to let him free them.

"I didn't say we were done."

She looked over her shoulder at him. "What does that mean?"

"It means I'm glad I have a higher bed than the ones in your cottage. It's the perfect height." He bent and picked up the vibrator.

She watched him walk to the bed and grab a pillow. He dropped it on the edge of the mattress and placed the vibrator on it with the rounded tip almost falling off. He turned the vibrator on, reached out and grabbed her arm.

She almost fell when he jerked her forward. She stumbled and then found herself bent over the bed. He grabbed her hips and yanked her down, putting her on her knees.

"What are you doing?"

One of his hands slid between her belly and the bed. He lifted her off her knees until most of her weight rested along his arm. He grabbed the pillow with his free hand and slid it under her, adjusted it and then lowered her. She gasped. The vibrator ended up right against her clit. The plush padding of the thick pillow kept the plastic handle from digging in to her stomach. She fisted her hands behind her back.

"I don't know if I can take this! I'm too sensitive."

"You're going to enjoy it a hell of a lot, sweetheart."

She nodded, sealing her lips. Oversensitive or not, she was willing to try it. Darkness had a way of making her want to push boundaries and try new things.

He shoved her thighs open, keeping her knees from touching the floor with his body pressed against her ass. One hand opened up on her butt as he leaned back a little, putting space between them. It kept her in place.

"You said I could fuck you. I'm going to."

She moaned when the thick head of his cock pressed against the entrance of her pussy. He entered her slowly, gripping her hips. He held her still while he started to move, thrusting deep.

The vibrations against her clit combined with being fucked made Kat unable to think. She wanted to claw something but her hands were still locked behind the small of her back. She found the carpet with her toes and tried to use that traction to shove upward to get away from the vibrator.

Darkness wouldn't allow it, his firm hands on her hips pinned her in place.

"Oh god," she moaned.

Darkness was in heaven and hell. Kat moaned louder and he fought the urge to come. He'd already been excited, watching her face while she climaxed twice. Now that she was under him, he was inside her and it was almost too much. She was wet and hot. Her internal muscles clenched tighter and he knew she was going to come again. He gritted his teeth, remembering too late that he hadn't put on a condom.

He wanted to shoot his seed inside her. Just thinking about it had his balls screaming for release. Kat cried out and her vaginal walls started to convulse around his cock. He shoved her forward enough to get her off the vibrator and stilled. His dick was steel-hard, ached, but he held back his own release. He took deep breaths, listening to Kat's breathing as she recovered. He withdrew from her body.

He grabbed the vibrator and turned it off, tossing it on the floor. He fisted his dick and rubbed it against the crack of her ass. He came hard. His semen coated her ass and lower back, even getting on her hands. He closed his eyes, shaking a little from the power of his release.

It would have felt better if I hadn't pulled out. He bit back a growl. It pissed him off. He knew better than to touch her without a condom. It would be a nightmare if he got Kat pregnant. She was someone he could never trust. She was FBI and while he could force her to stay at Homeland until she gave birth, afterward she'd have the choice to leave, alone. A Species child would never be safe in her world. Would she abandon a child for her freedom? Would she tell the world they were able to have children? He didn't know and never wanted to find out. It would put all the Species offspring at risk and that would be entirely his fault.

"Damn," she whispered. "Are you trying to kill me?"

Regret came next. "Was I too rough?"

She chuckled. "Nope. That was just way over the top. I think I lost brain cells."

He would have hated to have accidentally hurt her, regardless of knowing she wasn't who she claimed. He admired Kat. Most females would probably have protested his treatment. She seemed not to mind him needing to control the sex.

"I still can't tell you his name. What's next? May I have a few minutes first? I'm really sensitive."

He backed off and helped her get to her feet. "Let's shower."

She turned, showing the cuffs. "Can these come off yet? It's hard to wash your back otherwise."

He walked to his dresser and withdrew a knife. She didn't flinch when he approached and he saw no fear. He cut the cuffs. She grinned and rubbed her wrists. He turned and threw the plastic strip on the dresser.

"Follow me."

"I'm going to have to borrow something to wear to get home. I'm not doing the streak-back-to-my-place thing. I've seen your surveillance feeds. They film everything at Homeland. Do New Species have funniest-security-video shows? I don't want to be part of that footage."

He couldn't help but smile. He really liked Kat. It was a grim reminder, though, that he liked her a little too much. He paused at the bathroom door. "You shower first."

He didn't miss her reaction. Disappointment. She was easy to read when her guard was down.

"I thought we were going to do this together too."

He shook his head. "It's too personal."

He'd hurt her. He saw the flicker of pain in her eyes before she hid it. "Right. As if what we just did wasn't." She walked past him. "Whatever."

She flipped on the light and turned, gripping the door. "I guess I'll shut this. It would probably be too personal to watch me shower unless you think I'm going to steal your soap or towels."

He stepped back. "Go ahead."

Anger twisted her lips. "You really are a bastard."

She slammed the door. He was tempted to open it, to say something, but he stood there instead. Kat would leave Homeland soon and he didn't want to miss her. It was better if their time was limited to just sex. He wouldn't eat meals with her, share intimate grooming tasks with her or allow her to sleep in his bed.

He walked over to the chair and carried it back to the spare bedroom. The sound of water in the bathroom taunted him. He could be in there with her but instead he cleaned up the room, getting rid of all evidence of what they'd shared. Except her scent. It filled his room. It lingered as strongly as his memories of touching Kat.

The shower shut off and he put on a pair of sweatpants, not wanting to be naked in her presence. She exited the bathroom wearing a towel, her skin flushed from the warm water and her hair caught up in another towel that was wrapped loosely around her head. She looked adorable and he hated noticing.

"Do you have a robe?"

He hesitated. "I need that name, Kat."

"We've been over this."

"You tell me or I'll have officers come pick you up in twenty minutes. That means packing your suitcase and leaving Homeland. You won't be allowed back."

She stared into his eyes and he watched the color drain from her face. "You mean that?"

"I do."

Her chin lifted and her shoulders straightened. "You don't want to try to torture it out of me anymore?" She tilted her head toward the bed. "Round two might make me break."

She was baiting him to seduce her again and he wanted to. "Only if you give me the name."

A blush rose to her cheeks. "So now you're *withholding* sex for information?"

"Think of it as a reward. I won't ever touch you again if you don't tell me, Kat. That's how it's going to be. You know how good the sex is between us and won't risk losing that. I've been studying you."

"What does that mean?"

He hesitated. "There are cameras inside your cottage. I've been watching your every move since you arrived at Homeland. It's time to stop avoiding my questions. You don't like your boss and you have already betrayed his trust. Give me the name, Kat. Otherwise you will be escorted beyond our gates."

Her expression shut down. "I'll go pack." She tried to step around him to leave the bedroom.

He grabbed hold of her upper arm. "That's it? You'll just leave?"

He almost wished she hadn't looked up at him—pure pain showed in her eyes.

"You had me under surveillance as though I'm some criminal. I get what that means. I'm your assignment. I'm tired of this game, Darkness. I thought there was something between us but it was all chess moves to you. You win."

She jerked hard and he let her go. He hesitated then followed her down the hallway. "Kat?"

She stopped and turned. "What now? Do you want your towels?" She tore the one off her head and threw it at him. It hit him in the chest. "Don't ever say I took anything from you. God forbid you give anything to anyone."

"I warned you that I wasn't mate material."

"You did. I just thought you had issues. Instead you're ice cold inside."

"What does that mean?" He didn't understand.

"You're an excellent judge of people. You were trained to be. Was I that easy to read? Did you enjoy watching me when I wasn't aware of it? Did you profile me?"

"I don't know what you're talking about."

"Bullshit. Do I scream 'lonely' to you? I thought you wanted me because you were attracted to me. Instead this was just some mind game to you. No one can shut it down that fast if it's real. It wasn't though, was it? You played me."

He shook his head.

"Right. Spare me the token denial. I was just a job, right? Seduce the lonely chick and use sex to get her to open up to you. Great job. You did it. Now you can fry my ass for being stupid enough to fall for it. Go for it." She spun and stormed toward the slider. "Don't forget to add that phone call to your report. It'll end my career. Thanks for screwing me over in every way possible."

He moved before he thought, grabbed Kat around her waist and jerked her off her feet. He held her against his chest and refused to let her go when she struggled. He grunted when she elbowed him in the side and slammed her heel into his calf. Her head came back and nearly caught him in the jaw. Only his lightning-quick reflexes prevented the hit. He spun and stomped toward the couch. He twisted her in his arms and fell, landing on the cushions with her under him.

She threw a punch that bounced off his cheekbone. It hurt but he snagged her wrist and shoved it above her head. She tried to slam her other palm into his throat but he managed to capture it before she could make contact. He used his weight to pin her tightly under him until they were nose to nose.

"Shut up," he snarled.

"Fuck you."

She was breathing rapidly and her towel had come loose, revealing one breast. He lifted off her a little and stared at it. "You think I don't really want you?"

"Stop it. Game over."

He growled and glared into her eyes. She was furious too. "I didn't seduce you because anyone asked me to."

"Ah. You did that on your own. I'd pat you on the back but you are too strong." She tried to break his hold on her wrists but he just squeezed a little tighter. She stopped and he eased his hold enough not to hurt her.

"Calm down, Kat."

"Get the hell off me."

"I don't want you to leave believing I lied to you."

"We're dressed...well, I have a towel on at least. It's what we do, remember?"

"I could fix that."

"Don't you dare. I'm done being screwed by you." She glanced around the living room. "Are there cameras in here? Is your security team watching?"

She really believed he'd only bedded her to gain an advantage. He lowered his face and buried it against her wet hair. She smelled like him after using his shampoo and conditioner. It turned him on but he refused to give in to desire. She'd made it clear she didn't want sex any longer.

"No, Kat," he rasped. "It's just you and me here. No one is watching. Pretend no clothing is between us."

"Let's not. Get off me."

"I never wanted to get this close to a female again but I couldn't resist you. The smart thing was to never touch you at all."

"Whatever. I have packing to do, remember?"

She refused to listen. He should just leave it at that but he couldn't. Kat didn't deserve to hurt the way he'd seen in his bedroom. He'd been used before and it still hurt. He didn't want her to go through life believing he'd done the same to her. She'd given him her trust when she'd warned him about those agents. He wasn't certain why she'd done it but it couldn't be beneficial to her in any way. She'd said trust went both ways. He couldn't tell her NSO secrets but he could share one of his own with her. It would at least make them somewhat even.

"You asked about the female I mentioned while you were in interrogation and how I had to pretend you were someone else. Do you remember?"

She took a few breaths. "Yes."

"Darwin Havings was her boss. She told me he forced her to work for him and she was only there because she wasn't given a choice. They used her family as leverage. She was brought in because someone thought sex would be a good incentive to make us easier to control. She later admitted that her job was to teach me how to seduce females into obtaining information. She said she was a prostitute with the experience to train me to be a skilled lover but that was supposed to be kept secret."

Kat grew lax under him and he released her wrists, lifting up enough to see her face. She stared up at him, frowning. It beat the anger and hurt he'd seen before. He shifted his weight but kept her under him.

"They brought her in every few days to spend time with me and we would plot how to escape with my brothers." He swallowed. "I thought I could save them and her."

Kat lowered her hands and curled them around his shoulders. She didn't fight or hit him so he decided to tell her the rest of it.

"I believed she really loved me. I trusted her without question. We talked about everything. I told her about what they were making us do and all my fears. I found out afterward that nothing she said was truthful. She betrayed me from the start and it cost my brothers their lives."

Kat's lips parted but she said nothing.

"No one forced her to be there. She was paid a lot of money to gain my trust. I was the one who told her we had a weakness for females and children. That's why they sent us into that camp. The information she gained from me put us there so they could see how far we could be pushed to discover our limits. I got my brothers killed because I trusted the wrong person. I have to live with that."

"Darkness." Tears shone in her eyes.

He shook his head. "Don't. I don't want your pity. I'm telling you this because I swore to never allow another female to get close to me. I refused to mount any females they brought to my cell after I was taken back to Mercile. I'd think of my brothers and couldn't even get hard. My weakness for sex with the female got them killed. Mercile believed I was emotionally damaged so they stopped bringing females to me for breeding experiments. I've turned down every female who offered to share sex since we were freed. Don't ever accuse me of not wanting you, Kat. You're the first temptation I couldn't refuse."

Her hands slid down his arms, caressing him. "I'm so sorry."

"I am damaged. You're leaving Homeland today but go knowing that truth. I didn't touch you as a way to gain your trust or use what we've shared as a tool to deceive you. I did it because I couldn't fight the attraction I feel. I took control of the camera feeds because I didn't want anyone else watching you. You fascinate me."

"You just expect me to leave after that?" She shook her head. "No way."

He clenched his teeth. "Darwin Havings believed the female was a loose end. You know what those are. No one associated with that mess wanted her walking free to tell anyone about what had gone on in that camp. Never let it be said that cruel humans don't have a twisted sense of justice.

They thought it was fitting to let me be the one to kill her after giving her the impression that she'd been brought to me so she could watch me die. She took real pleasure in telling me how stupid I'd been to ever trust her and how disappointing it had been that she hadn't gotten to watch my brothers die as well. She said she should get an award for acting since fucking me had been revolting. You should have seen her face when the guards left her there alone with me. I killed her, Kat."

"I probably would have done the same in your place."

He saw no censure in her eyes and she didn't withdraw her touch. "I appreciate that but we both know it was wrong. I should have let the guards kill her. They were getting paid to follow orders. I did it for revenge."

"It was a difficult situation after what she'd just said to you. You reacted in the heat of the moment, caused by the pain you suffered from the senseless murders of your brothers. I think you're being too hard on yourself."

"It's who I am. It's what keeps me going and I can't change. I gave you all I had to give, Kat. This has to end. I can't get attached to you."

"I wouldn't mind."

"I would." He looked miserable. "I was jealous today. I wanted to rip out Jinx's throat. It wasn't a good feeling and I never want to experience it again. I like being numb. I never want to hurt again. You could do that to me if I don't stop it now. It's a risk I just can't take. I warned you that I'm damaged. That wasn't a lie either."

She surprised him by wrapping her arms around his neck and burying her face against his shoulder. "Thank you for that, Darkness."

He relaxed, lowering some of his weight, and closed his eyes. He wished the moment could last but he only allowed it briefly. He climbed off her.

"You shouldn't return home in a towel. I'll get some clothes."

"I don't have to leave. I still have classes to teach but I would insist on the cameras being removed from my cottage."

He refused to look at her. "I know you're FBI, Kat. So does the NSO. You shared information you shouldn't have with me so this is me returning the trust. *I'd* be in trouble if they knew I told you that. They wanted to figure out why you came by allowing you to keep up the charade. This thing between us ends today. Don't stay for me because I won't see you again after you leave this house. Go home before you do something that could get you in trouble with the NSO. I don't want to see you hurt. I'll be right back."

He bent, picked up her wet towel and walked down the hallway. He hung it in the bathroom before retrieving a shirt and shorts from his dresser. When he returned to the living room Kat wasn't there. She'd left. He cursed. He didn't place the call to Security. He'd leave it up to Kat if she wanted to stay or go but he'd keep his word. He'd avoid her. It was for the best.

Chapter Twelve

ဢ

Kat exited the gates, ignoring the jerks calling out to her from the sidelines. Her mood was foul enough that she was grateful not to have her sidearm. She might have been tempted to shoot a protestor in the mouth. The cab waited across the street. She just dumped her suitcase on the backseat and climbed in after it. She rambled off the name of the car rental company. The driver nodded and pulled away from the curb.

The NSO had known all along. That fact shouldn't have surprised her. Darkness had dropped enough hints. A lot of unanswered questions remained. Did they know her real name? Did Mason know her cover had been blown? If so, he'd be in a rage. She put on her seat belt and closed her eyes.

It was procedure to file a report. Mason would chew her ass up one side and down the other when she faced him. She just didn't want to deal with it. The short ride ended and she paid the driver. It only took a few minutes for her to retrieve her car from the parking lot where she'd left it.

She'd always followed rules. It was something she believed in. Life was messy but her job made sense of some of the chaos. She'd joined the agency to make a difference. To help put evil shits away and make the world a safer place. She felt as if Mason had placed her in the bad-guy category. The NSO had been victimized enough.

Darkness haunted her as she drove. Her guts felt as if they'd been ripped out. She believed what he'd told her. No sympathy rose for the bitch he'd killed. He might feel torn about it but it was cut-and-dried to her. That the woman had gotten close to him, yet hurt him that way, angered her. It just cemented her belief that purely evil people existed in the world—one less, thanks to Darkness. She grieved the loss of his brothers too, hurt for him.

"Damn." She sighed, gripping the wheel tightly. "I'm all fucked up."

Nothing made sense anymore. She just wanted to go home and lick her wounds. She took in her surroundings, realizing she drove aimlessly. It only took her a few minutes to establish where she was and get on the freeway. That's exactly where she'd go. Home.

It might be hours or days before Mason figured out she wasn't at Homeland anymore. She hadn't seen any of the three agents she'd recognized when she left though he might have other surveillance on the gates. She glanced in her rearview mirror, hunting for a tail. Her car could be tagged with a tracker too. She debated whether she should ditch it and get another rental but dismissed the idea. If Mason wanted her found, he'd do it. She didn't have enough cash to stay in a motel. Her identification and credit cards could be flagged.

She pulled off the road to grab some food at a drive-thru. It didn't help her upset stomach. The cause of that was knowing she'd never see Darkness again. He'd gotten under her skin in a big way. She'd always smirked when hearing one of her friends say that they'd fallen fast and hard for some man. That had never been her experience.

She'd loved before but her pride had always come first. It was a consequence of her childhood. The first step of acceptance was understanding the problem. Her parents had divorced when she had been eight, each marrying much younger spouses for their second marriages. Her mother had ended up with a serial cheater whom she'd made excuses for. It had disgusted Kat. Her father's wife had him by the balls too. She'd sworn that no one would ever make a fool of her and she'd walked away from any man who didn't conform to her ideal version of a boyfriend.

Darkness wasn't anything like someone she'd marry or want to spend her life with. He fell into all the "hell no" categories. He wouldn't support her career. Living with him at Homeland wouldn't fly. He couldn't leave the NSO to live in her world. He wasn't emotionally available.

"Understatement," she muttered.

There would be no playful shower moments in a future with him. No sleeping in on her days off, cuddled up against him. That would mean he'd actually have to let her get that close. A bitter laugh rose and she choked on it. Darkness wouldn't even let her touch him during sex. He always restrained her. He could be the poster guy for control issues. She had a lot of them herself.

They just made a horrible match. It didn't diminish the pain she felt. That ache in her chest and the tears gathering in her eyes pretty much were a reality bitch-slap. She'd fallen in love with him.

She blinked hard at the sight of her house when she pulled into the driveway, fighting the urge to cry. It wasn't something she did much. Seeing Missy's car helped her pull her emotions together. She turned off the engine, grabbed her suitcase and got out.

"You home?" Kat hollered when she entered the house. She dropped her suitcase inside the door and kicked it closed.

"You better be a hot handyman or my best friend," Missy called out from upstairs. "I have a gun."

"Don't shoot your imaginary weapon at me."

Missy rushed down the stairs. "I missed you."

They hugged and Missy leaned back, giving her a once-over. "You look like shit."

"Thanks. Your hair in a ponytail and paint smears on your sleeves isn't your best look either."

Her best friend grinned. "Someone abandoned me so I've been painting the spare room by myself. I'm lucky some of it ended up on the walls and at least I brushed my hair. You look like you hid from a brush."

"It's a long story."

"The kind you can't tell me? Just tell me you're not bruised to hell and back under those clothes. No bullet holes or anything, right?"

"I'm good."

"Boring kind of stuff, huh?"

"I wouldn't say that."

"Can you tell me anything?"

She shook her head. "You know how it goes."

"But you're good?"

Kat shrugged.

Missy inched closer. "You look sad."

"I am."

"I hate your job. Have I mentioned that before?"

"Constantly."

"Can we play twenty questions?"

"No."

"I had to ask. Are you hungry?"

"I stopped for a burger already."

"That's good since I ate the last of the pizza in the fridge. I didn't thaw anything out. I had no clue when you were coming home. Are you staying or did you just stop in to get a new set of clothes?"

"I'm technically still on assignment but I don't plan to leave the house any time soon." Kat glanced around the living room. "I like the bookshelf you put up."

"Thanks." Missy grinned. "I would take the credit but it was actually my brother-in-law. I couldn't make sense of the directions and Angela stopped by. He looked bored hearing us gossip so I did the sisterly thing by putting him to work."

"Good job."

"He was a grumpy ass about it but Angela told him to stick a sock in it." She bent and grabbed Kat's suitcase. "Come on. We'll unpack you. You don't have anything secret in here I can't see, do you?"

"Nope. Just dirty laundry."

"You unpack then. I'll watch. I am so glad you're home."

"Where's Butch?"

"The groomers. They are dropping him off in an hour. The pooch missed you but he's going to be pissed when he gets home. He's getting the summer cut and you know how sulky he is when we put him through that trauma. He takes it so personally."

Kat was glad to be home. It put back a sense of normalcy that she desperately needed in her life at the moment. She followed Missy upstairs and they turned right, moving down the hallway toward the bedrooms. A small sound stopped her. Missy turned.

"Oh. I forgot. I'm babysitting for George from across the street."

Kat backed up to locate the source and looked into Missy's bedroom. A small gray kitten with a yarn ball lay on the bed. It peered back at her. The cat's eyes reminded her of Darkness, despite their blue color.

"Butch loves Gus. That's the kitten's name. He's ten weeks old. Isn't he cute as hell? He's a nightmare on the curtains but they were ugly anyway. I put the litter box in my bathroom so no worries. I've kept your bedroom door closed, not that he leaves my room. He's kind of a chicken for being a cat. George's mom got sick and he couldn't leave Gus alone."

"It's okay."

"You're as white as a sheet. Don't tell me cats scare you. I know you're not allergic."

"I just didn't expect it." She forced a smile. "He's cute."

196

"I'm glad you think so. I plan to keep him. George kind of got stuck with him and wanted to find him a home. Butch adores Gus and I think he'd be heartbroken if he leaves." Missy batted her eyelashes. "May I keep him?"

"I don't mind. It's your house too."

"I knew we were best buds for a reason. You're home, Gus!" Missy opened Kat's door and dropped the suitcase by the closet. "Does that mean you'll clean the litter box too?"

"Don't push it. Your kitten, your shit."

"I can deal with that. Just don't bitch at me if he attacks your curtains too. We really should burn them. I think he hates flower prints, which I can't fault him for."

Kat glanced at her window. The curtains had come with the house. "No problem. It wouldn't be a big loss, would it?"

"Do you ever think we should feel ashamed? I mean, how long have we lived here? We still have boxes we haven't unpacked in the garage. You're gone more than you're here and my nose is usually shoved in front of my computer screen. I should just put a bed in the downstairs office since I practically live in there. We're workaholics who are too damn lazy to fix up our house. I figure, at this rate, we might do something nice to it within twenty years or so. I was only motivated to paint the guest room because my mom threatened to visit. You know she'd bitch if we stick her in a lime-green room."

Kat kicked off her shoes and sat on the bed. "We suck."

Missy sat down next to her. "You aren't okay. You didn't even flinch when I mentioned my mother. She drives you nuts."

Kat shook her head. "Nope. I'm not."

"Is it a chocolate kind of day or should I break out that bottle of vodka we were given at Christmas? How bad is it?"

"I don't even think both would help."

"Damn." Missy chewed on her bottom lip. "Did you shoot that asshole of a boss of yours? Should I bake cookies for the SWAT team that might come after you? It might distract them while you escape out the back."

"He's alive and well. I think. I'm avoiding him."

"Did you tell him you aren't a set of tits? I even want to punch him. I can't believe he thought we were getting it on. No offense but when I do get laid, he has to have a dick and actually be a guy. Your boss is a shitty agent if he didn't discover I write under a pen name after digging into our lives. My stories are about having hot sex with men. That would have been a clue, even for that moron."

"How goes the writing?"

"Good. I turned in my latest book and started a new one. It's about a hunky cat shifter. Blame Gus. I am. He's so damn cute."

Kat fell back and closed her eyes. "Stop."

"You like hearing about my stories. He's six feet tall, muscular and has these beautiful eyes like Gus. He's going to save this woman who gets her car stuck in mud and he has to take her home because a raging storm cuts them off when the roads flood. She's impressed with those muscles and jumps into bed with him. Fiction is way better than reality. Remember the last guy I slept with? Two minutes max of pushup sex and he couldn't find my clit to save his life. My girl is getting laid in style."

Kat reached over and used the back of her hand to swat Missy's leg. "Really. Stop."

"Real people have sex." She sighed. "Do you ever think about hiring one of those male escorts? I thought about it. Would you bust me? I could say it was for research purposes. Would that fly? You know, to see if they'd really have sex for money. I'm not a cop so I'm under no obligation to turn him in if he does. Then again, with my luck, he'd do bad pushup sex.

I guess I could pay him to read one of my sex scenes and tell him to act it out. I heard some of them are actors."

Kat sat up and opened her eyes. "I had sex."

Missy's mouth fell open.

"I broke the rules and went to bed with someone I shouldn't have."

"Another agent?"

She shook her head.

Missy gaped at her. "Your suspect?"

"No. Not exactly."

"That sounds ominous. Was he hot?"

"Scorching."

"Is he on a most-wanted list? Should I bake those cookies still? Just remember the window in the laundry room is the only one that opens when you make a run for it."

"No SWAT team is going to come. Sorry to disappoint you. I know you think they are kind of sexy. Can you be serious? I don't want to laugh."

"They are, in my defense. Why are you not okay?"

Kat didn't look away. "I fell for him but he's not the type of guy to settle down."

"You're not the kind of woman to settle down."

She hated the way it hurt. "He might have been able to change me."

"Oh honey. I'm sorry. Maybe he'll wise up and come knocking on our door."

She hesitated, almost wishing that were true. Darkness would never call to ask her back. He'd made it clear they were over. The urge to cry returned. "He won't. I breached protocol while I was undercover. I fucked up, Missy. I could lose my job and right now I don't even think I care."

Her friend reached out and took her hand. "Could you face criminal charges?"

"I don't think so. Not unless my boss wants to make up stuff just to get a little payback. I wouldn't put it past him. I'm supposed to still be on assignment but I didn't call in to tell him I left. I just needed a few days to get my head on straight."

"You were starting to hate your job. You know that, right? Ever since you got the dickhead for a boss you've been miserable." Missy took a deep breath. "You know you can trust me with your life. Talk to me. You need to get this off your chest or it's going to eat you up. It won't go any further."

Kat debated. She needed to tell someone. "I was sent to Homeland."

Missy squealed. "You went there! Oh my god!"

"Shush."

"Sorry. Go on."

"I can't go into detail but the guy was a New Species."

Missy yanked her hand free and clasped it over her heart. "You nailed a New Species?"

"Stop that."

"Just tell me."

She nodded.

Missy grabbed her. "I hate you right now. No, I love you. I do. Was he good in bed? Don't crush me."

"A 15 on the 1-to-10 scale."

"I knew it." Missy grinned. "You lucky bitch."

"Did I mention I won't ever see him again?"

Her joy faded fast. "Shit. He won't be coming to our door, will he? They don't leave that place." She rubbed Kat's arm. "I'm so sorry. What a bastard. I will never go all fan-girl over them again."

"Don't be so dramatic. It wasn't as if he didn't tell me it was only sex. I just didn't expect to feel so much and I really screwed up with my job because it pitted me against him. I chose him in the end."

"I heard the NSO is kind of like a different country. I don't think you sleeping with one is illegal and it wasn't technically on US soil. I think you're in the clear on that breach-of-conduct thing. I mean, you couldn't be fired if you went on a trip to Mexico and hooked up with a resident there. You're allowed to have sex."

"I was on the job and I shared information with him that I shouldn't have."

"That's bad."

"I know. Robert Mason is going to have my ass if he finds out."

"What are the chances of that?"

"I don't know."

"I'm getting the chocolate and the vodka." Missy rose. "Right now."

"Thanks."

"Then you're going to give me more details."

"You can't use it in a book."

"Damn." Missy narrowed her eyes. "That was me kidding. Think of this room like Vegas. What is said here, stays here."

"Thanks."

"Best friends forever, remember? I'm just glad you're talking to me. You hold too much in, Kat. I worry about you all the time."

* * * * *

Darkness slammed his front door. Kat had left Homeland. He'd reviewed the footage from Security. She'd hailed a cab after exiting the front gates. Justice and Fury had asked him why she'd left and he'd had to tell them something. He'd shared what she'd told him about the other agents but made it clear it could get her in trouble. He'd even volunteered the information that they'd argued. He just didn't tell them about what.

He walked over to the couch and sat, slamming his boots on the coffee table. The wood creaked and he leaned to the side to stare at the new crack along the top.

"Fuck."

He hated feeling as if he'd betrayed her trust. The agents who had posed as workers to fix the damaged front gates hadn't been able to do anything more. The humans had peered around a lot, their interest too intense, but hadn't attempted to leave the job site. He should have kept his mouth shut. Guilt and regret ate at him. So did another emotion. He'd never see her again and it left an empty space inside him.

He leaned back and closed his eyes, adjusting his arm along the side cushion. Something crinkled and he shifted, opening his eyes. A sheet of paper protruded from under the cushion. He pulled it out. It was from a notebook he kept on the kitchen counter to write down grocery lists when he ran low on supplies. The handwriting wasn't his. He read it and cursed.

Jerry Boris. You trusted me. I'm trusting you. K

She must have written it when he'd gone into the bedroom to get her something to wear. He stared at the name, enraged. Why would the FBI be interested in Jerry Boris? It raised all kinds of questions and alarms.

He jerked his feet off the table and stood. He paced the living room, gripping the note in his fist. She'd be in trouble for giving him that information. Otherwise she would have given it up in the bedroom. Why had she?

He stopped and smoothed out the paper, rereading. It angered him. Why couldn't she have just told him once she decided to share the name? *I would have tried to get more answers from her. I would have insisted she stay longer.* She'd intended the note be found only after she left Homeland.

"Damn it," he hissed.

He walked over to the counter and snatched up the phone and dialed Fury's extension. The male answered on the third ring.

"Fury here."

"I'm in over my head and I need help."

"Darkness?"

"Who else would call you to say those words?"

"Where are you?"

"At home."

"I'll be right there."

"Thank you." He hung up and resumed his pacing.

Fury must have left his office as soon as he hung up. The knock on the door came faster than expected. Darkness jerked it open and stepped to the side, allowing the male to enter his home. Fury's nose flared and he turned, a speculative look in his eyes.

"What?"

"You need to open some windows."

"Shit."

"You had sex with the FBI agent. You didn't tell us about that. I can still smell her. It's faint but I can pick it up."

"Put your canine nose away."

"Is this the cause of the disagreement you had with her?"

"Did you come to help me or to be annoying?"

Fury spun and walked over to the couch. He sniffed and then sat. "What can I do?"

Darkness crossed the room and took a seat on the coffee table. He hesitated, not sure where to start or what would help.

"You want her back?"

Darkness scowled.

"You think you're the only male who allowed a female to walk away and then regretted it? Should I make a list of names that come to mind? I could remind you about my history with Ellie."

"Spare me. I'm not like other males."

"Bullshit. You mounted her. That says it all. Do you think I don't make it my business to keep tabs on you? You wouldn't have let her get that close unless you couldn't refrain from giving in to your desire to have her. You think you're different but few males actually want to find themselves dependent on a female. They fight it. It's Species nature in most cases."

"That's bullshit."

Fury smirked. "We have trust issues. It's tough to admit we need or want anyone enough to risk pain. That's a common thread all Species share. Did you fall in love with her? Do you want us to get her back?"

"No."

Fury didn't look convinced.

It annoyed Darkness. "I don't want her to pay for trusting me."

"You do have feelings."

"I admire her and don't want her to be hurt because she took risks for me."

"We went over this. It's not as if we're going to call the FBI and ask them why they sent agents to Homeland. They want to pretend it didn't happen and we're good with that. We'll just be more careful, intensify our screening procedure and do more extensive background checks from multiple sources. We're always upgrading. All we can do is hope to prevent them from doing it again."

"I didn't tell you everything in Justice's office."

Fury sucked in a breath. "Okay."

"This is where it gets dicey."

"Shit." Fury leaned forward. "I'm listening."

"I want to protect her. I want that made clear. I got the impression she'd be in a lot of trouble and her career could end."

"Understood."

"Can I trust you? This might cause tension with the NSO. I'm asking you to keep this information between us. I don't know what to do."

Fury's eyes narrowed. "In other words, you're asking me to sit on information that should be shared."

"Yes."

The male leaned back and blew out a breath. "I love the NSO and I'd do anything for Species but there's one exception. That's my family. They always come first and foremost. You fall under that category. I won't betray your trust."

He stood and crossed the room, retrieving the paper he'd left facedown on the counter. He walked to Fury and held it out. The male took it and read the words. He paled. Darkness took a seat again on the coffee table.

"Kat implied she was given orders to search for a male at Homeland and help him leave. Those agents she identified at the gates may have been under the same orders."

"Why would the FBI want Boris?"

"She didn't know. I believe that. She seemed confused as to why the person who sent her here wanted that male but she thought it was personal."

"You think Boris screwed over someone in the FBI or that he might know something potentially damaging to them?"

Darkness shrugged. "It's a dilemma, isn't it?"

"That's putting it mildly." Fury leaned forward and laid the note down. "She trusted you not to share this information. I see why you called me. You're torn between us and not betraying that trust."

"I want access to Boris again."

"Why?"

"He has the answers. He'd know why the FBI has an interest in him. Give me an hour with that male and we don't have to involve anyone who could harm Kat in any way. Official channels would put her in harm's way. They can't get to him and discover she gave up his name to me."

"Does she know he's in Medical? She took a few tours. Did she see him?"

"She wouldn't have been allowed access to the basement area where he's being held and I kept close tabs on everyone she spoke to. I interviewed them to see what she talked about, trying to figure out why she was really here. She never asked about humans besides the mate hunters. Sunshine had that discussion with her. She never toured Medical either. I double-checked."

"We need to tell Justice."

"He might talk to the Senator and ask him to make inquiries. No. You said I could trust you."

"This is bigger than the female losing her job. Boris seems to be more of a problem than we thought. What if he had help from inside the FBI with his extortion scheme against the NSO? We paid him a lot of money to recover other Species. We need to find out everything we can to make certain that isn't a possibility."

"I don't know enough about Kat to understand all the risks she faces but I won't chance it. I refuse to allow her to pay for leaving that note. She wanted to help me."

Fury shoved his hair back, the frustration clear in his features. "Fine. You want access to Boris?"

"Yes."

Fury stood, paced. "I got an update today on his condition. He's not stable enough to leave Homeland and be transferred to Fuller." He paused, studying Darkness. "He could die if you aren't careful. He's not in the best health, especially after the last time you had a talk with him."

"Understood."

"I wouldn't mind if he died but I'd hate to try to explain why you were covered in his blood or why I put you there. We'd both be in front of Justice. Do you understand?"

"You'd tell him everything."

"No." Fury shook his head. "I'd break his heart by remaining silent. I gave you my word."

"He's your best friend."

"You're my brother." Fury hesitated. "Even if you won't admit the link, I'd stand by you and that means protecting your female too."

"She isn't mine."

Fury shrugged. "She's the first thing you've really given a damn about and put your ass on the line for. I owe her for that alone."

"She isn't mine," Darkness repeated. "You're making too much out of it."

"We'll see. Just keep in mind that we do know a Senator and could obtain her real name if she didn't give it to you. That means we could locate her and have her brought back."

"Why would we do that?"

"In case you decide letting her go was a mistake."

"It was for the best."

"For who?"

"Both of us."

"Let's go to Medical."

"You have a plan?"

Fury shook his head. "I'll just say I want to see Boris and you follow me in. I'll offer to give the officer guarding him a break." The male frowned. "You may not have an hour but we'll see how much time we can get. Work fast and try not to kill him."

"I'll do my best."

"You know you're going to owe me for this."

207

Darkness clenched his teeth. "What do you want?"

"Answers."

He nodded abruptly. The time had come for them to talk about the past. "Afterward."

"Of course."

Chapter Thirteen

∞

Darkness approached the cell that held the human. Boris lay in a hospital bed, the machines monitoring him making no sound as the male slept. Fury stayed near the elevator. Darkness unlocked the door.

Boris stirred. "It's about time. I need more morphine. I'm in pain."

"You won't be getting any relief from me."

Jerry Boris' eyes opened and he stared in horror at Darkness. "HELP!"

Darkness paused by the end of the bed and smiled coldly, making certain his fangs showed. "No one can hear you. I'm glad you remember me because we're not done yet."

Boris' fearful gaze darted frantically around the room, probably searching for the officer who was usually stationed outside his cell. It was easy for Darkness to read when the male realized no one was there to help him. Tears filled the human's eyes. No pity surfaced inside Darkness.

"What do you want?"

Darkness gripped the bars of the foot rail and rattled the bed a little. The male cringed and tried to pull his legs up as far as possible. "Let's talk about the FBI."

Boris panted and some of the blood drained out of his face. "I don't know what you're talking about."

"Yes you do." Darkness released the foot rail and straightened, inching around the bed. He studied every visible inch of Jerry Boris. "I was disappointed with our last conversation."

"I told you the truth. That cat girl is exactly where I said. You had to have found her. I bribed one of the guards on that estate and he verified she was there and that she was alive."

"I'm not here about the Gift." Darkness reached behind his back and withdrew a nail file he'd tucked into his waistband. He lifted one hand and used the tip to run along his thumbnail. "I was disappointed you survived." He paused and examined the metal point. "No one here likes you. I'm sure you don't have friends at Fuller either."

"You're going to kill me." Jerry's voice broke. "You said you wouldn't if I talked."

"I said I wouldn't as long as you gave me the information I wanted and didn't lie."

"I told you the truth!" The male scooted to press his body against the side rail opposite Darkness. "I told you everything I know."

"You didn't mention the FBI. I've been busy since we spoke, looking into everything about your life. They sent agents to attempt to take True's mate. You remember her, don't you? Jeanie doesn't like you either."

"I don't know why they wanted her."

Darkness lunged and grabbed the male's hand. Boris fought but not effectively enough to jerk out of his hold. "What did I say about lying to me?"

"HELP!" Jerry screamed again. The high-pitched sound was painful to Darkness' keen hearing.

He used the nail file tip to press just under the male's index fingernail. "Don't you hate dirt under your nails? Allow me to help you with that." He jabbed the point into the tender skin.

The male screamed again and flopped on the bed. Darkness glanced at the heart monitor, watching the numbers spike. He grinned and leaned in. "Tell me about the FBI, Boris."

The male whimpered.

"This is me being congenial. Do you want to see me pissed off? I could remove each fingernail and then start on your toes." He removed the metal and released the male's hand, wiping the bloody tip on the sheet. "Or perhaps one of your eyes. It's not as if you'll ever see daylight where you'll be sent, if you survive this conversation. Keep telling me lies and you definitely won't."

"I don't know what you're talking about."

Darkness chuckled. "Let the fun begin. I like hearing you scream, little man." He leaned over and grabbed the male's head. "Right or left eye? Do you have a favorite? I hate both of them so I'll allow you to decide." He waved the nail file in front of Jerry's nose. "Take a good look at me, human. Do you think I won't do it? I'm no longer amused."

Sweat broke out on the male's forehead and panic showed in his eyes. "Please, don't do it."

"I want you to tell me everything. I already know some of the details," he bluffed. He shifted the nail file and ran the tip over the male's cheek and down to the side of his mouth. "Lie once and you lose something. It's going to be painful. I would have brought a knife but you don't deserve being cut up quickly. I want you to feel everything."

The male whimpered again. "What do you want to know?"

"I want the name or names of your contacts in the FBI. I want to know why they give a shit about you. I want details. Why would anyone want to retrieve you from us? That plan failed, by the way. There is no rescue for you, Boris."

The male swallowed. Darkness dug the metal tip into the man's skin, opening a small cut on his chin. Jerry cried out. Darkness paused.

"Talk."

"My brother-in-law," he blurted. "Robert Mason. I was married to his sister. He'd try to help me."

"Why?"

211

Jerry grabbed hold of Darkness' wrist but failed to tug his hand away to remove the nail file from his face. It was a useless attempt since the human was weak. It angered Darkness though. He released the male's head and applied pressure on two of Boris' fingers until he felt bones break. Jerry screamed and lost his grip on Darkness' wrist.

"Don't touch me again," Darkness warned. "I've seen what you like to play with when you're alone. Keep talking and don't stop until I have heard enough. Otherwise, I'll take one of your eyes."

"Robert knew I worked for you." Jerry rushed his words. "He knew what happened while I was the director at Homeland. He sent some of his people to arrest Jeanie Shiver because I told him she was a lying cunt trying to help New Species get me fired from Fuller. I told him the NSO held a grudge against me because I had tried to prove they were incompetent to run Homeland." He sucked in a breath. "I warned him you assholes would make me disappear. And I did but he knows I'm here."

Darkness eased the pressure on the nail file against the male's face. "Keep going."

"I don't know what else you want me to say. Robert is family. He'd do anything he could to help me. He knows you bastards had it in for me."

"You extorted blood money for information to rescue our people. That's on you."

"You owed me!" Jerry cradled his injured fingers against his chest.

Darkness snarled. "You're owed death for what you've done. You allowed Species to needlessly suffer while you played games and tried to shift the blame to a female who only wanted to help rescue my kind. That makes you a piece of shit."

"Robert will get me out. He'll have a federal judge order you to hand me over to his custody."

Darkness straightened. "It's just paper here. Your laws don't apply."

"He'll get me. He knows where Fuller is. I told him."

That news irritated Darkness. Fury's soft growl was proof the Species had overheard their exchange. "Too bad you won't be sent there then." He lunged and gripped the male's neck. It was tempting to snap the bone. One good squeeze and a twist would end the male's life. He might need more information later though. He tightened his hold enough to choke off the human's air supply, watching his face change color and his eyes bulge.

"Darkness, enough." Fury spoke softly but his voice carried.

Several seconds passed before Darkness released the male and backed up. "You think on the matter. I'll be back. I want more information." He lifted the nail file to remind the jerk. "Next time I'll bring pliers. You don't need fingernails and you don't need eyelids if you don't have eyes. Or I could bring a sewing kit. I could practice putting stitches in you."

Boris whimpered and his body quaked. Darkness backed out of the cell and locked the door. He spun and stomped across the room. Fury stood next to the elevator with his arms crossed over his chest. He said nothing as he inserted his key to open the secure elevator. They stepped inside and waited for the doors to close.

"Would you have really killed him?"

"No. I just wanted him to think it."

"I smell his blood."

"It is no worse than a few paper cuts. I did break two of his fingers. He grabbed me so I grabbed back. We have a name and an association. We need to run the name Robert Mason."

"It will alert him if we look into him through regular channels. Word will spread among the medical staff about Boris' new injuries and I'm sure the human will protest what you did. Justice's father-in-law might be able to get information without raising any suspicions. Justice is going to find out either way."

Darkness considered it as they left Medical. Fury had sent an officer down to watch Boris again. "I could say I stopped in to check on the male and got the name. We leave Kat out of this."

"I assumed." Fury paused by his Jeep. "Let's go talk to Justice now. It's better he hears about our little visit from us before the officer calls it in."

Darkness climbed into the passenger seat. "Just remember that Kat stays out of this."

"We'll also ask for the names of all the agents who work with Mason. That way we'll at least find out your girlfriend's real name. I think the Senator would agree with that since this Mason might be a threat to the NSO if he's trying to get his brother-in-law back."

"She's not my girlfriend." He shot Fury a glare. "Are you going to drive or harass me?"

Fury started the engine. "Do you think Mason helped Boris with his extortion scheme?"

"I don't know but Boris' heart rate was too high. I needed to end the interrogation or he might have had a heart attack. That is one out-of-shape male. I'll go back later, when he's more stable. I got the information I needed most."

"We have a name," Fury sighed. "That's good."

Darkness silently agreed. Mason would have to be in a position to give Kat orders. He hoped pictures could be obtained of the agents involved with Mason. Otherwise he'd have to guess when he saw the list of names.

The drive to Justice's home was short. Fury parked at the curb, turned off the engine but hesitated. "Maybe I should call him outside."

"Jessie will want to know what is going on and it's her father we need to contact."

"Agreed." Fury slid out of the seat. "Let's go."

Darkness followed him to the front door and pressed the bell. Jessie answered. She grinned. "Hello. I didn't expect you two. Come on in. Justice is on the phone but he'll be off in a few minutes." She waved them inside.

Darkness peered around the cozy living room. Pictures of the happy mated couple adorned every wall. The place smelled of freshly baked cookies and the lingering scent of shared sex. He studied Jessie, noticing her dress was creased in a few places and her hair mussed. He hid a smile. She noticed his look and arched her eyebrows.

"Don't assess me," she whispered. "He had a rough day and I wanted to make it better. I know you can smell what we did but you don't need to be so obvious about it. You single males are too curious. Fury didn't do that."

"I'm smarter." Fury chuckled. "And have a mate who greets me at the door when I have a bad day. We'll avoid sitting on the couch. My nose tells me where you shared sex."

"Don't let your nose tell you anything else. Got it? Follow me into the dining room. I just took out some cookies. I'm baking a shitload of them for tomorrow."

"What is tomorrow?" Darkness pulled out a chair at the table and sat.

"We're flying up to Reservation in the evening. We're going to spend a few days in the Wild Zone. Justice needed a break and I demanded he take a few days off. You'd be surprised how friendly the residents become when you bring them oatmeal cookies. They love them." She smiled. "Do you want a few? By that, I mean a dozen. I know how you guys eat. I've been in the kitchen all day. I'm turning domestic. It's scary."

Fury grinned. "I'm taking over while they are on a mini vacation. You're good for him, Jessie."

"That phone has been attached to his ear, unless he's been in the shower, naked with me, or sleeping." She pointed a finger at Fury. "You better not call unless it's major, mister. I mean it. I want him to relax. He needs to have some fun without hearing bad news."

"I promise."

"Then it's your turn. You guys need a few days alone together. I'll babysit. Ellie said you're hardly home and you've been fighting with another male." She glanced between them. "I hope you two worked it out."

"We are getting there," Fury assured her.

"Good." She spun and went to the kitchen. "I won't ask."

"You're a good female," Fury called out.

"No need to kiss my ass. I said I'd babysit. I love kids." She returned with a plate of cookies, setting them on the table. "Dig in. I'll get Justice. I'm a pro at luring him off the phone."

She headed toward Justice's home office. Fury grinned at Darkness. He frowned back.

"What?"

"You should see the look on your face. You keep staring at everything."

"I haven't been inside Justice's home since Jessie moved in."

"Nor have you come to mine. This is what a mated home looks like. Did you expect something different?"

"I wasn't sure what to expect."

"Mine looks like this but with a lot of toys. They practically explode out of the boxes they are supposed to be kept in. You have to learn to watch where you step. Otherwise you curse often from pain and your child will repeat every word. Ellie has a sense of humor about it, luckily."

"You're going to allow Jessie to babysit?"

Fury nodded. "She does it whenever Ellie and I want alone time. Children can interrupt sex. Salvation does it often. We appreciate the break."

"You trust her?"

Fury's eyes narrowed. "Yes I do. I'd ask you to watch my son occasionally too but you won't have anything to do with us."

"You'd trust me with your offspring?"

"He's your nephew." Fury leaned back in his chair. "I would."

"I know nothing about children."

"You should learn. Salvation is pretty tough but you'd have to keep a close eye on him. He's fast and is prone to finding trouble." Fury chuckled. "He tried to leap off our roof after I dropped him off today. We visited Valiant and Tammy a month ago and he watched their son leap from one of the ceiling beams onto the couch. Noble is a terror with his claws and climbs everything."

That alarmed Darkness. "Is Salvation okay?"

"I went up after him and explained the differences between canine and feline. Ellie had called me. I was close. She had gone to use the bathroom and he was out the door that fast. She found him on the roof. I had a talk with him about how he could harm his mother if he ever did that again. She was ready to try to catch him."

Darkness winced. "He could have done damage."

"I know." Fury sobered. "It's tough for her to try to keep up with a Species child. She had to stop tussling with him after he bruised her badly. He didn't understand how strong he could be. I'm at work often. He grows bored. Some of my friends have come forward. They take him to the park to run and play games. It would be nice if he had an uncle who could take him out to play when I'm busy though."

"I'm not fit to be around a child." He scowled. "He could learn nothing good from me."

"We'll never know for sure unless you try. It might be good experience if you ever have children of your own."

"That won't happen."

Fury shook his head. "Says the male who is obsessed with a female."

"I'm not."

Fury snorted. "Justice comes."

Darkness turned his head, his keen hearing picking up the slight footfalls. "So does Jessie."

"Here we go," Fury muttered. "I hope he's not pissed."

"Why would I be?" Justice stepped into the dining room, holding Jessie's hand. "What have you two been up to now? I don't see any bloody knuckles."

* * * * *

"So there you have it," Kat announced. "He's totally wrong for me in every sense."

Missy buttered toast and dropped each piece on a plate. She turned, setting it down on their dining room table. "You'd have problems with any normal guy anyway. I can see why you'd be attracted to a New Species."

"I don't see it."

Missy sat. "Eat breakfast."

"You're bossy today."

"I'm grumpy. We didn't get enough sleep last night and I'm kind of jealous. The only guys who are interested in me are creeps. They find out what I do for a living and instantly assume I'm some kind of porn star/sex fiend. The only action I see is what my imagination comes up with."

"Did you hear the part where I mentioned how he's never going to see me again? He was a control freak too."

"You intimidate men so you need a strong, take-charge guy."

Kat lifted her toast and bit into it. She chewed and swallowed. "He's over the top."

"Says the woman who made her last boyfriend cry."

"He wasn't a wuss. He put his foot down eventually."

"He stood up to you right until you told him to shove it up his ass if he thought you were going to quit your job to make him happy. Then came the tears and the shitload of flowers he sent. I was the one who had to sign for them and read the cards to you since you were too swamped at work to make the drive home. Do I need to remind you of the begging that went on?"

"We still would have had the same issues. I did him a favor by not calling him back. He was too needy."

"You walked all over him. Let's just cut to the chase."

"Jason was a great guy."

"He was. He was too nice though. You need someone tougher than you are and those men are hard to find. You aren't the easiest person to get close to. You need a man who won't allow you to keep him emotionally distanced."

"Well, Darkness knows all about building walls and keeping people out. I could take lessons from him."

"Exactly. He made you feel when you didn't want to. That's what you need. You're both hardheaded and stubborn. It sounds like a perfect match to me."

"I don't want to talk about this anymore. I said more than enough last night."

"So you've reached the deny-he-means-anything-to-you stage now?"

"Shut up."

Missy threw a piece of crust at her. "Are you at the anger stage yet? We really need to do something about this kitchen and I'm not doing it alone. How do you feel about knocking out cabinets?"

"I'm not in the mood."

"You'd get to smash shit."

"Then we'd have to put up the new ones."

Missy sighed. "Right."

"We should just hire someone."

"You can afford that but I can't. Fifty-fifty, remember? I'm sorry. I'm hoping this new series I'm working on will hit a bestseller list. That stove is one of the things we most need to upgrade. I'm tired of having to light the burners."

"You'll get there."

"I'm a poor artist but at least I can pay my bills. Why did I quit my day job again?"

"Because we both have faith that you are an excellent writer. Give it more time."

Missy wiped her mouth with her napkin. "You should call Homeland and talk to this Darkness. You look miserable and you only left there yesterday. Just admit you have it bad for him."

"It was just great sex."

"Right." Missy rolled her eyes. "Because you haven't ever been exposed to hot guys before while on the job and you risked your ass for all of them." She stood. "Lie to yourself but don't forget who you're talking to. I see through your bullshit."

"I only knew him for a short time."

Missy rinsed her plate, turned and leaned on the counter. "Sometimes you just know when it's right. I believe that. Hell, I make a living writing books about it. I write from my heart and I'm hopeful that I'll meet some guy who makes me feel. Love is messy and terrifying, Kat. It's not going to be the guy who is your type or someone you can walk all over. You'd be miserable within a year. I've seen it go down before. This is the first time you've met a guy you can't control, who doesn't bow down to your strong will, and he made you take risks you never thought you would. Use that intelligence of yours and figure it out fast because let's face it, you've got it bad. This is the guy. Go after him."

"No. He doesn't want me. He made that clear."

"You don't want him either, according to you. You're both full of shit. This is the first time I've ever seen you lose it, Kat. It's for a reason. You really feel something for him and it scares the hell out of you. You're into giving reality bitch-slaps. This is me calling you to the mat. *POW!*" Missy grinned. "Bitch-slap delivered."

"You spend way too much time with fictional characters."

"Did you think I'd really slap you? Give me a break. You'd beat my ass."

"I'd never hit you."

"That's because you know I can't fight and it wouldn't be any fun whaling on someone who just lay there and screamed. Stop being such a wimp and call Darkness. You'd be all over me if I had it bad for a guy but was too chickenshit to give it a shot."

"He doesn't want a relationship."

"What's your motto? Oh yeah. Shit happens. Deal with it. Neither of you were looking for someone but he nailed you. You said he avoided all women and hadn't had sex in a long time. He broke his monkhood streak for you."

"Monkhood?"

Missy nodded. "Is he religious?"

"I don't think so."

"Exactly. He couldn't resist you. If he's as cold and controlling as you say, that's big. You are a robot when it comes to your job and you broke rules. Big. Huge." Missy pushed away from the counter. "Stop being a dumbass and go after him. You two sound well matched."

"I'll think about it."

"You do that. I'm going to go write. Give a yell if you decide to rip stuff apart. I have my own frustrations to work out."

"Are you okay?" Kat turned in her chair, studying her friend.

Missy paused by the door. "Don't blow what could be a good thing. I'd kill to meet a guy who flipped my switches and made me feel what I think you do. I get to watch other people live through books and out my window. One of us deserves happiness. Go full-out, balls-to-the-wall for this guy. Life is too short and regret is the worst thing to live with."

"You're thinking about Chris."

Missy teared up. "Yeah. I always do. I had my chance but lost it. He wouldn't have moved to New York if I hadn't been so set on finishing college before I married. What did I do with my degree? Nada. He and his wife just had their fourth baby."

"How do you know?"

"I looked him up on the internet. You should see the nice family photos. They look really happy. That could have been me with my arm around him. I have a dog and a kitten instead."

"You have me too."

Missy grinned. "I know, but regardless of what your dickhead boss thinks, I'm not doing you." Her humor fled. "My sex life only involves a vibrator. I know battery-operated-boyfriends don't leave their clothes on the floor or fart in their sleep but I'd take all the flaws that come with a real person any day of the week over being so lonely. You can't solve that for me."

"I understand."

"I know you do. So go after this guy, Kat. Get messy and be scared of having your heart broken. At least try. I would."

"I can't exactly storm the gates of Homeland and I won't be allowed back in. He made that clear."

"Call and bug him. Don't let him sweep you under the rug. Give him hell."

"I'll think about it."

"You do that." Missy left, going down the hallway into her office.

Kat closed her eyes and sighed. "Damn." She missed Darkness but her pride would take a hit if she tried to call him.

Chapter Fourteen

ജ

Justice peered at Darkness over his desk as he hung up the phone. He lifted the paper he'd written on and passed it over. "That is a list of every name Jessie's father could get. He called in lots of favors. He'll text the address if you can identify her by name. He wasn't able to get ages or descriptions but he could pull one or two files without raising red flags. That's everyone Mason could issue orders to."

Darkness accepted the list and read each name. One made him pause. The other names didn't come close. He reread the ninth name again. "This has to be her. Katrina Perkins."

"Are you sure?"

Darkness looked up. "She said everyone really called her Kat. With a K. Katrina could be shortened to Kat. She used the name Kathryn Decker to enter Homeland. Don't they attempt to keep the first names close to their real ones when they go undercover? That's what Tim told me. They use similar names because it draws their attention easier when it's spoken."

"Agreed." Justice picked up his cell phone and tapped the screen. "It should take a few minutes."

"I want to send four teams out to retrieve her."

Justice set down the phone. "Why do you want this female brought in? You're the one who argued we should release her in the first place."

"All the information we received on Robert Mason alarms me. He's been transferred seven times in four years. He kept requesting this post. I believe it was for a reason. You read the file. He hasn't asked to be reassigned elsewhere. It's possible he's been working with Boris. They would have been able to have face-to-face contact to avoid leaving any traces of their meetings."

"There are no bank records to show any connection between Mason and the payments we made to the false account Boris set up. Mason seems clean."

"There wouldn't be. Mason is a smart male who catches the mistakes of others for a living. He sent agents after True's mate and then he sent in Kat."

"We still aren't sure why."

"I know." Darkness closed his mouth.

"You assume he wanted information on Jerry Boris. I agree. They are linked by marriage."

"He has to know we're digging into his background by now. I don't want him to go after Kat in an attempt to silence her. Boris set up Jeanie. Mason could do the same with Kat. These seem to be males who don't mind hiding behind females and allowing them to take the fall for their crimes."

"You want to toss her into interrogation?"

That wasn't the plan but Darkness just lifted an eyebrow. "She might have answers we need."

"I understand. We'll wait for her file to make certain she's the right female. The last thing we need is to bring in the wrong one."

"Let's order the teams to prepare."

"Two should do it."

"I want four."

Justice frowned. "You think this female is that dangerous?"

"I believe Mason is. He has agents at his disposal. He could order her arrested or sent on assignment somewhere. He could also hire someone to take her out."

"It's possible if he really is working with Jerry Boris. I really dislike that male. You weren't able to confirm their association beyond the family tie while you were in Medical?"

"He showed signs of high stress. I didn't want to kill him. You asked me to try to keep him alive."

"I read the updated medical report. You broke two of his fingers and inflicted cuts."

"Just a few."

Justice leaned back and sighed deeply. "You should have had the doctor present if you wanted to question him further."

"It's done." Darkness wasn't about to apologize.

Justice regarded him with an unblinking stare. Darkness didn't blink either.

"Fury feels guilt. You're aware of that, aren't you?"

"The male has no reason to. Why are you bringing this up?"

"He took you to Boris. I have a feeling you used that guilt to get him to agree. I have a problem with that."

Darkness stood. "I don't use emotions to force males to do anything. I laid out why I wanted to speak to Boris and he agreed."

Justice stood. "Fury has a blind spot where you are concerned. We're both aware of it, even if he isn't. Family is very important, especially when shared blood is involved. It's rare. Don't use him again."

Darkness clenched his teeth.

"Answer the questions he has, Darkness. You owe him that much."

"I plan to."

Justice sat. "Good. Go do that now while we wait for this file to arrive. I'll contact you as soon as it comes and have Tim put together four teams."

"I don't want Tim there."

"Trey can take lead then."

"I'll lead them."

Justice seemed unable to hide his surprise. "You don't like to leave the NSO."

"I'll make an exception. I demand to be put in charge of retrieving Kat."

A calculated look entered the other male's expression. "I see. Fine. I have calls to make."

Darkness strode out of Justice's office but didn't leave the building. He sought out Fury. The male was on the phone when he opened the door but he waved Darkness to a seat. He hung up a minute later.

"What did Justice say?"

"I'm surprised he didn't call you as soon as I left him."

"We've already spoken. Did you find out the female's real name?"

"I believe so. Justice is having the Senator pull her file to make certain. He agreed I could have four teams to go pick her up. We're just waiting for confirmation of the name and face matchup."

"I'm glad. She'll be safer here at Homeland."

Darkness hesitated. Memories flashed through his mind—bad ones. "Her name was Galina. She was an attractive female in her early thirties."

Fury frowned. "That is Kat's real name?"

"No." Darkness blew out a breath. "She was the female hired to come into the camp where my brothers…" He paused. "*Our* brothers were taken after they transported us away from Mercile Industries."

Fury swallowed, the muscles in his throat working. "Go on."

"She was a tall, blonde female with pretty light-green eyes. I don't know if that was her real name but she was so frightened I could smell her fear. They brought her to where I was being held in handcuffs. The guards removed them and one of them pulled his sidearm, pointing it at her head. He said for her to do her job or he'd shoot her. They left her there with me. I didn't know what to think."

"She was a prisoner?"

"I believed so. She fell to her knees and began to beg me not to kill her. I wasn't in chains. We all had explosive collars around our necks. They threw one outside the camp when we first arrived to show us what would happen if we breached the perimeter. It exploded as it sailed past the marked line. They used a second collar around the neck of a dog to show us that they could be detonated at will when the man in charge pushed a button. The dog was small and there wasn't much left of it. No chains were required. We knew escape would be impossible. They were coded every six hours and without a password they auto-detonated so taking out our captors wasn't a possibility. The male in charge of the code wasn't in our camp but video monitored the entire site."

Fury grimly regarded him. "Is this too difficult for you to discuss? I really would like to hear it but I don't want you to suffer."

Darkness shook his head. "The female was hired to have sex with me. I didn't want to touch her but she started to cry, informing me they'd kill her and her family if she didn't do her job. Rejection meant death. She swore she had two small children being held and that in her younger years she'd shared sex in exchange for money with humans. It's why she was kidnapped and taken to the camp."

Fury nodded but didn't comment.

"It made me less inclined to touch her, knowing it was forced, but I felt pity for her. She begged and removed her clothes, telling me about her young. They were babies, according to her. Both were toddlers. I didn't attack her. I just stood there when she started touching me. I hadn't had a female in nearly a year. She unfastened my pants and I responded to her touch. It was the first time a female had put her mouth on my dick."

Fury shifted in his chair. "Understood. That's something I couldn't ignore."

It didn't make Darkness feel any less guilty. "I didn't resist when she was brought to me every few days. They'd already taught me how to inflict pain. She was there to teach me how to seduce females into giving up information. That and, according to her, to help keep my aggression levels lower since I was the most dominant of the males. Our brothers took orders from me."

Fury opened his mouth as if he wanted to ask a question but reconsidered and closed it.

"They did look like us. We were very similar but I was the tallest and most aggressive. They forced us to train together and fight. My reflexes were faster and I picked up the fighting skills easiest. None of the humans would dare spar with me. They were afraid I'd kill them."

"Was she sharing sex with our brothers too?"

"They brought in other females, never the same ones twice for them and with less frequency. Galina was assigned solely to me. I believe they wanted me to form a bond." He paused. "It worked."

"It would be natural."

Darkness wished it were that easy. "We began to plot how to rescue her young and get my brothers freed from the camp. They took her to the secondary camp where the male in charge of monitoring us was kept. She told me about the tent and the many viewing screens she'd seen. The guards were lax with her since she was a female. I began to teach her how to fight. There were no cameras inside the tent where I was kept. I was as desperate to save her young as she seemed to be. It was her plan, her insistence we could do it."

Fury leaned forward. "It went bad."

"Worse." Darkness broke eye contact and looked down at his hands, resting on his lap. Pain tightened his chest but he held still, enduring the male's curious stare. "The humans in charge were forcing us to kill other humans. They weren't American soldiers but threats to them. It was taking a toll on us all. We'd been reassigned numbers, one through four. I was number one. At Mercile we dreamed of killing our captors and the ones harming us but it was different out there. These were strangers. We didn't know what their crimes were or why we were being forced to kill them. We were given an order, a timed mission, and the collars would blow if we didn't return to the camp. They would send humans with us who could activate the bomb collars to make certain we didn't deviate from the mission."

Fury's hands on the desk fisted and he lowered them out of sight. "That must have been hellish."

"It was. It was breaking us apart inside. Four was more sensitive than the others. He hesitated during the killing. We tried to cover for him and hold him together. He grew mentally unstable but we were able to hide it from the humans. Two had anger issues. He enjoyed the killing a little too much. He saw all humans as the enemy. We tried to conceal his flaw. Three was like you, Fury." He smiled, a fond memory surfacing. "You remind me of him."

"How?"

"He was very reasonable but he was one to watch closely when he was angry. He'd think about it before he acted." Darkness chuckled. "He stood up to me and did it in a way I admired. Very clever and always had my back. We were the closest. We would talk often and assess the other two, working as a team to protect their flaws. He could make me laugh. He had a keen sense of humor." Darkness rose and walked over to the mini fridge. "May I?"

"Help yourself."

He removed a soda and opened it, taking a drink. He couldn't sit any longer and paced instead, avoiding Fury's gaze. Darkness didn't know how to tell the rest of it. The male's chair creaked and Fury moved in front of him.

"Just talk to me. I want to hear it all."

Darkness set the drink down. "I don't think you'll want a bond with me after you do."

"Try me."

"I trusted Galina. I opened up to her and talked to her. She said she loved me and I felt highly bonded to her. I shared my fears. We were waiting for a human named Darwin Havings to leave her campsite. He had a lot of guards with him and the security would lighten when he was gone. It would give her a real chance at reaching the male monitoring our camp, force him to give her the pass code to unlock our collars, and then we could take out everyone at our camp to reach hers. She'd given me detailed directions on how to reach her. It was only a few miles away. We planned to steal their vehicles from her location. She said she could drive and she had friends who could hide us. We'd work out the rest later."

Fury kept close, watching him.

"Havings was set to leave in four days. That was the time we planned to make our escape. She was able to get an exact time, stating she'd overheard some of his personal guards making the arrangements. All of us were excited. We had no idea what awaited us in the out world but we were ready to find out. It had to be better than being returned to Mercile or staying there, forced to kill for them. She left my bed to return to her camp and orders came to us that we were going out that night to attack another group of humans. No one was to be left alive."

"It went bad," Fury guessed.

"There were no males there." Darkness clenched his teeth and took a calming breath. "It was all females and their young."

Fury wavered a little on his feet. "It was kill or die."

"Those females and children screamed when we entered their camp, cowering and crying. We terrified them. They weren't armed and the few weapons they had in camp, they didn't even go for or attempt to defend themselves. They were too frightened and shocked by the sight of us. It would have been a slaughter. We refused and left. The humans on scene ordered us to turn around and go back. We ignored them."

Fury didn't hide his look of relief and Darkness didn't blame him for feeling that emotion. Dread showed on Fury's features next. "They killed our brothers as punishment."

Darkness could have just nodded. That was the easy way out. It would leave the male peace of mind to know they'd died for a good reason. "I wish it were that simple." He took a deep breath. "Sit down." He took his own advice and returned to the seat on the other side of the desk.

Fury sat. "Tell me the rest."

"We were returned to the camp and the human in charge was furious. He was someone I would have gladly killed with my bare hands. He ordered us to go back but we refused. We stood there in the formation they'd taught us, five feet from each other in a line. That human ordered the one with the device controlling our collars to step forward and he took possession of it. He said he'd set off the collars if we didn't kill. We stood there. Four died instantly."

Fury paled but nodded. He said nothing.

"Three knew it was coming. He didn't attempt to run. There was nowhere to go. We couldn't attack with success and twelve guards had their weapons ready to open fire if we moved. He died next."

"You can stop. This is too hard on you. I get it."

A lump of emotion nearly choked Darkness. "You don't. Two didn't die that way. I killed him."

Fury paled more. "Why?"

"Two roared out from his rage and told the human he'd return to that camp and tear them apart. He needed a target for his anger. I could see it in his eyes. Watching our brothers die stole what sanity he had left. He was no longer the male I knew. The human in charge laughed, saying he knew we had a breaking point. He ordered us to return to the camp to kill those females and young. I could see Two wanted to shed blood. I reacted as soon as the human in charge turned his back to speak to the ones under his command, congratulating them on their success. I lunged at Two and broke his neck."

Fury closed his eyes and Darkness looked away. He couldn't blame the male for not being able to stand looking at him anymore. He lowered his head and stared at his hands—the same ones that had killed his brother.

"Darkness, look at me."

He forced his head up and held the other male's gaze. Tears shimmered in his eyes but he didn't glimpse hatred there.

"I'm so sorry," Fury rasped.

"So am I."

"I would have done the same. You couldn't allow him to strike out at the innocent."

"There's more to tell. Don't feel compassion for me yet."

"Nothing could be worse."

"The human in charge was enraged and began to curse. I returned to my spot in the line. I thought he'd either detonate my collar or order the guards to open fire on me. I was ready to die. I'd lost my brothers and the grief was deep. I'd never felt such pain before."

"I feel it with you."

Darkness held his gaze. "They returned me to the tent. I didn't understand why they allowed me to live until about half an hour later. The human in charge entered with six guards and Galina. I saw her and knew it was punishment. They planned to kill her in front of me to make me suffer more."

"Fuck." Fury reached up and used his finger and thumb to wipe away tears that threatened to spill.

"I apologized to her. She was going to die because of my actions. I thought if I attacked that they would kill me and she might live. I tensed, prepared to do just that."

Fury sucked in a breath. "They probably would have killed her anyway."

"She laughed, Fury. She told me I should apologize for all the times she'd had to pretend to enjoy my touch when I revolted her. At first I believed she was just saying the words in order to stall for more time but she kept going. She had lied to me. All of it was a lie. She worked for them for money. She'd had young but assured me she'd given them away at birth since she wasn't the motherly type. I stood there stunned while she berated me for being stupid and how she'd shared everything I'd told her with Darwin Havings. They knew we had flaws and she was brought in to gain my trust to discover them. They'd sent us to that camp knowing it only held females and young to see if we'd become the weapons they wanted us to be. We failed."

Fury snarled.

Darkness looked at his hands. "She'd been told the test was over, the program closing down, and that they were going to kill me. Darwin Havings had promised she could watch me die and she'd come to see it. She voiced her disappointment over not witnessing our brothers' deaths."

He looked up then. "Darwin Havings entered the tent and told her she was fired. He wasn't going to allow her to sell the information about what she'd been a part of and he'd never trust a whore to keep her word. He looked at me and said she was one woman I shouldn't mind killing. They left her alone with me."

"You killed her." Fury's tone was soft.

Darkness didn't flinch. "I did. She pulled a knife and came at me. I could have disabled her without death. I didn't. She attempted to stab me in the heart but I was faster. It was over in seconds. They trained us to kill with efficiency. I made it painless and fast."

"She deserved to suffer," Fury whispered.

Darkness nodded in agreement. "I cared about her though. Even then, after learning what she'd done. I had trusted her, had made that fatal error. I cost our brothers their lives." He got to his feet. "I'm sorry." He spun, heading to the door.

He tried to open it but Fury's hand darted out to press against it. He turned and looked into his eyes, the male standing inches away. "Do you want to fight? I won't hit you back. I deserve a beating at the very least."

Fury surprised him when the male grabbed him and jerked him against his body. He thought he might go for his throat but the male just kept his arms around him. It sank in that he was hugging him. He hesitantly lifted his hands but didn't know what to do or where to put them. Males didn't hug other males. At least never where he was concerned.

"You're my brother," Fury stated. "I don't want to hit you and I don't want to cause you any more pain. You've carried this burden far too long. No more. Let it go."

He relaxed. "I can't."

"I wish I'd been there with you."

"I'm glad you weren't."

"Hug me back."

He still hesitated.

Fury slowly released him and stepped back a foot. "You can't make me hate you and I sure as hell don't hold what happened against you. To trust another isn't a crime. The blame was on that female. You're a better male than I because I would have made her suffer. Do you understand?"

"You wouldn't harm a female."

Fury leaned closer, staring deeply into his eyes. "I would have in that case. You were kinder than I would have been.

You have no idea the murderous thoughts in my mind when Ellie wiped that blood from her kit on my hands while I lay there helpless on that floor. It's a good thing I was paralyzed. I told you I kidnapped her to do harm. I wasn't ready to kill at that point but the payback would have been hell if my attraction for her hadn't prevented it. Galina got our brothers killed for a stupid test result and money." His breathing increased. "You were more merciful, Darkness. Trust me."

"I even failed you there then. I should have taken a more vicious revenge for our brothers."

Fury gripped his arm. "Don't say that ever again. I'm just stating that you think you should be punished for your actions but I don't see it that way. You never let them or me down. You did your best to keep them alive and survive. Their deaths are on those humans. There was no way for all of you to walk out of there alive from what you've told me. The test was doomed to fail if they believed our wills could be broken to the point of no return."

"I don't think I should be punished but there's no room for forgiveness or redemption either. Parts of me died with our brothers and that female."

"You've saved lives, Darkness. Focus on that. You just helped us locate a Gift. We rescued her today."

"Her condition?" He hadn't heard that news.

"She is surprisingly well." Fury grimaced. "The humans seemed to treat her as if she were a pet."

"No sexual abuse?"

"Not that we're aware of but the reports are still coming in. We don't like to go at them full-force with our questions when they arrive. Medical has done a workup, though, and she's very healthy. There are no outward signs of abuse or scars to indicate anything severe in the past."

"Good."

"There's one problem we didn't expect."

"What is that?"

Fury hesitated. "She wasn't pleased to see other Species. There was some trauma in her past involving a male. We have no details yet but let's just say Jaded set her off. She hissed at him and was terrified."

"That's not good."

"No. A human had to be assigned to stay with her. It was at her request."

"Trisha?"

Fury hesitated. "It's one of the male task force members."

"I don't like it."

"Nor do we but we want her to remain calm while she settles in at Homeland. We need to earn her trust. She feels more secure in his presence and that's the important part."

"Were the humans who were holding her caught?"

"Not yet. They were out of the country. We have the humans who were assigned to guard her and keep her prisoner."

"Do you want me to question them?"

"It's being handled. I want you to give yourself a break, Darkness. Leave the past behind and have a future."

He had no words.

"Kat isn't Galina."

"She came here under false pretenses."

"They aren't the same. Kat left that note and it tipped us off to a connection between Boris and Mason. I'm sure they didn't want her to do that."

"It could be a setup to gain my trust."

"Or she could have chosen to give her loyalty to you instead."

"No female would do that."

Fury smirked. "Not all human females are heartless. Ellie is a good example."

"She's special."

"Perhaps your Kat is too."

"She. Is. Not. Mine."

Fury dropped his hand away. "You care about her whether you're willing to admit it or not. You want her protected. She's a trained agent. She could handle herself if she's in danger but you won't leave that to chance. You want her here where you can be certain no harm comes to her. I think part of you just wants to see her again."

"Mason could order her killed to protect his own ass. He sent her in here after Boris. That had to have broken some of their laws. She could testify against him."

Fury nodded. "True." He moved away from the door.

Darkness opened it. "I'm going to go home and shower while I wait for the file to come in. I'm leading the teams to bring Kat here as soon as we have confirmation of her identity."

"Brother?"

Darkness slowly turned. "What?"

"There's a lot we don't know about each other but I plan for that to change. You aren't going to keep me distanced any longer. Is that clear?"

"It's better that way."

"It's not happening. Ellie and I are going to invite you to dinner soon. We'll keep asking until you accept." The corners of his mouth curved upward. "I can be very annoying."

Darkness muted a growl. It sounded more like a threat than an invitation.

"I do know you well enough to say you're spewing bullshit about not having an attachment to Kat. Denial is a waste of time but regrets never fade. You've got a second chance when she is returned to Homeland."

"I won't spend time with her. I just plan to bring her to safety." He exited the office.

"I never pegged you for being an idiot," Fury called out.

Darkness halted and turned, glaring at the male.

"You heard me. She might be your one shot at happiness. Be a smart male and acknowledge that possibility."

He spun before he could say something he regretted. Fury didn't understand. He had good intentions but Darkness would never be the kind of Species to take a mate. He wasn't fit for a female. He had no heart. It had been destroyed long ago.

Chapter Fifteen

ဢ

"Kat!"

She bolted upright, Missy's alarmed tone waking her instantly. She grabbed for the nightstand drawer, fumbled for the knob and yanked it open. She felt for her gun and grabbed it.

"Black SUVs just blocked off both ends of the street." Missy lowered her voice. "I was people-watching out the window and saw them. I was kidding about the damn cookies."

Kat kicked off her covers. "They wouldn't be SWAT. They use vans." She rolled out of bed. "You said black?"

"Yeah. No lights or anything. They are just sitting there and nobody got out."

Kat made out her friend's shape near the doorway. "Do you think they saw you?"

"No. I was trying to clear my mind before bed and sometimes that hunky guy down the street goes jogging at odd hours. That's when I saw them pull up. I got out of bed for a better look. There are two on each end of the street, parked side by side, blocking the road. Do you think they are coming to arrest you? They are other agents, right?"

Kat moved around Missy and entered the hallway. "I want you to go up to the attic and hide. Leave Butch and Gus in your room so they don't give away your location. Shut the door first to contain them."

"I'm not leaving you." Missy trailed her down the hallway.

Kat walked to the window and used the barrel of her gun to part the curtain an inch and peered out. She had a good view of one side of the street. Two dark SUVs were there. The doors were closed and they didn't have running lights. She studied the vehicles.

"I don't think they are FBI."

"DEA maybe? I told you I thought that guy four houses down looked like a pothead. Maybe he's growing plants and they came to raid his house."

"No." Kat had a bad feeling. She carefully let the curtain drop and spun. "Get in the attic. I mean it. You know the hiding spot I'm talking about. Don't come out for anything unless I give you the all-clear."

"I bet they aren't here for us."

Kat grabbed her arm. "The DEA doesn't use black SUVs with tinted windows or this strategy." She heard something and peeked out the curtain again. All the doors were open on the SUVs and men dressed in black outfits, including headgear, got out. She saw white lettering on their chests and the assault rifles cradled in their arms.

"It's the NSO."

"Are you sure?"

"They are coming for me. Get your ass up in that attic."

"Why would they do that?"

Kat shoved Missy, herding her toward the hidden attic entry. She paused at Missy's bedroom door, glanced in to see the curtains pulled back and enough of the streetlight poured in to assure her the dog and cat still slept on the bed. She closed the door and forced Missy forward.

"I don't know why they are here but it can't be good. Hide. I don't want you involved."

"I'm scared."

"I don't have time to argue."

She pushed the panel on the wall and it popped open. Missy hesitated. "Maybe you should put the gun away or hide with me."

"No." She nudged her friend inside. "Move!"

Missy ran up the flight of stairs, her bare feet quiet on the carpet. Kat closed the panel and shoved the table in front of it. Why would the NSO come? It wasn't for a visit. They were in full tactical mode and ready to hit her house in the middle of the night. It pissed her off.

She rushed into her room, grabbed a bottle of perfume off the dresser and entered the hallway again. She sprayed it a few times as she moved down the hall. Darkness had told her it interfered with their sense of smell. She hoped it would hide Missy's scent trail.

A soft pop sounded from below and she gritted her teeth, stopping at the top of the stairs. She took a deep breath and peered down. It was dark at the bottom but the first few steps creaked. She inched her elbow over and waited. Her heart pounded as she slid the safety off her gun and gripped it firmly with both hands. They thought they were going to surprise her but they were the ones who were about to be caught unaware.

Wood creaked and she jerked her elbow, hitting the light. The stairwell and hallway below lit up. She aimed at the first man who came into sight when she glanced around the wall at the top, keeping most of her body behind it.

"Freeze, asshole!" She hoped she sounded as angry as she felt.

The guy in full gear paused, his face hidden by the shielded helmet. She adjusted her aim, pointing it at his throat area. Two more men were behind him and they raised their weapons, trying to get a bead on her.

"You take one more step up and I'm going to shoot you. What are you doing in my house? What does the NSO want?"

A loud snarl sounded and a fourth man appeared. His gloved hands gripped the barrels of the lifted rifles and shoved them downward to point at the floor. His helmet tilted upward as he seemed to stare at her. "Don't shoot her."

She recognized that voice. "This is how you visit, Darkness?" She didn't lower her weapon. "What is going on?"

He released the weapons, reached for his helmet and tore it off to glare up at her. "Stop pointing that weapon at Trey."

"You break into my house and have the nerve to give me orders?" She inched away from the wall a little but kept most of her body shielded. "No. Why are you here?"

"We need to talk."

"My doorbell works. So does the phone. Have you ever heard of either of those things?"

"Put down the gun, Kat."

"No. Explain to me why you brought an assault team into my house. Did you come to arrest me? This isn't NSO land. That shit doesn't work here. You want me? Get a warrant and send real cops to haul my ass in. I'm not going in willingly."

Darkness scowled. "Please aim your gun at me at least. You're making Trey sweat. I can smell him."

She glanced at the man she kept her gun trained on. "Fine. Tell them to back off."

Kat adjusted the barrel of her gun, lowering it slightly so the guy felt safe to move. He backed down two steps, spun and walked out of sight. He muttered something but it was too low for her to catch. Darkness jerked his head and the other two men left him standing alone.

"May I come up?" Darkness took a step forward.

"Nope." Kat aimed at his thigh. She would hate to have to shoot him but it didn't mean she wouldn't if he left her no choice. "What is going on? Why are you here to arrest me?"

"What makes you think that?"

She tilted her head and arched her eyebrows. "Really? You brought four SUVs full of your task force guys and you breached my house as if I'm some dangerous felon. Give me a break."

"We didn't see any cameras."

"There aren't any. I have a dog and a cat. They let me know something was up." It was a lie but she didn't want to mention Missy. Both of the animals were dozing. Butch was a horrible guard dog. He was a wuss and slept like the dead when he went to bed. He'd lick an intruder to death if he were awake. "What are the charges?"

"I need you to come to Homeland with me."

"No."

He took another step and gripped the banister. "Put the gun down."

"Start talking or get walking, Darkness. You didn't do all this for a booty call. People use the phone for those these days, just so you know. I didn't do anything wrong but say too much. You told me to leave and I did. We ended it on good terms."

"You could be in danger."

"You mean from the group of heavily armed men you brought into my house? There isn't a second stairwell up if they are looking for it and the windows on this floor are painted shut. The last owner was an idiot and I never got around to unsealing them. That's the nifty thing about central heat and air. That is one thing in this house that works well. Tell them not to bother to try to sneak up behind me. They can't. I'll also be furious if they hurt my pets."

"I ordered them to stand by and we didn't come to hurt you."

"That was nice of you. What was the plan? Grab me while I slept?" She hated that they could have done just that if Missy didn't have odd habits to fight her insomnia.

"You're in danger."

"No shit." She tightened her grip on the gun. "You put me in it."

"Not from us. We came to make sure you were safe and take you back to Homeland where our security is much better."

"Who am I in danger from then? I'm dying to hear this."

"Robert Mason is the brother-in-law of Jerry Boris. That is their connection. Your boss is the brother of Boris' deceased wife."

"Okay. Who is Jerry Boris? What's the deal with him?"

"I'll tell you if you lower the weapon."

She knew it was a reasonable request. "Fine but you stay there or it goes back up, am I clear? I will shoot you in the leg." She lowered it to her side but was ready to lift it if he tried to rush up the stairs. She didn't trust him anymore and resented it. "Talk."

"Jerry Boris was the director of Homeland when it opened."

"I thought he wasn't a New Species."

"He's human. We didn't run Homeland at first. They did until we took over."

That was information she hadn't known. "Okay. Go on."

"He was removed. He didn't like Species and made trouble for a few of them."

"Not exactly a job he should have had from the sound of it. So you arrested him for being an asshole?"

"He was offered a job running Fuller Prison."

She remembered her boss mentioning that place. "What is that?"

"It's where we send humans who have done us harm. Most of them are ex-Mercile employees we hunted down. Boris was good for that job since it made him responsible for humans only. Someone thought it would be a perfect place to put him. It was a political move to make sure he stayed silent."

"Got it. He couldn't bitch to the press if he still technically had a job. Why aren't those jerks in a regular prison?"

"Your justice system is flawed."

She couldn't exactly disagree. "Go on."

"It's a long story."

"And the night isn't getting any younger, nor is this gun in my hand getting any lighter."

Darkness growled.

"Don't you dare. You're the one who broke into my house."

"Boris had undetected access to our computer systems at Homeland and he used information from the tip line we set up to recover lost Species. Some of them were stolen from Mercile facilities after the first raid. It was televised and gave others warning, allowing them to escape and take Species with them. We hunt for the ones taken. He gathered information from the tip line, verified the solid leads and then erased the messages. He forced the NSO to pay him to obtain the locations of missing Species."

"That's all kinds of fucked-up."

Darkness put his foot on the step. "I'm coming up."

Kat raised her gun. "Stay put."

He stepped back. "We learned what he was doing after he tried to set up a human to take the blame for his crimes. He was arrested and we are holding him at Homeland."

"Got it. So Mason wanted him sprung because they are related. That is so unprofessional. What a dick."

"We believe Robert Mason might have been working with Jerry Boris. It's possible he was aware of his activities and tried to use his position with the FBI to protect him. That female Boris tried to blame was at Homeland and FBI agents tried to take her from us. She was the only one who could identify Boris on sight. He was using a false name."

She never had liked her boss or thought much of him. To hear he might be involved with something so low didn't come as a shock. "Mason really has issues when it comes to New Species."

"He could hurt you."

She shook her head. "No way."

"What were your orders going into Homeland?"

She debated answering but she believed Darkness. Her boss was a lowlife. "He wanted some intel and for me to look for Jerry Boris. I knew it was personal. He made it sound like you guys were a bunch of thugs who were kidnapping innocent people when you weren't drugging and raping women."

Darkness' mouth dropped open.

"I didn't believe that. I was under orders to go so I thought I'd make the best of it. I'd have a little fun, relax, and I liked running the classes. I never searched for Jerry Boris or tried to dig up dirt on the NSO."

"What did you put in your report?" He looked pissed.

"I didn't file one. I also didn't exactly let Mason know when I left Homeland. I wasn't ready to deal with him yet. I planned to go in on Monday and write about how boring everything was." She shrugged. "You know, how I never left the guest cottage except to teach the classes and that I didn't learn anything important. He would have been pissed but he calls me a set of tits and thinks I'm doing girls. He's not my favorite person."

"Doing girls?"

"He thinks I'm into women. I don't need to tell you I'm not. I pretty much hoped this would blow up in his face. I don't know how he got his position. He's kind of a tool but orders were orders. My ass got sent to Homeland. I had to go. How did you figure out I was FBI?"

"Your false identity was flawed. Our males didn't make a mistake. I told you that to make you think we bought your story."

"Understandable. I wanted to believe that you believed. Game well played. You did drop some hints though."

"So did you." He sneezed.

"Are you okay?"

"I smell perfume. It bothers me."

"My roommate sprayed some on before she left earlier." They stared at each other. "I didn't agree with why I was sent in. Mason is an ass."

"Why?"

"You should hear his theory on dogs sometimes. I'm not repeating it. It was bad enough the first time I heard it, especially since I have one. I'm guessing that he skipped sensitivity training."

"Your boss could want to hurt you to keep you quiet once it comes out that we have linked him to Boris."

"He sent in other agents too. What do you think? He's going to turn ninja assassin and take us all out? They didn't get far but I'm guessing they had orders similar to mine. He's not going to try to silence that many agents."

Darkness turned his head and murmured something she couldn't hear. Her grip on her gun tightened. She frowned when he looked back up at her.

"Is your team getting antsy? Why don't you tell them to get out of my house? I'd also like to suggest you call next time if you want to talk instead pulling this shit. It's rude."

Glass broke somewhere behind her and she spun, startled. Movement caught her eye and she jerked back. Darkness leapt, moving faster than her vision could track. He grabbed her and tore the gun out of her hand. It hit the floor and he lifted her off her feet, slamming her back against the wall.

"You son of a bitch."

"I warned you I could do that. It's not my fault if you forgot I didn't have to walk up each step to reach you."

"Put me down!" She grabbed his shoulders.

"I'm taking you to Homeland, Kat. It would make everything simpler if you just complied."

"Nothing about you is simple, Darkness."

"I know. I want to make sure you're safe. I'm taking you in and keeping you there for as long as I feel it's necessary."

"Mason isn't going to come after me. He'll be too busy protecting his own ass if everything you've said is solid. I need to go to work on Monday."

"You could work for the NSO."

"Doing what?"

He shrugged. "We'll figure something out."

"You can't replace the years I have already put in or my pension benefits. Do you even know what that is?"

He leaned in. "Stop."

Her eyebrows arched. "Excuse me?"

"You're being difficult and trying to piss me off."

"You brought an assault team into my house." She leaned closer until their noses almost touched. "I'm already pissed off."

He growled and his lips parted. "Kat." It was a warning.

She looked down, seeing his fangs. It was a reminder of the things they'd shared and how much she missed him. He could have sent someone else to pick her up but he'd come himself. That had to mean something. The feel of him against her couldn't be ignored either. She totally understood a love/hate relationship at that moment. She hated how he'd gone about it but loved seeing him again.

Her gaze lifted. "Sex isn't going to make me any more agreeable to go with you."

He sucked in a sharp breath, not able to hide his surprised reaction at her words. "Who said I was trying to seduce you?"

"You've got me pinned to a wall and you're making sexy sounds." She lifted her legs and wrapped them around his waist. The holstered handgun strapped to his thigh dug into her skin so she adjusted that leg higher, hooking her ankles together behind his spine. "You could have just called if you wanted to fuck me again." She released his shoulders and fisted one hand in his hair. She yanked, jerking his head up and to the side since he didn't expect her to do it. She pressed her nose against his throat and inhaled. "What cologne do you wear? It smells good."

He stiffened but didn't jerk away. "It's just me."

Kat smiled at the sound of his voice deepening. "What was it you said to me? Oh yeah. You smell so good I could just eat you."

His hands on her hips loosened their grip and slid to her ass, firmly cupping her there. He pushed her tighter against the wall and she could feel his erection against her pussy through the layers of clothing.

"Kat, don't."

"I thought you were going to never see me again?" She ran the tip of her tongue across his skin, paused right under his earlobe. "Did you bring handcuffs, Mr. Control?" She nibbled on his earlobe. "Control this." Her hands started to roam his body wherever she could reach.

His chest started to vibrate and his fingers flexed. He made a deep rumbling sound and tried to move his head away. She gripped the other side of his face with her free hand and kept him there. She released his ear and went for his neck, kissing it and using her teeth to gently nip him. Her thighs squeezed his waist and she wiggled against him.

Darkness snarled low. "There're fifteen males waiting for us to leave."

"I rated a sixteen-man team? I'm flattered."

"I didn't know if we'd come across another team. I wanted enough males with me to assure that I could get you out. I think Mason will try to kill you."

She stopped kissing him and leaned her head back, staring into his eyes. He really thought she was in danger. It sank in that it wasn't just some ploy to see her again. Part of her was sad about that but the fact that he'd go to such lengths to make certain she was safe warmed her heart.

"You care about me."

He closed his eyes. "Can we discuss this later?" He glanced down the hallway. "We need to go."

"Darkness?"

His dark eyes narrowed. "What?"

"I'll go with you on two conditions."

"You don't have a choice."

"Two conditions," she repeated.

"What do you want?"

"I get to stay at your place with you if I return to Homeland since I'm in such supposed danger."

A muscle in his jaw clenched. "What is the second one?"

"You get to guard my back in the shower. In the stall with me."

"No."

"I might wash your back while we're in there."

He growled low. "I don't do that."

"I don't let a bunch of guys kidnap me but I might allow it to go down if you agree."

"No."

She licked her lips and liked the way he noticed. She pressed the muzzle of his gun against his thigh. Her thumb assured her the safety was on. "I stole your gun, sweetheart. You were kind of distracted. Do you agree to my terms after all?"

"You won't shoot me." He looked furious.

"I won't." She moved the barrel away. "That's beside the point. Don't ever underestimate me, baby. Meet my terms or I'm not leaving with you."

"I don't live with others or shower with them."

"I won't be coming with you then."

"I'll knock you out and take you over my shoulder. You'll wake at Homeland."

"You'd deck me?" Her eyebrows arched in question. "Possibly break my jaw or cause a concussion?" She didn't really believe it.

"I'll handcuff you the way I did before."

"I allowed that. That was just a token fight. One of us would get hurt if we really went at it. Agree to my terms or get out of my house."

"You're stubborn."

"You are too. I think it might be why we're attracted to each other. You want a woman with some give but not too much."

"That's not why."

"Really? Then what do you like about me?"

"Everything *except* your stubbornness. Human females are supposed to be more passive."

Kat chuckled. "You'd be so bored if I were."

"You're brave and you aren't afraid of me."

"I don't believe you'd hurt me. You're a good man, Darkness."

His scowl returned.

"You are." She shoved his gun back into the holster and reached up to caress his face. "Even if you don't want to admit it. You want me to go with you? We sleep together and share showers. I don't believe I'm in danger but if you want to cover my ass, it better be in the literal sense." She winked.

He eased his hold on her and helped her stand. "Let's go."

"May I at least change out of my pajamas first and grab a few things?"

"Why? According to your terms, we won't have a reason to wear clothing. I'll have the team retrieve your pets and seal the broken window. I had them toss a rock to distract you."

"Leave them. My roommate will come back in the morning. She can deal with the window too." She didn't want to involve Missy. She didn't believe her boss was a threat, regardless of what Darkness alleged. "The pets are more hers than mine anyway. I'll just push the table in front of my door so they can't get in there. The dog can twist a handle with his mouth and I don't want them having an accident on my floors if she runs late. Her pets, her piss."

She walked over to the table hiding the entry into the attic and gripped it. It would allow Missy to get out. "I'll go to Homeland with you. I know it's going to be fine. I'll just be there for a few days." The walls were thin so she was certain Missy could hear her. She shoved the table in front her door. "Let's go." The faster they left, the less chance of Missy being found.

Darkness took the lead. "Stay close."

"I plan to."

Chapter Sixteen

ಬಂ

"This isn't the front entrance," Kat announced, staring out the windows.

"No it's not. We have a few hidden ways in." Darkness sat next to her in the second row of seats. "This is a house we bought."

The SUV pulled into the garage and the doors closed. No light came on. The driver switched on a flashlight and got out. In seconds the overhead light came on. It was an otherwise empty space. Darkness opened his door and slid out. "Follow me, Kat."

She scooted across the seat, careful of her long sleepshirt, not exposing too much of her thighs. She stood and expected them to lead her inside the house. Darkness took her elbow, turning her toward an exterior door.

"We are going to the backyard and entering Homeland that way," he informed her softly. "I could carry you. I told you to put on shoes."

She'd wanted to leave her house fast. There was a long list of things she wished she could have packed. "I'm good." The yard was dark and soft grass cushioned her feet. "So far."

A low whistle sounded from one of the other three men. It was dark but she could make out shapes. A section of wall covered in what appeared to be vines opened, showing street behind it. The professional side of her didn't like that they had hidden ways into Homeland.

"I thought thirty-foot walls surrounded all of Homeland."

"They do."

She exited the backyard and saw the road wasn't wide and the massive wall stood across it. "That opens up too?"

"Nope. Not that section. We're going up."

"Great."

Ropes dropped from the top, hitting the ground. She watched a male grab hold of each one and climb hand over hand. Kat clenched her teeth. She hated to admit it but it had been a long time since training and she hadn't been in a nightgown the last time she'd had to scale a wall.

"I see a problem."

"I don't." Darkness turned her. "Wrap around me." He lifted her in front of him, chest to chest.

"You can't climb and hold me."

"I can. You're a hundred forty pounds."

"A hundred thirty-eight."

"Close enough. Just hold on tight and don't let go. The officers above us will grab you when I am within reach. They'll lift you the rest of the way to prevent your skin being scratched by the brick."

"Why couldn't we just go through the front gates?"

"Mason could be having them watched. We don't want him to know where you are. It's safer that way."

She hugged his neck and wrapped her legs around his waist. "My underwear is going to show."

"That's why I'm waiting to climb last."

"You're so thoughtful." She hoped he didn't miss the sarcasm.

"Let's just avoid talking right now."

She buried her face against his warm neck. His uniform was bulky. "You drop me and I'm going to be pissed."

"I'll make sure you land on me if we fall."

"That isn't helping."

"Trust me," he rasped.

That was the hell of it. She did. Otherwise she wouldn't have agreed to go with him. She'd wanted to see him again. "Okay."

"They reached the top. Ready?"

It was on the tip of her tongue to say no. "Sure. This should be fun."

"Don't make me laugh."

"I won't talk again."

"Good."

He released her and walked forward, paused and then a rope bumped her back. She clung tighter. His arms tensed and she squeezed her eyes closed. No way did she want to peek. It was insane for anyone to hold the weight of another while they climbed. They weren't even clipped together. He kind of jumped and she locked her thighs tighter around him, also being careful not to choke him in her fear. His arms tensed as he used his strength to pull them higher, hand over hand.

It went too fast. He stopped. "Reach up one arm."

"Fuck."

She lifted her head and peered up. Two dark figures were above her at the top of the wall. One bent and reached for her. She had to let go of Darkness and trust strangers. It wasn't her first choice but it was the only way to get up there. It took courage to ease her hold and reach out. A firm, gloved hand wrapped around her wrist.

"I have her."

"Give them your other arm and then let go of me with your legs," Darkness urged.

"I'm going to get even with you for this," she muttered

Darkness bent his legs, forming a kind of seat for her ass when she let go of him. Another gloved hand got a firm hold on her wrist. She eased the grip of her thighs on Darkness and the men pulled her up.

A third man suddenly appeared. He moved between the two when they brought her to the top of the wall. He gripped her hips and just lifted her the rest of the way. They released her the second she was on her feet. She tried to step back out of the way. One of the men growled and turned, hooking an arm around her waist.

"Careful."

She turned her head and gasped. There was a waist-high lip on the outside wall but there wasn't anything but emptiness behind her. A few steps more and she'd have pitched off the wall and fallen to whatever lay below.

"Thanks."

Darkness made it the rest of the way up and lunged, tearing her out of the grasp of the man keeping her immobile. "What are you doing, Book?"

"She almost backed off the wall."

"Thanks." Darkness suddenly bent and Kat gasped when his shoulder hit her hip. He rose with her secured there. One gloved hand yanked her shirt and held it in place high on the back of her thighs.

"Put me down." Kat didn't fight but she did frantically grab for some part of him to hold on to. It ended up being the lower edge of his vest. She was too afraid he'd drop her off the wall.

"Shut up, Kat. We're going to the stairs. It's the safest way to get you down."

She closed her eyes and hung there. It wasn't dignified and she mentally went over ways for payback. "I can walk."

"This isn't a well-lit section," another male informed her. "You almost fell once. We can see."

And I can't. She quieted and knew when they reached the stairs. From the sound Darkness' boots made when they descended, they were metal and felt a little rickety. She imagined the flimsy ones she'd once used to board a plane.

She was grateful she couldn't see. He finally stopped going down and paused.

"Thank you."

"It was good to have an adventure," the guy who'd spoken before responded. "Are you taking her to a holding cell, Darkness?"

"She's not a prisoner. This was for her safety. I'm taking her to my place. Will you let Security know, Book?"

"Of course. I'll also inform Supply that you'll need things for the female."

"I'll handle it." Darkness didn't put her down but spun fast enough to make her dizzy. He moved fast. He probably considered it walking but she'd have been jogging at that pace.

"Can you please put me down?"

"You're barefoot. We're not too far from the men's dorms."

"Great. You can walk me past a bunch of guys so they can see my bare legs and ass too."

"You're covered."

"How far are we from your house?" He kept walking and didn't answer. "Hello?"

He wrapped his other arm around the back of her knees, covering more of her skin. "The cottage next to the one you stayed wasn't my home. It's where I stayed to be close to you. I live in the dorms."

"Fantastic. Don't a bunch of New Species guys live there?" She pictured a fraternity house in her mind. "This just keeps getting better and better."

"I'm taking you through the backdoor. We shouldn't come into contact with anyone else this late. They are either on shift or sleeping."

He stopped and released her with one arm. A beep could be heard and she knew he had opened a door with his ID card. They entered a well-lit, tiled hallway.

"Put me down," she ordered again.

"You're testing my patience, Kat. I'm not in the best of moods. You demanded we share quarters so that's what you're getting."

He had a point. She'd thought they'd go to his house though, not a building full of other men. Kat winced, hoping he didn't have a roommate. That would be awkward. It would be worse if he didn't even have his own bedroom. They entered an elevator but it was empty. That was a relief. It opened and he stepped out onto a carpeted floor and strode down a hallway before pausing in front of a door.

Another beep sounded and the door opened. He carried her inside and bent, putting her on her feet. She stood and shoved her hair out of her face. The door closed and she turned, studying the small living room. A kitchen area was to the left and an open door was across the room.

"This is it. Welcome to my home." Darkness didn't sound happy. "It's a one-bedroom and considerably smaller than the guest cottages. The bathroom is through the bedroom. There's food in the fridge if you're hungry and drinks are there too if you get thirsty."

She turned to face him. "It's cozy though a bit sparse."

"All I needed was a couch, TV and bed. I don't spend much time here."

She swallowed, feeling nervous. "You don't need more than that. I get it. I'm not home much either."

He frowned and reached for the front of his vest and removed it. He just tossed it on the floor next to the door. "You would be more comfortable at your cottage. Tell me when you're ready to go there." He walked across the room and into the bedroom.

She followed. He flipped on the light and took a seat on a big bed. She watched him remove his gloves then his boots. He stood and pulled his shirt over his head, revealing his bare stomach and chest. His dark gaze pinned her where she stood.

259

"I'm going to shower. I'm sweaty after climbing the wall. I sleep on the side of the bed closest to the door and don't open my nightstand drawer. That's a rule."

"Dirty magazines?" She wanted him to smile. He looked angry.

"Weapons. Don't touch my guns, Kat. Am I clear?"

She nodded. "Why are you so angry? You're the one who forced me to come here."

"I wanted you at Homeland, not living with me."

He spun, stalked into the bathroom and firmly closed the door. Kat walked over to the bed and sat down. So much for him coming after her because she hoped he'd missed her. He got credit for keeping his word. He could have just dropped her at guest housing and left. Just because she was in his apartment didn't mean she was welcome in his personal space or that he'd be happy to have her there. He obviously wasn't.

The water came on in the other room and she stared at the door. She could imagine how the rest of the night would go. He'd come out and probably turn off the lights, ignore her. It was stupid. Mason wasn't a danger to her so she didn't need to be there. Darkness was just being paranoid.

She stood and walked over to the bathroom door. Her temper flared. She tested the knob and it turned in her hand. One deep breath and she shoved it open, stepping into the quickly steaming room. The door to the shower stall was glass and Darkness stood totally naked under the hot spray of water. He turned his head and his eyes narrowed.

She grabbed the bottom of her nightshirt, yanked it over her head and dropped it on the counter. Her thumbs hooked her panties and she bent, shoving them down. "I'll be damned if you ignore me."

He appeared shocked when she straightened and crossed the small room. She jerked open the door and stepped inside with him. He had to move to make room. A soft growl came from him but his cock stiffened and he kept glancing down her body.

She saw body wash on the shelf built into the tile wall and grabbed it. She dumped a handful on her palm and lifted her chin. "Turn around. I promised to wash your back, remember?"

He didn't move, seemingly frozen to the spot.

"Fine. I'll wash your front."

"Kat," he snarled and flashed fangs.

She went right for the good spot. She stepped forward and wrapped a soapy hand around his dick. He gasped and jerked, his back hitting the tile. She pressed up against him and rubbed his shaft.

"I want to make sure you're really clean." His shaft became more rigid in her hand, growing larger and thicker. Harder. Her hand trailed to the base and then to the tip. "You don't want to talk? Fine." She looked down between them and adjusted her stance until the head of his cock brushed her stomach. Water ran between them.

He didn't touch her but just stood there allowing her to play with him. She used her other hand to admire his abs. It was something she'd wanted to do forever and the lighting allowed her to see the way those muscles tensed and quivered at her light exploration.

He had a perfect cock. It reddened as it grew really hard. Some of the soap washed away, making her reach for the bottle again. She noticed the way he breathed faster. He kept his hands fisted at his sides, spine and ass pressed firmly against the tile. She poured out more soap and ran some of it over his stomach, trailing it upward to his ribs. She massaged his shaft again, even slipping her hand lower.

He snarled when she gently cupped his balls and he spread his legs to allow it. Kat felt victory and looked up at his face. His eyes were closed, his lips parted in an almost grimace. She lifted his dick higher and got even closer so the head and underside of his shaft rubbed against her stomach. Her attention focused on his nipples. She couldn't resist and went for one with her mouth.

"Fuck," he hissed.

She released that nipple and went for the other. It was about time he knew what it felt like to be tortured a little. He'd done it to her many times. She curled her fingers around his shaft and gripped him with enough pressure that she knew it would feel good. She stroked him up and down.

He wrapped his arm around her, one hand cupped her ass and his fingers dug into her skin. He shifted his hips, forcing his dick against her skin. She sucked on his nipple harder, raking her teeth over the pebbled tip.

His other hand fisted in her hair and he tugged. It wasn't enough to hurt but she released him with her mouth and looked up. He lowered his chin and stared at her. Passion harshened his features but hunger showed in his eyes.

"Damn you."

He closed his eyes and threw back his head. Hot semen shot across her belly. She looked down, watching him come. His stomach quaked, muscles rolling under the skin a little, but the sight of his cock held her attention the most. He came a lot. He released her ass and gently closed his hand over hers, urging her to let go of his shaft. She opened her fingers.

"You are so sexy," she admitted.

He took a deep breath, his chest expanding, and lowered his chin. His dark eyes snapped open and she spotted the yellow flecks in his irises. That was the Darkness she liked to see most. He released her hand and curved his fingers around her hip.

"Payback is a bitch, sweetheart."

He let go of her hair, reached up and grabbed the detachable showerhead. He suddenly moved and she would have slipped on the tiles but he twisted her and pressed back, pinning her to the cold tile wall. He moved in close, his body trapping her in the corner. His foot covered one of hers, firmly securing it between them. He let go of her waist and bent a little, hooking her under one knee. He lifted until she stood on one foot.

Kat grabbed at his arms to keep her balance. "What are y—ahhh!"

Water pressure slammed against her clit. It was shocking, sudden and felt amazing. He held the nozzle against her pussy. Kat gripped him tighter and locked her knee to keep from falling.

"Too much," she pleaded.

"Too bad," he growled. He dipped his head and pushed her face to the side. His hot mouth bit down on her throat. It hurt slightly but it felt good too. He growled, moving the nozzle a little to stroke her with the water.

"Fuck." She was going to come fast and hard. Her hips bucked and it only made it more intense. She just couldn't hold still. It was impossible with that much pleasure overload.

"Darkness!" She cried out his name when everything inside her exploded.

Her leg gave out but she didn't fall. The showerhead hit the tile instead and his strong arm caught her around the waist. He lifted her, releasing her trapped foot at the same time. She wrapped her arms around his neck and just panted.

"This is a disaster about to happen," he muttered.

"You caught me. The worst thing that can happen is if one of us slips in here."

Water sprayed up at them from the dangling shower nozzle. Darkness reached behind them and it shut off. "No. It's not, sweetheart."

She liked him calling her that.

Darkness held Kat and muted the roar that wanted to come out. To throw back his head and let out his frustration would feel good. Almost as good as her hands had been on him. His dick was hard again and he wanted to fuck Kat. Watching her climax always did that to him.

He used his shoulder to open the glass door. He stepped over the lip and onto the tile floor. Water would soak it but he didn't give a damn. She'd left the bathroom door open so he just strode out into the bedroom and tossed her on his bed.

She gasped, not expecting that. Hell, he could relate. He went after her, just dropping onto the bed. He grabbed her leg and shoved it out of the way, exposing her pussy. He needed to taste her. It beat the alternative. He didn't have condoms at his place and it was too late to go get any from Supply. He'd have to go to Medical, probably wake someone.

He buried his face and ran his tongue over her slit. The sweet flavor of her drove him insane. One of her hands dug into his wet hair, fisting a handful. He didn't care if she pulled it. Nothing was going to distract him. He fastened his mouth over her clit and used his fangs to push some of the tender flesh back to expose more of the fleshy bud. He flattened his tongue and rapidly rubbed.

Kat moaned and shifted her legs. One foot ended up on his back. She moved under him, her hips rolling. He pressed her down, pinning her.

Purrs tore from him and he didn't discourage the sound. It would add to her pleasure if he vibrated. He moved his hips, his dick hard and painful. It helped a little to rub against the comforter but being inside her would be better.

She came, saying his name. He growled and crawled up her, not gentle when he grabbed her arms and shoved them out to her sides. He used his arms to pin them there and he spread his thighs between hers, forcing them wider. He lifted his ass and shifted until the tip of his dick found heaven. He drove into Kat.

Darkness watched her face. She was wet, hot and nothing was between them. He fucked her hard and fast, unable to do anything less. He saw no pain though, just pleasure twisting her features. She tossed her head and made sounds that urged him to be even a little rougher than he should.

The bed creaked, his neighbor would hear the headboard slamming into the wall but he didn't give a shit. He'd beat Smiley if the male complained. Kat's pussy clenched tighter around him until he had to slow a little. She was so tight he had to fight to move. He growled, released one of her arms, reached down and snagged her behind her knee. He yanked up, making it easier for him to move.

Kat came. Her arm hooked around his neck and she threw her face against his shoulder, screaming out. He started to come but snarled and pulled out of her, turning his hips. His semen coated her thigh. He knew he hadn't done it in time. Some was inside her.

"Holy fuck," she panted.

"Are you on the Pill?"

Her eyes opened and she appeared confused. "What?"

He released her leg and grabbed her jaw. "Are you on birth control?"

She blinked, still looking confused. "No."

"Son of a bitch." He released her and rolled away, getting to his feet. The closest thing to hit was the wall. His fist slammed into it. Plaster gave way under his knuckles.

"Darkness?" Alarm sounded in Kat's voice.

She was to blame. She didn't know it but she was. He spun, snarling. "You shouldn't have come after me in that shower. You always have to push."

She sat up in the middle of his bed. Her nipples were beaded and there was gooseflesh on her still-damp skin. It meant she was cold now that they weren't distracted. He stomped into his bathroom and tore one of the towels off the holder. He spun and lost his footing on the slick tile, almost falling before recovering his balance. It was just another reminder of how she drove him insane. A large puddle of water tracked from the shower all the way to the carpet in his room. He made it to the bed and tossed the towel at her.

"Cover up. I can't see you naked right now." It just underscored what they'd done and how he'd lost control.

"What's going on?"

He clenched his teeth.

Her expression softened. "Talk to me. Please?"

He said nothing.

"We were having a great time and now you're tearing up your hand. It's bleeding. What did I do? Did I say something? I was kind of out of it."

He still said nothing. He couldn't. Wouldn't.

"You asked if I was on birth control." Her features went lax and she paled a little.

The quietness of the room became uncomfortable. Kat took the towel and got off the bed. He noticed red marks on her ass cheek when she turned, wrapping it around her. He'd done that in the shower. She might end up with a bruise. It was just another thing for him to regret.

Kat faced him once the towel was firmly wrapped around her middle, tucked tightly to keep it in place between her breasts. She cautiously approached him and just stared up at his face. He didn't move.

"Everyone will hear that we're sharing your place." Her voice softened in tone. "They probably heard us having sex too. We got kind of loud. The secret is out." He hated when tears filled her eyes. She blinked them back though. "You asshole."

That surprised him. She raised her hand and slapped him on his upper arm. He glanced at where she'd struck him then back at her. It had hurt but not enough to do damage.

"The condoms weren't because you were worried that someone would smell you on me. You can get me pregnant.

You should have told me. I'm not a moron. I can add up the clues." Her chin jutted out. "Deny it. Go ahead."

He clenched his teeth tighter.

She backed up and almost tripped. He moved, catching her arm to help steady her. She tore out of his hold and more tears welled. She blinked those back too. "I could have taken precautions. You and your damn secrets."

"Humans can't find out, Kat."

She spun away and wrapped her arms around her waist.

"It would put our young in danger. They could try to kidnap them and sell them. Mercile tried to breed us for a reason but failed. It helps keep some of the worst of the fanatics from coming after us when they think this generation will eventually die out."

The silence stretched again. He wished he knew what she was thinking. He calmed. "I will take you to Medical in the morning. There's a pill you can take to make sure you don't get pregnant. I lost control."

She refused to look at him. Her body quaked but he wasn't sure if it was from a chill or emotional since he couldn't see her face. She sucked in a breath and turned.

The anger wasn't a surprise when she glared at him. "There are children at Homeland?"

He said nothing. He couldn't tell her.

"Are there?"

"It's dangerous information."

Pain flashed across her face. "What? You think I'm going to tell the press? What part of 'I'd never hurt the NSO' do you not understand? Do you think so little of me that you honestly believe I'd put kids at risk? Jesus! Then to add insult to injury, you casually mention the morning-after pill? You really are a bastard."

He probably deserved that. He just didn't know how to respond.

Her hand opened over her stomach. "Don't worry. I'm a smart woman. I catch on fast. If your little slip in control has consequences, they won't be yours. You don't want to let anyone in. What's protocol?"

"I don't understand."

"What do you do if I'm pregnant?" She paled. "They can't force me to abort, can they?" She backed up, inching closer to the side of the bed to put space between them.

"No." He hated seeing raw fear in her expression.

She didn't relax by much. "I can't leave though, right? No." She answered her own question. "That's how you've kept a lid on it. You'd have to keep them all here or at Reservation. Hidden away so no one knows they exist."

Darkness frowned, not liking just how accurate her musings were.

Kat paced, hugging her waist. "Reservation. It's too risky to have them here. I was allowed in. That's why everyone needs an escort. No accidental run-ins with kids. Smart." She ignored him, seemingly lost in the thoughts she spoke aloud. "Shit." She stopped and stared at him with a horrified look. "Assholes like Darwin Havings would do anything to get their sick hands on infant New Species. They'd be able to raise them and twist their minds. He and men like him would do what was done to you and your brothers by making them kill."

Darkness nodded.

Tears filled her eyes again. "I get it."

He stood still while she approached him. He almost expected her to slap him again but she surprised him when she pressed her forehead against his chest. She just stood there. He had the urge to put his arm around her, only hesitating for a moment before following his instincts and doing it. She didn't flinch away.

"What's protocol?"

"I don't know."

"What do you do when you think you might have accidentally gotten someone pregnant or there's a chance of it?"

"I haven't had it happen before. We should go to Medical and get you tested, Kat."

"Right. Pregnancy test. They should be able to tell in a few weeks. I guess I'm not making it back to work on Monday." She laughed but it sounded harsh, bristly. "I might need that NSO job after all."

"Kat." He wasn't sure what else to say.

She lifted her head away from him but didn't look up. "I'm tired. I didn't get enough sleep last night and only about two hours tonight." She walked around him and entered his bathroom.

He tracked her with his gaze. She dried her hair then put her nightshirt back on. The panties stayed on the floor since they were wet. She turned and finally looked at him. "Do you have a spare toothbrush?"

"You can use mine."

She snorted. "Great. Now you're willing to share something personal. Forget it. Deal with bad breath until you can get me a new one." She exited the bathroom and crossed his bedroom, studying the bed. "We got the top blanket wet. Do you have a spare?"

"Yes. I'll get it," he offered.

"Why don't you go tend to your knuckles? They haven't stopped bleeding. I'll deal with this. Just tell me where it is. You still want the side by the door? I assume you do it for safety reasons."

"Top shelf in the closet on the right side. Kat?"

She paused. "Everything will seem better in the morning. That's a motto I really want to believe in right now. Just...let's not talk any more tonight."

Chapter Seventeen

✌

Kat still reeled from the night before. Darkness returned to his apartment with a few bags in hand. He closed and locked the door behind him. "I got you a few things."

"A toothbrush?"

"That and a few other things."

"Thanks."

He entered the kitchen and used the counter to remove the contents. "I'll make you food."

"I already had toast. Your bread is about to expire."

"That isn't a good breakfast. I know how to make omelets. I picked up eggs and ham and cheese for them. Give me ten minutes."

"No thanks."

His focus fixed on her. "You're still angry."

"I'm tired of playing verbal games with you. I'm not going to eat anything you fix me."

"Why? I'm a good cook."

She pointedly stared at the bags. "You didn't happen to stop by your medical center and pick up any pills to put in my food without me knowing, did you?" She watched his face for a reaction.

His mouth drew into a fierce line. "You think I'd do that?"

"I have no idea what you're capable of. I was thinking while you were gone. I want to be taken to guest housing. I'm voiding the terms I demanded. I don't want to live with you anymore. I have no idea how I feel right now but I'll be damned if you make a decision for me, Mr. Control."

He moved fast, dropped to his knees in front of her and leaned in. He growled. "I would never do that. It's your choice if you want the pill."

She'd thought of nothing else since waking. Darkness had slept with her but stayed on his side. She'd hugged the edge on hers, not wanting to touch him. It hadn't been a good way to spend their first night as roommates. The concept of having a baby was scary but she didn't hate it. The circumstances couldn't get much worse. His eyes were almost black and he looked angry. It wasn't anything new. "What if I am and want to have it? Are you going to make my life miserable?"

He paled. "Your life is in the out world. You'd abandon your child here?"

He might as well have spit on her. "Fuck you. No." A new suspicion hit. "Other women have done that?"

"No."

It made her feel slightly better but then the insult hit. "Just shut up now. I remember what you keep in your nightstand drawer. Don't make me shoot you."

He jerked back.

"You really think so little of me? That I'd go through a pregnancy and dump a baby with you? I want to be taken to guest housing now."

"I didn't mean it the way it sounded. I just can't see you being happy here. You said your career was the most important thing to you."

"It was. Then I blew it to hell because I thought you were special. My mistake. Lesson learned. Robert Mason is going to make certain of that, right before his ass is booted out too, when all the details come out of what he sent me here to do. Hear that sound? It was my career flushing down the toilet."

"I'm sorry."

"It's not your problem. I did this. I know where the blame lies."

He rested on his heels. "What can I do?"

"Take me to guest housing right after I borrow something to wear and brush my teeth." She stood, making sure she didn't bump into him. "Who do I talk to about getting hired?" She paused by the bedroom door and studied him. "Can you help me get a job here?"

"Yes."

"That would be great." She bit her lip. "Do I have to go to Reservation if I am pregnant?"

He shook his head. "There are young here."

She walked into the bedroom and paused, not sure what to do. Her life had turned messy. That reminded her of Missy. How was she going to explain why she couldn't ever come home? To lie outright would be necessary but it would break her heart. They were like sisters. Their house was half her responsibility. How would Missy make the payments? She couldn't do it without her. It would go into foreclosure. Her best friend would hate her and be homeless. Her knees weakened. She walked to the bed and sat.

"Cart before the horse," she muttered.

The chance of her being pregnant was small. *What are the odds?* She'd always had protected sex when she was dating someone and considering getting involved with them. She'd jumped into it with Darkness because he'd been that hot. It was also common knowledge that New Species didn't carry diseases and weren't able to have kids. That proved her theory that nothing was set in stone.

"Kat?" Darkness hovered in the doorway. "Are you well?"

"No. Just give me a few minutes."

He didn't leave but instead crossed the room. "Talk to me. I hate seeing you this way."

"I hate being this way," she admitted.

"What can I do? Just tell me. I'll do it."

She should have asked him to leave but instead she slid off the bed and he gasped when she threw herself at him. He wrapped his arms around her then moved them to the bed. He sat and she climbed on his lap.

"Just hold me and don't talk."

He rested his jaw on top of her head. She stayed there. His arms tightened and he adjusted her a little on his lap, moving them closer to the headboard until he leaned against it. It felt nice when he stroked her back. She relaxed.

"Talk to me, Kat. You're disturbing me."

That struck her as funny. She laughed, then sobered. "I am disturbed."

"I keep calculating the chances. They are in our favor."

"I know. It was one time."

"I will make a call and find out when the soonest time is that we can find out if you're pregnant."

"Okay. Talk about bad timing and two people who shouldn't breed."

He tensed. "The child wouldn't have deficiencies because you're human and I'm Species. My genetics would dominate yours. He'd be born Species."

She tensed too and looked up at him. "I meant because we're both workaholics and not exactly a couple in a relationship." She wiggled and got free of him. "Thanks for holding me. I'm good now. I almost forgot how anti-human you are."

He growled. "That's not what I meant."

"Deficiencies. Keep it up." She glanced at the nightstand drawer to make a point then looked back at him. "God, you're an ass. I'm going to shower. Will you please bring me that toothbrush and find something for me to wear? I don't want to

have to ride to the cottage in my nightshirt and wet panties."
She fled at that point, before she really got mad.

She slammed the bathroom door but didn't lock it. She
really wanted to brush her teeth and have something to wear.
It would be hard for him to bring them to her if he couldn't get
in. She turned on the shower and stepped inside, hoping it
would cool her temper as she adjusted the water temperature
to a little colder than she normally liked. Darkness just pissed
her off. He had moments where she remembered why she had
fallen for him then he blew it by opening his mouth.

Falling for him. Try fell. It disheartened her to know he'd
never really return her feelings. He wouldn't allow anyone to
break through those emotional walls of his. It had been foolish
to think that living with him and making him get to know her
better would work.

Darkness uttered a curse and reached for the phone
beside the bed. He dialed Trisha at home and she answered on
the second ring. "Hello?"

"It's Darkness. Are you busy?"

"No. What's up?"

"I need you to act as a doctor."

"That's what I am."

"I meant, I need confidentiality. I have a question."

"You don't want me to mention it to Slade, in other
words. Hit me with it. I'm curious. He already left so he won't
overhear anything."

"I made a mistake."

"Okay. What kind?"

He hesitated. "When is the soonest you can discover if a
female is pregnant?"

The silence on the other end lasted about ten seconds.
"Oh. You and that FBI agent? Okay." She paused. "Five days
from the time of your, um, accident. The condom broke?"

He clenched his teeth. "I refuse to discuss that."

"Fine. A blood test could tell us in five days. When did it happen? I can schedule you both to come in."

"Would it be accurate?"

"Yes. I've gotten results in three days but five for sure. Species hormone levels hit fast when a woman is carrying one of your kind. They also have accelerated pregnancies. You're feline so it would be a twenty-week gestation or thereabouts. It would mostly depend on how stubborn the baby would be. Some like to come a little early while others have hung in there an extra week or so."

"I don't want anyone else to know."

"Not even her?" She paused again. "There are options. You need to tell her. She has to make a choice."

"I informed her. She didn't want to take a pill."

"She knows you can get her pregnant? You're going to have to inform someone at Security, Darkness. What if she wants to leave? Or tells someone outside?"

"She understands the importance of keeping it a secret."

"It's still a risk. You understand that."

"I'll handle it but not right now."

"I take it that this accident happened recently?"

"Thank you, Trisha." He hung up.

Darkness stood, went into the kitchen and grabbed the new toothbrush. He paused next to his dresser to find Kat a T-shirt and a pair of his drawstring exercise shorts. He entered the bathroom and placed them neatly on the counter. He soaked in the sight of her with her head tilted back under the spray of water. The smell of conditioner filled the bathroom. His attention lowered to her breasts. His dick hardened. He turned before she caught him admiring her and left the bathroom.

He fled his apartment and went down the hall where he knocked on the door beside the elevator. Book answered, wearing a pair of boxers, obviously ready for bed after his shift. The male arched an eyebrow.

"Do you have condoms?"

"You don't have any? We all got issued some recently."

He resented being questioned. "I did but I threw them away. I didn't think I'd have a need for them." He had thought Kat wasn't coming back to Homeland.

A smile curved the male's lips. "Hang on." Book strode across his apartment and disappeared into his bedroom. He returned quickly, a box in hand. He tossed it and Darkness caught it. Book halted before him. "Anything else?"

"Thank you."

"I'm not surprised. You seemed to want to rip my arm off last night when I held that female to keep her from stepping off the wall."

"Could we keep this between us?"

"Sure. I'm glad you found someone."

He spun and walked away. Book chuckled. Darkness resisted slamming his door when he returned to his apartment. He didn't like to amuse other males. He locked the door and took the box to his bedroom. He put them in the drawer next to his two handguns and sat on the bed. The shower still ran in the other room.

Kat would leave. She'd remain at Homeland but no longer be in his home. That should have made him feel pleased. It didn't. She'd be alone. Other males from her classes would hear she'd come back. His memory flashed to the feline in the bar who'd offered to share sex with Kat. Others would too. He growled.

He'd hurt her feelings and insulted her. She'd taken his comment about the baby wrong. He hadn't meant it as an offense. He'd just wanted to assure her the child would be healthy and strong if they'd created one. He stood and walked to the bathroom door, put his hand on the knob. The water shut off in the other room. He remained still, listening to her moving around.

He released the knob and backed away, taking a seat at the end of the bed. He waited. She took her time but she finally appeared. Her skin was pink from her shower, her dark hair wet, and his clothes were baggy on her small frame. She paused when she saw him watching her.

"I'm ready to go."

He should just escort her to guest housing. They'd prepared it for her when he and the teams had left Homeland to pick her up. He stayed seated.

"You said he." She slightly tilted her head. "When you talked about a baby. He. Why did you say that?"

She'd replayed their conversation in her head, he guessed. "All Species children are male."

"No girls?" Her skepticism was clear.

"No. As I said, they get our genetics. Sons look eerily similar to their fathers. Almost miniature replicas. None are fully grown yet but it appears they might be that distinctly close. I haven't seen any of their mother's features in their faces."

Her expression softened. "He'd be the spitting image of you?"

It affected his breathing when her words sank in. His son, if he had one, would. He'd never considered having a child. He experienced unfamiliar emotions. Kat stepped closer, alarm showing widened eyes.

"Are you okay?"

"It just really hit."

"You're panting. Slow it down." She stopped in front of him and bent, her hands on his shoulders. "You're having a panic attack."

"I don't suffer from them."

"Yeah, well, you're doing a great impression. Just breathe in and out. Slow it down. Do you have a paper bag?"

He forced his lungs to work properly. "I'm fine."

"Every time I want to hate you for acting like a robot, you do something I don't expect." She hesitated and then surprised him by straddling his lap. He gripped her hips to keep her from falling back. "There's only a slim chance of me being pregnant, remember? Worst case, it won't be the end of the world. I'm pushing thirty so it's about the time that I would have been considering having a kid anyway. My mother will be thrilled. I'm not sure if that's a plus or a minus. I can't be around her for more than a day without wishing I'd been adopted. She's a really negative person." She stroked her hands down his arms. "I won't expect anything from you."

He didn't enjoy the emotions he felt then either. Anger. Hurt. But not relieved.

"Well, you helping me get a job here would be great. Either way, I'll probably need one and really soon. Do employees live at Homeland or elsewhere? I have to figure out living arrangements and see if I can afford to keep my best friend from disowning me. It's kind of a long commute from my house if I'm not pregnant. I can do it though."

"Disowning you?"

"I own half of that house you broke into. Missy can't make the payments on her own. I can't dump that on her. She's a starving artist." She smiled. "At least that's what she calls herself. She has plenty of food. It's just that she doesn't make what I do and her earnings can be erratic, depending on how her novel sales are."

"Novels?"

"She writes sexy romance stories." He looked bemused. "I need to call her at home. I won't mention anything about this mess. I just need to tell her I'm okay."

"You can't."

"She knows where I am." She hesitated. "She was there last night. I didn't want her involved so I had her hide. She won't tell anyone. She knows about us too. I trust Missy with my life, Darkness. We've been best friends since the ninth grade. We both had crappy home lives and bonded in a big way."

He licked his lips, debating. "You'll be angry and I don't want you to be."

"What does that mean?"

"Will you be calm?"

"I am."

He still hesitated. She was in a good mood, on his lap. He didn't want her to yell or hit him again. It didn't hurt but that was beside the point.

"A team performed a sweep of your house last night after we left. Only three teams returned with us to Homeland. One remained to make certain no one came after you. We stationed them there."

She paled. "Is Missy okay?"

"She's fine. Snow caught her but he didn't harm her. I heard about it this morning when I left to run errands."

"You waited until now to tell me?" She looked angry. "Where is she?"

"At your home. The team is there with her. I spoke directly to Snow. He's a good male. She was only frightened for a few seconds when he sneaked up behind her. He realized she lived there because her scent was everywhere and she was barely dressed. He knew she wasn't an intruder. He swore she was fine with having the team there and that she hadn't demanded they leave."

"He's New Species, right?"

"Snow is but the other three members of the team are human."

She appeared to calm. "Well, that should excite her. She always wanted to meet one. She's not handcuffed or anything, is she?"

"No. They gave her free roam of the house. They will stay there in case anyone comes after you. She'll be protected. I wanted them captured if anyone showed up."

She shoved, surprising him enough that he fell backward. Kat climbed up him, reaching for the phone on his nightstand. "I'm calling her just to make sure."

He snagged her waist and rolled, pinning her under him. "She's fine. Your phone lines aren't secure. I'll set it up if you insist on speaking to her."

Kat didn't struggle and her supple body made him aware of her as a female. His borrowed T-shirt outlined the shape of her breasts, holding his attention.

"Don't get that look."

He glanced up to discover her frowning. "What look?"

"You know the one. Your eyes are changing color again. I have a one-mistake-a-day limit and we reached it already."

"I got condoms."

"That was nice of you. A little presumptuous too. What makes you think I want to have sex with you?"

"You demanded to live with me." He liked a challenge and Kat always provided that. "Did you assume I wouldn't touch you?"

"I told you I voided the terms. I'm going to guest housing."

"Are you?" A spark of humor surfaced and he grinned. "Only if I allow you to get up and leave."

He almost expected her to claw him when she reached up and cupped his face. She caressed him instead. "I don't understand you. You know you're confusing, right? One minute you're cold, the next you're hot."

Her assessment was dead on. "It's your fault."

One eyebrow arched. "Really? Why is that?"

"You drive me crazy. I don't know if I should let you leave or not." He wanted to be honest. "You also confuse me."

"At least we're feeling the same things." She stared at his lips. "Is kissing still off the table? You've got the best mouth."

"I'm not ready for that yet." It was how he felt and he wanted to be honest.

She slid her hands up and her fingers played with his hair. "At least you're letting me touch you. That's progress. You have the silkiest hair. I like how warm you are too, as if you're always running a fever. I was cold last night but I didn't know how you'd react if I curled up to you. Would you have let me do that or would you have gotten out of bed?"

"I would have held you but I knew you were angry. It's why I stayed as far away as possible."

"I'm surprised you didn't hide the knives. You're not the most trusting person. I was joking when I threatened to shoot you."

"I'm learning that."

Kat held his gaze. "I'm not *her*, you know."

He didn't like being reminded of the past. The *her* she referred to was clear—Galina. "I'm aware."

"Can we make some new rules?"

"Why?"

"I'm tired of walking on eggshells and you being wary of everything I do or say."

"It's difficult for me to trust."

"I get that. Really, I do. People lie to me all the time in my line of work. We're not on duty though. This is just you and me, Darkness. I'm willing to climb out on a limb for you. Can you at least try to do the same for me?"

"I don't know. What do you want?"

"No more lies. Clothed or when we're naked. I don't want us to have to analyze everything we say to each other. Good, bad, whatever. We'll just say it the way it is."

"No one can ever be that candid."

"I can be with you. I'll tell you how I feel too. You might not be comfortable with that but one of us has to do it. It won't be easy for me either, so remember that. You make me want to take risks. I'm hoping I inspire you to do the same one day."

Kat always amazed him. He wasn't sure how to respond.

"Here goes." Her breasts pushed against his chest when she inhaled deeply. She blew the breath out before she spoke. "I was attracted to you and thought I could just be happy with sex. I didn't expect the things you make me feel. They range from anger to frustration to just wanting you to hold me. I can't seem to get close enough to you but I want to. I don't want a series of one-night stands or whatever you want to call it. I want more."

He reacted the same way he had when he'd realized they might have created a child. His breathing increased rapidly and his heart pounded. He couldn't speak, wasn't even sure what to think.

Kat gripped his cheeks. "Slow your breathing. Don't have another panic attack. I just said what I want. I know you're not ready for that. This is me expressing my feelings." She sucked in a breath and blew it out slowly. "Do what I do."

She kept breathing that way and he mimicked her. It helped a lot and the unpleasant physical difficulties passed. Kat smiled. She caressed his cheek.

"That's a compliment to me."

"That I'll listen to you?"

"That I make Mr. Control lose it."

"That's why I can't give you more." He didn't want to hurt her but she wanted honesty. "I don't have panic attacks."

"Didn't. Past tense. You've had two."

Anger stirred. "I can't do this." He tried to lift up and away from her but she refused to release his face. He paused.

"It's scary and messy when you start to fall for someone, Darkness. I heard that from someone who gave me a reality bitch-slap. This is yours. You can physically haul ass away from me but it's not going to stop you from thinking about me or admitting that I've gotten to you. It's a two-way street." She opened her hands. "It's your choice if I stay here or move to guest housing. Can you at least think about it for five minutes before you make a decision?"

He rolled off the bed and strode into the living room. He paced, considering her words. She didn't follow him. He kept glancing at the door but she allowed him space. He cursed. The urge to punch something surfaced but he refrained. Kat drove him insane. His first instinct was to ask her to leave but he admitted deep down that he didn't want her to go. It was the most torn he'd felt in years.

Chapter Eighteen

ℰℴ

He was still in the apartment but the silence in the other room unnerved Kat. What would Darkness decide? She stayed on the bed to give him time to think.

She sat up after about five minutes, slid off the bed and tentatively crept to the doorway. Darkness paced between the kitchen and front door, his expression stormy. She leaned against the doorway, watching him. He was a handsome man but not her type. Missy had been right. She had no idea how to manage him. She didn't even think it was possible. He was a wild card and she couldn't even hope to predict what he'd do next. His nose flared and he stopped, turning his head her way.

She smiled. "Still thinking?"

"You can stay."

Her smile widened. "Good."

"I can't promise you anything, Kat."

"This is a start."

"I've never lived with anyone before. I could be bad at it."

"I'm willing to chance it. I'm probably no picnic either. I'm pushy and you piss me off. That means I'm going to get in your face. Forget that whole docile thing I've heard you guys expect from women."

"I'd hate that."

"Good."

"You'd be terrified of me if you weren't so brave."

"That's a good term to use."

He arched an eyebrow in question.

"Some people would call it something less flattering. Like stupid to not run when you're angry." She stepped away from the wall. "Are you still willing to make omelets? I'm hungry. Birds eat bread. I actually have an appetite."

"I'd never drug you with anything."

"That was a cheap shot. Sorry. I just know how much you'd hate it if I ended up pregnant."

"I'd make a bad parent and a worse mate."

"Let's forget about it for now. Why worry about something that probably won't happen? You picked up condoms. We'll use them."

"I called one of our doctors. A blood test can answer that question in five days."

"That's fast."

He entered the kitchen, yanked open the fridge. "So is a pregnancy."

"What does that mean?" She followed him in, wanting to help.

"Let's discuss that if you are pregnant. The less you know, the better."

"You mean it's classified and you're afraid I'll tell someone."

He held the egg carton in his hand and nodded. "Don't take offense. I have to inform the NSO that you're aware of the children."

"Will it help if I sign a blood oath of silence?"

"We aren't that severe. A confidentially clause would do. That would alleviate some of their worries. Your laws in the out world don't hold up here but ours do in yours."

"That sounds fair." She chuckled. "Sarcasm."

"I got that." He smiled. "We'll take any advantage we can get."

"I don't blame you. New Species got the shit end of the stick for most of their lives. It's about time the tables were turned."

He laughed, the sound deep and wonderful. It lit up his expression too. She loved seeing it.

"I've never heard it put that way before."

"Graphic, yet effective, to get the point across. What can I do?"

"Stay back. The kitchen is small. We'd be bumping into each other otherwise." He paused. "I have to warn you that I only know how to put together a few meals well. Cooking was new to us and I only took an interest in learning to make what I enjoy eating most."

"Is it a short list?"

"Omelets, bacon, steaks and grilled ham and cheese sandwiches."

"I know how to open cans and reheat what's inside them. I never learned how to cook. Missy kept me fed. She is a fantastic cook and loves to bake. I like everything you said. How do you feel about canned corned beef hash and soups? I've got that down pat."

He chuckled. "There's always the bar. They serve excellent food. At Reservation they have a cafeteria with huge buffets every day. Most of the males there don't cook or have kitchens in their homes so they feed everyone."

"We won't starve. That's a bonus."

"It is."

"Tell me about Snow. Any chance he'll mate Missy and bring her here? She could feed us."

He gawked at her.

"What? It's a valid question. She's single and always complains about how lonely she is. I've seen your guys. She wouldn't stand a chance if he decided to bring her home. She'd probably drive the SUV for him."

"He's single but I have no idea if he wants a mate."

"He might if she makes him cookies. I told you that girl can bake. Does he read?"

"I assume so. Why?"

"She writes hot sex in her books and is forever asking everyone she meets to read them. I hope he has a good sense of humor."

"He reminds me a little of myself."

"Shit. That's not good."

He scowled.

"Missy isn't like me. We're polar opposites. She is passive. He wouldn't walk all over her and break her heart, would he?"

"I don't know."

"Would you kick his ass for me if he does?" She grinned, teasing him.

A dark eyebrow rose and he shook his head. "You're joking."

"Not if he really breaks her heart. I might try to kick his ass for real then. Would you back me up? Maybe hold his arms so he doesn't pulverize me with a few punches?"

Darkness sobered. "No one would dare hit you."

"Why is that?"

"I'd kill them."

He wasn't joking. She realized that. "You're so hot when you talk that way."

He set a pan on the stove and looked away. "Do you want to eat or end up on my bed?"

"That's a tough decision." She meant it.

"We'll eat first. You said you were hungry. Stop distracting me."

"But it's so fun."

A smile curved his lips. "Do you want me to overcook your omelet?"

"No." She turned. "Do you have a washer and dryer? We need to do something about your damp comforter and I could use some clean clothes that don't smell like they just came out of a bag, which they did. Thanks for picking me up some things."

"I'll handle it after we eat. They are downstairs on the first floor."

"Just tell me where to go and I can start the laundry."

"No."

At his sharp response, she swung around to look at him. "Is it breaking a law?"

"This is the men's dorm. The first floor will be flooded with males at this time of day."

"Women aren't allowed?"

"They are but you won't be walking around without me."

"Right. I need an escort. I just assumed that it would be fine as long as I kept inside the building."

"That's not why. Some of them will approach you for sex." His tone deepened to a growl. "You want the truth? I'd hurt someone."

She smiled. "You are jealous."

That earned her a glare.

"I would never accept. You're the only man I want."

"I'd still hurt them." He focused on the pan. "Stop distracting me. I'm not an expert at this. I'd like the first meal I make you not to be a disaster. I'm attempting to impress you."

"Strip out of your clothes if you ruin breakfast. I'll still be impressed."

He softly cursed and licked his thumb. She knew he'd burned it. She couldn't help but laugh. "Sorry. I'll go into the bedroom. Call me when it's ready. You okay?" She turned, heading toward the other room.

"I'm fine. I heal fast."

Kat grinned as she entered the bedroom and stripped the bedding off the mattress. It needed to be washed too. He wouldn't let her do laundry but she could at least get it ready for him. Her morning had started out bad but it had gotten a lot better. Darkness was letting her stay. They were both making an effort to see how living together would turn out.

She searched his room and found an empty laundry basket in the bottom of his closet. It was sad to see only his uniforms hanging on the closet rod. She glanced at the tall dresser, assuming he folded most of his casual wear. She tossed the bedding into the plastic container, hefted it up and carried it to the front door where she set it down.

"That smells wonderful."

"Do you want ham and cheese?"

"Yes." She went after the towels they'd used and his outfit from the night before, minus his vest, and added everything to the pile. "Where are your dirty clothes?"

"I washed them yesterday. I had time to kill while I was waiting for your file from the FBI."

That crumpled her good mood. She approached the counter. "My file?"

"Yes."

"How did you get that?"

He plated their food. "We have a contact in your world who was able to obtain it."

"Who?"

"Senator Jacob Hills."

The name was very familiar. It clicked. "His political platform is the NSO and your civil rights. Isn't he also the father of Jessie North?"

"Yes."

"Did you read anything interesting about me?"

"You have a good record. There is no criminal activity in your background and your previous supervisor seemed to like you from his evaluations. You aren't very close to your family." He paused. "You—"

"That's enough. I sound so boring. It's bumming me out."

He lifted both plates and came around the divider. "I usually eat with a plate on my lap."

She accepted the one he offered. "You need a coffee table." She just sat on the floor.

"I can acquire one today. I'll take one from another apartment."

"Just like that? Nobody is going to mind you stealing theirs?"

He chuckled and sat across from her. "Not all of them are occupied. We transfer back and forth from Homeland to Reservation."

"We need drinks." She rose and grabbed two sodas after learning what he wanted. She sat again. "I have a question."

He peered at her. "You have many of them. What do you want to know?"

She glanced around. "Does someone else live here when you're at Reservation?"

"No. I spend most of my time here so it's a permanent residence."

"Okay."

"Why do you ask?"

"I was just wondering where I'd live if you have to go there." His expression tensed and his eyes darkened. "What? You plan to stay that long?" She dropped her gaze. "Let's eat. This looks really good."

They ate in silence. They were almost finished when the phone rang. It startled Kat but Darkness just got to his feet and answered it in the kitchen. He spoke low and then hung up.

"I have to go."

"Is everything okay?"

"Fury wants to talk to me in his office. He's taken over while Justice is on vacation for a few days."

"Where do you guys go?"

"He went to Reservation with his mate." He picked up his plate and put it in the sink. "Don't leave the apartment or make calls. Can I trust you to do as I ask?"

"Yes. I want to talk to Missy but I will do it when you get me a secure line. I heard you earlier."

He looked uncertain.

"Trust me," she urged. "I won't leave the apartment or touch your phone. Even if it rings. I understand your need for security and procedure. I might not be a big fan of it and think it's a bit paranoid but rules are rules. I have to follow them while I'm at Homeland."

"Thank you. I'll be back soon." He walked over to the door and picked up the hamper.

Kat watched him go and finished her omelet. She'd keep her word.

* * * * *

"What can I do for you?" Darkness sat in Fury's office. He'd made a few stops on his way.

"What took you so long?"

"I had errands."

Fury leaned forward and braced both elbows on the desk, resting his chin on his fists. "Is there something you want to tell me?"

"No."

"I took over for Justice, remember? I read all the security reports."

"Nothing happened in the out world. One team is still there but I checked on my way here. They are fine. It's quiet and no one has attempted to break in at the home they are occupying."

"What about Katrina Perkins?"

"She's here. I was able to retrieve her."

Fury frowned. "You didn't take her to guest housing. I had a spare officer without a job since he'd been assigned outside duty to keep an eye on her." He lifted his head and tapped a finger on a file. "This is a report of a disturbance at the men's dorm. The male below your apartment reported loud noises coming from your home. He was too afraid to approach your door. He's a primate from Reservation, only here for a few weeks a year."

That angered Darkness and he decided to speak to the male who'd dared complain.

"Don't. I can almost read your mind. You have Katrina Perkins at your home. She's not at guest housing so I'll assume she's still there."

"I didn't break any rules. I asked one of the males to keep an eye on my door. Kat is secure. I followed protocol."

"This isn't official, damn it. You're living with her?"

"She insisted. Those were her requirements to return to Homeland with me."

Fury's eyes widened. He recovered from the astonished look fast. "She's a human female. You could have subdued her easily and just forced her to go with you."

"I didn't want to do that."

The male had the nerve to laugh. "And the disturbance in your home? I take it she wasn't happy there?" He studied Darkness. "I don't see injuries."

Darkness growled low and stood. "I have better things to do than be the brunt of your amusement."

"Sit down. That's an order."

Darkness froze. "You said this wasn't official."

"Not for the NSO. Family business. What is going on? Talk to me."

"What is wrong with everyone?" Frustration rose. "Why does everyone require me to talk? She's here and fine. I'm not breaking rules by having her in my home and I had a male watch her since she's not a mate. That's all you need to know."

"Please sit."

Darkness slammed his ass in the chair and it groaned under his weight. He crossed his arms. "It's none of your business."

"I care anyway." Fury stood and rounded the desk, taking a seat in the chair next to him. "Is this better? We're just two males having a conversation. Talk."

"She wanted to stay with me. There's nothing else to say."

"You don't allow anyone to get that close."

"I told her that."

Fury schooled his features. "Is there anything else going on?"

"No." He avoided meeting Fury's curious gaze.

"Trisha called."

Darkness snarled. "So much for confidentiality."

"She just said we needed to speak. I'm the closest male to you. What does she know that I don't? Did you lose your temper and harm your female in some way?"

Darkness shot to his feet, resisting the urge to punch him. "I'd never harm Kat."

Fury stood. "I never thought you would do that with intent but you wouldn't be the first male who worried they might have harmed one in the heat of passion. Trisha was worried and knew to contact me. You're a difficult male who refuses to seek help from anyone. What is going on? Will you please tell me? Should we go outside and fight until you're willing to open up to me again?"

Darkness sat. "I won't fight with you."

"Good. Ellie hates it when I mess up my hands. She likes to hold them and scabs aren't her favorite texture." He sat and turned his chair to face him. "Why is Trisha worried about you? Her intentions were good. She cares. We all do."

Darkness grimaced. "It's annoying."

"I understand but we have to stick together. It's all new. Are you attracted to Kat?"

"You're playing shrink?"

"I'm being a friend and brother. It helps to discuss things with others who have experienced them. I fought emotions for Ellie. Is that what is happening to you? It may feel as if you're losing your mind because love makes you question your sanity. It's normal. You aren't injured, Kat isn't, so that means you must have contacted Trisha to evaluate you. You're not suffering a meltdown."

"That wasn't it."

Fury's silence, as if he were waiting for an expanded explanation, calmed him a little. He took a deep breath and blew it out. "I lost control."

"How? Did you lose your temper and throw things?"

He gripped the arms of the chair. "Sexual control."

"Humans aren't as fragile as we imagine. They aren't made of glass. Ellie can handle me. She enjoys rough sex at times."

"I came inside her before I completely pulled out." He spoke softly, a bit humiliated to admit it. "It felt too good and she was biting me. I lost it."

Fury paled. "She's not on birth control?"

"No."

"Shit. Do you want me to smell her? I could tell you if she's ovulating." He leaned forward and gave him a sympathetic look. "You'll need to talk to her if she is."

"She's a smart female. I had a fit of temper afterward. I didn't have to tell her. She figured it out."

Anger twisted Fury's features. "You should have informed me right away."

"She's not going to betray that information."

"She works for the FBI. For Robert Mason." Fury stood so fast it knocked the chair over. "You hardheaded asshole. You're putting Salvation and every other child in danger. I'll have her brought in. She needs to be put on lockdown until we can be certain."

Darkness lunged out of the chair and tackled Fury. They both hit the top of the desk. He snarled in his face and barely resisted punching him. "No one goes after Kat. She isn't going to put your son or others at risk."

Shock whitened Fury's features but he grabbed hold of Darkness' shirt and shoved some of his weight off. "Get control of yourself."

Darkness let him go and rolled away to stalk across the room, putting space between them. "She stays with me."

Fury slid off the desk and glanced at the mess of papers that had ended up on the floor. He glowered at Darkness. "I wasn't going to hurt her."

"She does work for the FBI. That makes her very aware of the kind of dangers our children could face. She is willing to sign confidentiality papers to assure us of her silence. We spoke of it already. Have them drawn up but don't send anyone after her. You do and they'll end up in Medical."

Fury fixed his shirt and kept his distance. His anger faded and he masked his features. "You trust her that much?"

"I do." It sank in slowly to Darkness that he wasn't just defending Kat to keep her safe. He believed she would keep her word. He really did trust her. "Fuck." He moved forward and bent to pick up the scattered paperwork. He hadn't meant to go after the male. "Sorry. I'm on edge."

"It's caused by fear."

Darkness' head snapped up. "You're wrong."

"That female might be carrying your son. You can't just ignore it."

"I'm not going to grow alarmed unless there's a reason to be. It was one slip."

Fury had the nerve to snort. It turned into an outright fit of laughter.

"What is funny?" Darkness straightened, dumping the rest of the files on the desktop.

"You are."

"I resent that."

Fury closed the distance between them and gripped his arms. "You can't expect me to believe you just set that information aside and you're not obsessing about what you're going to do if she's pregnant. You don't want anyone to get close to you but you might have no choice. That will be your son. You're terrified."

Darkness tore away from his hold and considered slamming him on the desk again. "No. I frighten others. I don't experience fear."

The male got in his face. "You're not so different after all. Denial is the first step to falling in love with a female. I know the signs. I saw it in my mirror after Ellie came into my life again." He backed off fast, getting out of punching range. "You trust her when you don't even trust me and I'm blood."

Darkness spun. "Send the paperwork to my home. I'm done here."

"Mate papers?"

He halted at the door and turned, his look deadly. "Confidentiality agreement. You knew what I meant. Don't fuck with me, brother."

Fury leaned his hip against the side of the desk. "Tell your female I said hello. We'll be sure to invite her to dinner too, with you."

"Fuck you." Darkness stormed out and slammed the door.

His keen hearing didn't miss the sound of more laughter from the male. His hands fisted and he wanted to hit something.

Chapter Nineteen

Kat knew when she was being avoided. Darkness definitely stayed away from his apartment as much as possible. An officer had been posted outside in the hallway. She'd been instructed to stay inside or a New Species would stop her.

Boredom was a terrible thing. She flipped channels and almost threw the remote at the television. Nothing was on that she wanted to watch or that could distract her. For the past three days Darkness had left early, stayed away and only came home late at night. They had sex but it involved handcuffs. He kept her facing away from him, restrained so she couldn't touch him. She couldn't say it hadn't been fantastic, just controlled and a bit cold. He didn't want to talk, just went right to sleep afterward. He would hug the edge of the bed, his back to her.

The door opened and she turned her head, surprised to see him while it was still daylight. She hit the mute button and stood. "Hi."

He slammed the door. "Hello. I need to change my uniform. It's unusually hot today and I sweat while on patrol." He strode across the living room toward the bedroom.

Her temper boiled. "I'm done."

He swung around, pausing. "Excuse me?"

"That's the most you've said to me since the morning after you brought me here. You're gone all the time. I'm losing my mind."

"You wanted to live with me." His mouth tensed into a grimace. "I work long hours."

She closed her eyes and counted to ten. He was gone when they opened. Kat stormed into the bedroom and caught him stripping out of his uniform. A fresh one lay across the bed.

"I want to be escorted to the gates. I'm going to need some money to get home. You didn't let me grab my purse."

"You're not leaving." He sat on the bed, removing his boots. "We're still working on getting Robert Mason taken care of."

"What does that mean?"

"Justice decided to go through proper channels since it's the FBI. We don't like to make enemies and we need to stay on good terms with them. We've been assured they are investigating him and he's been suspended for the time being. They took his passport away too, preventing him from leaving the States."

"I'm no longer in danger then. Even you can see that. I'm going home."

He rose to his full height. "You can't."

"I can. I only came here to spend time with you. That's not happening."

He frowned. "Mason could still be a danger to you."

"While he's under investigation? He's an asshole but not a complete moron. I told you he's not going to kill me. I bet the other agents he sent to Homeland are fine too, right?"

His lack of response was a good enough answer. He'd have smugly informed her if something had happened to the other agents just to prove his point. Silence spoke volumes.

"I want access to a phone then. I'll call Missy and have her come get me."

He made a point of staring at her stomach. "It hasn't been five days." He looked into her eyes then. "You aren't leaving until you take that test and it comes back negative."

"Fine." She tried to be reasonable. "Understood. Will you escort me to guest housing or should I ask the guy in the hallway?"

He removed his boots, stood and unfastened his pants. "Your cottage was assigned to someone else. We have visitors. You'll stay here."

"Find me another cottage then."

He removed the pants and put on the clean pair. "There is no guest housing available. This is it."

Kat wanted to call him a liar but with the way he'd been acting, he seemed as if he wanted to be rid of her. It also could explain his foul mood. He was stuck with her. "Great. Wonderful." She spun away, marching back into the living room. Two minutes later Darkness exited the bedroom.

"I'll see you later."

"Right." She refused to look at him. "Don't bother waking me when you come in. I'll sleep on the couch."

"Why?" His tone came out gruff.

She glared at him then. "I'm done just being screwed by you."

His nostrils flared and he advanced a step. "You wanted to share quarters with me."

"That was before I knew the only interaction we'd have was you waking me up by snapping handcuffs on my wrists and fucking me. You don't even talk during. I'd rather just skip it."

"You enjoy it."

"I also enjoy talking, spending time with someone and not being avoided. You don't give a damn about my needs. You seem to be punishing me, Darkness. I've had enough. You get the bedroom and I'll take the couch. Make sure you set up that appointment for me to get a blood test the day after tomorrow. I'm out of here the moment we're in the clear."

"I'm not punishing you."

Some of her anger faded. "That's how it feels. I didn't come here to be driven out of my head. I haven't left your apartment since you brought me here. The only outside time I've seen is standing on your balcony. I'm not big on television but it's the only entertainment I have. I'm going stir-crazy. I thought we'd be able to get to know each other better."

"I know every inch of you." His expression was ruthless when he jerked his focus up to stare into her eyes. "I've learned everything you like."

"I want more than just sex. I'm pretty sure I made that clear."

"I told you I don't have anything else to give."

It hurt. She didn't want to fight with him anymore. He was stubborn and determined to keep her at arm's length. "You win. I give up. I thought there was something more between us but I see you're never going to allow that to happen. You can sleep alone from now on. That should thrill you." She spun, entered the kitchen.

He lingered for a few moments but then the door opened and closed after him. She fixed a sandwich and took a seat on the couch again. The dull ache in her chest was disappointment and sadness. She'd given it a shot at least, knew she couldn't regret making the effort. Darkness wouldn't meet her halfway.

Her appetite fled and she cursed. She dumped her food in the trash, walked to the door, opened it and leaned out. A New Species sat in a chair about ten feet away holding an electronic device. He peered at her curiously.

"Do you need something?"

"I'm not allowed to leave the building, right?"

He stiffened in his chair. "Correct."

"Does this building have roof access?"

He hesitated. "Yes. Why?"

"I need to stretch my legs. That balcony isn't big enough to do that. I'd like to see some sunshine and breathe fresh air. Can you take me up there? That technically wouldn't be breaking the rules, right? Don't make me beg. It wouldn't be pretty."

He hesitated a moment then closed the device and laid it against the wall. He stood. "Just promise you won't try anything."

"I don't have wings to fly and I sure as hell wouldn't jump because of Darkness."

The guy grinned. "I'm Field."

"It's nice to meet you." She stepped out and closed the door. "Call me Kat. It's short for Katrina."

He indicated the direction and fished out his identification badge from his front pocket, swiped the lock and opened a door. The stairwell led up. He went first and she followed. He had to swipe the card again at the top and push a flat ceiling panel up.

"We don't use it often. Just stay away from the edges. It's a long fall down and the sides are sloped. They didn't install safety walls to enclose the space."

Kat sucked in a deep breath as she stepped out into the sunshine. It was a warm day, just as Darkness had said. The view from the roof showed her more of Homeland. She could even spot the tall walls that enclosed it from the outside world. The park showed to the left, in the distance.

"Thank you." She flashed him a smile.

"I understand feeling closed in and needing an open space. I could contact Darkness to see if he'll allow me to take you somewhere else."

"Don't bother. This is great." She walked a few feet away from the door and stretched, turning her face into the sun, eyes closed. She just stood there. A light breeze stirred. It felt great to be out of the apartment.

"Have you left his home at all?"

"Nope. He's gone all the time." She turned to look at him. "Is he friendly to everyone?"

The guy's expression showed his surprise. "Um…"

"That was a poor joke."

He smiled. "Darkness is Darkness."

"That's a polite way to put it." She turned to enjoy the view.

"He's a good male. Just…not very outgoing."

She nodded.

"He's respected by all."

"I'm sure he is."

"May I ask you something?"

She faced him. "Sure."

"Are you going to teach more classes? I enjoyed the one I was able to attend."

She didn't remember him. There had been a lot of faces though. "I don't think so. I'm going home in a few days and doubt I'll be back."

"That's a shame. I don't work in Security but everyone who does liked your classes."

"What do you usually do or are you not allowed to say?"

"I'm a nurse." He grinned. "Darkness asked me to be one of your guards. I'm well acquainted with human females. He knew I wouldn't be a threat to you in any way."

"A threat?" That piqued her interest.

He blushed. "Some of our males wouldn't understand what you living inside his quarters means. Darkness didn't want any males to make the mistake of believing you were available for them to approach since you're not his mate. He has earned a reputation of not being the type to grow attached to others. Our males are used to our females sharing sex with other males. Our females don't have monogamous relationships. Some males would be confused about your status."

She let that information settle. "I'm not anything to him but an annoyance."

Field shifted his stance. "He threatened to rip off any body parts we touched you with. He cares about you. He also handpicked every male assigned to stay outside the door. Medical is short-staffed today because I'm here instead."

That surprised her. "Why would he do that?"

The guy swallowed and glanced away, looking uncomfortable. "You live with him. May I speak freely?"

"Sure."

"You're the first female Darkness has shared sex with since we were liberated. He avoided them to the point that others believed he might be interested in males." His cheeks flushed. "Please don't tell him I said that. He has a temper. I'm not a good fighter. It's why I chose nursing as a profession. He'd pull me into the training room to get even."

It confirmed what Darkness had told her. "I won't repeat anything you say. I swear."

Field stepped closer and lowered his voice. "I was also ordered to tell you that there is no guest housing available if you asked." He licked his lips and glanced back at the open door, then gave her an intense stare. "That is a lie."

Her mind reeled a little.

"He wants you to stay with him. I assume from those orders he gave me when he left that you might ask to be moved. He doesn't talk much but it's clear that you matter. He's a good male. He's just difficult to relate to. He keeps everything inside."

She approached him and kept her voice low. "He asked you to lie to me?"

He nodded. "He is known for his honesty. I was surprised by the order. My take on it is that he's desperate to keep you inside his home. He might not feel comfortable admitting that to you or even know how."

"He's never there. Don't you think he'd spend more time with me if that were the case?"

"He's Darkness. I'm telling you this because I'd hate for him to lose the one thing he's shown interest in. I would tell a female she was important to me, but him?" Field sighed. "He'd assign you officers he knew would be too afraid to touch his female and ask them to lie so she believes there are no other options but staying in his bed. Do you understand? He's proud and stubborn. He might be afraid of rejection. I know you care about him. I am friends with Book. You demanded to live with Darkness. He overheard your conversation in your home when they went to bring you to Homeland. Species hearing is excellent. Don't give up on Darkness. I believe he's worth the frustration and anger he must make you feel."

"He keeps pushing me away."

"Push back. He won't harm you. I'd bet my life on it. He needs a very strong female to handle him. I know what your job in the out world is. A weak female wouldn't have chosen to work for the FBI. I do have human female friends who also chose male-dominated careers. You're used to facing adversity. The male is worth it. You obviously couldn't find a male worthy of you until now. Darkness would be."

She studied his pretty eyes. "Thank you for telling me all that. I won't rat you out. I appreciate it."

"We all should come with instruction manuals." He grinned. "It would be so much easier to relate to each other, wouldn't it? I have an advantage since I spend a good amount of time with human medical staff. Darkness isn't typical and he's lost a lot more than most. It makes him extra stubborn about allowing anyone to get too close."

"I know that too well."

"His heart is larger than he'd like anyone to know. I've seen such thoughtfulness in some of his actions. You just have to push past his resistance."

"I needed that pep talk. I was about to throw in the towel. Let's go back to his apartment. I have to think up a new game plan."

"You might want to reword that in the future. Species would believe you mean that in a literal sense, that you're playing with his heart, but I understand." He grinned. "Keep your eye on the ball and knock that sucker right out of the park. He cares about you."

Kat laughed.

* * * * *

"All is well?" Darkness studied Field. The male stood, nodded and tucked his ebook reader under his arm. "Thank you."

He strode to his door but paused before entering. He liked coming home to her in his bed but Kat would be sleeping on the couch. It was his own fault. He couldn't blame her for being resentful of his treatment. She was stuck in the small space and that would irritate anyone. He waited for Field to pass him in the hallway before he opened the door.

His vision adjusted to the dim room. She hadn't left on any lights for him, another sign she still resented him. He closed the door and crept across the room to stare down at the couch. Kat wasn't sleeping there. He frowned and approached the bedroom. The door stood open and no light showed. He hesitated at the entry.

She lay on his side of the bed, almost falling off the edge. He leaned against the doorframe, accepting that it was relief he felt. She was there, in his bed. He backed up, removed his vest and tossed it on the couch before removing his boots. His feet hurt from pulling so many extra shifts. It had kept him busy though, away from Kat. He stripped out of all his clothing and returned to the bedroom to stand at the end of the bed, his gaze locked on her form. She slept on her stomach, her bare arm and back revealed where the covers didn't reach. She hadn't put on one of his shirts as a barrier against his touch. Her hair was thrown above her head, spread out across his pillow. One of her hands curved into a loose fist inches from her face. Each slow, steady breath was proof that she slept peacefully.

He wondered if she'd drifted across the bed in her sleep or purposely taken his space to cause irritation. He grinned, guessing the second. Kat liked to push him when she was angry. Sometimes her rebellion was loud and obvious but she had a talent for small displays of defiance.

He inched closer until his thighs pressed against the bottom of the bed. He wanted to crawl toward her and flip her over. He needed to get his handcuffs. That's what he'd done to her every other night.

He snapped them on her wrists and hooked them through one of the slats of the headboard. He hesitated, despite his dick stirring. He wanted Kat. The condoms were in the drawer next to the bed. He'd brought more in case he went through the box.

She straightened and her legs slid a few inches apart as she settled more firmly on her stomach. There was no change in her breathing. She slept on. He rounded the bed, crouched next to her and captured a lock of her hair on his fingertip. He leaned in and inhaled.

He'd ordered personal grooming products of her choice. The peach scent would forever remind him of her. The fruit fit her personality. Soft, sweet, delicate, with a hard core at the center. Mouthwatering to taste. He closed his eyes and admitted to himself that she'd changed him. Become a part of him. A tinge of resentment washed through him but when he opened his eyes again and stared at her peaceful features, the emotion changed to longing. He'd miss her when she was gone.

"Shit."

She stirred and opened her eyes. He held still but released her hair. She frowned a little, blinking, but then he must have come into focus. "Hi."

"You're on my side of the bed."

"I know." She lifted her head and looked at the clock on the nightstand. "You're later than usual. It's after one."

"I needed to do some thinking."

She sat up, clutching the covers to her breasts. One hand reached out, searching for the lamp. He caught her it, held it. She had no choice but to sit still.

"Don't. I like it this way."

"I'm not surprised with that name. Darkness—I get it."

He smiled. "That wasn't why I chose it."

"It should have been."

She didn't attempt to tug her hand free. He liked touching her. "I am sorry for earlier."

She sighed. "Is it easier to admit you're wrong when I can't make out your features?"

"Yes."

She scooted over. "At least come closer."

He rose and sat on the edge of the mattress. "I haven't been fair to you."

"I know." She surprised him when she leaned his way and rested her forehead against his chest, her other hand curling around his forearm. She stayed there, close. "It's not easy for you to share anything with anyone."

"I don't mean to hurt or anger you."

She turned her head and rubbed her cheek over his skin. "You mean to piss me off. I'm guilty of doing the same to you. It gets a reaction and that's better than the silence. We need to work on our communication skills. We have only two volumes—high or mute."

He let go of her hand and wrapped an arm around her waist. He liked her in his arms. He rested his chin on top of her head. It seemed to fit there. "I can't change."

"I'm not asking you to. I just want in."

"No."

She tensed in his hold. "No discussion about it, huh? No give and take?"

"I warned you from the start, Kat. You're a temptation I couldn't resist but I'll never be the type of male you need. I can give you sex. That's it. I want to be honest. I spoke to Justice today and we can find you a job with the NSO. Our people like you and enjoyed your classes. He'll take you on as a full-time instructor."

"Teaching them about security? You have a task force for that."

"To teach them about humans overall. We owe you a debt for how you handled those humans in the van. You were correct. They could have inflicted a lot of damage before we took them out. We weren't prepared for that kind of assault. We are now."

"I, um…" She paused. "I have to think about it."

"You could live at Homeland or drive to your own home at night. It would be your choice. It's always dangerous working for Homeland. You'd have to be very aware of your surroundings to make certain no one followed you to your house. It's less dangerous at Reservation. There's a much smaller population of humans. The nearby residents like us there but I realize it probably wouldn't be your preference to move so far away." He ran his hand up and down her spine. "I'd prefer you live at Homeland. We could still see each other."

"Are you asking me to keep living with you?"

"No. You'd be assigned your own home. I could visit you after my shifts sometimes."

"I see." She relaxed. "You'd be able to fuck me and then leave whenever you were in the mood." Her wounded tone indicated that wasn't an option.

"I can't offer you more."

She pushed him and he dropped his arm. She rolled away and scooted to the other side of the bed. "I'm tired."

"Is that not enough for you?"

"You know the answer already. You're a bright guy. Good night."

She pulled up the covers, hiding her body from his view. The way she drew her knees up and kept her back to him left no doubt that she didn't want to be touched. He was disappointed but not surprised. Kat wanted a male who could give her all the things she needed. That would never be him.

He stretched out on the opposite side of the bed, flat on his back and stared up at the ceiling as he'd done thousands of times before. The sound of her ragged breathing hurt him. She didn't cry but her distress was clear. He'd let her down.

"I'm sorry." They were tough words to say.

She sniffed. "Don't be. I was the one who wanted to change things."

He wanted to reach out and touch her. He didn't. "You deserve better."

"I agree."

He shifted his focus back to the ceiling. Her breathing eventually slowed and he knew she slept. He couldn't find that peace from his turbulent thoughts. It took awhile but he finally nodded off...

~ ~ ~ ~ ~

Kat straddled his lap, grinning down at him. She was naked, her breasts bare. He reached up and palmed them. She arched her back, pressing against his touch more firmly. They were both bare. His dick was hard when Kat wrapped her fingers around the shaft. She lifted, adjusted the position of his dick and sank down on him.

He groaned at the feel of her hot, wet pussy. Tight. He stared at her face. She was stunning. Her cheeks were flushed with passion, her beautiful eyes half closed. She held his gaze and moved on him, taking more of his dick, lifting up, slamming down. The pleasure tore through him until he couldn't remain still any longer. He trailed his hands down over her ribs, curved them around her hips and held her there while he thrust upward, fucking her harder and deeper. Moans tore from her parted lips, driving him on.

Kat leaned forward and her hand stroked his stomach then upward to play with one of his nipples. She pinched the tip between her forefinger and thumb. The sharp sensation almost made him come but she wasn't there yet. He clenched his teeth, ignoring the way his nuts tightened and wanted to explode. He adjusted his hold on her and pressed his thumb against her clit, rubbing.

Kat moaned louder and her pussy tightened almost painfully around his shaft. She reached up near his head with her other hand. He thought she planned to grab hold of his shoulder for support but she clutched the pillow under his head instead. He closed his eyes, just enjoying the feel of being inside her, of having her ride him.

"Darkness?"

He opened his eyes at the sexy sound of her voice but it wasn't Kat on top of him anymore—Galina straddled him. She held a knife in her hand and the blade reflected light as it arched downward. The tip of it buried deep in his chest. Agony ripped through him and he roared out from the force of it…

~ ~ ~ ~ ~

"Darkness!"

Kat's voice came from his right and she clutched his biceps. He was sitting upright in the dark, on his bed. He was breathing heavily and sweat soaked his body. He'd had a nightmare. It was fresh, crisp in his mind. It took every ounce of control not to strike out. He locked his body into position, only allowing the movement of his chest as he panted.

"Are you okay? I think you were having a nightmare." She rubbed his arm.

"Don't," he managed to get out. He fought the urge to knock her away. "Stop touching me."

It helped when Kat pulled her hand away but it could have resulted in tragedy. He might have attacked Kat. His chest was intact. His heart was not pierced by Galina's blade. She was dead. He'd killed her. It wasn't her in his bed.

"Try to slow your breathing," Kat murmured. "It's okay."

He lunged to the left and stood. "I have to go."

He bent, grabbed his discarded clothing and fled the bedroom. He just put on his pants, carrying his shirt out of the apartment. He needed to distance himself from Kat. He could have killed her. He wasn't fit for a relationship with a female.

Chapter Twenty

ß

Kat's mood was grim as she waited for the blonde doctor to enter the exam room. She glanced at the clock on the wall. The minutes ticked by slowly and she was certain that had been the longest twenty minutes of her life. The door opened and she tensed. It wasn't Doc Alli, as she had introduced herself, who entered. Darkness stepped inside the room.

He looked handsome in his uniform. His features were harsh though, and his dark gaze pinned her where she sat on the padded exam table. "Hello."

That's all he has to say to me? She hadn't seen him since he'd rushed out of his bedroom the night before last. Later Field had shown up, looking apologetic and regretful, to inform her that he'd been instructed to move her to guest housing.

Darkness no longer wanted her in his home. It had hurt but she hadn't been that surprised. "Should I thank you for showing up to get the results?"

"Have you found out yet?"

She shook her head. "Still waiting."

He leaned against the wall and crossed one boot over the other. His silence pissed her off. She managed to remain seated but was tempted to stroll the five-foot distance between them and smack him. It might have felt good but in the end, she used words instead.

"Next time have the balls to kick a woman out of your place yourself."

He frowned.

"You heard me."

"I felt it was best to have a clean break."

"What are you going to do if I'm pregnant?" She arched an eyebrow.

He growled and looked away. "I don't know."

"Me neither. We agree on something else."

"You and the child would be taken care of."

"That had better not be a threat."

His dark skin paled slightly and he glared at her. "You know I'd never harm you or allow anyone else to. I meant the NSO and I would make sure you were both provided for and protected."

"From a distance."

"You would stay at Homeland or Reservation."

"I take it that, wherever I chose, you'd be in the other location?"

He said nothing. It answered her question. She'd pegged it right. The door opened and Doc Alli entered. "The pregnancy test is negative." She folded her hands as if she were nervous, glancing between the two of them. "I'll leave now." She turned to go.

"Are you sure?" Darkness pushed away from the wall.

"Yes." The blonde paused. "I'm certain. The hormone levels would have been spiked if she were carrying a Species baby. I could do an ultrasound but it's not necessary."

"Thank you." Darkness allowed her to leave.

The door closed and Kat slid off the edge of the table, her legs feeling a bit shaky. She hated the disappointment she felt at the news. It would have been the worst circumstances to have a baby but part of her had started to warm to the idea. Another part of her was thankful. Darkness would get his wish. They had a clean break. There was nothing to bind them together.

"That's good."

She peered up at him. *Is he trying to convince me or himself?* "I won't keep you from your celebration. I have a taxi to catch." She walked to the door and gripped the handle.

Darkness suddenly stepped behind her and flattened his hand on the door to keep it shut. She could feel him close. If she turned, they would have touched. It kept her still, wondering why he wasn't opening the door for her.

"Kat," he rasped.

Tears filled her eyes. She hoped he'd say he was willing to try to have a real relationship with her, that he'd changed his mind. She wasn't going to hold her breath. "What?"

"Have you considered the job with the NSO?"

She refused to face him. "I have. I appreciate the offer, but no. I'll either stay with the FBI if they allow it or find work somewhere else after the investigation is complete. I'm going in later today to speak to the supervisor in charge. I plan to go home first and get some real clothes." She glanced down at the NSO-issued T-shirt and sweatpants, minus their logo. "This isn't my best dress-to-impress look."

"Do you need anything?"

A long list formed in her head, starting with him dropping to his knees and begging her to stay. "Nope. The NSO assured me they'd pay for a taxi to take me home. That's all I need. My escort is going to take me from here right to one of the side gates. They wanted to avoid anyone seeing me leave."

"I..."

She blinked back tears and turned. He was so tall and big. She'd always remember that about him. And the way he always smelled so good. "You what?"

Pain flashed in his eyes or maybe that was wishful thinking on her part. "I wish you well, Kat."

"You too." She spun. "I have to go if that's all you want to say."

He released the door and stepped back. She twisted the handle, jerked the door open and strode down the hall at a rapid pace. *Don't fall apart. Don't give him the satisfaction of knowing he hurt you.* She repeated it in her head until she located her escort near the front door.

"Let's go."

The male nodded and led her out to a waiting Jeep. She was leaving Homeland and never coming back. That should make Darkness happy. She'd be miserable but that wasn't his concern. It hardened her heart a little. The gate turned out to be a door in the wall with a single New Species officer manning it. There were three heavily armed ones on the walkway atop the wall.

"Just walk through the alleyway and through the gate to the house directly across. A taxi is waiting in front of that house. He'll believe you're a resident there. He's already been paid." The officer forced a smile. "Please don't reveal the location of the house to anyone. Both gates to the back and front have been unlocked for you."

"Thank you. I won't tell anyone." She meant it.

The instructions were clear. She left Homeland, crossed the alley and walked through a nice, landscaped yard to the front gate, avoiding the house altogether. A taxi was parked in the street. The woman driver grinned as she took a seat in the back.

The driver rattled off Kat's address. "That's correct, right? Your mom said you had a fight with your boyfriend when she called. She already paid by credit card so I don't mind to wait while you get more of your things."

"I'll come back later." Kat leaned back. It was a good cover. "He needs time to cool off."

The driver put the car in gear. "I'm sorry, hon. Men can be such assholes."

"Yes they can." Kat thought of Darkness. She had no one to blame but herself for hoping for more with Darkness. It didn't ease the heartbreak any. "I don't feel like talking."

"Sure. I get it." The woman turned up her radio—a country tune.

Kat touched her stomach. It should have been fantastic news that she'd avoided an unplanned pregnancy. The idea of having a little mini-me Darkness had been on her mind often and she'd started to like the concept. He had to be feeling the exact opposite.

The taxi stopped in front of her house and Kat thanked the driver and got out. It was nice to be home. The paint was chipping and the windows needed to be replaced, but it was home. Missy would be happy to see her. She had to ring the bell since she didn't have keys.

Missy answered and instantly grinned. "You're home!" She hugged her hard. "I missed you."

"I meant to call but wasn't able to." Darkness had made sure of that. "Are you okay?"

Missy released her and tugged her inside, closing and locking the door. "I'm great. It's clear, guys. It's just Kat."

A uniformed man stepped into the hallway from the living room. He held a handgun and the white NSO lettering on his vest indicated who he was. His features revealed he wasn't a New Species. The second guy who stepped into the hallway from the kitchen was. He was a tall, white-haired male with unusually light-blue eyes.

The sight of them pissed Kat off. "What are you still doing here?" She addressed the nearest officer, avoiding looking at the New Species again.

"We were assigned to guard the house in case anyone showed up."

Kat's temper snapped. Darkness wanted a clean break and so did she. "Get out of my house."

"We're under orders," the man argued, holstering his weapon.

"Kat," Missy whispered, "it's okay. There're four of them. Two are sleeping right now, while these are on duty. They are here to protect me."

"I can do that." She got in the uniformed man's face. "Get out of my house. Don't make me pick up the phone and call the police. I will. Get your team and go. I'm home. Did you take my guns?"

"No."

"Then get out. You have five minutes." She inched around him, grabbed Missy's wrist and yanked her toward the kitchen. "I'm going to fix myself a sandwich and you'd better be gone by the time I'm done eating. Go back to the NSO."

"Kat," Missy protested.

She halted when the New Species blocked her path. He growled low and his strange eyes narrowed. "We are under orders to remain, Miss Perkins."

Kat released Missy and shoved her finger into the center of his vest. "You tell Darkness to go to hell. He wanted me out of his life and I am. That means you guys are out of my house."

Confusion flitted across his face.

"Be gone in five minutes or you can explain to the police department and probably the news hounds with their ears to their scanners about why you are here. I don't want or need NSO protection. You don't want to draw attention that you're here. I would call that a fair trade. Get lost!" She shoved him to the wall and stormed into the kitchen.

"Kat, they are nice. They're worried about Robert Mason. They came here to keep us safe in case he shows up."

She spun, trying to cool her temper. "He's not going to. I'm the least of that asshole's problems. He's been suspended and is under investigation. He abused his position, wasted money and agents' time and I never want to hear anything about New Species ever again. Am I clear?"

Missy studied her. "Oh, Kat." Pity showed in her expression. "I'm so sorry."

"Don't," she warned. "Not another word." Her tone softened. "I don't want to talk about it. I don't want to talk about him. I just want to eat and get on with my life, okay?"

"Sure." Missy nodded. "I'm going to thank them and say goodbye."

"You do that." Kat yanked open the fridge, glancing at the clock over the stove. "Five minutes, Missy. I mean it. I want them gone."

"Okay, Kat." Missy left her alone.

Kat withdrew a soda and one of the packaged salads Missy liked so much. The heartache would fade eventually. He hadn't left her with any other options. Pining away over a man who would never allow himself to get close to her would be a waste of time. She'd taken a risk, fought for him, but it was a losing battle.

"Damn," she whispered. It wasn't going to be easy to get over him. Not one bit.

* * * * *

"What would you have preferred I'd done? Hog-tied and gagged her to keep her from calling the police department?" Snow crossed his arms over his chest. "She was angry at you. That was apparent."

Darkness snarled. "You shouldn't have left."

"They had no choice." Fury took Snow's side. "They were dismissed. We don't have jurisdiction to stay inside a home without the owner's consent. We have eyes on Robert Mason. He's been to his attorney's office and home. He's made no move to retaliate against your Kat."

"She's not mine," he hissed.

Fury stepped in front of him. "You're right. She's not. You sent her away. She's a trained officer. You saw firsthand how well she can handle herself at our front gate." He glanced at Snow. "Did she have weapons at her home?"

"Two handguns and a shotgun in her closet." Snow took a seat. "We left them there."

Fury turned his head to stare pointedly at Darkness. "She's armed. She can handle a single human male if the need arises."

"The security at her home was a joke." Darkness wasn't willing to concede. "At least allow me to send a team out to install a system."

"No." Justice's chair creaked. "I was willing to place a team on site but Katrina Perkins has made it clear she wouldn't welcome more assistance from us. We must respect her decision."

"I'll pay for it myself." Darkness held the feline male's calm stare.

"No," Justice repeated. "Snow, you're excused."

The male left, closing the door behind him. Justice sighed loudly and leaned back. "You should have asked her to stay if you are so worried about that female, Darkness."

"I didn't think she'd kick out our team."

Fury snorted. "You wanted her out of your life. Let her go."

"She is at risk," Darkness argued.

Fury took a seat and shook his head. "You can't have it both ways, brother. She's not some defenseless human. You were drawn to her because she's tough. Mason has made no indication he's a danger to her. The FBI has him closely monitored as well. They shared their findings so far. His relation to Jerry Boris might have been the only reason he searched for him. They haven't found anything so far to indicate he knew or was a part of what Boris did to the NSO.

Humans can be fiercely loyal to family. Do you know what I think?"

"I don't want to know." Darkness shot him a dirty look. "I'm leaving now." He spun and marched to the door.

It came as a surprise when Snow waited just outside the building. The male approached with a grim expression. "You care about that female."

"I don't want harm to come to her." He refused to admit more.

Snow licked his lips and glanced around, before slipping his hand inside his vest. He offered a card. "Here."

Darkness glanced at the numbers written on it. "What is this?"

"The access code to the camera feeds we set up outside Katrina Perkins' house. I didn't remove them. The interior cameras were stripped but you'll have a full view of the front and back of the property."

Darkness pocketed the card. "Why did you leave them?"

Snow hesitated. "I liked Missy. She was sweet and I wanted to keep an eye on her. I think it matters more to you than me. I frightened her too much to pique her interest."

"Thank you."

"You're welcome." Snow looked as if he wanted to say more.

"What?"

"You had a female. Why give her up? Was it due to all she'd lose coming to be a part of our world?"

"I'm not a fit mate."

Understanding dawned in the other's male's face. "It's difficult to get over the past. There's no point of a future if you can't let it go."

"It's not that simple."

"We adapt," Snow reminded him. "We aspire to always become more than we were meant to be. Don't you hold that goal as well?"

"I'm too damaged."

Snow nodded. "All of us are to certain degrees. Some damage is visual, some scarred deep into our souls. It's part of being Species. You are not the least likely male I've met to take a mate. Valiant has Tammy."

"He at least was willing to take a mate."

"Willing and being able to succeed are two different things. They made it work. That's one male I couldn't live with." Snow smiled. "Do you think she's deafened by now, hearing his roars? He isn't the most patient or calm male."

"He wouldn't frighten her."

"He scares me, along with the Wild Zone residents and they aren't exactly what I would consider sane. It speaks volumes, doesn't it?"

Darkness had a flashback of a moment with Kat. He could almost hear her voice. *We have two volumes. High or mute.* "I'm not him."

"You're more rational. He allows his feelings out in a big way. Too much so. He doesn't know balance."

"Nor do I."

"Have you tried?"

"I'm not going to discuss this."

"You care about that female. It's a fact. Have you considered that she'll meet some human? What if he hurts her? Humans can cheat on a female. They carry sexual diseases too. I went to one of her classes. Domestic violence is a problem in their world. I'd guess she wouldn't seek a weak male to breed with. He could do serious damage or kill her."

"Enough." The things Snow described enraged him.

"Have you watched their news? They showcase home-invasion robberies, rapes, murders and random acts of violence. We don't have those issues inside our borders. The walls around us protect our females from the violence of the out world. It's our duty as males to keep them safe. Your female isn't here."

"She isn't my female," he snarled.

Snow smiled. "You wouldn't have lost your temper before meeting her. You would have calmly corrected me. She's already changed you."

"I'm the same male."

Snow shook his head. "Perhaps you should go home and take a good look in a mirror. You're in denial. Lie to others but not to yourself."

Darkness watched the officer stalk away. He clenched his fists, angry. Everyone kept giving him advice and that wasn't the first time he'd been accused of not being honest. He went home and slammed the door. Faint trances of Kat's scent lingered in the bedroom. He breathed through his mouth and entered the bathroom, flipping on the light. He gripped the counter, leaned in to take Snow's advice.

The same male stared back at him in the mirror. He noticed no physical changes. He had forgotten to get his hair cut, the strands now long enough to rest on his shoulders. The last thing he wanted was to resemble Fury or the brothers he'd once lost. He made a mental note to get that done soon and strode into his bedroom. He studied the bed, memories of Kat unavoidable.

He missed her. It would fade over time and he'd get back into his normal routine. Go to work, come home and be alone. He'd stare at the ceiling until he fell asleep. Nightmares would wake him at some point. He'd shower and begin his day over. It had become an endless cycle that no longer held any appeal.

"Son of a bitch," he rasped.

He opened the closet and withdrew a locked case. Kat hadn't attempted to open it. He'd checked. He put in the right combination and withdrew the laptop. Within minutes he had it plugged in and pulled up the secure feed — the front and back views of Kat's home on split screen. He removed his boots, got comfortable and sat on the bed, placing the device on his lap.

There was no sign of life until the sun went down. Lights came on and off in the house, allowing him to track movement. A blonde woman paused in front of a lit window on the second floor in the front. That had to be Missy. She peered out and turned, her lips moving.

Darkness hated the way he hoped Kat would step into sight. The light went off and time passed. He got up and fixed a light meal. Returning to the bedroom, he ate while keeping watch over Kat's home. The laptop fit well on the nightstand, facing his bed.

The phone rang and he answered. "Darkness."

"How are you?"

"I'm fine, Fury."

"Would you like to come over for dinner?"

"I already ate."

"You could join us tomorrow."

"I'm on duty tomorrow night."

Fury sighed. "I'll call again in a few days."

"You do that." He hung up and put on silky pajama bottoms.

It was early but he lay down and turned on his side, his attention on the laptop screen. He might not allow himself to be part of her life but he felt better watching over her. It beat staring at the ceiling. That excuse made him feel better.

Chapter Twenty-One

∽

"I'll get it! It's for me," Missy called out from her office.

Kat glanced at the clock over the stove. It was past eleven. She wondered if Missy had a late-night craving for pizza or Chinese food. They'd eaten dinner early and her friend was determined to write most of the night away. It usually annoyed her when they got food deliveries so late but she didn't have to go to work early in the morning.

"Yeah, it's my food," Missy yelled.

Kat poured a glass of milk and took a sip. She'd said goodbye to Darkness and filed her report about Robert Mason. It hadn't been her best day. The front door closed, the sound soft but distinctive.

"This smells so good." Missy walked in carrying a pizza box. "Want some?"

"Nope. I'm going to bed in a few minutes."

"I ordered extra bacon and cheese."

Kat grinned. "You're such a bitch. It will go from my lips directly to my hips if I eat this late."

"So what?"

"Give me one piece." Kat set down her glass and grabbed two paper plates from the cabinet. "A small one."

Missy dished it out. "Are you okay? You've been in a foul mood since you got home from work."

"They brought in a new guy to take over Mason's position. He's pissed. I got a lecture and had to file a very detailed report. I'm suspended with pay. They are going to call me when they are done with the investigation."

"Did they suspend the other agents sent to Homeland?"

She took a bite and chewed. "Yeah. Chavez was furious that any of us would, and I quote, 'listen to a moron'. I had to agree. I should have flat-out refused to go undercover but we were all between a rock and a hard place."

"Screwed if you do, screwed if you refused direct orders."

"Exactly."

Missy grabbed a soda. "I'm going to eat in my office. Do you want to join me?"

"No. I know you need to finish your book and send it to your editor."

"I've got three days to hit this deadline and I don't think I'm going to get much sleep. It's for an anthology series so it has to be in or my story won't make the cutoff date. They'll have to pick someone else to be a part of it."

Kat lifted her plate and glass. "I'm going to bed. I'll see you in the morning. Try to get some sleep, okay?"

"Yeah. Can you check on Gus and Butch on your way?"

"They are probably sleeping. I swear you own the laziest pets ever."

Missy chuckled. "They turn hyper in the middle of the night. It's a good thing I keep odd hours."

Kat headed upstairs and stopped at Missy's door to peek in. The dog slept on Missy's pillow but the kitten was on the floor, chewing one of Missy's shoes. Kat winced, grateful it wasn't one of hers. She closed the door to keep the little destroyer of fashion from going to her bedroom next.

The doorbell rang again. Kat turned.

"I've got it," Missy yelled. "It's probably the pizza guy again. I asked for sauce but he didn't bring it. He must have just remembered."

Kat went to her room. She flipped on the light with her elbow and crossed the room to her night table. She placed her food down. The front door slammed loudly. She paused, listening. Missy didn't call out. That was odd. Her friend always let her know who'd been at the door. It was a habit Kat insisted on.

She walked out of her bedroom and down the hall. "Missy?"

A chill ran down her spine when she didn't get a response. She backed up and rushed inside her room, grabbed her service weapon and crept back down the hallway. She paused at the top of the stairs.

"Missy?"

Seconds ticked off. Kat strained to hear anything below but it remained quiet. "I am calling 9-1-1 and I have a weapon!" she yelled.

"Hang up the phone or I'll kill her," a familiar voice threatened.

Kat's knees nearly buckled. She had to be mistaken. "Mason?"

"You fucking bitch!" he shouted. "Get down here."

Panic set in. Why would Mason be at her house? Obviously Darkness had not been paranoid by believing her ex-boss would come after her. She fought to remain calm. "I'm not doing anything until I know Missy is okay."

"Talk," he grunted.

"Kat?" Missy's voice was soft and strained. "He's got a gun to my head."

"That's enough," Mason ordered. "Toss down your gun."

Kat tried to think but all she could imagine was him shooting Missy. "Why are you here, Mason? What do you want?"

"This is your fault. I trusted you to do a job. What did you do instead? You screwed me over. You told those animals I sent you. You shouldn't have fucked me over, Katrina."

She bit her lip. Normal tactics weren't going to work with him. He'd had the same training, knew the same tricks. "That's not true. Let's talk about this, Mason. Okay? I didn't do anything. I went to Homeland to look for that man you wanted me to find. I couldn't get any information." She tried to slow her hammering heart. "I went in to file a report and that's when I learned you'd been replaced. What's going on? They wouldn't tell me anything."

"I'm under investigation. I want you down here now, Kat. If I hear sirens or see cops, I'll kill this bitch. I have nothing to lose. I want your gun or she's dead."

"I'm trying to figure out why you're here." That was honest. He could have gone after any agent but he'd chosen her. "Do you need help?" She changed tactics. He was apprehensive and hated the NSO. "Did those New Species find out we were trying to bust them and came after you?"

Silence. Kat prayed he'd fall for it. He had to be desperate to show up at her house. Was he seeking revenge? Just a random target for the shit storm he'd brought down on his own head? Missy's life depended on being able to manipulate him.

She didn't like the silence. "Who else knew you sent me in? It was just me that went in there, right? Nobody else? I sure didn't leak anything," she lied. She'd just enlarged the suspect pool to include the agents he'd sent in as the work crew. "Who did you tell about Homeland?"

"I want your gun." His voice sounded calmer.

"Okay." She ejected the clip and the chambered round and put on the safety. "I'm going to send it down."

She flung the clip first, then the gun a second later, keeping close to the wall, protecting her body. She did glance down though, identifying Missy's bare feet with Mason's shoes right behind her. He was using her as a shield and kept them out of the line of fire.

"I want your backup gun too," he demanded.

"It's in my bedroom. I just grabbed my service weapon. May I get it?"

"Ten seconds." He began to count.

Kat fled down the hallway and jerked her second handgun off the top shelf of the closet. She snagged her cell phone from the charger and hauled ass down the hallway. She made sure she made a lot of noise so he could hear her every movement and know where she was. The last thing she wanted was for him to get twitchy with a gun to Missy's head.

She shoved the gun under her armpit and activated the phone. Her first instinct was to dial 9-1-1 but they might come in with sirens or lights. It was also possible her ex-boss was listening to their channels. "I have it," she called out. "What is going on? Talk to me, Mason. I'm a little leery of sending my last gun down to you. You might kill my girlfriend anyway."

She scrolled through numbers and found the one she'd programmed in when Mason had sent her on assignment. She hit the icon, using her shoulder to hold it against her ear as she gripped her gun.

"Send that gun down!"

"Not until I know you're not going to kill us both."

"You've reached Homeland," a cheerful deep voice answered. "How may I help you?"

"I want that fucking gun," Mason yelled.

"I know you have a gun to Missy's head, Mason. Just tell me why you're at my house. I only went to Homeland as Kathryn Decker under your orders. Let's talk. I'm not giving up my gun until I know what you want or you could kill us both."

"Shit," the guy on the phone growled.

"I'm going to count to ten and you either toss down the gun or your girlfriend dies. One, two…"

"I know you record these things," she whispered. "He's going to shoot Missy if he hears sirens. Don't call the police or she's dead. Just mute your side and keep recording."

"Nine," Mason yelled. "Send down that gun."

Kat shoved the phone down the front of her pants, into her underwear and removed the clip from the gun. "Here it comes. Clip first. Just calm down." She leaned out and threw it. It bounced on the steps. "Gun next." She pitched it.

"Get down here." Mason sounded pissed.

She raised her hands, palms out. "I'm coming."

Mason had Missy in a choke hold, keeping her in front of him, his gun pressed against her temple. Kat moved slowly, taking in his black clothing. She paused midway down the stairs. "I want to help you. You need to tell me why you're here and what I can do for you."

He turned the barrel of his gun away from Missy's head and pointed it at Kat. "Turn around."

She slowly spun, lifting her shirt to show him that she didn't have a weapon tucked in her pants. They were baggy but a weapon would be too heavy and bulky to hide. "See? You have both my guns." She kept eye contact with him. "Tell me what this is about."

"All you had to do was get Jerry out of there."

"I tried to look for him but they had me watched at all times. They put an ankle monitor on me," she lied. "No one would tell me anything and I couldn't go ten feet without them knowing exactly where I was. I think you were right about them. They are hiding something there. Their security was way over the top. May I call you Robert?"

"No." He glared. "All you had to do was one fucking thing, Perkins. Bring me Jerry."

"I tried. I really did. Are they after you now? What can I do to help? Do you need a place to lie low? Money? I don't keep cash here but I can get some. I want to help you." She hoped she looked sincere. "Are they going to come after me next?"

Mason's angry expression wavered slightly but his gun didn't. "That bastard transferred the money. I have to get him."

"Jerry? What money?"

He pressed his lips into a white line, rage reddening his features. She hoped he'd have a heart attack. That would solve the problem. He glanced around and Kat took the opportunity to look at Missy. She was terrified but seemed unharmed. Kat focused on Mason again.

"I can't help you unless I know the situation. What are we looking at? I assume the NSO is after you. Someone in our department turned on us." She wanted him to think of them as a team, not enemies. "My ass is on the line too."

"You're not suspended or under investigation. I had to go in today and saw you leaving. That's how I knew you were out. What did you tell them?"

"I didn't. They did put me on suspension. They want me to come in on Friday and file a report. Your replacement was in a meeting." She didn't want him to know she'd already told them everything. "You were there? You know I wasn't there long then."

He looked uncertain. She decided to push.

"What can I do? You don't have to hold a gun on Missy. She'll do whatever I say. We're the men in our families, remember?" She was willing to use his words against him.

"I have to get Jerry. He's transferred the money."

He'd said that before. "Okay. What's the plan? I'm with you. The NSO obviously owns the FBI. They are calling the shots. That means both of us are going to be in a world of shit."

The gun lowered slightly. Mason seemed to consider her words. "We need to get Jerry."

"Okay. Why does he matter? If the NSO is after us, we should leave the country."

"Not without my money." Rage twisted his features. "That stupid bastard couldn't have done any of it without me. Half of that two and a half million is mine. He's going to open his big fucking mouth eventually or he's using them to hide behind. I thought at first they grabbed him but the more I think about it, he might be setting me up too, like he did that girl. I'm not going to prison."

She wasn't sure what girl he was talking about but the rest was starting to make sense. "That's a lot of money."

"I set up the false identities he used, made sure he covered his tracks and told him how to funnel all the money so it couldn't be traced. That asshole made it so I couldn't access it and now he's trying to take it all." Mason studied her. "I'll split the money with you. Fuck Jerry. I'll kill him as soon as I know where he transferred the funds. Are you in, Perkins? We're screwed otherwise. We're going to prison or worse. Jerry and those damn animals aren't going to win."

"I'm in."

He lowered the gun all the way and shoved Missy forward. Kat descended the rest of the stairs and grabbed her arm, tugging her behind her. She kept hold of her. Missy might try to run and it would cause Mason to shoot her. He kept a tight grip on his weapon.

"We need to figure out where he's staying and get to him." Mason paced. "How much of Homeland did you see?"

"A lot of it. They gave me a tour with a guard." She wanted him to think she was useful or he'd kill them both. "Do you want me to draw it out? I saw some nice homes where they probably put VIPs. He's probably there if they are hiding him."

He shot her a shrewd look. "Any weaknesses in their security?"

"I think I could find a way in. I saw a back gate for delivery trucks. It wasn't guarded well." It was bullshit but he might fall for it. "We could steal a delivery van and borrow some uniforms. They don't check identifications since they have a high turnover of employees for those types of businesses. I even saw a few of them so I know what is ingoing."

"They just let them drive around Homeland?"

She nodded. "Yeah. They only guard the walls. The inside is clear of guards. It's just that they kept that ankle bracelet on me and assigned two guards who were always on my ass."

"They hit on you, didn't they?" He stared at her shirt. "You have nice tits."

It took a lot for Kat to keep her cool. She rubbed Missy's wrist with her thumb, trying to reassure her. "You know it. They didn't stand a chance though."

Mason paced again. "We're going to get Jerry and he's going to get us that money."

* * * * *

Darkness jerked awake when his phone rang. He opened his eyes, stared at the screen of the laptop a few feet away. Lights were still on inside Kat's home. He answered the phone. "Darkness here."

"This is Book. We have a situation. Get to Security now."

"Are we under attack?" Darkness was off the bed in an instant, moving fast to his closet. He threw it open to grab a uniform.

"A call came in and it's still live. Your female is currently planning on breaching Homeland with someone named Mason. He's at her house and has a gun to Missy's head. She's lying to him, I assume, since most of what she's said is bullshit."

Darkness nearly dropped the phone and spun toward the laptop. "I'm looking at her house."

"He's inside." Book hesitated. "Bluebird is transcribing what we know so far. Kat called in saying Mason had a gun to Missy's head and to record the conversation. We're doing that. She also said not to call the police. Mason will shoot them if human police arrive. We put a trace on it immediately. It's a cell but the tower is in the location of her home and I verified the sound of her voice myself. It's real."

"Wake a pilot and get a helicopter ready."

"We're already on it. We're up in ten. I'll fill you in. Move!" He hung up.

Darkness dropped his cell on the bed and rushed to dress. He almost forgot the phone but grabbed it and his boots, not taking the time to put them on. He threw open the balcony door, scanned the ground below and leapt, landing on the grass. Pain shot up both legs but nothing broke. He ran toward the helicopter pad.

Kat was in trouble. He'd warned her Mason was a danger. She'd ignored him and sent away the team he'd assigned to guard her. His rage grew as he ran, spurring him on. The sound of the helicopter blades assured him they hadn't left without him but were preparing to take off.

Trey Roberts and Book met him. He was surprised to see the human there so fast but he shifted his attention to Book, panting. "Give me the details." He sat on the ground and put on his boots. There weren't enough males yet to make up a full team but he hoped they hauled ass. He wanted the helicopter in the air.

"It sounds as if he was the brains behind Boris," Trey answered instead. He held his phone, reading the screen. "I'm getting the transcripts texted to me. My guess is that Mason and Boris were partners. He tried to access the money they ripped off from the NSO but he's bitching about how it was transferred to another account. Boris fucked him and he wants to find him in order to get the millions they extorted from the NSO."

Darkness stood, stomping his boots on the ground since he hadn't put them on well. "We recovered the money. I beat it out of Boris. Mason doesn't know that?"

"My guess?" Trey glanced up from his phone. "Boris used online banking. He probably transferred the money to the account info you got out of him but had already blocked Mason from the money. He probably did it before he came here after Jeanie Shiver. Greedy fucker. He wanted it all. Now Mason is flipping out because he's under investigation and wants a way out. That money would assure him a good life somewhere else."

More males rushed to the area and Darkness threw up a fist and then pointed to the helicopter. He was taking charge of the team. He didn't care if he stepped on Trey's toes or anyone else's. Kat was in danger. "Let's go."

They climbed inside the helicopter and Darkness grabbed a headset. "Get us in the air," he demanded of the pilot, twisting in his seat to glare at the male.

The pilot nodded and faced forward. They lifted off and Darkness put on his seat belt. He glanced at the dimly lit faces of the males who'd come. They were six in all. He touched his head and all of them put on their headsets.

"Pilot, land us eight or ten blocks away. The human will still hear us but maybe he won't connect the dots because of the distance. Are you patched in to Security?"

"It's Darren, and yes I am, Darkness."

"Have them find you a landing site. I don't care if we have to stop traffic in a street. How far out are we?"

"Ten minutes if I really push it. They want to know if we want police assistance." The pilot waited for instructions.

"No," Trey answered. "This guy could have a police scanner. I'd have one and this guy is smart. We'll steal a car. It will be faster than jogging."

Darkness was ready to run it but using a vehicle would be faster. "You know how to do that?"

Trey grinned and touched his sidearm. "Yeah. Leave it to me."

"Thank you for reaching Homeland so fast."

Trey cleared his throat. "I was already here."

Darkness frowned. "Tim sent you this late? Why?"

The human broke eye contact. "Tim didn't send me. I was already at Homeland when this went down. Let's talk about it later." He glanced around at the other males. "It's personal."

Darkness let it go. He trusted the male. It didn't matter why he'd been at the NSO in the middle of the night. He was more worried about Kat. Was she alive? He saw Trey remove his phone and scan the screen, reading texts. He should have had Security send the transcripts to his phone.

"Trey? Is she alive still?"

The male looked up and nodded. "She's drawing him maps of Homeland. He hasn't fired the gun. They are apparently in the kitchen and she just asked Missy to make them coffee. I can't tell this guy's mood from reading dialogue but he isn't threatening to shoot them again. He's more focused on getting that money."

Darkness could breathe easier.

"We're almost there," the pilot said. "I'll do a hard touchdown. We found a park. The house is eight blocks north. I'll get directions."

"I'm on it," Trey announced. "I know the area. I dated a girl who lived nearby once and know where that street is. I had them text me the exact address. I'm pulling up a map now just to make sure."

Darkness released his belt and held on to the seat. Book sat closest to the side door and opened it. The air blew in and amplified the sound of the helicopter blades. He turned his head as the helicopter banked sharply and lowered. It went down fast, as Darren had warned. Streetlights came into view and a small building he identified as a public restroom sat in the distance. The helicopter landed with a jarring bump. He tore off his headset, barely taking time to hook it to the wall.

He was out third in line and turned to Trey. He didn't enjoy turning control over to the human but he wasn't sure where Kat's home was. The streets confused him and most of the homes looked too similar. Trey motioned the helicopter to take off and pointed toward a street. He ran and Darkness followed. The sound of the helicopter faded.

They reached a street lined with homes. Trey turned left. "Damn."

"What?" Darkness caught up to him.

"I thought there'd be more traffic. Wait. There's a car." He threw up a fist and they all stopped.

A small four-door sedan drove toward them and Trey rushed into the path of it and withdrew his sidearm, aiming it at the driver. He pointed to his vest with his other hand where the NSO white lettering showed. The driver slammed on the brakes.

Trey approached the driver. "I'm with the NSO," he yelled. "You're in no danger. Don't panic. Put down your window."

It was a female and Darkness could see her fear. She lowered the window and Trey leaned in. "I'm really sorry about this but we have an emergency. We need your car."

She shook her head, still pale.

Darkness approached. He tried to appear friendly. "Human, this is an emergency. Let us have your car. You will get it back."

"Promise." Trey reached inside and opened the door. "Just take off your belt and scoot in the back. You can drive away once we're out. There's a man holding a couple of women hostage. He'll kill them if the police show up. We're all NSO."

The woman stared at Darkness. He wasn't wearing a face shield. He could see her terror. Her hands shook as she reached down and unfastened her belt. "Please don't hurt me."

"We just need a ride," Darkness assured her.

She nodded. "Get in."

"We need something bigger. All of us won't fit," Book assessed.

"We'll fit," Trey announced. "It's just going to be cramped."

Trey helped the woman out and got in the driver's seat. "Darkness, passenger seat. Lady, you can sit on his lap."

She gawked at Darkness.

"The rest of you get in the back. Three can fit across in the seat and one of you can huddle in their laps."

"This is undignified," Jinx growled. "But let's do it."

Darkness grabbed the female's hand. It trembled in his. He hadn't taken the time to put on gloves. "It will be fine. You're with six well-armed males. Thank you for your assistance."

He led her to the other side of the car and got in. The female paused but climbed on his lap. It was a tight fit but one glance in the back as four males tried to squeeze into the space designed for three humans made him grateful to be in the front.

Trey grinned, slamming the door. "See? Let's do this."

The back doors closed and Darkness slammed the passenger one too. He hooked an arm around the female when Trey punched the gas and executed a tight U-turn. Trey removed his phone from his vest pocket and turned on the screen. A map showed.

"Thank you..." Trey paused. "What's your name?"

"Amber." The female relaxed against Darkness.

"You're helping save two lives." Trey took a sharp turn. "If you really feel the need to report this, give us twenty minutes before you call the police. This jerk could have a scanner. If you call Homeland instead, we'll reward you, okay?"

"Yes." Amber gripped Darkness' arm when Trey took another turn fast.

"Ever wanted a tour of Homeland?" Trey slowed. "It's yours if you just don't call the police. I promise. Tell them Trey Roberts said so. Okay, Amber?"

"Yes." She was still pale but seemed less fearful.

"I'm sorry about the gun but we really needed a ride fast." He pulled to the curb and put the car in park. Trey turned and grinned at the woman. "I'm Trey Roberts. That's Darkness holding you. You've been fantastic. Just call Homeland. We'll show our appreciation."

"I won't call the police."

"You're a doll." Trey winked at her. "This is where we get out. Thanks, Amber."

Darkness threw open the door and the female scooted off his lap. She stared curiously up at his face. He smiled. "Thank you, Amber. You're doing a great service to the NSO tonight."

She smiled back. "Good. I'm pro-Species."

"Drive safely," Darkness rasped.

She blushed. "I will."

He spun toward Trey. "Let's go. How far?"

"It's just up this street." Trey glanced at Amber. "Turn your car around quietly and keep out of this area. There could be gunfire."

She rounded the car and got inside. Following his orders, she drove in the opposite direction. Trey took point and Darkness followed. They stayed on the grassy lawns to avoid making noise. Trey halted and pointed. Darkness recognized the front of the house. They had arrived at Kat's.

Chapter Twenty-Two

ॐ

Kat watched Mason. His mood swings were a sign of high stress. He didn't trust her and he shouldn't. He kept a tight hold on his gun. She'd gotten a close enough look to know the safety was off. He tapped the weapon against his thigh and kept glancing at Missy, frowning. She didn't like it one bit.

"We need to talk." He shot a pointed stare at Missy. "But I want her in sight."

"Okay." She got up from the table, moved slowly, to avoid making him jumpy. She entered the hallway.

He approached Kat, pointing the gun at her chest. It was clear he expected her to try to disarm him. She put her hands on the doorway so he felt more secure. Mason turned enough so he could keep them both in his view.

"She's a risk."

"She'll do everything I say." Kat's worst fear had come true. She'd wondered what Mason was thinking and now she knew. "We've been together for a really long time. She's completely submissive." She used the term he'd probably understand best.

"I need to know you're a hundred percent committed. You have nothing to lose otherwise." He kept his voice low.

Dread made her stomach cramp. "What do you have in mind?"

"Kill her."

She hoped she masked her horror. "I think that's a bit drastic."

"Bullshit," he hissed. "I'm facing prison or worse if those animals get me. I need to know I can trust you. Kill that bitch."

She could understand his logic, as messed up as it was. She'd be wanted by the police for murder if she killed Missy. Recovering Jerry Boris and making him give up the money would become a survival strategy. They'd need money to obtain false identities to leave the US for a non-extradition country where a few million could provide a lifetime of luxury.

"Kill her," he whispered. He lifted his gun to her head. "Or I kill you."

"Fine. Hand me the gun."

He took a step back. "Do I look stupid to you?"

She wasn't surprised he hadn't fallen for it. "I'll get one of mine then."

"So you can shoot me?" He shook his head. "Bare handed."

"That's cold." She straightened her shoulders. "But you said there were millions involved. I'm sure I could get over it."

He smiled. Her opinion of Mason had never been good but now he was no better than a turd in the toilet to her. To kill a loved one over money was as shitty as a person could get.

"You kill her and we'll leave. I know which company we can use to get inside Homeland. We should hit them early. It's the best time."

He was right. Most people weren't at their most alert—sleeping or just have woken—if they entered Homeland around seven in the morning. That would be the time most delivery trucks started to roll in. "Okay. I get half though. Right? Don't fuck me, Mason."

"I won't. I could use you, Katrina. You're smart. We would have an easier time traveling as a couple." His attention dropped to her breasts.

Her skin crawled at the way he looked at her. She'd never allow him to touch her. "You're right." She smiled, pretending he was attractive to her. It was one of the hardest acts she'd ever put on. "We'll need to depend on each other."

"We will." He glanced at her breasts again. "In every way."

Yuck! She forced the revulsion back. "I'll do it now. I don't want her to see it coming though. She could scream. Our neighbor calls the cops every time we get in an argument." She wanted him to keep believing her and Missy were a couple, one with domestic problems. "I'll wait until her guard is down and move in behind her. Let's do this in her office. It's the farthest from that side of the house."

"Do it." He backed up and kept his weapon trained on her.

Kat crossed the kitchen. Missy leaned against the stove and met her gaze. *Trust me,* she mouthed.

"How are you holding up, honey?" She stopped in front of Missy, taking her hand.

"Scared," Missy whispered.

"It's going to be okay." Kat knew Mason stood about six feet behind her, watching and listening to everything. He couldn't see her face though. She glanced at the counter, looking for a weapon.

The stove caught her attention. "Why don't we go into your office? You can write while we talk."

"Okay."

Kat put her arm on Missy's waist and slid her hand to the knobs on the stove. Mason wouldn't be able to see that. She twisted all of them. Missy's eyes widened but Kat squeezed her hand, giving her a stern look. She felt a little proud of her best friend when she smiled.

"I should get some writing done," Missy bravely got out.

The slight sound of gas filling the stove could be heard but she doubted Mason would pick it up from across the room. He'd smell it soon though. The oven was old, on their list of things to replace. The pilots never lit on their own. She tugged Missy away from it and turned, pulling her behind her.

Mason backed into the hallway, giving them a wide berth. Kat led her friend to the room across from the kitchen. "She likes to light candles when she writes. It makes her relax." She addressed Mason but kept a hold on Missy. "I'll light a few."

Missy paled. Kat pushed her against the window that faced the backyard. "Where do you keep the lighter? Is it still in your desk?"

"It's in one of my drawers," Missy whispered, catching the hint.

"Mason might be interested in what's in your drawers. He doesn't know you. Right, Mason?"

Mason took the bait. She'd implied there might be a weapon. He moved around the big desk and bent, keeping the gun on them. His attention was diverted, though, when he yanked open the top drawer on the left of the big desk. There were four drawers in all. Kat knew how messy they were. He'd have to dig around. He bent a little more and Kat used the opportunity to grab the lighter off the shelf next to Missy's scented candles.

Missy grabbed her arm, her fingers digging in. "We should feed the dog and cat soon."

Kat winced. There was no way to save the animals. It was Missy's life on the line. She knew her friend had guessed at what she was doing and had said it to remind her that they were upstairs. "They aren't a priority right now."

Tears filled Missy's eyes and Kat had to look away. It hurt her too. The smell of gas reached her nose. Mason slammed one drawer and had to crouch to open the one under it. His gun rested on the desk, pointing their way. Kat moved to get between Missy and that gun. She glanced at the curtains. They were horrible, the same flower print that matched most of the house. The home had been a dream of theirs but they'd buy another one. Missy couldn't be replaced.

"Nothing." Mason moved around the chair and opened the other drawer. He suddenly tensed. "What is that smell?"

"What smell?" Kat gave him a blank stare. Time was up.

He sniffed and rose, moving toward the hallway door. His gun wavered and Kat spun, praying the lighter lit on the first try. She pressed it against the curtains, pushing down on the tab. A flame burst forth. The second she realized the curtains were on fire, she dropped it and wrapped her arms around Missy.

"What the fuck?" Mason yelled.

Kat shoved Missy away from the flames that shot up the curtain to keep her from catching fire. The window was single-paned since they hadn't replaced them for more efficient ones. Missy had installed a thick blackout shade, the only thing that stood between them and the glass.

A gunshot rang out as Kat spun, using all her strength to hurl both of them through the window. They slammed into the glass and when it shattered there was nothing but luck, the shade and their clothes to protect them.

Darkness approached the house with the team, motioning for them to separate and surround the house. The sound of a gunshot fractured the night. He froze, terrified of what it meant. It was immediately followed by an explosion at the back of the house. There was a blinding blaze of light and the windows along the front of the house blew outward. The sound was deafening and set off car alarms along the street. They honked and beeped, flashing lights.

"Move," Darkness roared. "Get in there!"

Any plan to sneak in and take out the male was forgotten. Darkness rushed to the side gate and jumped, not caring what was on the other side. He landed on concrete and stared horrified at smoldering chunks of the building. The back of the house had been destroyed—a flaming open wound of jagged destruction. Flames shot upward from inside, reminding him of a torch in one area. Dark smoke choked him as he rushed to enter, prepared to go into the burning house after Kat.

His peripheral vision caught movement and he froze, whipped his head in that direction. A bare arm rose from what appeared to be a section of wood paneling. The hand was small and appeared female.

"Kat!" He rushed toward her, dodging smoldering and burning debris.

Blood smeared her palm when he grabbed hold, using his other hand to grip the wood on top of her. He threw it aside. It wasn't Kat staring up at him when he dropped to his knees. She had blonde hair and terrified blue eyes and wore a long nightshirt. Cuts and fresh blood marred her limbs but she didn't appear to be critically injured.

"Where is she?" She tried to move but cried out.

"Kat?"

She nodded. "The house blew up and it ripped me right away from her." The female tried to sit up again but collapsed flat, whimpering.

"Stay down," Darkness ordered.

Book was at his side in an instant, tending to the female. Darkness rose and frantically searched the yard. A large piece of roof lay crumpled about five feet away. A bloody bare foot poked out from underneath the edge. It was small and lifeless.

"Kat!" He was terrified when he bent, afraid of what he'd find. The roofing appeared heavy, about eight feet long and five feet wide. It had sustained profound damage. His fingers hooked an edge and Trey rushed to the other side to help him move it.

"Now," Trey urged.

They lifted at the same time and threw it to the side. It wasn't as heavy as it had appeared. Darkness stared down and pain tore him apart. He'd found Kat. His knees collapsed. She was on her side, one hand over her face as if she'd tried to protect her head. Blood from a gash on her forearm smeared her skin. Blood covered her chest but he wasn't sure if it was from the first injury or worse. Her sleeping pants were torn up, red-stained in spots.

"Fuck," Trey hissed. He grabbed his phone. "Airlift them to Homeland or call for an ambulance?"

Darkness wasn't even sure if she lived. He breathed in, the stench of smoke was overpowering but he could smell her blood. It took a lot to reach out and touch her. He gently gripped her arm and moved it. Blood covered her cheek. Her eyes were closed and he wasn't sure if he breathed while he checked for a pulse. He pressed his fingertips against the column of her throat. He didn't feel anything.

"No!" he roared out in anguish. Her arm twitched and he snarled. "Airlift." He just wanted to get her to Homeland.

"On it. Don't move her," Trey demanded.

Darkness bent over Kat, shoving away debris. "Kat? I'm here. It's Darkness."

Her eyes remained closed but she was alive. He wanted to pick her up and cradle her in his arms when something inside the house blew. It was a smaller explosion but enough to make him fear more of the home would come crashing into the yard. He turned, evaluating the house again. Both floors were gone on the back of the house. Flames had spread to other sections.

"This is Trey," the human yelled. "We need that helicopter to turn around. Land it right in front of the house if you can. We have two injured females. Alert Medical. Severe trauma." He paused. "The fucking house exploded."

Darkness blocked out everything but Kat. He put his body over hers but kept all his weight off. He wanted to protect her from more hurt. Someone grabbed his arm, jerking it. He turned and snarled, looking into Trey's eyes.

"Let me help her. I have some medic training. She's bleeding." The male released him and tore off his vest, then his shirt. He started tearing it into strips.

Darkness knew Trey was right. Kat needed help but he was frozen, his mind blank.

"Move," Trey repeated. "We've got to stop the bleeding or she's not going to make it."

He backed off a little. Trey took over. It made Darkness feel helpless, something he hated. Kat made a soft sound of pain when Trey moved her bleeding arm and wrapped the sleeve of his shirt around the wound, using the ends to tie it.

"It's too tight."

Trey frowned. "Do you want her to bleed out? Look for something flat that we can tie her to. The helicopter wasn't expecting a medical emergency. We don't have a backboard on it. I asked."

Sirens grew closer. Darkness didn't move away from Kat. He watched Trey carefully wrap the cut on her ankle, the source of the blood on her foot. Darkness knew he should handle the humans and take control of the scene. New Species were in danger if he didn't. He just couldn't leave Kat. He couldn't even follow Trey's directions on how to help her. It was as if he'd shut down until he gently held her hand on the ground next to his knee. It wasn't bloody but it was lifeless.

Trey stood. "I've done all I can. I'll find something to use as a backboard or grab one from an ambulance. I'm going to send the paramedics to her. I'm sure they'll come with the police. Everyone along the block must have called for assistance."

Darkness ignored him, staring at Kat's face. Her eyes remained closed. "Kat? Can you hear me? I'm here."

It was his fault she lay there on the ground. He'd sent her away from Homeland. She'd be sleeping safely in his bed otherwise. He visually examined her body. Every cut, every trace of injury rested squarely on his shoulders. She'd wanted him to give a relationship between them a chance. He'd shut her down.

"Kat," the soft female voice whispered.

Darkness turned his head. The blonde female crawled to his side. The raw fear etched on her features might have reflected on his own face if he were able to look in a mirror. Tears fell freely down her face and he envied her ability to cry. He hurt enough to but his eyes remained dry.

"She saved me," Missy sniffed. "She blew up the house because I think Mason was going to kill me." Her shoulders rocked as she fought tears. "She threw us through the window before it blew up," she gasped, crying. "She put herself between me and the glass. We hit the ground and she rolled on top of me. When the house went, it just tore her away. I should have held on tighter. I should have..." She stopped talking, dissolving into gut-wrenching sobs.

Darkness realized he should try to comfort the female but he couldn't. He turned his head, staring at what once had been a home. The entire back side of the house was exposed to show the burning interior. The roof had collapsed inward where it hadn't been blown outward. Kat had done that to save her friend. He wanted to kill Missy. Pure rage hit but he didn't strike out at the blonde. Kat had to love her to sacrifice her own life.

Moisture filled his eyes, making his vision blurry. He leaned down, getting close to Kat's face. He detected her breathing against his lips. It was shallow but she lived. He just didn't know for how long. She was dying. Sirens stopped nearby. His brain began to function and a new target for his rage surfaced. He leaned up and turned his head, grabbing hold of Missy's shoulder. He shook her once.

"Where is Mason?"

She lifted a shaking finger at the destroyed house. "We were in my office. He was near the door. He smelled the gas and walked toward the hallway. He shot at us when Kat threw us through the window. It blew up."

He could see she was in shock. He was torn between going to hunt for Mason, if anything remained, and staying by Kat. His legs decided it for him when they refused to work. He just stayed on the ground next to her. He didn't want her to die alone. Not Kat. He bent, pressing his face close to hers.

"I'm here, Kat. Don't leave me."

"Over here!" Trey yelled. "This way."

"Please open your eyes," Darkness urged, watching, hoping she'd do it. "You're a tough female. Don't let that bastard win. He wins if you die."

Something heavy crashed next to them and Darkness jerked his head up, snarling at the threat. A human female in a dark blue uniform was on her knees on the other side of Kat, a medical kit gripped in her hand. Her eyes widened and she paled.

He glanced down, realizing what kind of uniform it was. "Help her. You're a medic."

She nodded, seeming to snap out of the fear he'd instilled. "What's her name? Do you know?"

"Kat. She's mine. Don't let her die."

Trey gripped his shoulder. "Darkness, back up. There are more of them. They need access to her and you're in the way."

He looked up at the male. "I can't."

"You have to." Trey bent, staring into his eyes. "Let them help her."

"My legs won't work."

Trey glanced down him. "You broke something?"

"I can't move. I can't leave her."

Pity flashed in the male's blue eyes and he bent, wrapped an arm around Darkness. He hoisted him up, grunting a little in the process. "Fuck, you're heavy. Lock your knees."

Darkness did as he said, found himself standing again. Trey kept hold of him and forced him back. Three more humans crouched around Kat, shoving debris away from her to get access. Two more humans helped Missy move about five feet away, asking her to lie flat so they could examine her.

Book showed up. The male had dark smudges under his nose and around his mouth, as if he'd breathed in a lot of smoke. He carried a dog in one arm and a kitten in the other.

They were alive but seemed too petrified to move around. They just lay on the male's forearms, clutched against his chest.

"You went in there after them?" Trey shook his head. "Crazy fucking Species."

Book frowned. "Missy was hysterical and worried about them."

"I can't believe they survived." Trey eased his hold around Darkness' waist. "You good now?"

He remained standing. "Where is that helicopter?"

"It's waiting." Trey released him. "You didn't hear it? Darren set it down at the end of the street. He didn't want the blades to affect the fires here."

"We need to get Kat to Homeland."

Trey hesitated. "They'll want to transport her to the hospital."

"Homeland," Darkness snarled.

Trey walked away and crouched next to the paramedics, softly talking to them. He couldn't hear the words. A bunch of humans were yelling and he turned his head, staring at the ones he hadn't noticed until then. Firemen were putting water on the house and police were moving debris, looking under it for other victims.

Trey returned to his side, looking grim. "She's critical. They can't find any breath sounds from her left lung. It's the side she landed on. She might have possible crush injuries. Internal bleeding." He paused. "Her vitals are bad."

Darkness kept his knees locked. The paramedics laid out a backboard, put a cervical collar around Kat's neck and turned her against the board. They used restraints to wrap around her head and body, even her legs, to keep her immobile.

"Darkness," Trey murmured, "they don't think she's going to make it. I'm so sorry, man."

NO! He shoved Trey away and stomped to the humans lifting Kat on the backboard. He glared at the female he'd frightened. "You have an ambulance in front?"

She nodded.

"Trey, team, grab Missy. Let's go." He turned, studying the animals in Book's arms. "Bring them too."

"You can't all ride in the ambulance with her," the human female informed him. "There's not enough room."

"They are going to go to the helicopter and wait for your ambulance to drive Kat to them. I'm staying with her." He shot Trey a furious glare. "You don't take off without us. Inform Homeland we're coming. I want all our doctors on standby and tell them to get the healing drugs ready."

Book stepped forward. "She's human."

"She isn't going to die," Darkness snarled. "I won't allow it."

Trey paled. "Do as he says."

"I can't allow you to do that," the human female protested.

Darkness snarled at her next. "What is your name?"

"Heather."

"I'm your worst fucking nightmare, Heather. Realize that and stop arguing with me. Do as I say. You come with us in the helicopter. I insist. You can work on her and keep her alive until our doctors have her."

"Fuck," Trey muttered. He raised his voice, deepening the tone. "That's official NSO orders. We have jurisdiction. We're taking over the scene and your ambulance." He pushed forward and stopped before Heather. "You are working for the NSO now until further notice. Let's go. You heard him."

Darkness glanced at Trey. The male shrugged. Both of them knew they were overstepping their bounds but he appreciated the male backing him up. Darkness inclined his head, acknowledging the debt.

"Tim and Justice are going to hand us our asses," he muttered low enough that only Darkness could hear. "But what the hell. That's your woman."

Darkness stayed with Kat as they loaded her into the ambulance and drove her down the street. The helicopter had come down in a four-way intersection. Cars were lined up, traffic blocked. A lot of them were outside their cars. Darkness ignored them, yelling out orders for the paramedics to carry Kat to the helicopter. Heather looked frightened but she boarded with them.

Missy sat next to Book. He held her against his body, as if she had a hard time sitting upright without assistance. Two of their males had her pets on their laps. The dog looked fine but the kitten appeared terrified, its claws digging in Jinx's vest. He petted its back, his face lowered, lips moving as if he talked to it.

Darkness took the floor after helping secure the backboard along the bench seat. He kept close to Heather since they couldn't buckle in. He gripped the underside of the bench and glared at her.

"I'll make sure you don't fall. Keep your attention on Kat. Don't let her die." He had to speak loudly to be heard.

"This is insane!" she yelled. "She needs to be taken to a hospital."

Trey closed the side door and crouched next to them, grabbing a strap since there was nowhere to sit. He snatched a headset, yelled at the pilot. "We're a go. Fly like you've never flown before, Darren."

The helicopter lifted straight up, fast. They banked hard. Darkness hooked an arm around Heather when she swayed but she fisted the sides of the backboard, clinging to it. He focused on Kat's face. She was breathing but her complexion was too pale. She had to survive until they reached Homeland.

Heather drew his attention when she gripped his hand. He turned his head, peered at her. She moved it to her belt, making it clear he should hold her there. He fisted it at her spine. She opened her medical kit and began an IV. He admired her courage and skill as she worked under pressure.

Fury believed he'd been drawn to Kat because she was a brave female. He felt no attraction to Heather, despite her pleasing appearance. Memories of Kat surfaced. She'd drawn him like no other. It wounded him, seeing her lying on that backboard when other images were so fresh in his mind — her laughing and even glaring up at him in anger. Such life had sparked in her eyes.

He might never see that again or hear the sound of her voice. He'd be left with nothing except bitter reminiscences, knowing everything could have been different if he hadn't denied how important she'd become to him. He'd wanted to protect her but he'd left her vulnerable instead. Emotions rose, almost drowning him in grief.

He fought to draw air, the pain crushing him from the inside. He wanted to roar out his rage at the unfairness of it. Part of him wanted to beat on something until his fists bled. Another part of him knew he'd never forgive himself if he lost her.

Don't leave me, Kat. Don't die. Keep fighting, he silently urged her. *I'll do anything if you just stay with me.*

Chapter Twenty-Three

෩

"Why is it taking so long?" Darkness cradled his bleeding fist, ignoring the hole he'd just put in one wall.

Fury sighed. "Do you feel better? Allow Paul to bandage that. You're going to slip on your own blood."

Darkness refused to stop pacing. "They've had her for ten hours."

"It takes time," Fury reminded him. "You insisted on them giving her the healing drugs. They had to put her in deep sedation and stabilize her heart before they operated to stop the internal bleeding. No news is good news. It means she's still alive."

He halted. "Maybe they are afraid to tell me."

Trey sipped his coffee. "I would be."

"You're not helping," Ellie muttered.

"Would you want to tell him? He's scary when he's pacing and randomly striking out at walls." Trey arched his eyebrows. "They'd tell you though. I was trying to lighten the mood. She's hanging in there."

"Why are you even here?" Darkness glared at the human.

"I want to know how your girlfriend is. I'm rooting for her."

"Shouldn't you be at the task force meeting?"

Trey hesitated. "I wasn't invited. I'm suspended for a few days."

"Tim suspended you?" Darkness growled. "I'll take care of it."

"Easy there," Trey murmured. "You want someone to pulverize but it had nothing to do with you or what we did on scene last night."

"Why are you suspended?" Fury frowned. "I haven't heard anything about it."

"It's between Tim and me. I broke a rule of his. He's pissed but he'll get over it. I'm not saying anything more." Trey grew quiet.

Darkness resumed pacing. Justice entered Medical and Darkness glared at him. "Do you have something to say to me?"

Justice glanced at Fury.

"No word yet." Fury looked at the clock. "She's a fighter."

"For a human?" Darkness snarled. "Is that what you meant?"

Fury lifted his palms. "Stop. You are looking for a fight and I'm not giving it to you."

"Don't look at me." Justice shook his head. "I read the reports and I don't have a problem with anything your team did. We returned the paramedic to her home. She'll have a good story to tell and was very understanding of the stressful situation. There won't be any problems with the human authorities. I did want you to know that the police recovered a body from Katrina's home. It's Robert Mason."

That saved Darkness the trouble of hunting the male down and killing him.

"Are they sure?" Fury looked skeptical. "I saw some of the news coverage. There wasn't much left of that house."

"They had positive identification. He was a priority since he's FBI and because of the association to the NSO. They pulled dental records and immediately compared them at the coroner's office. Jessie's father put pressure on them too. It's him. There's no doubt. His body was heavily damaged but enough was left for them to make other distinctions as well." Justice walked over to the pot of coffee and poured a cup. He turned, studying Darkness. "We're getting heavy inquiries from the press about what went down last night but it's being handled. Her family is in communication with Missy. We won't allow them access to Homeland but Missy assured them everything was being done for Katrina."

Darkness scowled. He didn't know much about Kat's family. He hadn't asked. "They wish to see her?"

Justice nodded. "They have to fly in. They are living in other states. She had Missy listed as her medical contact at the FBI. That was lucky for us since the female is here and hasn't protested anything our medical staff has done."

"She probably doesn't realize how dangerous that healing drug is," Fury rasped.

Darkness glared at him.

"I'm not saying you did wrong by demanding she be given it," Fury quickly stated. "I'd have made the same decision." He shot a meaningful look at Ellie. "I just hope her friend is kept unaware of the side effects."

"What are they?" Ellie inched closer to her mate.

Fury took her hand. "It was tested on Species but when they tried it on humans it caused heart attacks and massive strokes. It was too powerful for them to withstand."

"Think massive amounts of amphetamines," Trey added. "I learned about it when they put True's mate on it after she was shot. It accelerates the healing process but it can also raise the heart rate too high, causing severe arrhythmia and heart attack. The patient can also stroke out because their blood pressure goes through the roof." He stared at Darkness. "You had to take the risk. I'm sure she's still here because of the drugs. It's given her a real chance at survival if they can just keep her stabilized. It's got to be a fine line between keeping her vitals high enough to keep her alive but low enough to combat the side effect of the drugs."

"Well, Jeanie is great now." Ellie smiled. "The drugs saved her. We just need positive thinking. They'll save Katrina."

"Kat," Darkness growled. "She likes to be called that."

"Don't," Fury growled back. "You want to pick a fight? Not with my female."

"I'm frustrated." Darkness calmed. "Sorry, Ellie."

"It's okay." She kept her smile in place. "You wouldn't be the only Species to ever get testy with me."

The door across the room swung open and Doc Alli came out. She'd changed from her scrubs to a shirt and shorts set. Her sandals were quiet on the floor as she approached. Her expression masked her emotions but she locked gazes with Darkness, walking directly up to him. She stopped.

"That's one tough lady you have in there, Darkness. I didn't want to come out to give you news until I was sure she was going to make it, barring unforeseen circumstances."

He let the words sink in.

Doc Alli grinned. "It was touch and go. I won't lie. We had a hell of a time figuring out what dosage she could withstand but giving her enough to help her. The paramedics on scene were wrong. Her lung was bruised but it hadn't collapsed. She had hairline fractures along her rib cage on that side but they've mended. We also didn't find any internal bleeding so we didn't have to operate. She just got bruised to hell, has a severe concussion and needed stitches in three places. She lost a lot of blood from those sites, which explains her scary vitals when she came in. She was suffering from extreme shock. She's Trisha's blood type. That was lucky. Treadmont insists on keeping all mate blood types on hand just in case one of us ever needs it."

"May I see Kat?" He was afraid to believe her.

"Yes. I'll take you back. We have her hooked to a lot of monitors. I want you to be prepared for that. Treadmont and Trisha are staying with her. She's healing so fast we already had to remove the stitches so you won't see those. Next time we'll just use staples if we ever have to use the healing drugs on one of us. We're keeping her sedated to manage her heart rate and blood pressure. We brought her around once to make sure she…"

"She what?" Darkness didn't like the way her grin faded and worry flashed in her eyes.

"She took a severe blow to the head. We had to put her down fast when her heart rate rose too high but we wanted to make certain she was okay. The scans we did when she arrived showed some swelling but it's gone now." Doc Alli reached out and placed her hand on his chest. "We were worried about damage."

"She's fine though, right?" He felt sick.

"It was a closed head injury. You got her to us fast and we immediately began the drugs. We think we caught it in time before she suffered permanent injuries. The scans look great now. There's no bleeding. We've been running scans every hour to watch her. The last thing we wanted to do was open her up. We don't have a neurosurgeon at Homeland but we had one on standby from one of the nearby trauma centers in case he was needed."

"What if there is damage?"

Doc Alli chewed on her bottom lip.

"Just tell me."

"We have been consulting with the neurology department. If there was damage and it's mild, she might not remember what happened to her. Short-term amnesia is a possibility. It could cause some personality changes. Irritability. Mood swings. Depression." She paused. "There could be some mild physical issues. Blurry vision, headaches and some weakness to her limbs. We'll watch for verbal clues too. Slurred speech or trouble identifying words, spoken or heard."

Darkness closed his eyes. It hurt. *It's my fault.* He couldn't stop repeating that thought in his head. He should have kept Kat at Homeland, handcuffed to his bed, instead of pushing her away. She'd wanted him to meet her halfway but he'd refused to even try.

"Darkness?" Doc Alli patted his chest. "She's tough."

He opened his eyes. "You said you brought her around once. Did she seem fine?"

"She opened her eyes, looked confused, but then her heart rate climbed too high. We put her back under. She never spoke. It was too fast. Sedatives are hard to shake off and we just didn't have enough time to allow her to become coherent." She dropped her hand. "Do you want to see her?"

"I do."

"Follow me." She spun and quickly walked away.

Darkness stayed on her heels. They had two operating rooms and that's where she took him. Doc Trisha and Treadmont were in the large room, both sitting on chairs. They looked worn out and had changed clothes as well. Doc Trisha smiled at him. It looked forced. Doc Treadmont just dropped his head, watching something on a laptop.

Kat lay still on a padded gurney. They had the rails up on each side of her. She wore a hospital gown. A thick blanket covered her to mid chest. Her finger was covered with a plastic clip and a green thing was taped to her upper arm near her elbow. It pumped fluids and drugs into her system. The leads of a heart monitor ran under the top of her gown to her chest. She breathed on her own but still looked too pale.

He stood at her bedside. Her other arm was bandaged where he knew she'd suffered a deep gash. It was wrapped loosely around her arm. He frowned.

"It's healing," Doc Alli informed him. "We keep peeking at it so it's best not to tape it to her skin. Do you want to see her other injuries?"

He jerked his head in agreement.

Doc Alli lifted the blanket and Darkness growled. Kat had been on her side when he'd found her and too many bodies had been in the way when the paramedics had strapped her to a backboard. They'd covered her with blankets to keep her warm against the effects of shock. He realized her hip and thigh were damaged.

The wounds looked as if she'd been cut by a thick blade. The skin was marred by multicolored bruises, a natural progression of the healing process. It was in the advanced stages. They'd already started to become yellow.

"I don't know if it was from flying debris from the blast or if she landed on something," Doc Alli explained. "She got nailed on both sides, either way. Her left side was cut up like this but she sustained the worst damage on her right side. Her arm, her head and the ribs."

Darkness leaned over, noticing how his hands shook when he carefully gripped the top of Kat's gown and peeked under it. Circular pads attached the monitor leads above her breasts and more lines ran to her lower ribs. There was bruising under her right breast. He let go and straightened.

"It looked a lot worse when she was brought in." Doc Trisha moved to the other side of the bed. "The minor cuts and scratches on her have already healed. Not even bruises remain." She met his gaze. "We have a decision to make. I'm going to go talk to her friend."

"What decision?" She had all of Darkness' attention.

"To keep her on the drugs until she's fully healed or not. At this rate that will be complete by tomorrow night. The other option is to take her off them and allow her to heal naturally the rest of the way. If that's the decision, we'll flush out her system to remove the healing drugs."

"How is she handling being on them?"

Doc Trisha shrugged. "Good, considering she's almost in a coma." She glanced at Doc Alli.

"I told him. We're all worried about the closed head injury." Doc Alli took a breath. "We're anxious to wake her up and see how she is."

"She's not critical anymore," Doc Trisha informed him. "It would be safe. Her worst enemy was shock from the blood loss she suffered and the trauma of her injures. We've battled both those and won. We're going to talk to Missy and let her decide."

Darkness shook his head. "Keep her on them. Kat would hate being contained in Medical. Let her fully heal."

"It's not up to you," Dr. Treadmont stated.

Darkness whipped around to glower at the male.

"It isn't. They are guests at Homeland and her best friend is listed as her next of kin. Her records were forwarded to us."

He backed away from the bed and advanced on Treadmont. "You'll do as I say. Keep her on the drugs."

Doc Alli grabbed his arm. He stopped, not wanting to drag her. She stepped around him, putting her small body between him and the male.

"We'll keep her on them but if she starts to show signs that the drug is too much of a strain, we'll stop them. I think that's a reasonable compromise."

He growled low, glared at the male doctor, but calmed. "That's fine."

He shook off her hand and returned to the bed, watching Kat sleep. He didn't plan to leave. He didn't trust Treadmont anymore. It angered him that the male would disregard his wishes when it came to Kat. He'd put her in danger but he'd also make sure she fully healed before they allowed her to wake.

"We're going to keep her in here while she's on the drugs." Trisha caught his eye. "Okay? We'll move her to a room once we're ready to wake her up."

"Yes."

Kat would want to know Mason was dead. Her next question would probably be about her friend. He reached out, taking Kat's hand.

"How is Missy?"

"She's fine," Doc Alli assured him. "Some bruises and cuts but nothing serious. She just needed a few bandages and ice packs. We have her in one of the rooms."

"They have pets." He remembered that. "Where are they?"

"Book took them home. I checked them over. I'm not a vet but they seemed fine." Trisha moved away. "He's going to keep them at the men's dorm until Missy and Kat are ready to leave Homeland."

Darkness lowered his voice in case Kat could somehow hear him. "They don't have anywhere to go. Their house was destroyed."

"I'm sure the NSO will help them find a new place." Alli reached over and patted his arm. "She's going to be okay, Darkness. Why don't you try to get some sleep? You've been up all night. We're going to bring a few cots in here and take shifts napping. I'll have one brought in for you too."

"No."

"Darkness?"

He looked down at Obsidian's mate. She peered back at him with a determined look. "I'm used to dealing with growly, stubborn guys. You don't frighten me. You want to stay here? You take a nap. That's not up for debate. We'll wake you if anything goes wrong. Kat is sleeping. Get the rest while you can."

He understood the logic of it and caved, nodding.

She stepped back. "Good."

* * * * *

"What a mess," Justice said and sighed, taking a seat in the waiting area.

"It could have been much worse." Fury pulled Ellie closer. "He's still in denial but he has strong feelings for that female."

"You think that's denial?" Ellie didn't look convinced. "I was afraid he'd go insane if she died. I had Paul put a tranquilizer gun on the other side of the counter in case we needed to knock him out."

"Darkness is stubborn. We may be brothers but I'm the smarter one." Fury turned his head and placed a kiss on Ellie's forehead. "I stopped fighting my feelings for you."

"It's a circus outside the gates." Justice reached up and rubbed his forehead. "Reporters, police detectives and FBI all want to interview Darkness and the team. I told them they are at Medical. I let them assume everyone needed to be treated for injuries."

"I'm at Medical and so is Darkness." Trey stretched his arms, adjusting in the chair. "So it wasn't exactly a lie. Do you want me to do the bullshit verbal dance? Just tell me what you want them to know."

Justice seemed to consider it. "Is that before or after you give some human female a tour of Homeland?"

Trey cringed. "Sorry about that. I can explain."

"Save it. Jinx already did. It was smart. She didn't contact the police or press charges. We're sending her a basket of NSO merchandise and arrangements have been made for her to visit Homeland next weekend. We'll have to explain that she can't take photos unless we approve them but I'll have Flame or Smiley escort her around. They can stop at the bar and have lunch. It's a small price to pay for not reading headlines stating 'NSO team carjacks lone woman'. You know some journalist would imply we were kidnapping females to bring to Homeland."

Fury snorted.

Justice dropped his hand and focused on Trey. "Tim is pissed at you. Do you want to tell me why?"

"Nope. It's personal."

Justice appeared guarded, studying Trey. "We can't tell anyone about the call that came in from Katrina's home. They'd want a transcript of it. Book assured me Katrina was only planning on sneaking into Homeland as a tactic to stall the male until help could arrive. I agree. I'd rather not have to explain that to the press. They tend to twist the truth."

"No shit," Trey muttered. "They'd think the FBI was plotting to overtake Homeland instead of it only being one crooked agent who partnered up with his brother-in-law to get money off the backs of incarcerated Species."

"Exactly." Justice sipped his coffee. "The FBI would like to keep a lid on the Mason investigation. It will make them look bad."

"Screw them." Trey frowned.

Justice chuckled. "Always think two steps ahead, Trey. We could hand the real story to the press or we could have the appreciation from the government. Which sounds more helpful to the NSO? Mason is dead. We have Boris in custody." Justice paused. "They'll owe us and we could always release the details later, if the need arises."

"We score brownie points," Ellie added. "I get it."

Justice grinned. "That's one way to put it."

"Yeah. I get it too." Trey spoke to Justice. "What story do we tell them? Those TV hounds aren't going to disappear until they get something or they could just make up shit. You know it won't be flattering."

"Our public relations team is working on it. So far they believe we should release a statement saying Katrina Perkins is a consultant for the NSO, assigned by the FBI to assist us. We do get a lot of death threats from across the US and other countries. It sounds reasonable and she did stay at Homeland for a short time. We state that she was supposed to check in but didn't. The FBI and NSO both sent teams to check on her."

Trey nodded. "I see where this is going. Katrina and Missy were overcome by fumes from a crack in a gas line. Mason reached the home first and forced his way in to check on them. The house blew up and we arrived on scene. The only thing that pisses me off about that scenario is Mason is going to look like a hero who died trying to save a coworker."

Justice inclined his head. "I agree that it's distasteful but it would explain why our team arrived there and it doesn't cause a corruption scandal for the FBI. We both get to walk away from this with good press. I'm certain they'll be willing to remain silent on the matter or agree with our version of events."

"I can spin that." Trey stood. "Do you want me to handle this?"

"Go see our public relations team first. We pay them a lot of money so put them to use. They set up in the conference room in our office building. They'll help you manage the press and I'll have to make a statement within a few hours too. I'll let Tim know I put you in charge of handling the task force side of this. It will seem more official to have a member of the team address the press."

"I'm on it," Trey said as he left Medical.

Justice turned to Fury. "What do you think is going on in your brother's head regarding Katrina?"

"Hell if I know." Fury shrugged. "Darkness resists emotional attachments but he seemed really shaken that she nearly died. He'll either realize what she means or just grow more stubborn to keep her at arm's length. I have no idea which way this is going to go. I'm just happy she didn't die."

"He left Homeland to go into the human world. That's big." Ellie glanced at them both. "He has to care a lot about her. He refused to go after that Gift he worked so hard to find."

Fury pulled Ellie closer. "I know. We'll have to wait and see how this goes."

"I hope whatever his future holds, no more explosions are involved. I'm almost afraid to think of the consequences if he does make her a mate." Justice grimaced.

Ellie frowned. "What does that mean?"

"Shit seems to blow up when Katrina is nearby," Fury muttered. "That's one dangerous or unlucky female."

A door opened on the other side of the room and Sunshine stepped out. She glanced around then addressed Fury. "Is it safe?"

"Trey won't be back and our guests are surrounded by staff to keep them where they are."

"Come on out," Sunshine crooned.

Salvation rushed out of the room toward his parents, holding a paper. "I drew this for you."

Ellie slid away from Fury and opened her arms. "Come show Mommy!"

The boy hugged her and grinned, holding up a picture he'd drawn with crayons. "That's you and Daddy."

Justice laughed. "You both look so thin."

Ellie laughed. "We're stick people. I love them."

"Sorry to interrupt," Sunshine stated. "He's hyper and it's tough keeping him contained in an office."

"Thank you for babysitting him." Fury pulled his son onto his lap. "We both want to be here for Darkness."

"It's okay." Sunshine came closer. "I love spending time with him."

"We're going to be here a few more hours." Fury glanced at the clock. "I want to make sure Darkness doesn't snap if the female's condition changes. You could take him to our home."

"He wanted to stay close to you." Sunshine held out her hand. "Salvation? How would you like to watch a movie with me? I am having someone drop off my laptop."

"What movie?" Salvation wiggled off Fury's lap and ran to Sunshine. "I love movies."

The tall Species female lifted him, held him close. "Any movie you want. That's the neat thing about the internet. We can rent them. Let's go back into the office until it arrives." She glanced around, obviously on alert. "I'd feel better if we were in there. There are hu—"

Fury cleared his throat and shook his head. "He doesn't understand the need for secrecy."

Sunshine nodded. "Right."

Chapter Twenty-Four

ဢ

Kat opened her eyes. The first thing that came into view was a paneled ceiling. She blinked, trying to make sense of why it was there instead of the popcorn one of her bedroom. Memory surfaced fast. She turned her head and stared at a monitor to her right. Her heart rate was normal according to the number.

She'd jumped through a window with Missy and then there'd been pain and a loud noise. The gas must have ignited. She looked down her arm—an IV in her arm and an oxygen sensor on her index finger. Fearful, she moved her legs, shifting her feet on the hospital bed. They were there and intact. Her other arm ached and she turned to see a loose white gauze bandage wrapped around her upper arm.

I'm alive. Missy? Oh god! Panic set in and she tried to sit up. It was easier than she thought it would be and less painful. *This isn't a hospital.* She recognized the layout. *It's their Medical center. I'm at Homeland?* She was alone in the room with the door partially open to a silent hallway.

Something dark moved at the bottom of her bed. It was just a flash of what looked like black hair and then she gasped, almost falling over when a boy popped his head up. Dark eyes with unusually long, thick eyelashes peered at her. He lifted up a little, his fingers gripping the foot railing. She took in the shape of his nose. He blinked, his expression curious.

He looks like Darkness, except for the shape of his eyes. It might just be the coloring and skin tone but she saw a resemblance. He lifted up more, revealing his mouth. It was closed but that downward slant was a frown. He didn't talk, just continued to watch her.

Kat cleared her throat. "What's your name?" She smiled, hoping he wouldn't leave.

"Who are you?"

"I'm Kat."

"You don't look like one."

He had a gruff voice for a child so young but it was clear he was New Species. She pegged him to be about five years old, from what she could see of him. "It's just a name. I'm not a real cat."

He ducked and disappeared. She held still, knowing he hadn't left the room. She'd have seen him go with her clear view of the door. Something bumped her bed on the left and he straightened. He looked at her from a few feet away, glanced at the monitor then at her face.

"You're hurt?"

She assessed her body. A blanket covered most of her and she wore a gown. "I think I'm mostly okay. I feel good."

"You're in Medical." He reached out and touched the plastic clip on her finger. "Does that hurt? It is pinching you."

Kat held still. "No. It's not on tight."

He pulled it off and the machine beeped. He growled, dropped the clip on the floor, but then looked back at her. His eyes were big, almost fearful.

"It's okay." She resisted laughing. "Monitors make weird noises. You didn't hurt it and it can't hurt you. You didn't tell me your name."

"Salvation."

"That's a nice name." She glanced at the door, wondering where everyone was and why the boy was in her room. She couldn't see New Species allowing children to roam free in Medical. It wouldn't be safe with all the drugs and supplies he could get into. "Where's your mommy and daddy?"

"I sneaked away." He lowered his voice. "Sunshine fell asleep. She was watching me. My parents are in the waiting room. I crawled behind the counter so they couldn't see me. They were talking."

Kat was tempted to push the assist button on the hospital bed. She would bet his parents wouldn't be happy to find he'd slipped away from his babysitter. She didn't want to get him in trouble though. "You should go back to her. She'll wake up and be worried if you aren't there."

"She snores."

Kat laughed. "Really?"

He smiled, his expression adorable. "Loud. It woke me up."

The door suddenly moved and Darkness filled the space. "Salvation."

The boy jumped, spinning to face the snarling voice. Kat shot Darkness a warning look. "Don't scare him."

"He should be frightened. He knows better than to run away from someone watching him." Darkness entered the room, focused on the boy. He pointed toward the hallway. "Run to your father. He's to the left."

Salvation took off, moving fast for a small boy. He was out the door in a flash. Kat gawked at Darkness. "That was mean. You shouldn't have used that tone."

"He shouldn't have been in here. We were looking for him. Sunshine woke to find him gone. Everyone scrambled to search the building."

"He's just a little kid. He can't be more than five years old. What child doesn't explore his surroundings?"

"He's three and he's Species. It's a safety issue."

"Three?" She was stunned. "He's just a baby then." *A big one.* "You scared the crap out of him."

Darkness walked to the end of her bed. "Our children aren't clumsy, helpless individuals for the first years of their lives. He crawled at three months, began running by the time he was six months old, and spoke complete sentences before his first birthday. He was reading and doing what most of your children learn in school by his second birthday. You may see him as a baby but he's not human. He knows there's no excuse for him leaving the care of Sunshine and understands why he must follow rules. They are there for his protection."

She let that sink in. "Do they age faster?"

Darkness growled. "No. We don't age in dog years."

"I didn't mean it that way."

"I keep telling you we're different from you."

She took a calming breath. "I'm not going to argue with you. Where is Missy? Is she okay?"

"She's fine."

Kat closed her eyes, her fear alleviated. "Thank you."

Darkness snarled. "You nearly died saving her. Don't thank me. I just arrived in time to see the results of your efforts. You were dying."

She glanced down her body. "I feel okay. A little sore but—"

Another snarl tore from Darkness and he lunged, getting in her face when he stalked to the side of her bed and bent. "We gave you Species drugs to heal you. You were bleeding out when I found you. Motionless. Near death."

Darkness' eyes were almost black and his lips parted, revealing his fangs. Kat held still, assessing what he'd told her.

"You saved me. Thank you."

"You risked your life for another. I don't want your thanks. Missy said you turned on the gas and ignited it to blow up your house. She also said you used your body to shield hers from glass and falling debris. Don't ever do something like that again."

"She's my best friend." She tried to figure out the source of his anger. "You would have done the same. Mason ordered me to kill her and it was the only thing I could think of to do. He had the gun."

He backed off a few inches. "Just don't do it again."

He was worried. She found it touching. "The house?"

"Destroyed."

It didn't come as a surprise. "Mason?"

"Dead."

"Good."

"I would have killed him if he'd still been alive when I arrived."

"The explosion took him out?"

"Yes. He was found in the rubble after the firefighters were able to put out the fire."

More details came to mind. "How upset is Missy — at me?"

"She stated you did everything to save her."

"I meant about Butch and Gus. That's her dog and kitten. I couldn't save them. Mason would have shot her if I'd refused to prove I was all in as his partner. He wouldn't let me get close enough to disarm him or even attack so she could make a run for it."

"They survived. Missy told one of our males they were still inside the house and that crazy bastard went in after them. Book is lucky he didn't get killed. The back of the house was gone and the front was about to collapse and was in flames. He found them under a mattress that had pinned them against a wall next to the window he jumped through to reach them. It probably protected them from most of the blast."

"Please thank him for me. I don't think she'd have ever forgiven me if they'd died."

Darkness growled again. "She owes you her life. How are you feeling?" He seemed to search her eyes, looking for something.

"A little groggy and sore." She glanced at her arm. "How bad is it under that gauze?"

"You will be fine. They were worried about damage to your head."

She reached up, examining her hair and the shape of her head with her fingers. "It feels intact. Do I look bad?"

"You're pale. You also have all of your hair. They didn't have to operate but you suffered a blow to the head. There was swelling."

"Was?"

"The Species healing drugs were effective. The open wounds have closed and most of your bruises have faded."

"Open wounds?" She glanced at her arm again. "There's more?"

"Your hip and upper thigh were sliced open."

Kat shoved back the blankets and lifted her gown. She found more gauze on her right side. Darkness gripped her gown and jerked it down. "Anyone could walk in. You have nothing on under that."

"I don't care. I want to see what happened to me."

Darkness straightened, crossed the room and closed the door. He twisted the lock and returned to the side of the bed. He lowered the rail and offered her an arm. "I'll help you up. The doctors said you can stand and use the bathroom with assistance. You could suffer dizzy spells and weakness for a day or two. There's a mirror in the bathroom."

Kat swung her legs over. "I'm a little shaky."

"You almost died."

She allowed him to help her out of bed and into the bathroom. Darkness helped her remove her gown and she stared in the mirror. Gauze covered her arm and two places on her hip and thigh. Her ribs appeared discolored under one breast. She turned, staring over her shoulder.

"It was much worse," Darkness rumbled. His tone revealed his anger. "The drugs have worked very well on you."

Darkness gently removed the gauze on her arm. She watched him, not surprised at how tender those big hands could be. He tossed the bandage in the trash and Kat stared at the reddened skin. Faint marks revealed stitches had been there. She swayed on her feet.

Darkness bent, scooping her into his arms. "You should have stayed in bed."

"How long was I down?"

"Just since last night."

"That's amazing. I didn't know there were drugs like that in existence."

"Only Species have use of them."

"You should share them with the world. Do you know what a miracle it is that I've healed this fast?"

A muscle along his jaw jumped, his anger clear. "Mercile did trials on humans. The results were deadly. We're much sturdier than your kind. You wouldn't have been given the drug either due to the risk of death but you were so injured there was nothing to lose. It's amazing you're alive." He carried her to the hospital bed and laid her on it. "You're going to have to take it easy for a few days. Your body has endured a lot, Kat."

She let that information sink in. "I feel good."

"It took three of our doctors all night to make sure they didn't sedate you to death in order to keep your rapid heart rate and rising blood pressure from killing you while you were on the drugs. It's lucky you made it, Kat. You may feel as if you're fine but your body has probably never suffered such stress."

"Thank you. I take it that you asked them do it?"

He hesitated. "You were dying anyway. It was your only chance."

"Please thank everyone for me."

"It's their job."

The subject was closed. He didn't seem willing or able to accept her gratitude. She changed the topic to a safer one. "I'd like to call Missy."

"She's down the hall."

"She's here at Homeland?"

"Where were we supposed to send her? Your home was destroyed." He got her a fresh gown and helped her pull it over her head then tugged it down until she was decently covered.

"Thank you, Darkness."

He backed away. "Stop thanking me. Was I supposed to allow you to be sent to a human hospital to die?" His tone deepened into a snarl. "Was I supposed to just trust them to do everything they could to save you? I thought you were dead when I found you under the piece of roof that landed on you."

"A roof landed on me?"

"Only your foot was free of it. That's how I spotted you."

"Thank goodness I wasn't wearing ruby slippers. Missy says I can be a witch at times."

Darkness scowled. "What does that mean?"

"Sorry. That's my bad attempt at humor."

"It wasn't funny!" he roared.

Kat started.

Darkness panted, backing away. "You rest." He didn't yell that time but he still looked enraged. "And don't mention the boy to anyone. You shouldn't have seen him."

"I signed the confidentiality agreement. He's cute. He won't get into trouble, will he? I swear I won't tell anyone about him."

"He better not have gone to Missy's room. I need to check. It would make her a security risk."

"She'd rather die than put a child in danger. I know her as well as myself. She's my best friend. Don't threaten her,

Darkness. Just explain the situation or I will if Salvation paid her a visit. She'll keep it a secret."

"Stay in bed and allow your body more time to heal."

He spun, unlocked the door and was gone. Kat leaned back on the bed. "Shit." She'd nearly died. Darkness had saved her life. All those facts were sinking in. He was also trying to pick fights with her.

So much for our clean break. She was right back at Homeland. If she believed in signs, it would be a flashing neon one. She and Darkness weren't done. *Not by a long shot. And I'm not sorry about it. I just think he is.*

Darkness located Fury and Salvation down the hallway. He approached. Fury whispered to the boy, chastising him about his behavior. He was on the floor, on his knees at the boy's level. Darkness caught the end of their conversation.

"That's why you can't roam, Sal. That human knew about our children but what if she didn't? You're too young to understand but we have enemies. You need to trust me. I'm your dad."

"Sorry." Salvation appeared contrite.

Fury ruffled his hair and pulled him into his arms. "You just need to be more careful."

Darkness halted a few feet from them. "Did he visit Missy too?"

Fury looked up and shook his head. "No. Just Kat. How did she take it?"

"She thinks he's a baby."

Fury grinned. "Ellie does as well."

"I'm no baby." Sal growled, showing his fangs.

Darkness bent. "Then follow orders and don't go against your father's rules. Adults know boundaries."

Sal leaned heavily against his father, a little fear flashing in his eyes. "I'm not an adult. I'm a young male."

Fury hugged the boy to his chest and rose to stand with his son in his arms. "Is this going to be a problem?"

"Kat won't say anything about Sal. She understands why Species children need to remain secret."

"Good. How is she?"

"Much better but weak."

"It's to be expected. Trisha and Alli have gone home to their mates. Treadmont wanted to be informed when she woke."

"Why?"

"To check on his patient. He is the only doctor on duty right now."

"She's well."

"There's no neurological damage?"

"She's a little," he searched for an appropriate word, "mellow, but I think it's from the sedative."

"Ted can determine that better than you."

"She's fine. She's just not as focused as normal. There's no slur to her speech, no loss of mobility in her limbs and her memory is intact. Those were the things they said to watch out for. Tell him to avoid her room."

"Why don't you want Treadmont to see her? He's a good doctor."

"He wanted to take her off the healing drugs."

"Okay." Fury frowned. "Because it's dangerous for humans."

"He was going to leave the choice to Missy."

"She is her friend."

"It was my choice but he didn't respect that."

Fury's eyebrows rose. "You're not her mate. Or are you?"

"I need to go."

"Where? Back to her room?"

"She needs rest. I have things to do."

"What is more important than staying with your female while she's in Medical?" Fury grinned.

"Stop that."

"What?"

"Being amused."

"She's yours. Admit it. You usually deny that when I say it."

Darkness was irritated. "I'm not playing word games with you. Kat and Missy have no home. I don't want her working for the FBI any longer. That means they are going to need housing. Kat will work for the NSO. I have arrangements to make."

"You're keeping her." Fury chuckled. "I'll have mate papers drawn up. Congratulations."

"Don't make me curse in front of your young." He darted a glance at Salvation then glared at Fury. "Stay out of my business."

"Whatever you say, brother."

"Keep your son away from Missy. That would actually be helpful."

"But Sal can have free access to Kat?" Fury had the nerve to chuckle again.

Darkness snarled and stormed out of Medical. Fury was purposely being aggravating. There were details he needed to take care of before Kat and Missy were released. He jogged toward Security, hopeful that a little exercise would release some of his anger.

He entered and scanned the room, taking note of everyone on duty. He needed to ask a favor and Bluebird seemed the most likely to do it. She had said she wanted to be helpful. He approached her. She turned in her chair, her smile instant.

"Hello, Darkness."

He glanced around and crouched, lowering his voice. "I need a list of all available homes at Homeland."

Her eyebrows arched, her surprise evident.

"In the Species section. Is there anything open?"

She recovered and turned to face the monitor. Her fingertips flew over the keyboard as she hunted the information he wanted. "Always. Why do you want to know?"

"Don't ask questions."

She paused, turning her head. "They are usually for mated couples. Did you take one?"

"No."

She swiveled back around. "See the highlighted dots? Take your pick." She pointed to one. "True and Jeanie are normally in residence at this one though it comes up in search as available because we removed them from the system when we thought the FBI was coming after her."

"Which one is the most distanced from others?"

She gave him the information. "Is it just curiosity or do you want me to mark it as being used?"

"I'll take it."

"Okay." She frowned. "You no longer wish to live at the men's dorms? Some males have private homes. You'll live next to Brass when he's at Homeland. He's a single male."

He debated giving her an answer, realized she deserved one. "I want more privacy. Recent events have left me irritated with certain males."

"You know anyone would have assigned you the house if you'd just asked. Why come to me as if you don't want anyone to know?"

He clenched his teeth but calmed. "I can't do anything without everyone discussing it."

"Everyone worries because we care about you."

"I'm tired of it. This will allow me to come and go as I wish, without it being commented on."

"Understood."

"Do they still allow Species-friendly human females to stay in the women's dorms the way Ellie did?"

"We don't need a new house mother but yes, it would be okay for Katrina to stay there if you wish. We're human-female friendly."

"Are there any apartments open?"

"Always. We are fewer than the males."

"Is there anyone willing to give a tour of the dorm?"

"I can do it." Bluebird smiled. "I'd like to get to know Katrina better."

He scowled. "Thank you. I'll see when Treadmont is going to release his patient."

"Just call me." She winked. "You have my number."

He fled Security, his mind working. He didn't have a lot of time and there were many things to do. He called Book on his cell phone. The male answered on the first ring.

"How are Missy's pets?"

"Fine. The dog sleeps a lot. He's lazy." Book chuckled. "The kitten on the other hand has managed to open the closet door and destroyed a lace on my boot. He seems to be teething."

"Get them ready to be moved. Missy should be checked out of Medical soon. She'll want her pets to go with her."

"Okay." Book hesitated. "They have no home to return to."

"I'm aware." He hung up, taking one of the Jeeps parked outside of Security.

Chapter Twenty-Five

∞

"What do you mean, Missy is gone?" Kat shrewdly assessed Dr. Ted Treadmont. He had a gruff personality, was obnoxiously direct and did not have a good bedside manner.

"Darkness checked her out a few hours ago."

"Where did he take her?"

"You need to answer my questions before I answer yours." He tried to shove a light in her eyes again.

She blocked him by grabbing the mini light and snatching it out of his hand. "Where did he take her?"

"I don't know. He doesn't answer to me. That's one rude Species. I reminded him that I hadn't officially released her but he told me he'd put me in one of the beds if I didn't get out of his way. He wouldn't even wait for a wheelchair. He snarled something about how her legs weren't broken and she could walk just fine on her own. Now behave before I call in a nurse to hold you down."

"I wouldn't do that if I were you," she warned. "I feel fine."

"You suffered a closed head injury. I'd like you to answer some of my questions and I need to check the dilation of your pupils. You could have suffered brain damage."

"I'm starting to see why Darkness snarls at you. I'm good."

"You're testy. That's an indication that you could have neurological problems."

"My only problem is that you keep annoying me. You think Darkness is rude? I just want to know where my best friend is."

"I don't know. He probably drove her to the front gates."

"Shit." She shoved at the blankets over her lap and reached over the side bar to release it. "Move."

"You're not going anywhere."

"I have to find Missy. She'll be freaking out." *My emergency kit is in the trunk. I have enough clothes for both of us. We'll need to get a hotel room and figure out our next move.*

She got the side rail down and slid out of bed. The doctor tried to stop her but Kat pushed him back. She felt stronger as she stood there. No dizziness.

"Get back in that bed, young lady."

"I need something to wear. I'm not going to exit your gates with my ass exposed." *I'll sweet-talk the taxi driver into taking us home. I can pay him after I bust into my trunk. I'm sure he'll do it if I promise him a fifty-dollar tip.*

"Get back in that bed or I'm calling a nurse."

"You do that. Maybe he or she will find me some scrubs or something else to wear."

Dr. Treadmont muttered a curse and turned toward the door. Kat made it to the bathroom and stared at her reflection. She was still unusually pale but splashing water on her face helped. She found a toothbrush in the cabinet, unsealed it, brushed her teeth and used her fingers to comb her hair. Voices in the other room assured her the doctor had made good on his threat. She walked out, prepared to do verbal battle.

Darkness and Dr. Treadmont faced off against each other. Field, the New Species she'd spoken to before, hovered by the door. She paused, taking in the scene.

"You don't threaten Kat," Darkness growled.

"She's not released from my care," Treadmont shot back. "Field? Make him leave this room."

Field's eyes widened and he backed up closer to the hallway. "No way."

"Hey," Kat interrupted. "Darkness, where is Missy? You didn't just leave her outside the front gates, did you?"

He turned to look at her. "No. She's safe."

Kat leaned against the door. "Thank you. I was imagining her out there with those protestors."

He frowned. "You believe I'd put her at risk?"

"Dr. Treadmont implied you might have. You left, I took a nap and woke up to him trying to play twenty questions. I'm not in the best mood. Then I wanted to see Missy and he said you'd taken her away. You weren't exactly thrilled with what I did to protect her from Mason." Suspicion hit. "She's not locked up or something, is she?"

He growled. "No. She's with her pets. Some female Species are looking out for her."

Kat blew out a relieved breath. "I'd like to be taken to her." She looked at Field. "Can you find me something to wear? Scrubs, whatever. Just something that isn't open along the back."

He nodded and fled out the door. Dr. Treadmont threw up his arms and spun, following him out of the room.

"Nobody listens to me. I'm just the damn doctor who stayed up all night and most of the day to look after my patient."

"Thank you," Kat called out after him. She lowered her voice, stared up at Darkness. "He's kind of pushy."

"He's good at what he does."

"Obviously. I'm still here and you told me I was in bad shape. I just didn't like the bright lights he tried to flash in my eyes and his attitude. What paperwork do I have to sign to get released? I need to get Missy and myself home. Well, to what is left of our house. To my car. It should have survived. I have to get the suitcase out of the trunk and check us into a hotel."

Darkness blinked but said nothing. Kat inched around him, walked to the door and peered down the hallway. Field carried a small stack of folded clothing. He paused in front of her.

"I hope these fit. I went to the doctor's lounge where Trisha and Alli keep spare leggings and T-shirts. You're all about the same size. The pants might be a little short on you since you're taller than them."

"Thank you." She accepted them and backed up, closing the door.

Darkness remained by the bathroom as she dumped the clothes on the bed and reached behind her, feeling for the ties of the gown. "A little help?"

He brushed her fingers aside to do it. "That's your plan? Check into a hotel?"

"Yeah. I have savings. Tomorrow we'll hunt for a rental. The pet deposit is going to be expensive but I can manage it. Missy is going to need a computer too. She goes a little nuts if she can't write for a few days. I know she's got online backup for all her work. That's one less worry. She can do that anywhere as long as there's internet and electricity. I have an extra debit card and credit card hidden in the lining of the suitcase. We'll be fine. I just hope my insurance covers what happened to the house. I doubt it since I pretty much blew it up but the police reports will help. It was done under duress."

She yanked off the gown and put on the shirt. The leggings were tougher to get on over the bandages but she managed it. Kat looked down. "I don't suppose you could find me a bra in my size? I feel kind of weird without one. Shoes would be good too." She turned to look up at Darkness.

"The police weren't told the truth."

Kat tilted her head. "What?"

"No one wanted the truth about Mason or what really happened leaked to the press. They would have twisted it into negative things about the FBI in general and the NSO."

"They'll think I blew up the house to defraud the insurance company. There will be an investigation on what caused the explosion."

"It's been handled. It will be deemed as an accident."

"The NSO is going to cover it up?" That stunned her. "They can do that?"

"You can tell our legal department your concerns and they'll help you deal with your out world and the insurance issues with the house. Don't worry about that right now."

Kat gaped at him. "Do you understand that I would be arrested if I filed a false claim? If they prove I turned on that gas and lit the curtains on fire? It's a crime to destroy your own house and then collect insurance to cover what you still owe on the mortgage. I don't want to go to prison. The press can kiss my ass. I'll tell them the truth."

Darkness sighed and bent, scooping her into his arms. "You talk too much."

"Put me down."

He ignored her, carried her to the door, and shifted her in his arms to grip the door handle. He used his foot to shove it all the way open and strode down the hallway. Kat wrapped her arms around his neck.

"I can walk. Are you taking me to Missy?"

"Eventually. We need to talk first."

She studied his severe expression. He looked angry and determined. "Fine. Just don't bitch at me again about putting my ass on the line for my best friend."

"I don't bitch."

"No. You growl and snarl."

His mouth tightened into a white line but he said nothing. The lobby was empty. The exit doors slid open automatically and he carried her outside. She glanced at the sky, realizing the day had almost passed. The sun was still up but it wouldn't be for long. He stopped in front of a waiting Jeep and deposited her on the passenger seat.

"Thank you."

He rounded the vehicle and climbed into the driver's seat. "Stop that."

"Sorry. That's what people say when other people do something nice for them. It's called being polite. You should try it sometime. Where are we going, if not to find Missy?"

"You'll see."

"Okay." She put on her belt. "We're playing the few-words game."

He started the engine and threw it in gear. She gripped the seat with both hands, wondering what he was up to. She realized he wasn't headed toward the front gates.

"Where are you taking me?"

"I didn't want anyone eavesdropping on us. We have some things to discuss."

"Fine. That still doesn't answer my question."

"I'm taking you to my house."

They passed the men's dorm. Kat turned her head, frowning at him. "Your house is back there."

"I moved."

"To where?"

"Someplace where no one can overhear if there is yelling."

"Great." That didn't sound good. She knew he was furious that she'd risked her life and that he'd had to go to a lot of trouble to save it. She was grateful for all he'd done. He was probably due a little temper tantrum.

A small guard shack appeared on the left, with gates across the two-lane road he turned onto. He slowed and a New Species stepped out of the building. The officer reached inside as he waved them forward. The gates swung open slowly to allow them to enter an area of Homeland she hadn't seen before.

"What is this?"

"The Species living area. It's similar to human guest housing but the cottages are bigger."

"I didn't know they were separated."

"Now you do."

She dug her fingernails into the seat. Darkness was really irritating her. He drove down one street of nice-looking homes, turned right and then made a left. He pulled into the driveway of a pretty, brown single-story home. He turned off the engine and set the parking brake.

"Don't move."

"Okay."

He got out and walked up the sidewalk to the front door. She had no idea why he was making her wait there unless he had to visit someone first. He returned a minute later and approached her. He just leaned over, unfastened her belt and lifted her out of the seat. Kat hugged his shoulders as he carried her up the walkway.

The front door stood wide open and he entered the house then used his foot to slam the door. He stopped. Kat glanced around. It was an open living space, showing off a living room, dining area and a bar that separated them from the kitchen.

"Nice place."

"Thank you." He strode across the room to follow a long hallway.

"Where are we going?"

"My room."

They passed one open door on the right. Probably a guest room. The door across from it looked like a bathroom from the quick glimpse she got. He paused at the end of the hallway and turned, making sure she didn't hit the doorway as he took them into the master suite of the home.

"It's much bigger than your apartment."

"It's a two-bedroom, two-bath. It's not as big as some of the homes in the Species living section but it is the one I chose." He approached the bed and bent, setting her on the edge of the bed. He let her go and straightened, backing up a few feet.

She got comfortable and took a deep breath. "Okay. You brought me here. Let me have it. Go ahead and yell at me. Tell me what I did to piss you off. I'm ready."

"You're not allowed to risk your life for anyone else's. You came too close to death. That's unacceptable."

She was surprised by his rational tone. "We've already had this fight. Missy is my best friend and Mason didn't give me much choice. Where is she?"

"I set her up in an apartment inside the women's dorms with her pets. She's fine. A friend of mine is going to make certain she's comfortable. The females will look out for her and will acquire everything she needs to set up her new life here."

That wasn't the answer she'd expected. "The NSO is okay with that?"

"I said I'd get you a job at the NSO. I made inquiries and you no longer need to work for the FBI. Give your notice. You and Missy are a package deal. You care for her. That means we care for her as well."

They wouldn't be homeless. It would be tight living, sharing a one-bedroom apartment with Missy but they'd done that right after high school. Missy would probably take over the living room as her office. It wouldn't interrupt Kat's sleeping time. It also meant she could kiss the investigation regarding Mason goodbye and all the stress that came with it at work. The police couldn't touch her if they did charge her with arson. It was almost too good to be true.

Darkness had made it all possible. "I don't know how to thank you enough."

"Stop saying that," he growled, his eyes flashing anger.

It pushed her into feeling a bit of temper too. "Fine. Fuck you. Is that better?"

"Only if it's an offer."

That remark knocked her for a loop. She gawked at him. Darkness came forward and crouched next to the bed, pinning her legs between his spread ones. She stared into his eyes, stunned. He had that hungry look she remembered too well.

She flattened her palms on his chest. "Uh-uh. I'm not doing this again. We made a clean break, remember?"

"Things change."

"But you don't. We don't want the same things. You made it clear that it can't ever be anything but sex to you. It's more than that to me."

He put his hands on the bed next to her hips and leaned in. "I'm going to kiss you, Kat."

"You don't kiss."

"I'll make an exception for you."

She stared at his lips. They parted and he ran his tongue over them before inching closer. She leaned back, wondering if it was payback for angering him. He'd had to go to a lot of trouble for her. First to save her life then to get her a job and home with the NSO.

"Don't."

"Why not?" He spoke softly, his gruff voice sexy.

"This is just cruel."

"I don't understand."

"Yes, you do. It was hard enough walking away once."

He lifted one hand and reached behind him, digging something out of his back pocket. Metal clanked and he showed her a set of handcuffs. She glanced at them then stared into his eyes.

"No."

He arched one eyebrow.

"I'm not going to allow you to hook me up to your headboard and do this dance again."

He tossed them across the room. "I'm going to allow you to touch me all you want. I removed them to make a point. I won't restrain you anymore."

"You're such a bastard. What did I ever do to deserve this?"

"You got under my skin." He rose, the movement pushing her flat on her back with her hands still on his chest, just inches between their bodies. He climbed over her, trapping her under him. "You nearly died. When I lifted that roof off you I couldn't detect your breathing at first. I thought I'd lost you forever."

"So this is how you decide to get even? Give me what I want then regret it right afterward?"

He had the nerve to smile. "I lost control the last time you touched me."

"What makes you think it won't happen again? You're that smug?"

"I was too focused on how good your hands felt to remember to use a condom. I could have accidently gotten you pregnant."

"Yeah, that was five days of waiting I'll never forget."

"This time will be different."

"No. I'm done with casual sex."

"There's nothing casual between us."

"My point exactly."

He lifted one leg and gently nudged hers. She locked them together, shaking her head. "No."

"Spread open for me."

"Darkness, don't seduce me just to be an asshole."

"I'm not."

"Right. We have sex and then what? You tell me to leave again? That the job offer and living in the apartment were just bullshit?"

"You're not living in the women's dorm."

"You said that's where Missy was."

"She is. That's her new home."

"She gets to stay at Homeland but I don't?"

"You're going to stay here with me."

She had to be hearing him wrong.

"This is our house," he said as he nudged her leg again. "Our bedroom. Our bed." He rolled over suddenly, taking her with him. "And there will be no more regrets."

Kat ended up sprawled on top of him. She spread her legs and straddled his lap, pushing against his chest until she sat atop him. "What kind of game are you playing?"

"I'm not. You're important to me. I don't want to lose you."

He looked sincere and it made her angry. "Are you kidding me?"

Darkness growled, his mood matching hers. "Do I look as if I'm telling a joke? I got us a house. We shouldn't have to live in the men's dorm where other males can hear everything through the walls."

"You don't do relationships. You don't let anyone get too close to you. What changed? I almost died? That's what you're saying?"

"Yes."

"What about tomorrow or next week when you get over the fact that I had a close call? You shut down again and build up the walls? No thanks."

He sat up, almost knocking her off his lap. His arms hooked around her waist and he jerked her tightly against his chest until they were almost hugging. "I tried to resist the emotions you bring forth. I regretted it when you left Homeland."

"Which time?"

"Both."

"But you let me go a second time."

"What do you want from me, Kat? I got us a house and I promise not to restrain you during sex anymore. I'm offering to share my life with you."

"Do you want a list?"

"Yes."

"You're never home. I lived with you before."

"I'll work fewer hours and spend more time with you."

She wanted to believe him. "You don't like to talk. I do."

"I'm talking to you now."

"That's only because you want to have sex. That motivates any guy to be a chatterbox if he thinks it's going to get a woman's pants down."

"You want proof that I'm going to do everything to be the kind of male a female mates?"

She couldn't believe he used that word. "Mates?"

"Mates," he growled. "That's what you want."

"It's not what you want."

"I want you."

"For sex."

"Work with me this time, Kat." His tone softened. "I'm trying."

Tears filled her eyes and she blinked them back. "I don't want to get my heart stomped on."

"I won't hurt you."

"You won't mean to. That, I believe."

Darkness was frustrated. He'd expected Kat to allow him to kiss her and just agree to move in with him. Instead she was sitting on his lap and he felt as if he were holding her in place. She might put space between them if he allowed it. He wasn't going to.

She wanted him to talk to her. It wasn't easy to express his feelings. Losing her wasn't an option. "I feel things for you."

She wiggled on his lap. "I feel. You're hard."

"You're in my arms."

"I need more than just sex."

"I had a nightmare when you were sleeping next to me."

"I bet."

He flashed his fangs. "May I finish talking?"

"Sure."

"You were on top of me, touching me, and it turned into a nightmare."

"This is just getting better and better. I'm sorry that's traumatizing to you."

He rolled, pinning her under him again. This time she couldn't close her thighs—his hips pinned them open. He was careful to keep most of his weight off her and was aware of her bandages. He didn't want to hurt her in any way.

"It was about that female who betrayed me. I trusted Galina. She tried to stick a blade in my heart after I learned she was the reason my brothers died. In the dream you became her and she actually killed me. I'd let my guard down for you and I died in the dream because of it."

Kat's expression showed sadness. "That's rough."

"It motivated me to keep you distanced. I thought I could ignore the emotions you stirred in me and they would fade if you weren't a part of my life. They didn't. You said it would happen and you were right. Distance isn't going to make me want you any less. It just makes me miserable when you're gone."

Her hands massaged him through his shirt. "I can relate to that."

"You almost died and all I could think about was how much I regretted sending you away. I wouldn't have the chance to have you in my life again." He swallowed against the lump in his throat. "What do you call it? It was a reality bitch-slap."

Her lips curved and she smiled. "It was, huh?"

"Yes. I saw a future I didn't want. You wouldn't have been in it. It won't be easy for me to change but I'm motivated to try. All I have to do is think about going to bed without you beside me and knowing you won't be the first thing I see when I wake. It's a bleak outlook. I want you in my life. You will make it a better place."

"Damn." She shifted her hands to his shoulders, curving them there. "Kiss me."

"Are you going to live here with me, Kat?"

"I'm all in if you are. I'd have you shake on it but I really want that kiss. You have the best mouth. Have I ever told you that?"

"It's been awhile. I might be bad at this."

"I'm willing to risk it." She grinned. "I'm willing to risk everything when it comes to you."

"Me too."

Darkness lowered his face, focusing all his attention on her mouth. He could remember some of the basics. He'd been taught how to kiss but it had been a really long time. It was important that he do it well for Kat.

She closed her eyes when their breaths mingled and her lips parted. He gently covered hers with his. They were soft and so Kat. He darted his tongue out, tracing the inner line of her full bottom lip. Her fingernails dug into his shirt urging him to continue. Her tongue met his and he growled, his control slipping. He took full possession of her mouth, kissing her deeply.

It all came back to him when she moaned, meeting his passion. He rolled, making sure they didn't break the intimate connection. He tore at her shirt, careful not to get her skin with his fingernails. Material ripped and she shifted, helping him remove it from her body. She tugged, trying to destroy his shirt.

They rolled again once she was bare from the waist up. He helped her by using his nails to claw at his own shirt. She hooked her fingers inside the holes, stronger than she seemed when she shredded it apart. Her hands spread across his skin, almost frantically exploring every inch. He hooked the waist of her leggings, shoving them down her hips. He hit gauze and halted, afraid he'd hurt her.

Kat let him go and reached down, shoving at them herself. He rolled them again, almost right off the bed. He growled, breaking the kiss, and lifted up. "Damn. We should move to the floor."

"Only if you're on the bottom. Rug burn is a bitch." She lifted her hips, getting her pants down, and kicked them away.

His allowed himself to admire the length of her beautiful body. He removed what was left of his shirt, tore off his boots and shucked the pants. Her bandaged wounds only served as a reminder of how close he'd come to never touching Kat again. "You're mine," he snarled, lunging at her.

She didn't flinch or seem alarmed. Her arms opened and she wrapped them around his middle when he came down on top of her, her nails raking down his back. She spread her thighs wide to accept the girth of his hips. He ached to take her, to be inside Kat and know her warmth. The smell of her arousal was strong enough to know she was as ready to be taken as he was to take her. He wanted to kiss her again and went for her mouth. She twisted her head at the last second, preventing him from making contact.

"Stop!"

"What?"

She adjusted her hold on him and pushed against his chest. He lifted up a little and she turned her head to stare at him. "Condom. I'm not going to have you destroy our new bedroom walls or mess up your hands. You might have forgotten but I haven't. Tell me you have some."

"I do. They are in the nightstand drawer."

"Get them."

Darkness held her gaze. "No." He adjusted his hips, brushing the tip of his dick against her pussy, finding the right spot. He pushed forward slowly, entering her. She tensed, her nails digging into his chest but a low moan broke from her lips.

"What are you doing?"

"Not allowing anything to get between us ever again."

Her legs lifted and wrapped around the back of his thighs. She locked them, her thighs gripping his hips to hold him in place. "I could get pregnant."

"I'm willing to risk it. You thought Salvation was cute, didn't you?"

Kat appeared stunned and turned-on at the same time. "He's adorable but what are you doing?"

"Proving that I'm serious about you and making our relationship last." He shifted his hips, thrusting forward despite her attempts to keep him still. Her pussy gripped him as much as her legs did but he still managed to sink every inch of his dick inside her body. "I'm all in, sweetheart." He nudged her face aside and nipped her throat. She moaned and caressed him. "Relax and enjoy this. It's the first step in mating. I'm claiming you in every way."

Kat eased her grip on him and lifted her legs higher, wrapping them around his ass. "You better not regret this. I'll kill you. I remember what else you keep in your nightstand drawer."

He nipped her again. "I'm certain. I love you, Kat. You won't have a reason to shoot me."

She twisted her head to look up at him. "Say that again."

"I won't give you a reason to shoot me."

Her mouth opened and she didn't hide her outrage. He chuckled.

"I love you, Kat."

Tears filled her eyes. "I love you too. Now fuck me. Lose control."

"That's going to happen a lot. No more restraint."

"Good."

He let go of the past. Kat was his future. He started to move on top of her, being gentle. Her moans were music to his ears. He loved the way her hands glided across his skin, her nails raking down his spine. Her nipples hardened, rubbing against his chest. He braced one arm and lifted up just enough to reach between them, found her clit and rubbed. Her pussy clamped tighter around his shaft and he clenched his teeth, fighting the urge to come. He waited for her. Kat's vaginal walls clenched and squeezed his shaft, milking him. He drove deep inside her, roaring out as he emptied his seed.

He rolled over onto his back, taking Kat with him so she lay on top of him. They were both panting and spent. He smiled, kept his eyes closed and didn't stare up at the ceiling. He was focused on the female in his arms. Life was good.

Kat brushed a kiss next to his nipple. "Do you want to hit something?"

He chuckled. "Nope."

"What if I do get pregnant? Are you going to freak?"

397

"Probably, but only because I'm not certain what kind of father I'd make."

"A good one. I know that."

"I trust you, Kat."

He meant it.

Epilogue
ဆ

Fury opened the front door and grinned. "It's about time."

Darkness gripped Kat's arm, steering her inside the home. He glanced around the living room. Pictures adorned the walls and the smell of food tempted his appetite. It was a very domestic scene. Salvation sat in the middle of a pile of multicolored plastic toys. The boy waved.

"Hi!" Kat pulled away from Darkness and approached the boy. She just dropped down to her knees beside the mess and picked up a block. "What are you going to build?"

Fury closed the door and stepped next to him. He lowered his voice to a whisper. "Ellie is in the kitchen. She's worried about overcooking her pot roast so it is too dry. I told her it would be fine. You will like her food."

Darkness stared into the male's eyes and kept the same low tone. "Can she cook?"

"Better than we can." Amusement lightened his features. "She teaches the females. She's just nervous because you've finally agreed to have dinner with us. She knows it matters a lot to me." He looked at Kat. "Does your female cook?"

"We often eat at the bar."

His brother laughed. "Understood. Get comfortable."

Darkness crossed the room and took a seat on the couch. Kat was playing with Salvation, using blocks to form some sort of structure. He enjoyed seeing her interact with a Species young. She still considered the boy a baby at the age of three but she'd learn if he wanted to show off his physical prowess by playing rough with her. He wouldn't allow it to happen. She could get hurt.

Fury sat in a chair a few feet away. "You look happy."

"He is." Kat turned her head. "When he isn't trying to pretend otherwise. You know how he can get."

"I do." Fury relaxed in the chair. "How are you adjusting to Homeland, Kat?"

"I'm loving it. I start teaching classes next week."

"I didn't want her working Security," Darkness confided.

"He's afraid I'll blow shit up." She winced, glancing at Salvation. "Sorry. Stuff. Shit is a bad word."

"He's heard way worse." Ellie walked out of the kitchen. "Don't worry about it. My son could probably teach you some you've never heard before. We don't sweat a few occasional slips. It's when people start combining them that we draw the line." She pointed at Salvation. "Don't give her an example."

Salvation giggled. "Darn."

Ellie winked at him and moved behind Fury's chair. She bent, coming up with a gift bag. "We have a present for you both."

Darkness tried to hide his surprise. "Is a gift exchange expected?"

"No." Fury pulled Ellie onto his lap. "My mate just wanted to do something to show how happy we are for both of you."

Kat climbed to her feet and took a seat next to Darkness on the couch. "That's so sweet."

"It's nothing major but it's becoming a kind of tradition around here." Ellie leaned forward and passed the bag to Darkness. "Careful. It's breakable."

Darkness handed it to Kat. "You reach inside." He was afraid he might damage the gift if it were fragile. He watched her face, liking the joy she expressed.

Kat opened the bag and removed a glass frame. Darkness leaned in, pressing his body against her smaller one. He enjoyed touching Kat and found any reason to do it. It wasn't a photo inside the frame but a copy of their signed mate papers. Kat turned her face and lifted her chin. Tears glimmered in her eyes.

"Look." She held it as if it were precious. "How cool is this?" She shifted her attention to Ellie and Fury. "Thank you!"

"We keep ours over our bed." Fury pointedly stared at Darkness. "Just glue it to the wall. We learned the hard way that it can fall down if the headboard bangs too much."

Ellie blushed. "Too much info. They could have figured that out themselves without you mentioning it."

"I'm his brother. It's my job to help him avoid making the mistakes I have." Fury snorted. "We went through three frames before I made sure it couldn't fall." He nodded at Darkness. "Use super glue. Just plaster the entire back of it directly to the wall."

Ellie wiggled off his lap. "I think the roast should be done. Ready to eat?"

"Do you need help?" Kat rose to follow and placed the framed document down. "I suck at cooking but I follow directions well."

Ellie's eyes widened. "Do you want to learn? I give cooking classes at the women's dorm."

"That would be great. My classes are going to be held at the bar."

"What are you going to teach?"

Kat flashed a playful look at Darkness. "According to him, it's to reiterate how all humans are criminals." She laughed. "Human nature. It seems a lot of New Species are curious about us. I'll give Security some tips but I want them to be able to ask me anything they want."

"Not everything," Darkness reminded her. "The males better watch what they ask."

401

Kat arched an eyebrow. "No one is going to hit on me. They are too afraid of you. I don't tell you how to do your job. Ditto, baby."

Ellie grabbed her hand. "Come with me. He's going to start snarling. Did he warn you about how possessive a mate can be?"

"No need. I caught on fast."

Darkness watched the females enter the kitchen. He stared at the frame Kat had placed on the table. It was proof that he'd taken every step with his female. They were mated and not using condoms. She could get pregnant. He studied Salvation. The young male was content with his blocks.

"This life might be yours soon," Fury rasped. "It's fantastic having a mate and a child."

Darkness stared at his brother. "I still don't know if I'm going to be good at it."

"Is making Kat happy your first priority?"

"Yes." He could answer that without hesitation or thought.

"Do you love her?"

He nodded. "With everything that I am."

Fury leaned forward. "You have a family. You're never going to be alone again. It is a good thing, isn't it?"

Darkness contemplated his life before and after Kat. He also felt grateful he'd finally allowed Fury into his life. "Yes."

"You'll do great then." Fury stood. "Let's go eat. You know this is going to become a regular event, right? We want you over at least once a week to share a meal and Ellie celebrates human holidays. Deal with it. I do. It's not so bad." He scooped his son off the floor and tossed him at Darkness. "Catch."

Darkness was amazed that the boy laughed. He hugged him close, cradling him against his chest. "You throw him at people?"

"He likes it. I knew you wouldn't drop him. Tell him, Sal."

The boy beamed. "I love it, Uncle Darkness. It's fun!"

Something inside Darkness' chest melted. The trust the boy showed, the way he relaxed against him, felt right. He suddenly wasn't so afraid of the concept of having young of his own.

"It's not so alarming, is it?" Fury regarded him. "I can see it in your eyes. Tomorrow Sal and I are going to the park. Meet us there at seven in the morning. You'll need some practice before it happens. I had none." He laughed. "It worked out but I'm going to give you an advantage for when your time comes. What do you say?"

"I'll be there."

Fury opened his arms. "Do you want to toss him back?"

His hold tightened on the boy. "I think I'll carry him into your dining room."

Fury winked. "Good. You know your mate is going to see you with him and all bets are off if you have talked her into waiting to have babies. We make adorable offspring."

Darkness was willing to risk it.

Also by Laurann Dohner

ଌ

eBooks:

Cyborg Seduction 1: Burning Up Flint

Cyborg Seduction 2: Kissing Steel

Cyborg Seduction 3: Melting Iron

Cyborg Seduction 4: Touching Ice

Cyborg Seduction 5: Stealing Coal

Cyborg Seduction 6: Redeeming Zorus

Cyborg Seduction 7: Taunting Krell

Cyborg Seduction 8: Haunting Blackie

Lacey and Lethal

Mating Heat 1: Mate Set

Mating Heat 2: His Purrfect Mate

Mating Heat 3: Mating Brand

Mine to Chase

New Species 1: Fury

New Species 2: Slade

New Species 3: Valiant

New Species 4: Justice

New Species 5: Brawn

New Species 6: Wrath

New Species 7: Tiger

New Species 8: Obsidian

New Species 9: Shadow

New Species 10: Moon

New Species 11: True

New Species 12: Darkness
New Species 13: Smiley
Riding the Raines 1: Propositioning Mr. Raine
Riding the Raines 2: Raine on Me
Something Wicked This Way Comes Volume 1 *(anthology)*
Something Wicked This Way Comes Volume 2 *(anthology)*
Zorn Warriors 1: Ral's Woman
Zorn Warriors 2: Kidnapping Casey
Zorn Warriors 3: Tempting Rever
Zorn Warriors 4: Berrr's Vow

Print Books:
Claws and Fangs
Cyborg Seduction 1: Burning Up Flint
Cyborg Seduction 2: Kissing Steel
Cyborg Seduction 3: Melting Iron
Cyborg Seduction 4: Touching Ice
Cyborg Seduction 5: Stealing Coal
Cyborg Seduction 6: Redeeming Zorus
Cyborg Seduction 7: Taunting Krell
Cyborg Seduction 8: Haunting Blackie
Mating Heat 1: Mate Set
Mating Heat 2: His Purrfect Mate
Mating Heat 3: Mating Brand
New Species 1: Fury
New Species 2: Slade
New Species 3: Valiant
New Species 4: Justice
New Species 5: Brawn
New Species 6: Wrath

New Species 7: Tiger
New Species 8: Obsidian
New Species 9: Shadow
New Species 10: Moon
New Species 11: True
Riding the Raines 1: Propositioning Mr. Raine
Riding the Raines 2: Raine on Me
Something Wicked This Way Comes Volume 1 *(anthology)*
Something Wicked This Way Comes Volume 2 *(anthology)*
Zorn Warriors 1 & 2: Loving Zorn
Zorn Warriors 3: Tempting Rever
Zorn Warriors 4: Berrr's Vow

About Laurann Dohner

೮ು

I'm a full-time "in-house supervisor" (sounds much better than plain ol' housewife), mother and writer. I'm addicted to caramel iced coffee, the occasional candy bar (or two) and trying to get at least five hours of sleep at night.

I love to write all kinds of stories. I think the best part about writing is the fact that real life is always uncertain, always tossing things at us that we have no control over, but when you write, you can make sure there's always a happy ending. I love that about writing. I love to sit down at my computer desk, put on my headphones and listen to loud music to block out the world around me, so I can create worlds in front of me.

೮ು

The author welcomes comments from readers. You can find her website and email address on her author bio page at www.ellorascave.com.

Tell Us What You Think

We appreciate hearing reader opinions about our books. You can email us at Service@ellorascave.com (when contacting Customer Service, be sure to state the book title and author).

Why an electronic book?

We live in the Information Age — an exciting time in the history of human civilization, in which technology rules supreme and continues to progress in leaps and bounds every minute of every day. For a multitude of reasons, more and more avid literary fans are opting to purchase e-books instead of paper books. The question from those not yet initiated into the world of electronic reading is simply: *Why?*

1. ***Price.*** An electronic title at Ellora's Cave Publishing runs anywhere from 40% to 75% less than the cover price of the exact same title in paperback format. Why? Basic mathematics and cost. It is less expensive to publish an e-book (no paper and printing, no warehousing and shipping) than it is to publish a paperback, so the savings are passed along to the consumer.

2. ***Space.*** Running out of room in your house for your books? That is one worry you will never have with electronic books. For a low one-time cost, you can purchase a handheld device specifically designed for e-reading. Many e-readers have large, convenient screens for viewing. Better yet, hundreds of titles can be stored within your new library — on a single microchip. There are a variety of e-readers from different manufacturers. You can also read e-books on your PC or laptop computer. (Please note that Ellora's Cave does not endorse any specific brands.

You can check our website at www.ellorascave.com for information we make available to new consumers.)

3. *Mobility.* Because your new e-library consists of only a microchip within a small, easily transportable e-reader, your entire cache of books can be taken with you wherever you go.

4. *Personal Viewing Preferences.* Are the words you are currently reading too small? Too large? Too... ANNOYING? Paperback books cannot be modified according to personal preferences, but e-books can.

5. *Instant Gratification.* Is it the middle of the night and all the bookstores near you are closed? Are you tired of waiting days, sometimes weeks, for bookstores to ship the novels you bought? Ellora's Cave Publishing sells instantaneous downloads twenty-four hours a day, seven days a week, every day of the year. Our webstore is never closed. Our e-book delivery system is 100% automated, meaning your order is filled as soon as you pay for it.

Those are a few of the top reasons why electronic books are replacing paperbacks for many avid readers.

As always, Ellora's Cave welcomes your questions and comments. We invite you to email us at Service@ellorascave.com or write to us directly at Ellora's Cave Publishing Inc., 1056 Home Avenue, Akron, OH 44310-3502.

Make each day more *EXCITING* With our

Ellora's
Cavemen
Calendar

✞ www.EllorasCave.com ✞

Discover for yourself why readers can't get enough of the multiple award-winning publisher Ellora's Cave. Be sure to visit EC on the web at www.ellorascave.com to find erotic reading experiences that will leave you breathless. You can also find our books at all the major e-tailers (Barnes & Noble, Amazon Kindle, Sony, Kobo, Google, Apple iBookstore, All Romance eBooks, and others).

www.ellorascave.com

CPSIA information can be obtained at www.ICGtesting.com
Printed in the USA
BVOW05s0325300115

385629BV00001B/19/P